To Malik...

Best Wish...

THE GOBBINS

Stewart J. Wilson

13/9/99

MINERVA PRESS
LONDON
MONTREUX LOS ANGELES SYDNEY

THE GOBBINS
Copyright © Stewart J. Wilson 1997

ISBN 1 86106 381 4

First Published 1997 by
MINERVA PRESS
195 Knightsbridge
London SW7 1RE

3rd Impression 1998

Printed in Great Britain for Minerva Press

THE GOBBINS

Dedicated to
June, Jeremy and Timothy

All characters and events in this book are fictional
and any resemblance to actual places, events or persons,
living or dead, is purely coincidental, with the exception
of the terrorist cease fires in 1994.

Contents

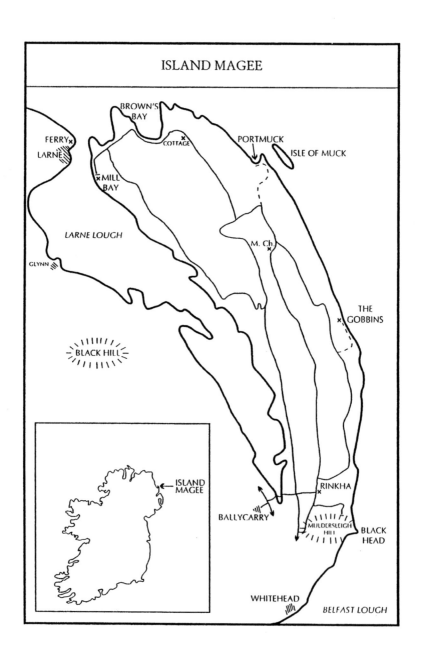

List of Main Characters

Washington

General Gene Laskie	Covert Operations, The Pentagon
Captain Mark Hudson	Laskie's Secretary
Colonel Charlie York	Security, Covert Operations
Captain David Becker	The 'Banker', Covert Operations
Captain Henry Black Feather	Library/Surveillance, Covert Operations
Major Nicholas Bishop	General Duties, The Pentagon
T. J. Smith	CIA
Guy Adams	CIA
Stan Hill	CIA
Lance Green	CIA

Dugway

Major Simon MacBride	Officer in charge, Dugway
Captain Thomas Hunter	Strategy, Dugway
Lieutenant Owen Croft	Security, Dugway

THE EUROPEANS

Island Magee

Major Edward de Courcy (UK)	Anti-terrorist team, N. Ireland
Major Lee Elmer Sutton (US)	Anti-terrorist team, N. Ireland

Ballycarry

Mrs Susannah Lacy	Strategy, UVF – sister of Lt Owen Croft
Joseph Lacy	UVF supporter, brother-in-law of Mrs Susannah Lacy

Belfast

'The General'	Head of UVF
Martin Richmonds	Bank manager, accidental involvement in the proceedings
Supt Stephen Richards	RUC
Temple Spooner	Editor, *Belfast Telegraph*
Willis Chapman	Reporter, *Belfast Telegraph*
Professor Geoff Withers	Medical Professor, Military Wing, Musgrave Park Hospital

Cushendall

William (Liam) Magee	IRA
Jarvis McBrien	IRA

Others taking part are minor players, and are not listed.

Prologue

The professionally made poster, announcing the European Journalist of the Year – 1995, was displayed on the dark brown wooden notice board at the main entrance to the Culloden Hotel, Craigavad, Northern Ireland. Beneath the poster's title there was a colour head-and-shoulders photograph of this year's recipient – Willis Chapman, *Belfast Telegraph*.

The dining room was full of representatives from the major daily newspapers published in Europe and a few special guests from the United States. There were television cameras in place, recording the whole scene for a seven-to-ten-second slot in the local news programme later that night.

The dinner had started. Having mingled over a few drinks beforehand, the guests were in jovial form – all but one, that is.

Willis Chapman was not enjoying himself. The great honour of the award coming to Northern Ireland for the first time did not make him feel any better. Chapman enjoyed the dinner. He ate slowly to make it last and to put off for as long as possible the moment when he would rise to give his acceptance speech.

The salmon starter was delicious. Usually he couldn't afford such luxuries, but as the editor was paying, he decided to relax – over the meal, that is. The surroundings were beautiful and, despite the past twenty-five years, appeared to have escaped damage from terrorism. The weather was good – a clear day, little cloud, warm for June. The gardens around the hotel were spacious and set out well. There was a good view over the lough to County Antrim, where he could see Carrickfergus clearly, and the chimney at Kilroot Power Station that towered over everything.

"How did all this start, Willis? How did you get the story?" said one.

"Yes, Willis, spill the beans. Tell us how you did it."

Chapman was at the top table. The window with the view was to his right, so when looking at the view his immediate neighbour, a hack from one of the London-based tabloids, caught his eye and used the opportunity to put the question which was echoed by the *Guardian*'s man opposite him.

He noticed that the next course was being served. Good.

"I'll tell you later," Chapman said as an excuse, as the waiter placed a large plate before him.

"Mind the plate, sir. It's hot – very hot," a comment that he repeated word perfect as he went round the table.

"Go ahead, Willis, how did all this start?"

The President of the National Association of Journalists, sitting at Chapman's left, interrupted this conversation.

"By the way, Willis, in your short – I trust it *will* be short – acceptance speech, you won't be too provocative, now. Especially when the TV cameras are here. Understand?"

Ms Winnifred Townsend was one person who liked to keep up appearances. Being President, her priority was making sure that she didn't let the side down, and Winnie expected others to act similarly.

"What do you mean by 'provocative', Winnie?" Chapman knew how to annoy her.

"Good old Willis," the hack to his right butted in, "always the reporter. Answering a question with a question." Those who heard enjoyed the remark and started laughing. The top table was round, making it easier for the eight who sat at it to communicate.

"Now listen, Willis, this is a chance to get good publicity and I want you to use this opportunity properly."

'Getting a little agitated now is our President', thought Willis.

"Don't worry, Winnie. I'll use the opportunity properly."

"That could mean anything!" The hack was enjoying this and by laughing managed to stir the pot.

The waiters arrived in convoy, the first carrying one of the meat dishes. The choice was steak, beef, or vegetable lasagne for the vegetarians. Chapman took the beef. There were three slices – thick too. There was a choice of croquette, boiled, baked or chipped potatoes.

"Croquette and a boiled, please," requested Chapman and watched them being deposited on his plate.

The vegetables were not the usual offering of peas and carrots, but broad beans, French beans, sweetcorn, and roasted turnip.

"A few of each will do nicely!" Chapman requested, and he got them.

That was good, thought Chapman. He was no longer hungry, just a little bloated. The wine was dispersed freely, with orange juice and other fruit juices for the drivers. Chapman kept to apple juice. He didn't want to ruin his speech. The sweet trolley was offered and Chapman played safe and had some warm apple pie with cream. Coffee and chocolate mints rounded off a satisfactory meal. The hotel had provided a Toast Master, who prompted the President and kept things moving smoothly when it came to the speeches. The toasts were completed, and silence greeted the President as she rose to speak.

"Fellow journalists and special guests," she began. The prepared text was read without error and was forgotten as soon as it was delivered. Fortunately, she restricted the delivery to six minutes and ended by announcing, "I now call upon the Northern Ireland Secretary of State to make the presentation. Mr Secretary."

The polite applause saw the Secretary rise from his seat where he sat to the left of the President, and when the noise cleared he delivered some unusually short and humorous few sentences before declaring, ". . .it is with real pleasure that I present Mr Willis Chapman with this certificate according him the title 'European Journalist of the Year'. Mr Chapman." The Secretary, standing with a generous smile and scrolled certificate, shook Chapman's hand and made the presentation. The applause, mixed with a few shouts and stamping of feet, seemed to go on for far too long.

Chapman reached for the sheet of paper – his speech – from his inside jacket pocket and waited. Here goes, he thought, I might as well be hung for a sheep as for a lamb. He cleared his throat and with every eye upon him, began.

*

Chapman entered his editor's office the next morning at 8 a.m. and asked, "Do I still have a job, Mr Spooner, or am I sacked?"

Temple Spooner, Editor for the past six years, wasn't about to lose the current European Journalist of the Year just because he spoke the truth as he saw it.

"Sit down, Willis," and he offered him the chair away from the desk to avoid Chapman interpreting the desk as being a barrier between them.

"No, Willis, you still have a job as far as I'm concerned. It's a pity you didn't tell me what you were going to say before you said it. You know, if you had only told me, I could have had another scoop!" That was Temple Spooner, always thinking of circulation. "I trust you have proof. If not, I can't help you."

Chapman handed over a copy of the manuscript he had brought with him.

"I think," Chapman began, "you would like to read this – it's a copy. The original is in a safe place. By the way Mr Spooner, I—"

"Forget the Mr Spooner bit. . . call me Temple. . . okay?"

"Thanks, Temple. I was just about to say how much I value your support. None of this would have been done without it." Chapman gestured towards the manuscript. "I would welcome your views on whether it is worthy of publication. It might be another 'scoop', as you put it."

Chapman left Spooner to decide whether to read it or not and took the rest of the day off.

Spooner started to read selected paragraphs from various pages before he made up his mind that perhaps there was something here after all. He lit the DO NOT DISTURB SIGN and started from the beginning.

DECLARATION

We the undersigned declare that the information disclosed in the attached paper gives a true and accurate account of events that took place in our presence either solely or jointly during the period commencing on or around August 1990 to August 1994 inclusive.

(signed)   J. E. de Courcy
Susannah Lacy (née Croft)
Lee E. Sutton
M. Richmond

(witnessed)   M. Cole, solicitor (dated)

I, Willis Chapman, declare that the information in the attached paper was obtained by interviewing the above persons.

Interviews were held with other persons who preferred not to sign the above declaration. They both assisted with the story, and were, on several occasions, able to confirm the veracity of the events described herein.

(signed)   Willis Chapman
(witnessed) M. Cole, solicitor (dated)

Chapter One

One month after Iraq had invaded Kuwait in August 1990, a small
deputation of British and Northern Ireland civil servants involved in
the Prevention of Terrorism legislation arrived in Washington. It
began the previous year with President Bush offering an exchange of
views at civil servant level, which were accepted by Prime Minister
Margaret Thatcher.

Nothing was reported of the event. There was no reason for the
media to be interested. The people were non-entities as far as the
Administration in Washington was concerned: ordinary people doing
what they felt was in the best interests of their country, meeting other
ordinary people doing the same thing. It would be forgotten as soon
as it was over. The separate governments wouldn't remember. Some
future historian might turn up an obscure reference to the meetings but
that was as much as anyone could expect, and it is likely that the
meetings would be interpreted as being necessary to maintain the
'special relationship' between the two countries.

Most of the business was carried out informally over breakfast and
lunch, with most of the time used spending taxpayers' money on small
but expensive gifts for the hosts. One such gift was not bought using
taxpayers' money but acquired from a small but upmarket wholesale
jewellers in Edinburgh. Acquired, not purchased, as it was one of
four such items stolen during a planned armed raid, and subsequently
passed on to one of the Northern Ireland civil servants. He brought it
with him to Washington just in case there was a use for it.

On the second day over breakfast, the civil servant was engaged in
conversation with the person beside him. He got the hang of his
opposite number's accent long before the American managed to
understand him.

"We are the same in many ways," he continued and skilfully drew
out a parallel between living in Northern Ireland where the
Government and people of the Republic of Ireland were trying to wipe

the North's existence off the map, and the treatment of the American Indian by the 'white man'. Being white himself, the civil servant quietly assured his Indian neighbour that he had nothing to do with the maltreatment of the Indian nation and neither had his forefathers. He cited illogically that the Indian lifestyle was destroyed by the likes of the Republic of Ireland immigrants, not the Northern Irish, who stayed in Northern Ireland to continue the fight for their survival. His gamble paid off as his interested host asked for more information. He readily gave it over the next few days mentioning one-sided atrocities such as Enniskillen on Remembrance Day, which was recollected by the Indian.

"Sure do remember that one."

"Ethnic cleansing is not the way civilised people should behave, yet it continues with the perpetrators receiving help and encouragement from the Irish-American lobby and such like". He took the stolen object from his pocket.

"As a personal token from a representative of one repressed people to another, please accept this in remembrance of our meetings," and he quietly handed over the boxed gold Rolex.

His host was impressed. The civil servant seemed to want to keep this quiet, so he pocketed the watch and thanked him, saying that if there was anything that he could do to help, just ask. The Indian slipped him a business card with his name and address shown.

"Let's keep in touch, Captain Black Feather," suggested the civil servant, who, with reciprocity in mind, gave Black Feather one of his cards.

"Sure thing, Mr Johnston," said Black Feather, placing the card in the same pocket as the Rolex.

They kept in touch over the years by sending greetings, usually by colour postcard, the latest of which advised Mr Johnston, ". . .*sending you something of interest by separate mail. . .*".

The something of interest was a file of papers marked 'Ireland 6'. Using his contacts, Johnston managed to verify the information contained in 'Ireland 6', and decided to bring the matter to the attention of his new Head of Strategy at the next meeting of the Council. To clear the way open in case Council decided to publish the 'Ireland 6' information, Johnston acknowledged the safe receipt of the file from Black Feather by colour postcard saying ". . .*thank you for the gift. The peoples of the six counties rejoice. Should I publish your manuscript?. . ."*

The reply was polite, but short, *"You can do what you want."*
The postcards were destroyed on both sides of the Atlantic, and their existence impossible to verify.

Chapter Two

Democracy, freedom, and responsibility are linked by invisible threads of interests that are shaped by background, culture, and ambition. Something had to be done to hurry matters along. Forget about the democratic rights of the majority, what of freedom for the minority? The minority were suffering as they always suffered, but now power was available to change this, and this power will be used. It could not be traced back: that would be bad for democracy and freedom in this country. No, it would be kept quiet. Let others have the praise as long as those who really matter knew who made it happen. Advancement would surely follow, and, who knows? – the top job could be his. Head of Covert Operation, CIA. That would do nicely! He was good, in fact very good. It was his idea that proved correct in the Gulf. It was their stupid stubbornness that robbed him of a great victory, but he would be back, and how. He was livid at the time, which was probably why he was transferred out of Washington. So convinced was he that he was right that he risked being kicked out altogether, but his skills were needed so he was kept on. The oil fields were the key. They were the only reason for going in. The fact that Iraqi forces had swept aside the Kuwaitis didn't matter, it was the oil that mattered. If that was so, his plan to protect the oil was valid. He reasoned, and reasoned well that, should Iraq feel that they were losing, they would blow up the oil fields. To prevent this, he recommended that troops should be deployed into two areas at the same time: north-west of Kuwait, which they did, and in the immediate vicinity of the oil fields, which they did not. And what happened? The oil wells were set on fire. Remember the fires? The pollution? The dead wildlife in the Gulf? Still, it was considered too dangerous.

So he was moved to Dugway, where he could work on covert plans for submission to Washington, and if they were considered worthy, he might be invited back. He wasn't even the boss. The boss was filling in his time awaiting retirement, but he had the right background, and that was good. He could use this background as a lever.

The resource of an angry mind would overcome the resistance of a democratic system. Anger that could be controlled and channelled to achieve the task.

They met in Major Simon MacBride's office, which was a cordoned off area of the open-plan second storey of the two-storey building. After pleasantries, discussion on the reliability of this or that machine was voiced and problem-solving with contributions from the engineering team adding value. After about an hour Major MacBride, rubbing both hands together, would say:

" Okay, that's it – get on with it."

The engineers would salute and leave. The two of them were now alone.

Capt. Thomas Hunter would stand when the engineers stood, and watched as they left to return to the warehouses of equipment. It was now or never. Now – the time was right.

"Might I have a word, Sir? I have an idea I would like to run by you."

" Okay, Thomas. Let's get a coffee, and you tell me what's on your mind." Major MacBride rose from his chair, and moved to a side table where he poured two coffees into white plastic disposable cups from a heated jug that always seemed to be in the offices of those holding senior rank. MacBride nodded to Hunter.

"Let's assume," Capt. Hunter began, "that we could do something to improve matters in a foreign country, for the ordinary people, without getting involved. Would that be considered good or bad for the US of A?"

"That depends what it is you propose to improve and what country."

"Well. . .," he pretended to need time to think, but he had already invested time on this one and was just making sure that he didn't blow it by choosing the wrong words, ". . .for over twenty years there has been trouble in this country, but the political parties involved both directly and indirectly – including Washington – have achieved very little, nothing in fact."

MacBride stopped fiddling with his coffee cup and started to show interest. "You say over twenty years? There is only one place, no two, but the Middle East has always been a problem."

"I was thinking of the political goodwill it would give us if we sorted out the Irish problem."

"Ireland! You're talking of my old country, boy, tell me more."

"I didn't know you had Irish connections," lied Hunter.

"Sure have, son. My grandmother on my mother's side was part Irish as she had a cousin that came from Donegal, no less," smugly stated MacBride.

"You have one over me, Sir. My connections are somewhere in mid-Europe. Belgium, I believe. But you – part Irish – congratulations, Sir." Now I have him. He has fallen for it, and I'll not let him go. Careful now, not too much, he might cotton on.

"It goes away back, of course but there's some Irish blood in me for sure." MacBride was proud of this nebulous connection.

"A pity about the Irish blood spilt in Ireland. I wonder if my ideas could help?" suggested Capt. Hunter.

"Is this a covert operation you have in mind?" asked MacBride.

"Only a few thoughts at this stage, Sir, but yes. Nothing connected to us. . ."

"Hold it. I'll introduce you to the *room* – come with me. First relieve yourself of the coffee, son," as they went to the bathroom.

*

"I like your ideas, son," gestured MacBride by patting Hunter on the back. "See you in a day or so," as he made his way to the jet which was preparing to take off for Washington. "Work on this some more, son – OKAY?"

This just might work, thought MacBride. Old Major Bishop in Washington would help – after all, he was as much Irish as himself and would give him all the backing he needed. Something to do again, great. MacBride was getting tired of Dugway, even though he had only a year to do. But this – he could go out on a high. This might even get him promotion which would lift the pension – happy days!

The journey was a good one. He was in buoyant mood so the journey was bound to have been good. The attitude effects the total.

You feel good, everything is good. You feel bad – well, the bad days are about to end. He had arranged the flight quickly – he had to as it would be another week before the next one – so he made sure that Major Bishop was there. It would be bad planning on his part if, having travelled to Washington, he found that Bishop was on vacation.

*

There were four who considered themselves Irish, and this fact gave them sustenance during their tours of duty in Vietnam. Only two of them got out alive – MacBride and Bishop. They would meet at least annually and reminisce of past days, both good and bad, and end up well fed and watered. So well watered, that MacBride couldn't remember how he had got back to Dugway last time. His head hurt for days.

This was different. Now there was a job to be done and this job would help the old country, so there was no need to drown past memories in alcohol.

"An' how the bogs of Donegal are you, Paddy?" It was Nicholas Bishop, as big as ever and beaming from ear to ear as he greeted his buddy from the old Vietnam days.

"Hi, Nick, just the same, and that toupee of your still going strong?" It was their little joke, always the same. It was reassurance and gave each of them comfort in each other's company. That was no toupee. Bishop had the thickest of hair with no sign of baldness, unlike MacBride who was decidedly thin on top but with plenty around the sides.

"Ever heard of hair dye, Nick? It might help." Bishop's thick hair, once jet black, was now quite grey. Very respectable looking and it added to his authority. Laughing, they both left together in the direction indicated by Bishop.

"The car's over there. Don't say too much 'til we get to the office, the chauffeur is new. And hands off – she's mine!"

The car was parked where cars shouldn't be, but being painted with army insignia and with chauffeur in full uniform – sergeant, complete with peaked cap – the police kept their distance. In fact the police kept other cars out of the way.

"There it is, what do you think of my girl there, eh? Not bad, eh?" as they were offered the back seat by the sergeant and climbed in. The sergeant closed the door behind them, went round the back of the car, got in and drove off, guided by approving nods from the two cops who also thought she was not bad.

From the back seat, Bishop continued the banter. "You haven't answered me, Simon," pointing at the sergeant, making sure she couldn't see him.

"There are occasions in which the dynamic structural posture of an event in military clothing fully meets the overall organisational concept, and that's one of them."

"You mean you approve?" Much laughter in the back seat for a mile or so before it was interrupted by Bishop.

"Sergeant, I want to go to Entrance 5. Wait by Security."

"Sir." Her reply was polite and without emotion as safely but quickly within the speed limit she drove them to where ordered.

The guard at the gate checked the passes of the driver and Bishop.

"He's with me," said Bishop pointing to MacBride and all were allowed to enter.

At the single-storey square building the car stopped. The sergeant got out of the car smartly and opened the rear door for Bishop to climb out.

"Wait," said MacBride. "I'll get out too. Been sittin' too long today, what with the plane journey," and climbed out. "You'd go ahead, Nick, I'll wait here." It gave him a chance to get a better look at the sergeant. She sure was a looker. Great figure and all that goes with it, with just a hint of perfume. While he entered the security building, Bishop heard MacBride ask, "How long have you been driving the major around, Sergeant?" He didn't wait to hear the reply, as he knew that MacBride wouldn't get far – he'd seen to that! He was allowed in; his pass gave him the authority; power – he liked that. He made his way to the desk, which was manned by a corporal, another woman. 'Not in the same class as my sergeant,' thought the major.

"Phone," he ordered as he rubbed finger and thumb together.

The corporal immediately lifted a phone having a long lead which was hidden from sight behind the desk, and with one movement placed it on top of the desk with the dial toward Bishop and, lifting off the handset, offered it to him.

"Thanks, Corporal," as he dialled internally. It was answered quickly.

"Hi! Major Bishop here. I want a room – small one is okay – any available?" He waited a few seconds and saw outside through the darkened glass that MacBride had given up talking to the sergeant. I bet that has sickened him, he thought.

"I'll take it – say three hours – okay?" It was confirmed and Bishop replaced the receiver and left the corporal to return the phone to its home behind the desk.

"Office, Sergeant," as he returned to his seat in the car.

MacBride was quiet – some change in a few minutes. "I bet I got you, eh?" goaded Bishop and, continuing, said, "Let me tell you something. I told my sergeant everything – okay?" Of course, MacBride hadn't a clue what was happening but expected something.

"Is that so? What exactly have you said this time, Nick?" The sergeant was listening as she pulled the car up into the space allocated for the vehicle.

"Just sit there a minute, Sergeant. I told my sergeant how you used to work with us in Washington before they threw you out to Dugway for making a grab at the girls!"

"Whaaat!" and both laughed as they watched the sergeant realise that she too had been set up.

"So that's why you hardly spoke to me, is that right, Sergeant?"

"Yes, Sir – no, Sir." As they laughed the sergeant joined in and it added to her beauty. They left her behind to do whatever sergeants do, as they entered the air-conditioned corridor to walk the one hundred yards to Bishop's office.

"The room is available first thing tomorrow – 0830 hours, okay?"
"Sure!"

"Let's go and meet a few people," as they entered the green door marked COVERT – EXTERNAL – ALL PASSES TO BE SHOWN, they displayed their passes, which were swiped into the ID machine and, once confirmed, handed back.

"I've booked you into one of the company's flats as requested. You were lucky, Paddy, there was one vacancy. The key will be waiting for you at Reception – okay?" They passed a row of glass-fronted rooms, some with their vertical slotted blinds drawn, keeping secret their contents, and headed for the office at the end.

"Any messages, Sue?" Bishop enquired of his secretary, who stood as Bishop approached.

The captain acknowledged his arrival. "No, Sir," as the two men walked past her and entered his office.

"Assuming you need some money for whatever you guys at Dugway are up to, I suggest we ask one of the finance guys to join us tomorrow – agreed?"

"What would I have to tell him, or her?" enquired MacBride.

"It will be a him. Everything – but it's a room job – okay?"

Hesitantly, MacBride answered, "Yeah, we'll need some capital. Do you know what funds will be available?"

"Not much," said Bishop. "All budgets were cut following the success in the Gulf, but there are always exceptions, especially if it's good, and you wouldn't be here unless the idea has legs, right?"

MacBride didn't say anything, he just nodded. He didn't like the idea of someone else getting involved. The more there were involved the greater the risk of a leak, and a leak meant failure. Bishop noticed the uneasy demeanour of his Irish friend and moved to eradicate his worries.

"It may not be approved, but if that happens, it dies. Nobody will know. If it gets the green light, only the *room* will know, okay?"

MacBride remained motionless except for a notional nod that signified understanding, not agreement.

"Let's give it a go, okay?"

"Okay," resigned MacBride.

"Good." Bishop picked up the phone and browsed through the internal directory – he never could remember extension numbers, but then as there was a list he didn't have to.

"Hi, David – yep, that's right – are you free 0830 tomorrow for say three hours? We need to talk. The *room* – No. 2 is booked – okay? Good, good – and have some figures at the ready – we need some capital – okay – bye," and he hung up.

"Now," looking at his watch, "I'll have to go, Paddy. My wife has invited a few people out this evening and I promised to be there – you know. You wouldn't like to come too, would you?"

"No thanks, I've arranged something with your driver!"

Bishop looked up sharply.

"Only joking, you go home to your wife, I'll slum it in the flat."

They left together and, as they passed the captain, Bishop ordered:

"Car – tell Sergeant I'll drive, she can knock off," and without looking at anyone he made his way out. The captain passed on the message to the garage.

Chapter Three

To gain entry to the *room* a strict procedure had to be adhered to. The three entered, led by Bishop who had the electronic key. Bishop made sure that all was in order before commencing the expected small talk. A quick check – yes – the row of lights was in order, the white board and markers in place, and the table and chairs set out. Bishop was now ready to begin.

"Right," he said. They sat down in no particular order, but as it was a round table no seating plan was needed. ". . .this is Major Simon MacBride from Dugway and this is Captain David Becker from the bank. Major MacBride has an idea, and as it's a good one he flew up here for one purpose, to bring us up to speed!"

Becker thought he knew of MacBride. "Major Simon MacBride? I've heard of you, you were in Vietnam and did good. Don't you have that Captain Hunter on your staff at Dugway? The ideas man whose oil fire predictions were ignored?"

"You've done your homework – yes. It's one of his ideas for discussion only at this stage, that brings me here." He paused, and realising that it was now his show, started to introduce the project.

"It's sorting out the problem in Ireland without getting involved."

"Without getting involved?" queried Becker. "We're already involved with funds to Irish this and Irish that – it's costing a bomb and getting nowhere—"

"Hold it – let's wait 'til we hear the plan, okay?" interrupt Bishop.

"Suppose," said MacBride as he approached the white board lifting a black marker, "we describe the problem simply as follows." He drew three lines from top to bottom dividing the white board into four sections and headed the first column on the left *IRA*.

"These people want a united Ireland and have organised themselves from around 1970 into an effective armed unit, with political support on the nationalist side called *Sinn Fein*. They have support in this country from the Irish National Caucus and from the

NORAID people – not to mention the Irish American lobby. But," pausing for effect, "no support for their military actions here or in Ireland, or in Britain, and especially not from each of the governments."

Moving to the next column, he headed it *UVF*. "The *Ulster Volunteer Force*, a party of militant terrorists from the loyalist side. They," he pointed to the board, "the UVF, were virtually wiped out in the First World War at the Somme. Before my time." There was mild laughter in the room.

MacBride continued. "These people want to keep the link – no, it's stronger than that, the union with England. It's called the United Kingdom – England, Scotland, Northern Ireland, and the other one called. . ." he was struggling to remember.

"Wales." It was Becker who helped MacBride out of his memory lapse.

"That's right – Wales. Well, these people," pointing to the UVF section on the white board, "are nowhere. They have support, but nothing to write home about. They have a few handguns, but no large beer and no real strategy. These people have their own culture which means they don't attack, only defend. There have been exceptions – there are always exceptions. The majority of the population are unionists, they don't want anything to do with these guys – the UVF." He had their full undivided attention, so he continued.

"Here," the third column he headed *USA*, "we have the problem of not wanting to be seen to get involved. Politically it would finish the Administration, especially after the help the Brits gave us in the Gulf. Yet there is support for the United Ireland idea here."

The others nodded in agreement.

"Lastly we have the Brits," as he headed the last column on the right *GB*. "They are involved in Northern Ireland and have lost a lot of army personnel not to mention local cops, civilians, and of course capital. It's communicated widely that they will continue to back the majority, that is the Unionist people, who are in the majority. But. . ." pausing again for effect, ". . .it's no secret that they would like out. Out of the problem means out of Ireland. So here is our idea. Let's help them get out."

He stopped. Nothing was said, but he still held their complete attention.

"The IRA have gone quiet in relative terms. They've had some bad press, especially following Enniskillen, and are believed to be regrouping and rethinking their strategy. The UVF can't do much as they have nothing to do it with. A few tit-for-tat killings, the same as here in LA or Chicago—"

"Or in Washington, like last week, believed to be drugs-related," interrupted the money man.

"Yeah, well you know how it is – a few get killed, nobody gets worried about it. Go ahead, Simon," said Bishop.

"We assist the UVF to do something big against the IRA, who in turn will be instructed by us to do nothing. Instead of reacting violently, the IRA will use the publicity machine, assisted by us at this end, to force the Brits to sort this lot out," pointing to the UVF column. "That means going in hard and taking a few of them out." MacBride pointed again to the UVF column. "There are only a few anyway. The result will be a massive backlash from the ordinary loyalist people against the Brits, who in turn, realising that they can't win, will pull out. Result? United Ireland." He replaced the marker, sat down and waited. MacBride didn't have long to wait.

"How much did you have to drink last night, Paddy?" asked Bishop. "That's the wildest one I've heard yet."'

Good ol' Bishop, thought MacBride. I expected him to say something, but not that good.

"You said contacts? How do we make contact? Firstly, the IRA, explain," sought Becker.

"That's where the beauty comes in. My man in Dugway, Captain Hunter, has connections with the IRA in Northern Ireland. This can be checked out."

"Okay, if that stands up, what of the connection to the UVF? Who?"

"Nothing worked out yet. But it's only an idea at this stage. If the idea is accepted, we go for the detail. Well?"

The three discussed the plan, with amendments coming fast and furious for the next hour. Their discussions ended abruptly.

"How much would you need, Major? My budget is limited." It was the banker's way of saying that it could be done if the price was right.

"Not too big, it would frighten them off; not too small, they wouldn't bite. Say, one million dollars in total spread over the full operation which should last six months."

Bishop raised his hands and stood up. "No more – let's see if we can meet here tomorrow, okay?"

"Okay," agreed Becker, "but leave it until the afternoon. I need to see about the money and have your man and his IRA connection checked out. Say 1600 hours?"

The white board was cleaned, the exit button pressed, and within five minutes they were into small talk as they headed for the latrine.

Becker headed into *Covert Intelligence* and quickly spelt out what he wanted, saying, ". . .and make it quick, but don't miss anything. If the connection is there, I want it proved, and this is unofficial, so no copies for the file. Savvy?"

Who are these guys, thought the banker, and how do they think of these corny ideas? Still, each to his own, and in the past their ideas have proved good enough to keep them on. One million? He would need approval for that, small beer as it was. Another one million job. I'd better ask for more and then I can always cut back if necessary.

Chapter Four

"Is the Boss in? I need to see him," enquired Becker of one of the secretaries.

"Yep – but not in a good mood, he's just back from a staff meeting where the Secretary of Defense blew down one of his projects. You still want to see him?"

Blast it. I don't need him in a bad mood, it could be the end of the million dollars. "I'll see him – how soon?"

The secretary, a captain called Mark Hudson, got up and, touching the side of his nose with his right forefinger, responded, "There are ways, just hang on," as he knocked and entered the office.

"Coffee, Sir? I have freshly baked cookies here, they're good, I've had two already," as Hudson offered a cookie he lifted from the trolley recently placed inside the door of the Boss's room.

The Boss was General Gene Laskie, a bull of a man who didn't much care for rank and treated everybody the same. Everybody in the Army anyway. The civilians who called themselves politicians didn't rate high on General Laskie's opinion poll.

"Why not, Mark? I need something," he said despairingly. "Save me from politicians! All they are interested in is their continual existence." He took the coffee from Hudson, his secretary, and a cookie.

General Gene Laskie had a large office, rectangular in shape, two sides having a double glazed partition, enabling the general to keep an eye on who was about. The blinds could be closed in sections or in total to keep prying eyes at bay when needed. There were three tables, the general's, one for the coffee and cookies, and a third for conferences. At the wall to the right as you entered the office was a steel door to the *Room*. Computer terminal, telephones, and paper shredder made up the bulk of the equipment the general used.

"Okay, Mark, what do you want?" asked Laskie. "More trouble?"

"It might be something interesting, Sir. Can you see Captain Becker? He's outside."

"Wheel him in – no, wait." He got up, cookie in hand, took a bite and, moving to the door, opened it and shouted, "Charlie, get your ass in here pronto," then, looking at Becker, "Hang around – this concerns you too."

Colonel Charlie York, the security man, hearing his name being shouted across the room, muttered, "It's happened again." York stopped his form-filling exercise, lifted the folder marked *PROJECT CHINA 4*, and made his way to the Boss's office.

General Laskie waited for him at the door and just as he arrived returned to the coffee tray and lifted a second cookie from the table. "These are good," he commented.

"Good luck," Secretary Hudson said to Becker as he closed the door behind them.

"Project 'China 4' is dead," Laskie announced to the men standing there.

Becker and York looked at each other in silence, then Colonel York, for clarification purposes, ventured, "Dead, or shelved?"

"Dead, that means dead. It's from the top. Something to do with Prime Minister Major not making it too good in London and possibly losing the next election. If that happens, the President doesn't want us anywhere near Hong Kong, Canton, or anything to do with 'China 4'. okay? So that's it. David, what have you spent on it so far?"

Becker noticed the word 'you', implying it was his fault. "Two million to date gone, another two million committed, the next instalment due in seven days."

"Cancel it. No more, and that's a direct order." Seeing that York was holding the file, he reached out for it and was handed it without a word being said. He opened the file and, taking the red pen from his desk, wrote on the inside cover, as was usual in such cases, '*Cancelled on instructions from Secretary of Defense*', dated it, annotated the time, signed it, and gave it back to York.

"For the library, I guess. Pity, I was getting into it," commented York. "I'd better pull out the team," he said and made to leave.

"Phone from here," instructed Laskie. "Use this one," pointing to the blue phone. "It'll get though quicker," and he left him to get on with the call. The others were silent while the call was made. It was quick, efficient, and the project was dead.

"David, what have you that's new? Charlie, hang around, it's not often that David comes up with an idea on a Tuesday! It's usually Friday when I want to get away to golf that you have your ideas, right?"

"Thank you, Sir," he said, pretending to be hurt, but it didn't work.

"I'm looking for around two million max. I might get away with 1.5 million."

Silence. Silence was the usual response when asking for money. It put pressure on those asking to produce the why, what, when, and whom answers.

"It's an idea from the *Room*. Can I talk here?"

"The *Room*, eh? Who from?" asked Laskie.

"From that guy, Captain Tom Hunter in Dugway. Remember the oil fires in the Gulf."

"Remember! That guy was good. Too hard to deal with, but good. We'll use my *Room*." Laskie pointed to the nondescript steel door in the wall to his left. "First – a visit to be comfortable, gentlemen," as the three left for the usual routine in getting ready for a session in the *Room*.

Routine is vital for safety. The routine was audited, inspected, and checked continuously. It was seen to be working, especially in this part of the Pentagon. Security was automatically advised when the Boss used the *Room*. The routine of entering was the same. In the Boss's case, he had his own key, not produced by a machine, but a six-lever precision-tooled job produced from solid brass that was kept in a wall safe which opened using two codes, one code being a four-figure number entered into the telephone dial-type keyboard forming part of the safe door – the other keyed in by Security from their office in the basement. Security knew to enter their code because Hudson had phoned to tell them when the Boss and the others returned from the bathroom.

*

"I'm ready – okay? Let's have it and not too long," instructed Laskie.

The banker kept it short. "It's Ireland, a plan to end all the terrorist crap by forcing one side – Loyalist – to take on the other –

Nationalist – without the other fighting back. The resultant pressure from the Nationalists should force the Brits to attack the loyalists. The backlash from the Loyalists will force the Brits out, and leave Ireland for good. That's the theory. We don't get involved, only fund the Loyalists to get it started."

"What is your initial reaction to this, David?" asked Laskie.

"Sounds too juvenile, but the more juvenile it is the greater the success rate. It could work, but who would run it?"

"We could control it from Dugway," suggested York, "but have it run by the Irish Loyalists. That way there is no contact. No contact – no comeback."

"I want one of ours on the team in Ireland," insisted Laskie. "I don't want egg on our faces if it goes bad. I'll give you one million and that's it. And a man we know in on it. If you need more capital, the progress needs to be measurable. Can you handle that?"

"Thank you, Sir. Yes, I can handle that."

"One last thing. Give control to Major MacBride in Dugway. If he blows it, we know nothing. If he succeeds, we get the points." Laskie waited for their reply, it came in unison:

"Agreed!"

As Laskie pushed the exit button, he turned to Becker. "David, get yourself down to Dugway and have Captain Hunter go over his ideas with you. Just to give you a better handle on it, okay?"

Becker nodded as they all left the *Room.*

*

Colonel York proceeded to get involved in sorting out the finances and recruited the assistance of Captain Taylor from Personnel to find a body to meet General Laskie's condition. To find someone, not necessarily to tell him everything, not even to tell him anything – let Dugway do that – just find someone suitable. He also had the task of checking out Captain Thomas Hunter.

Captain Taylor entered the library suite, half of which was nothing but computer terminals feeding from a mainframe in the second basement, the other half full of files. Paper everywhere. Everything was in order, everything was indexed and controlled but very time consuming. All necessary. Files held paper authorisations.

Computers held no authorisations – nothing that could stand up in court anyway.

"I'm looking for someone, not particularly active at present, who is able to do a job of work. Have we anyone not attached to anything traceable in say, Ireland or GB?"

The operator on the nearest terminal acknowledged the captain by responding, "Let's take a look." It was a simple task for the operator, but as usual he managed to give the impression to Captain Taylor of making the job look complicated.

"This is Ireland, four there at present," he indicated by pointing to the screen.

"This is GB – ten there, four England, one Wales, five Scotland and the islands. It's the oil that gets them to Scotland, not to mention the whisky and the golf. . . Officially this file doesn't exist," continued the operator. "It's showing people we have purposefully forgotten about for the time being." He scrolled through the list of names with Taylor looking over his shoulder.

"What's that?" Taylor pointed to a list of names headed 'Bodyguards'.

"Just as it says. We have a few of our good ones who are now considered past it acting as babysitters for people who did good for us. You don't want any of them, they're not up to it – usually suffering from stress or something physical, and not 100% cured."

"Hold it. Stop this thing moving." There it was. A name and a place in Ireland. That would do. He decided to check it out. "Get me details of that one," pointing to the screen. "All you have in, say, one hour."

The operator took note of the file number on the screen.

"Something else," as Taylor referred to his notes. "Check out a Captain Thomas Hunter. He's at Dugway. See if there's any connection to the IRA, and keep it quiet."

*

One hour later, Captain Taylor handed Colonel York enough information to keep him busy for some time.

"There is an IRA connection, Sir. It's in the top folder," explained Taylor. "The rest is to do with the guy who's past it. The 'bodyguard'. okay?"

Colonel York took a passing glance at the paper in his hands and expressed his appreciation.

"I hear 'China 4' is dead. Is that right, Sir?" How news travels fast in a secured area.

"It's dead, so don't mention it again. Do you hear?"

"Sir," replied Taylor, who backed off and left Colonel York to digest the information in the files. Past it he might be, thought Colonel York, but this bodyguard is *exactly* what we need. It would be easy to deny all of this. Who would credit anyone appointing a 'has been' to a job if it went wrong? If it came good, who would give a 'has been' the credit? Beautiful – he liked it. It would stand up to audit because there is nothing to audit. Colonel York read some of the juicy history of Major Lee Elmer Sutton, and having committed to memory the important facts he tore off the first sheet which gave a summary of the man and fed the rest into the shredder.

Down to two sheets. Not bad. This should keep the Boss and Becker happy.

Captain David Becker was after different fish. He was the banker for these covert jobs and was always thinking of money and budgets. To think of money is easy when it is all abstract. It's different when it is personal finances. This was not personal, and the amounts were so big that they didn't mean anything. How many millions in Vietnam? For Star Wars? It doesn't matter. Nobody cares about the big ones. The smaller jobs were different. Unless you had protection. The authority for the big amounts come from government. No worries there except for the Government. Becker didn't like the small one million jobs as people tended to remember those and were quick to question them. The *Room* decision was his protection. He could direct funds from 'China 4' and use the sale of land routine. That one usually worked and pointed the finger elsewhere.

He worked on it until he was satisfied that he was ready to advise General Laskie.

Chapter Five

The indigenous population of any area is controlled by that area's ability to support it. Buffalo are more numerous where the food for buffalo is greatest, providing the enemy is missing. Disease and man are the enemy. To a lesser extent, weather conditions are an enemy unless you plan for the weather. Man, too, has his enemies of weather, disease, and other men. The destructive power that man has for fellow man is governed by levels of greed. The greater the greed, the greater the destruction. White men are greedy and always have been and always will be. It's part of their logic for existing. Henry Black Feather was taught to believe, encouraged to believe, and had experienced enough maltreatment from the Whites at West Point that he believed with conviction, the belief his forefathers held about the white man. The Indian would never return to the old ways and enjoy the old culture as long as the white man existed, and their existence was not in doubt for they were numerous, and able to fight disease and to survive in weather conditions in ways the Indian could never equal. Yet the hurt of his people remained deep within him, a hurt that gave him a quiet pride and strength enabling him to succeed. He was the first Indian to get there and his tribe rejoiced in his success.

Before leaving to take up his position of trust, Black Feather was honoured by becoming the fourth member of those now living who were permitted to celebrate the life of their great forefather, Crazy Horse, at his burial place. Black Feather was one of them, yet remained separate. The work was interesting within his capabilities and financially rewarding, but not socially. Socially, he was still an outsider. When the work stopped, he didn't exist. Black Feather lived as his people lived which was frugally, with a regard for the environment and willingness to help the underdog. He learnt a great deal from the white man and some day the white man would regret teaching him. There was no anger, only hurt.

It was easy to remove the files, and easy to let them know that the files had been removed. Black Feather had read many files when working in the library. He removed files and returned them to the library as part of his duties, and had decided that there were at least a dozen more he could use. He would need to act soon as security in the area was bound to be increased. That could mean a rotation of duties and a transfer from the library to. . . say. . . surveillance?

*

"I'll buy that, the connection to the IRA is proved – agreed?" asked Laskie.

"Agreed," York replied. The Boss was in full flow. Quick, but missing nothing.

'That's why he's the Boss,' thought Becker. The Boss liked working in the *room*.

"Next?"

"I recommend a Major Lee Elmer Sutton as our man to meet your condition, Sir. You have read the summary?" The general nodded and said nothing, so Becker continued. "His military record is not in question, only his current physical state. Although passed fit, he has not fully recovered. Believed to be some reaction to the oil fire fumes in the Gulf. The clincher for putting him forward is that he is already over there and has been accepted by the Brits and the local police as okay."

The Boss moved back in his chair, body language that Becker noticed and made full use of.

"All we have to do is brief him – or, in reality, let Dugway brief him. What Dugway tells him is no concern of ours – he's expendable – the whole Dugway set-up is expendable."

"Whose payroll is he on?" asked Laskie.

"Attached to 'Pensions – Overseas Section'," replied York.

"Couldn't be better," commented Laskie. "What about our budget, David?"

"I could transfer some of 'China 4's' unused capital to cover the one million, but one million is a bit tight. How about one and a half million, Sir?"

The Boss looked at him while he thought. The silence in the room was unnerving and he knew that. He used the technique a lot. It gave him real power – staying quiet – while he watched for the reactions in front of him. He was happy with the banker's news. The banker had a good record, and on this one had produced the goods quickly. "One and a quarter, maximum – no more – even if it means pulling out – okay?"

"Right." Becker always answered 'Right' when he knew he was lucky to get something. At least it was over the magic million. The Boss didn't usually remember those projects, but this one would have no records.

Then it happened. It sometimes did, but it was never expected.

The panel lights – all of them – started to flash. The lights on each panel on each wall flashed and all out of synchronisation. That way none could miss it.

"What. . .? Blast. . .! Okay, we're finished anyway, let's get out of here." General Laskie pressed the exit button. They were out quickly and the noise hit them. The security systems had gone berserk, people moving about everywhere, grabbing jackets from the backs of chairs, files on desks were put into drawers and locked, exits were being used as the evacuation took place, and all accompanied by the harsh fire sirens.

"It's a fire, General." It was his secretary, Captain Mark Hudson. "Evacuation procedure in operation, Sir."

A fire? In here? Something was wrong. This place was fireproof, at least as far as he was concerned it was. Probably an electrical fault, he reasoned as he placed the key to the room in the wall safe, closed it, and together with York and Becker made to leave, stopping only to lift a cookie from the coffee trolley.

The complete building was evacuated. Imagine it, the Pentagon with all that top brass and political clout. General Laskie saw the Secretary of Defense with two heavies making their way to a nondescript limo and tried without success to attract his attention. Pity, he thought, as he wished to have a quiet word about 'China 4'. Blast it. The general wasn't one for four-letter words when five would do. In fact, he didn't use that sort of language. He believed it was a sign of weakness. If you could not use good plain American to express yourself, especially in this job, then you shouldn't be in the job. Looking around, he noticed quite a few using their mobiles, and, pulling rank, he managed to persuade a burly sergeant to lend him his.

"Only for one call, Sergeant," as he dialled Security. Security knew it wasn't the general's phone as they were able to monitor any call coming in from army issue mobiles via the LED near the handset.

"This is General Laskie here, Security. My phone's in the office. What's goin' on?"

"Fire, Sir. The system automatically came on once the smoke was detected."

"Where, man, where?"

"Library."

Blast it. That library. I wonder what's gone? If it's the lot, there will be big trouble.

"Any damage?"

"Believed to be minor, Sir. Only two sprinklers came on."

"What! Only two! Why evacuate the whole damn building, then?"

"Ideal opportunity, Sir. I decided to have a fire drill."

The Boss couldn't believe it for a moment, then his rational side took over. "Good for you, a great idea. Look, I'm going home, you can catch me there – okay?" as he switched the mobile off and returned it to the sergeant.

"Thanks, Sergeant. Have you your car nearby?"

"Over there, Sir." He pointed to a wreck of a Ford.

"That will do – come on, give me a lift home – it's only a few miles." He took the sergeant by the upper arm and led him through the crowd to the car.

The sergeant drove him home following the general's directions, but he knew the way anyway as he had been on duty there many times.

"You're home early, dear." It was his wife greeting him as he climbed out of the Ford.

"Thanks for the lift, Sergeant – yeah, honey – where you goin'?"

"To the club, remember? I said at breakfast—"

"Oh, sure, I remember – getting some practice in before the tournament – wait for me, I'll change and come with you – okay?"

"Okay," resigned Mrs Laskie, "but I want to win this time, it's my turn!"

'He always beats me at golf,' she thought, 'it's not fair. Even with the handicap, he beats me. Always manages to put me off just at the wrong time – still, who else would have him? I still love the big oaf, even after thirty years,' she reflected.

Laskie didn't take long and, lifting his clubs into the trunk of his wife's car, got in beside her as she drove off.

"A blasted fire today, honey – imagine it – a fire in our place! The whole lot was evacuated for a blasted two-sprinkler fire."

"Should you be here? Won't they want you for inquiries or something?"

"Sure will. But I picked up the spare mobile," tapping his pocket. "If they want me, they can ring – hey, watch that kid."

"I see him – and don't try and tell me how to drive, I've passed the advanced – remember?" She enjoyed mocking him. He had failed his advanced driving test and refused to do it again.

It was a good day to be at the club as there weren't too many about, allowing them to go round by themselves.

"You start, honey."

"All right, Gene, but no funny business. The usual? The winner buys dinner?" He nodded as he watched her prepare. She was some kid and still managed to attract him. He never needed anyone else and was content and relaxed in her presence.

"Any ideas for a vacation, honey?" he asked. "Where would you like to go this year?"

"Don't interrupt me – I'll tell you when you tee off – now shut up."

Her back swing was good. The down swing was. . . shall we say, interrupted.

"Blast you, Gene. You did that on purpose," as the ball moved ten yards. It was the mobile. Its shrill tone gave forth at the wrong time and put her off. He answered it.

"Yeah? Who. . .? What. . .? Okay, I'll be right over," and with one move, pocketed the mobile and replaced his driver into the bag at the back of the trolley.

"Sorry, honey, duty calls. See you for dinner."

"Blast you, Gene, blast you. Well, you are paying for dinner and we're going to Charlie's place."

"Charlie's? He's a bit expensive, honey, how about—?"

"No, Gene. Charlie's it is. You've cheated me again, so it's Charlie's," as the general walked back to the clubhouse. She shouted after him, "Charlie's – meet me there at eight. Don't be late."

He waved confirmation and noticed her retrieving the ball, replacing it on the tee and striking it beautifully, long and straight down the middle.

Margot Jane, the ladies' captain, arrived on the tee and saw her drive. "Lovely one, Belle. May I join you?"

Good, thought Laskie, she's got company.

*

"What's up?" Laskie asked his secretary as he entered his office, still dressed in his golfing gear.

"New uniform, Sir?" joked the secretary but with a straight face.

"Cut it. Why bring me in? What's up?"

"Trouble, Sir." It was Becker. "Captain Black Feather tells me that something fishy happened about the time of the fire. I'll show you," as they proceeded to the library. The water damage was minimal, so was the smell. Little smoke damage too. Very odd, thought Laskie. Security and the boys from the lab were there.

"Look at this, Sir." Black Feather picked up a file cover – half of it left, the other burnt. The name, *Project China 4*, could still be read. Black Feather opened it. Nothing – blank – no contents, no evidence of contents and the inside cover from it also blank. Laskie tore it from Black Feather's hand.

"I annotated on this today. This is *not* the 'China 4' file."

"We know, Sir," said one of the lab boys. "The 'China 4' file is missing. This is set up to look like the original. May I. . .?" The laboratory technician stretched out his hand for the file which Laskie gave him.

"York, Becker, Black Feather – my office! Now!" ordered Laskie. "Secretary, get me Surveillance – I want his butt in here now," and, seeing that the cookies were finished, "and organise fresh coffee and cookies."

They went over all they could in a systematic and thorough manner, checking and cross-checking. Who was in or near the library at the time of the fire? What did whoever do with the file and when? Did Surveillance see anyone leave, carrying a file? A stupid question. The videotapes showed nearly everyone leaving with a file of some sort. Who did the person on security duty know in the library? Who was weak on security clearance? Why was the file taken? Who would benefit from it? What were the chances of it getting into the wrong hands, and if it did, what were the likely consequences? Was the place searched and by whom in case the file was parked somewhere for collection later, and of course, were there any clues from the lab on the fake file? Plenty of questions – few answers.

The time went quickly, and Laskie was starting to get cold in his golfing gear. The air-conditioning was too strong, he thought, and he needed to get home and change in order not to be late for Charlie's. He must be there at eight, or 2000 hours as he preferred it, and anyway, Charlie's did a decent 10 oz steak. The thought of it made him hungry, so he wrapped up the discussion and went home, carrying the mobile he remembered to lift from his desk.

'We have a loose bullet,' he thought. 'Who could it be? Who would risk taking a file from his section? They all knew the penalty, should they get caught. There was no democracy in this game, only protection. That's what it was about – protection. Anyone caught fooling around – no second chance – immediate – swift shot without a trial followed by surgery to remove the bullets. Then the cover-up. So far it had worked, and over the past ten years there were four – now it would be five. The cover-up worked. ". . .Terrible accident in the line of duty. . . no, he felt nothing. . . yes, we will look after the funeral. . . yes, the pension is half salary." It was cold, uncaring, and so protective of the system. The system came first. The people? Who cared about the people as long as the system was protected? After all, the democratic way of life for all citizens was at stake.' Thinking of 'stake', he decided he would have his with sautéed onions and baked potato and found himself at the house, parked behind his wife's car.

He changed, having had a welcome shave and shower, and was ready first. Belle took time to ensure that she was made up real good. After all, one never knew whom one might meet at Charlie's. It was a classy joint and those who dined there were classy people. Fortunately she had phoned and booked a table. It was packed. Belle was looking well – very well, thought Laskie, as Charlie himself led them to their table.

"Thanks, Charlie. I'm going to enjoy this, especially as Gene is buying," as Charlie gently pushed the chair in behind her and offered her the serviette.

"Yeah, thanks, Charlie. Is the steak good?"

"Yes, Sir. I would also recommend the salmon, straight in from Canada this morning."

"Oh good, Charlie, I'll have that," said Belle. "But not just yet, Charlie, leave us for a minute, will you?"

Charlie nodded and gave Laskie the wine list and each a menu.

"Guess what, Gene, I beat Margot Jane real good today – that's the first time this year. Three holes it was. . . good, eh?"

"Sure is, honey, you would probably have beaten me. What do you want to drink? How about the house red?"

"No, I want the white, okay? Just a glass." The small talk continued until they were ready to order. The meal arrived, and the small talk ended.

Mobiles usually ring when you don't want them to, and before they finished their meal Laskie's phone let out its shrill tone, which was loud enough for those at the next table to turn round and glare.

"Gene, don't you dare leave me. Tell them you're not going in 'til morning. That's an order, honey." Belle was annoyed and Laskie knew it.

"Okay, honey – unless it's the President," he whispered. "He said he might ring." He spoke into the phone, "Yeah?"

"Sorry to disturb you, Sir. I thought you should know before you come in tomorrow – another file is missing."

Laskie recognised Hudson's voice.

"Which one?"

"'Ireland 6'."

Chapter Six

"What sort of a place are you running here, Mister?" shouted Laskie at the unflappable Colonel York. "I want to know it all, now." General Laskie didn't like his free time being disrupted and last night was too much. Charlie did a good job with the meal, but it was ruined by bad news. Four senior officers gathered around him, seated, shirt sleeved, showing evidence of little sleep and needing a shave.

"Total of files missing is two, 'Ireland 6' and 'China 4'," York advised. "The sequence looks like this. Both files were. . . were removed—"

"Trouble with words, Mister? They were stole – stole – say it," shouted Laskie.

"Yes, Sir, stolen. Time was probably minutes before or after the fire. The dummy file was prepared in advance, but deliberately left partially destroyed."

"Deliberately? Why?" the general demanded.

"To let us know that the files were removed. . . stolen, Sir."

Nobody moved or spoke. They just waited for Laskie to shout again. All he did was nod for York to continue.

"The fire was started by matches. There were three matchsticks recovered. The duty list, Sir, gives names of those on duty or who had entered the library within twenty-four hours before the fire."

They all examined the list, a copy of which was placed in front of each of them.

"It was Captain Black Feather who alerted us to the fire. He was—"

"He's here, isn't he?" asked Laskie, pointing to Black Feather.

"Yes, Sir."

"You tell it, Captain."

Black Feather in his calm midwestern accent had the ear of the general and was prepared.

"I had just finished my coffee in the rest area and was returning to the library where I noticed smoke, so I hit the alarm bell."

"Anybody around at the time, Captain?" asked Laskie.

"No, Sir, not that I saw,"

"Okay, Captain. You continue, Charlie."

"Thank you, Sir. The lab boys have found nothing unusual. The fire was small, about four or five sheets of paper with some rubber bands. It was the bands that produced the smoke and the smell."

The general said nothing as he waited for security to finish. There was an air of resignation around the table. The unsaid admission that they had blown something made them feel that they didn't quite know what to do next.

"What's the information on the audit trail of the file, Charlie?"

"'China 4' was ready for filing, and had left your section and arrived in the bucket. The bucket was delivered to the library and joined the queue. It was next in the queue for filing when the fire broke out. The 'Ireland 6' file hadn't been looked at for six months, that's when it was signed off as being completed. The authorisation sheets show that nobody has had access to it since then. It was found to be missing when the library was checked after we got back in, Sir. That was some job, Sir, it took us hours. Since then, the complete library has been searched twice."

"Is that why the ceiling's open?" The general pointed to gaps in the ceiling where ceiling tiles had been removed near the lights.

"Yes, Sir." Silence reigned for a few minutes with Laskie looking at each one in turn trying to size up whether the culprit was before him. "Any ideas. . . anybody."

"'China 4' looks deliberate, but 'Ireland 6'. . .," suggested York, ". . .might still be found – you know – caught inside another file by mistake. That's what the boys have been doing all night."

"How far have you gone on this, Charlie?"

"In-house only, Sir."

"Take it the whole way. Any problem with that?"

"No, Sir, but. . .," York's hesitation focused all eyes upon him, ". . .it could be bad if we brought in outsiders. Bad for morale and bad for our future."

"Shove it, Mister. Take this the whole distance – that's an order. You need to leave now and organise it?"

"Yes, Sir," and both York and Black Feather made to leave.

"As you were, Captain," Laskie addressed Black Feather. "You stay and help out here. Hudson, get me T. J. Smith on the phone – use this one," as Laskie pointed to the blue phone.

"CIA, Sir? Are you sure?" asked Hudson.

"Better we tell them before they tell us. Any more ideas? Come on now, what can be done to help stop this?"

"Would duty rotas help?" asked Captain Black Feather, who explained, "We could vary the time people are in the routine jobs, which would mean that those in the library this week wouldn't know where they would be working next week. That might remove the risk of boredom and lessen the chance of theft."

The blue phone rang and Hudson took the call. "It's CIA, Sir," and transferred the receiver to the general.

"Hi, T.J. – bad news. It looks like I've got a loose bullet. Can you get over here? Sure, I'll arrange it. My boys are taking it all the way. . . yes, all the way. . . okay," and he hung up, only to make another call immediately.

"Security? Tell the gate to expect visitors soon. It's T. J. Smith," and Laskie hung up.

"Well, Mister," addressing the Indian. "Anything more to say on the rota change idea?"

An hour or more passed before the CIA arrived, affording the meeting time to arrange and agree changes to duty rotas. "It was your idea, Captain, so we'll start with you. Okay? Hudson, put everybody where we can get to them fast. These CIA guys will want to repeat what we've done."

That went well and it was a good move to start and report the fire, thought Captain Black Feather. Hudson, in consultation with another secretary, had outlined the proposed changes and Black Feather ended up in spook territory – Surveillance.

The CIA were all over the place and repeated the search carried out since the fire and began interviewing all those appearing on the duty list. General Laskie was in conference with Thomas James Smith and Colonel York, and were determined to find the person or persons responsible. It would be an impossible task as Black Feather had decided not to do anything that might point the finger in his direction. He would of course get rid of the evidence – evidence which was already off the premises. During the fire evacuation, 'Ireland 6' was placed in the mail and 'China 4' in the tribe's safe deposit box. Black Feather knew that his apartment would be searched and expected to see evidence of this when he returned there later that day.

Laskie could see the anger from his wife as he pictured in his mind's eye the MPs and CIA going through everything at home, and was grateful that his policy of never taking work home would ensure a blank result for the searchers. Her anger! What to do to pacify her? Now that would be hard. Belle had had it with anything to do with government since his move to the Pentagon four years ago, and he would seek a transfer once this episode had been resolved. What value were the files anyway? 'China 4' had barely started before they pulled out. There was little to see on that one. 'Ireland 6' was different. In the wrong hands the whole administration could be forced to go down, and him with it.

*

They entered the *Room* at 1600 hours as arranged. It was going well, very well, MacBride thought. Then the topic of an additional person on the team arose to satisfy the general's condition to keep control of the money, or at any rate that's how MacBride saw it. The rest was fine. What he didn't know was how the connection Captain Hunter had with the IRA was going to work. That was his problem, anyway. He knew that Hunter wouldn't give him details – still, what he didn't know he could deny.

The banker continued, ". . .Give control to Hunter. It's his chance to come good if the thing comes off and it keeps your hands clean," he said to MacBride. "Of course, if it falls apart, tell him he's on his own, and so are you, MacBride," said Becker.

"Do you have a file on it?" queried MacBride.

"Not yet, but we'll open one to record progress. 'Ireland 7'."

"Is 'Ireland 6' complete? I remember doing something on that one," stated MacBride.

"Yes, we closed that one last year some time. I think that's it. Any questions?" Becker was keen to get out of the room.

"The money – how soon and how do we get it?"

"The usual. Phone me and quote the file, and it's the 'sale of land' routine, so you'll need to give me the destination details and four day's notice – okay?"

"Four days? That's good, and how much?"

"First draw down $330,000, say around £220,000 British – okay?"

They continued for an hour or so, going over the information again and again until all was clearly understood. Finally the banker finished with two headline stealers.

"By the way, there's a limit. One and a quarter million – that's it – and no additions. And secondly – make sure your team in Ireland uses the money to buy their supplies from us. That way we know what they've got and we get some of our money back. Pretty neat, eh? All you do, MacBride, is get our man over here to Dugway and brief him where to obtain the supplies. The usual place in Spain, and Covert Operations will assist with transport – unofficially, of course. The file on Major Sutton shows that he's done this sort of thing before. So if that's all – good luck."

They left the room and, without any pleasantries between the Irish majors, MacBride left that night and returned to Dugway.

Chapter Seven

"That's real good, that is," snarled Captain Thomas Hunter. "Don't you see it? Wake up, man, it means we're dead! That's all, dead! If it comes off, we're ignored; if it doesn't, we're ignored. Where's the incentive to continue?"

MacBride accepted Hunter's outburst as being typical of a small man. "Achieve the objective is the incentive. If you succeed, the IRA will not ignore you. And with their political clout, you could be welcome anywhere."

Captain Hunter was feeling down. His depression had hit him hard, and MacBride was trying to pick him up. He explained the whole set-up that was agreed in the *Room* and left nothing out. That was the problem. If he had not mentioned that it was he and he alone who was to organise the project, Hunter might have felt better.

"They still can't accept that I was right and they were wrong about the oil wells – can they?"

MacBride said nothing. Captain Hunter suddenly changed. His eyes grew bright. "You're right, Major, but it's when this comes off – not *if* – *when* – that the publicity will get me back in there – I can feel it."

MacBride let him revel in his imagination before bringing the discussion back to earth.

"It will be up to, you, Captain, to brief Major Sutton, and as he is working with some Brit, your brief needs to be worked out real good. Should he catch on – well. . ."

"I know, I know – it will be good, Sir. Sorry for the outburst earlier, but I have put plenty of thought into this and—"

"Sure, Tom – okay, cool it and let's sort out the brief. The capital is fine, delivery is the land sales routine. So. . . what do we need? A bank?"

"That's easy," interrupted Hunter, "a bank and two solicitors – one here, one over there – and the system explained to Major Sutton."

MacBride listened to Hunter. He's back on form, he thought. But I'd better not let him shoot his mouth off again. "There's more, Tom. You need to cool it real good when you brief Sutton. I say again, one word out of place and—"

"I know, Sir. I do break up at the wrong time, don't I? Well, it's okay now – I'm ready for this – it's the big one."

The plans for the project were discussed over the next two hours, including minor details. An integral part of their strategy was the purchase of arms, the bank, and the solicitor they would use, which had to be near the field of operations but not in the field. The North of England was decided – Carlisle.

"When do you want Sutton over here," asked MacBride.

"Next week. Can we get him that quick?"

"No problem – I'll arrange it, but the rest, the brief and all, that's your baby."

"Yes, Sir, that's okay. I'll see that you don't – I mean, shouldn't – get in too deep."

"I don't like what you're implying, son."

"Nothing offensive intended, Sir. It's just that if you have put me in charge, *you* don't need to get involved – that's all, Sir."

Boy, thought MacBride, he knows how to get in and out of holes fast

"There's one more item, Captain. The guy in Washington who's providing the money is coming here to talk to you about the whole set-up. Use the *Room* and give him all the information he wants – okay?"

"Yes, Sir. Will you be with us?" he asked MacBride.

"You bet, son."

He pressed the exit button. That evening, Security took the secret surveillance tape home with him and made copies as usual. It was now time, Security felt, to do something, and he started to make travel arrangements.

*

Captain Hunter's earlier communication with Liam Magee of the IRA needed updating. Changes forced upon him introduced hindrances. The IRA weren't interested in failure. He would only be tolerated as long as his ideas produced success. He wasn't one of them, and changes to agreed plans could remove confidence, remove success, and remove him. He wasn't going to let that happen. Especially on account of some two-bit player of a major who didn't have the courtesy to look him in the eye during the brief in the room. He would contact Magee using their system, doing it their way. He felt he still had their confidence. After all, the 'Ireland 6' project was his idea and it produced results. They were so pleased with 'Ireland 6' that they insisted, albeit at his expense, to visit them and take part in their commemorative celebrations of the rising last Easter. It didn't occur to him that he was being assessed during his stay for possible recruitment as one of their overseas operatives and was rejected as unsuitable.

Two documents were prepared which would be posted separately, two days apart. The first would give details but nothing of time or place. The second would give time and place. They wanted it that way. He gave it to them that way. No copies would be kept and it would be handwritten. He complied. It was urgent, so he prepared them quickly and, using envelopes already addressed and stamped, mailed one letter that day and set the other aside in a safe place for later. Hunter now saw two options. Success would offer the first option – the Pentagon. The second, something big within the IRA. He was sure of that. Why not? The IRA looked after their own and success would make him one of them. The failure option did not need contemplating. He never failed. In matters of strategic thought, he was the best. He would prove it again. Captain Hunter wouldn't be captain for ever. He was on his way and it was upwards, and nobody could stop him – not even Major MacBride, who, if he tried, would find himself minus a head.

*

Meetings are boring when nothing interests you. The tape of this meeting was far from boring, and the Security man, Croft, had been listening for less than one minute. It was agreed to accept the strategy that not too many would die unless mistakes occurred, then the dead would increase. But death was necessary to achieve the objective.

Lieutenant Owen Croft listened to the tape from the driver's seat in his vehicle, which was parked off a secondary road outside Dugway, Utah, and was engrossed. Dugway was a restricted area, west of Salt

Lake City, where the proving grounds sorted out men and machines, making them ready for war.

Croft's anger was evident, but only showed in the white of his knuckles gripping his 4×4 Shogun's steering wheel.

". . .it will be necessary to up the ante as soon a possible – agreed?"

"Agreed," said Becker.

"To do this the operation requires the UVF to wipe out an IRA active unit in the area. The reaction from the IRA must be curtailed. That's *vital*." Captain Thomas Hunter paused to let this sink in. The other two were listening in the windowless room, protected, cold and bare except for the chairs, table, and white board. Major MacBride sat motionless, staring into space, eyes fixed on nothing, but hearing and understanding everything. This is a dirty game we are at, playing with the lives of people you don't know, and won't meet, and with consequences you can always deny. Nothing to do with me.

Captain Thomas Hunter continued, ". . .the political clout that Sinn Fein will generate from this will lift their supporters to raise more funds, increase their recruits, and at the same time anger their supporters here in the Irish National Caucus and in the Irish American scene. Pretty neat – eh? Major North has nothing on us!"

Chapter Eight

The room should have been protected; there should not have been any chance of anyone knowing what went on there, except for the participants. The room was booked for the duration of the planning and the briefing of the exercise, authorised by Major MacBride, who had authority. Nobody outside the three men involved entered the room, which formed part of the Dugway complex. Dugway had two rooms, each available for planning covert operations, each protected. There were no telephones in the room, therefore no bugging of phones, and no access except by the door, which could only be opened by Security, who observed entrance procedures via TV monitors in the control room. Electronic credit-card sized keys were used once then destroyed. Security was responsible for maintenance, which was limited to checking the air and electricity supplies and cleaning. No paper was allowed in or out of the room and no notes taken. The white board was wiped and cleaned after each meeting by one of the participants before Security was allowed in to clean up, which was a token dusting of the area and a full check of the emergency systems. The room was in use from 0830 hours that day and Security, having checked the ID of Major MacBride, authorised the issue of the key, which was produced by a machine built in to the wall that separated Security's control room from the entrance passage. Major MacBride lifted the key from his side of the entrance passage and turned right to face the metal door of the chamber. The door accepted the key and opened, allowing the three to pass into the chamber. The door closed behind them. The chamber was small – three feet wide by six feet long. MacBride inserted the key into the inner door, which opened automatically and allowed them to pass into the room. When the door closed behind them, the lights came on. They were now isolated in the room.

The row of lights in the panels beside the door were all lit. Good, thought MacBride. All is in order. Should any one of the lights fail to glow, then either the bulb had failed or there was a problem.

Light 1 was red – all okay for air-conditioning;
Light 2 was green – all okay for air purity;
Light 3 was orange – all okay for emergency exit systems in case they had to evacuate quickly;
Light 4 was blue – when it flashed, it let those gathered there know that there was a message for someone.

The panel of lights was duplicated on each of the walls so that those involved in the meeting were more likely to see them should they start to flash. Beside the door, at shoulder height, was a separate button marked EXIT.

"How soon can we transfer the funds?" MacBride asked Captain Becker, the banker visiting them from Washington.

"Just give the word, it will be done. How much will you need for the first tranche?"

"Let's keep it low to start with, say $300,000 – that'll be about 200,000 in British pounds," replied Captain Hunter. It was Hunter's show and he was making sure that they knew it.

Security listened intently to the tape, thinking, as he did so, how best to get this information to his sister.

The tape machine was his idea and only he knew of it. The recorder was a good model of professional specifications, having two recording decks, each with twin recording heads and set so that when one side of the tape was finished, the other side would record automatically, and when that tape was finished the second tape would start recording. The resultant tapes could be played in any cassette deck. The set-up was his idea too. Each blue message light in each of the rooms was rigged to a small but sensitive microphone placed there during one of his maintenance routines. The only light connection into the security area was the blue light, the others were routed elsewhere.

So that's it. Set one side against the other using $300,000 as the carrot!

"Is the transfer of this capital being arranged?" enquired Hunter of Becker.

"It can be ready as soon as next week. We will use a bank in Carlisle, England. We have organised a solicitor to act for us. He has been told that it is sale proceeds of real estate, so we will make sure that the documents cover this."

"Good – that's very good. I'm impressed. Is the set-up this end okay?" asked MacBride.

"The transfer will be made to your solicitors as agreed – they will get confirmation in writing," advised Hunter, "and the bank will get the funds into the solicitors' account the same day. Have you asked for cash? The UVF won't like a banker's cheque!"

Becker and MacBride burst out laughing, with Hunter joining in.

Security listened to the rest of the tape which lasted eighty-five minutes. The meetings in the *Room* were usually less than three hours duration, as that was as long as was practical. Those around the table had to go to the bathroom some time, and there were no such facilities in the *Room*. Security was not permitted to leave the control room when a meeting was in place, but he had contingencies – a plastic bucket, which was very useful at times.

The meeting had ended, so MacBride cleaned the white board then pressed the exit button. The panel lights started to flash, and in a matter of seconds the inner door opened, allowing Croft to enter with his cleaning/maintenance trolley. Amid silence, Security cleaned the white board with quick drying solvent, wiped the table and chairs, quickly mopped the floor with a separate white cotton cloth, and gave each of the light panels the once-over. When he had finished, MacBride inserted the key into the door, permitting all, together with the trolley, to leave. The key was retained by the mechanism in the outer door and all headed fairly smartly to the men's room. One hour later, Croft had removed the tape and placed the cassette into its plastic case. He would make two copies and arrange to store them at different sites, as he had done in the past. There were now about a dozen tapes, all covering this particular operation, the objective to achieve by covert means death and injury to many for the benefit of a few. Force the Brits out of Ireland – force Sinn Fein/IRA into destroying the UVF. False claims and counter claims, false evidence planted here and there. The strategy was proven. It worked before in the Gulf; it could work again in Northern Ireland, and that was Hunter's strategy.

Croft's anger gave way to despair – what could he do? If the great American democratic system was against you, who would be for you? Where could he engage help? He was a good electronics man, not a strategist. He started the engine of his 4×4 and drove slowly towards his apartment in Midvale, south of Salt Lake City. It was a comfortable place, not too big as he was not a family man, there was only his wife and himself. The secure parking area was at ground level and was large enough for two vehicles, a chest freezer, the fuse box, storage, and a long workbench. The bench had more than the average person's collection of gadgets and tools, which were kept spotless and set out systematically. There were no windows, but good overhead lighting made working conditions good. In addition to the usual power points there was a telephone extension and a small sink with hot and cold running water. Croft parked in the usual place, beside his wife's BMW 3 Series, and, pressing the button on the wall, looked to confirm that the garage door behind him closed and locked itself. The entrance to the apartment was through a metal covered door directly opposite the BMW's front wheel, and was opened using a five-digit code tapped into the electronic lock. Most of those types of locks had four digits – not Croft's. Five gave him better protection, and not only that, should anyone key the wrong number by mistake, sixty seconds had to pass before the lock would accept a second attempt.

His wife, Mary Lou, was home. She finished early today as manager of the historical Stage Coach Inn, close to Lake Utah, and was beaming as Owen reached the top of the ten stairs from the garage and entered the living quarters.

"That smells good – what is it? T-bone?" He pecked Mary Lou on the cheek, and made his way to the shower, carrying the paper bag containing the tape. She blocked his way and with a glint in her eye put her arms round his neck and drew him towards her. As they embraced, she whispered in his ear, "How would you like to be a father in seven months time?"

He stepped back involuntarily, looked at her middle, with open mouth and somewhat shocked. Me, he thought, a parent? Time stood still as he thought quickly of the education system, medical care, and jobs for his child. Then, as the news sunk in, he said, "Are you *sure* is everything okay? Here, sit down and take it easy, Mary Lou." She enjoyed the moment.

"Don't fuss, Owen, I'm fine," and she found herself sitting on Owen's lap in the living area. The old chair groaned, but it always did that.

"The doctor confirmed it today at lunch time, so I took the rest of the day off and thought we would celebrate." Kissing him on the forehead, she pushed herself free, ". . .now have your shower, while I finish dinner."

What wonderful news! His eye caught the bag containing the tape as he went to shower, so he lifted it and quickly put the tape into the machine in the study, checking that the copying tapes were inserted correctly and depressed the appropriate buttons. He liked T-bone and it was just right as was the sweetcorn and baked potato with sour cream and butter. During the meal, Croft noticed how well Mary Lou was looking – no, not well, that wasn't adequate, blooming. That was it – she was overflowing with happiness, and so was he.

Croft tidied up after the meal while Mary Lou slipped into something more comfortable. Finishing the chores, he moved to the study and noticed that the tape copying had finished. First he removed the original, secured it in the safe behind the fuse box in the garage, and put the copies in separate envelopes. His supply of padded envelopes was getting low. He made a mental note to get more.

"Let's go out for a romantic walk in the forest – our usual walk okay?"

"Sure, I'll change my footgear." The comfortable Nike trainers – quite new – were retrieved from the communal shoe cupboard and, once they were laced, he donned his woollen jacket.

The Uinta National Forest was only across the road from the apartment, but the 4×4 was taken and driven down Interstate 15 to Provo and there to their quiet walk area in the forest.

"This is nice," she said quietly as they walked arm in arm along their favourite path. "How do you feel about the baby, Owen?"

"Sure, I can't believe it. You are just. . . just. . ." He was not normally an emotional person, but was overcome and started to smile and cry at the same time – his eyes filling.

"You are a big softie," she said as she hit him hard in the midriff and, laughing, started to run ahead. He was winded, but recovered quickly and ran after her.

It's the simple things that give most pleasure, he reflected. If only the people in Dugway could see him now. Dugway! The tape! The enjoyment was not to be spoilt – not now, as he forced it all from his mind and caught up with her.

Chapter Nine

The war lived within him, devouring him of needed energy and positive attitude. The walk from the cottage, their base of operations, to the sand in Brown's Bay was only half a mile or less, but that was enough. It was still dark; sunrise was still an hour away and the lack of heat about the place added to the bleakness. He had served his country well and deserved better. The current set-up was satisfactory enough. The cottage, or base of operations as the Brit put it, had the basics of heat, light, running water and bathroom, but it wasn't home. It wasn't what he expected, and it certainly wasn't what he deserved. Promotion to the rank of Major was the least they could have done. Being captain while doing the duties and being responsible for a major job during the Gulf War was exciting. But the war was over. He was ill and then they made him Major: sick, but they gave him the task of looking after the other major. Two majors, but he knew he was the subordinate. Nothing was detected during the medicals, and there were many medicals, including the shrinks. He would get over it in time was the prognosis, and to encourage this they would appoint him to a quiet covert operation in Ireland. Would he be interested? Yes? Good. The chain of command would be simple. Just the two of you, he was told, both majors but as the Brit was the older he would be in charge. Of course, he was told, there may be occasions that he would be contacted to help them out on this or that.

It wasn't the Brit's fault. In fact, the Brit was all right and he, Major Lee Elmer Sutton, could work with him. That wasn't the problem – it was the occurrence of the headaches and unexplained lethargy, yet he had been passed fit. Fit? He wasn't up to it, and they knew that. Why else transfer his salary to pensions, yet not pension him off? There was something wrong. The ethics were out of the window this time.

There were others worse than him. He could have been like them. Totally useless they were, unlike him. He was only partially useless.

He put it down to the dust in the desert. The dust from the tanks that had been destroyed using the depleted uranium shells. He kept out of it as much as possible while others took delight in examining their handiwork. The others were now worse than him.

His head was clearing as he saw the Larne ferry leave on its way to Stranraer. He stood up, looked around and, moving away from the wooden seat, made his way back up the hill to the cottage.

"Bacon and toast all right, Elmer? We've run out of eggs." The major was cooking breakfast and had already shaved.

"Sure, Edward. I'll have a wash up," and switched on his razor.

"How's the head, old boy?" asked Major James Edward de Courcy.

"Not bad. It was hell earlier, but it's okay now."

The cottage was divided into sections rather than rooms, with each section made from hardboard supported by strips of plywood to keep the bulges in check. The main area was used as kitchen, food store, office, and sitting room. The other areas gave them a small bedroom each and a bathroom. Luxuries were limited to a table, stools, an easy chair each, a television and radio, and, of course, telephone. The tools of their trade were kept hidden beneath the floor in a waterproof section under the shower tray that hinged up to allow access. The space was large enough for their small arms, two rifles, ammunition, and satellite link phone, and a small but high-powered radio. Any documents that were considered delicate were also stored there.

The phone rang. Sutton picked it up and heard, 'Contact us using the dish. Third number,' and the line went dead.

"Sounds like we're in business, Edward. They want me to use the dish."

The shower tray was lifted and the satellite link phone retrieved and set up behind the cottage where it could not be seen from the road. The third number on the list of contacts was input and Sutton waited for the connection.

He hung up, switched off, folded the dish and returned the kit to its hiding place.

"We're on vacation, Edward, start packing."

"Vacation? Where to?" asked de Courcy.

"Las Vegas, Edward, all at Uncle Sam's expense."

"Pull the other one, old boy."

"I pick up the tickets and the money from the Consulate's office in Belfast, tomorrow, and we both fly out at the weekend – how about those apples, Major?"

"Tell me more, old boy, that sounds good."

The lethargy had left him now and he was positively full of energy. He told the major of the briefing that was to take place somewhere near Las Vegas and some new project that would interest them both, and offered them the opportunity when they were there to take in a few shows.

"Ever been to Vegas, Edward?" It was never Ed or Eddie, always Edward. When relaxing or off duty, they would use first names; when on duty in the Gulf, it was always rank. It worked that way for them and let each know when business was the order of the day.

"No, never. I suppose it's a den of iniquity, old boy."

"Sure is, Edward, so you will find yourself at home. No eggs, Major?" as he finished off the toast and bacon. De Courcy smiled and said nothing. He was aware of Sutton's illness that was getting worse as the months passed. This trip would pick him up and give him new life. He recognised the tune the American was whistling, with his mind obviously at home somewhere in the mid West, 'Oh, give me a home. . .' that was the tune, and subconsciously de Courcy joined in. They both knew the words and the duet lasted while they tidied up.

"Remember the nights under the stars in Iraq? We would be singing that song and your boys would join in. We had some good days then."

"That's how I know the words, old boy. Yes, the good days, but they were not all good. The destruction all around made me uncomfortable at times." De Courcy became quiet as the memories came back. Then he continued, "We gave them a complete pasting. They didn't have a chance, not a chance, and being war it was either them or us. It's the loss of life that gets me. Who knows what contribution to medicine, arts or sport has been lost to humanity, during the action on the ground. . . what was it. . . 100 hours?"

"Yeah – they were hit real good. We needed to win that one, Major. Okay, you guys were already in a winning streak, what with the Falklands success, but we lost Vietnam, so we needed to win something. It's a pity it had to be so easy. That takes the reward out of it. It could be your turn to lose the next one."

"The next one?"

"Ireland. It only takes some IRA squad to get the hold of a nuclear device. The threat to set it off is all they need. You guys would pull out and that's a fact. The killings in the past around the borders and even in the towns didn't arouse the population, but a nuclear show – wow!" He sat down in the easy chair, hands behind his head, eyes closed. "What a mess that would be, Edward," sighed Sutton.

"What if the device went off in Las Vegas?" jested de Courcy. That brought Sutton up shortly.

"Look, Edward, there are enough nuts around for that not to be funny," and he returned to his relaxed position.

"What are we at today, Edward?" asked Sutton.

*

The use of words by those whose language is classified as English differs not only between generation, but between peoples living a few hundred yards from each other. The language used by the doctor in Whitehead bears no relation to the farmer in Whitehead, but both speak English. The Americans gave up English a long time ago, and speak an amalgamation of eastern and western tongues that may be defined as American. Sutton regarded himself as speaking American and enjoyed trying to annoy de Courcy by refusing to use the Oxford University standard. The major was past trying to correct him, so he ignored the grammatical errors being voiced by his sidekick. After all, as someone mentioned on more than one occasion, 'If it ain't understood, it ain't good English'.

"There it is, Edward. A thousand bucks each and we travel first class," as the cash and air tickets were dumped on the table. "It's only for three days, though. Not bad for three days – huh?" as Sutton pointed to the money.

"Pack a spare shirt anyway, Elmer, we might get lost if we're lucky."

"Travel light is right. Hand luggage, I guess, will be all we need and no uniform."

Major de Courcy examined the tickets, noticing that the departure times from Belfast to London were early. The first flight out no doubt, but he was grateful to accept the free holiday.

"On the basis that there is no such thing as a free lunch, I wonder what your boys are up to? I haven't contacted my people recently, so I'd better do it now."

"Your people? You mean Lisburn?"

"That's right, a quick phone call will do, but not from here. I'll use the public phone at the Rinkha while you get some eggs."

*

"Very disappointing old boy, very disappointing," declared de Courcy. Las Vegas in daytime is a grey, unattractive and characterless place. He expected better.

"This is a night-time joint, Edward. Just wait until it's dark." Sutton smacked his lips. "Home at last - nothing like home to make you feel good."

"I thought you were from Texas, old boy."

"Yes, Sir, Texas is home too. Fort Worth to be exact, but anywhere in the States is home for me. Great place, huh?"

"Not my cup of tea this. Even Brown's Bay is preferable, just look," as he surveyed all about him outside the hotel. White walls, grey walls, high and low, nothing interesting in sight - no shops restaurants or wide open spaces with views.

"Take it easy, Edward, this is just hotel country. It's cheaper here than in the centre. Wait till you see the centre with its lights and all the shows, just wait."

Sutton was back to his lively self, enjoying the proper accents, the cars on the proper side of the road, and proper fast food.

*

"What time is it, Edward? I've not changed my watch."

De Courcy changed his watch before the plane landed, and rather than tell him the time, took his watch off and handed it over.

Sutton adjusted his battery-powered watch to match the major's ageing mechanical Omega.

"Thanks, Mac."

"Mac?" queried de Courcy.

"I must be thinking of a big Mac. Want one?"

"No, Elmer, I want to sleep."

"Here. . ." as he returned the Omega. "Where did you get the antique watch?"

Looking at the gold coloured chronometer complete with gold coloured strap, he silently agreed that it probably *was* an antique. As he fastened it in place his mind went back many years.

"Present from my wife Hilda – the year we married. It keeps good time and I've become attached to it."

"Yeah? Well, I've to call someone up in Salt Lake City – duty calls – back soon," and Sutton left the major in the reception area.

Sutton phoned the number he was given by the Consul in Belfast and listened attentively to the instructions he was given. That caused the headache to return.

"You're on your own, Major, for the next day or so. I am being taken to some restricted military area near Salt Lake City. I leave tonight."

Chapter Ten

They were picked up at the hotel at eight. The car stopped to drop the British major off at Glitter Gulch. Sutton left de Courcy looking open mouthed at all the lights and sounds of the real Las Vegas, and disappeared into the wilds of somewhere called Nellis Airforce Base. The direct military flight to Dugway took forty minutes and by 2200 hours Sutton was in his room in order to be ready for the morning meeting at 0830 hours. He was shown the canteen and given two vouchers. One voucher was for the evening meal, the other was for breakfast. He didn't sleep well and didn't much fancy home after all. Perhaps de Courcy was right. Brown's Bay was a lot more civilised than this. The amenities might be better here, but the quality of life right now was not as good. The headache was a little easier but it came with monotonous regularity – morning and evening – and he was not looking forward to the morning.

He was met during breakfast by MacBride, who sat with him and talked pleasantries while he ate.

"Sorry to bring you all this way for a few hours, Major, but we have something to help you and the important work you are doing. It's not really my show. You will be briefed. . .," looking at his watch, ". . .in about half an hour. See that door?" as he pointed to the left. "To the left of it is Security. There is a sign, so you cannot miss it – I'll meet you there at 0830, okay?"

"Yes, Major, at 0830."

"Fine," and with a pat on the shoulder, MacBride left him to enjoy his waffles.

*

The three entered the *Room*. Sutton was aware of their false friendliness and tried not to show his reticence.

It was his first time in the *Room*, and he knew it would not be his last.

"This is Captain Hunter, Major, who is in charge of the project. The fact that you outrank him is immaterial. You are working for us, not the British, and don't forget it," said MacBride, who, having got that over, relaxed a little. "Your record is damn good, Major; in fact it's because of your record that you have been chosen for this little exercise. Captain Hunter will fill you in. Okay, Captain?"

"Firstly, I want to thank you for coming so promptly. Secondly, you are the only person able to do the job, which makes you the important guy; and lastly this meeting hasn't taken place," were Hunter's opening remarks .

"Come again?" asked Sutton.

"It's official, Major," confirmed Hunter. "There will be no record of this meeting, or of any other meeting we have here, but this is for real, and could do you a lot of good." Not bad for an opening, thought Hunter, who was pleased with himself.

"Back off, Captain. I've come a long way as ordered – that's right, *ordered* – and no small backroom captain is telling me that there is going to be no record of this meeting."

"Easy, Major," MacBride interrupted. "The captain's right. The security of this thing is so tight that we are not permitted to record this. It comes from the Pentagon."

"The Pentagon. How do I know that?"

"I'm telling you, Major, that's why. Now just sit and listen – go ahead, Captain."

"Yes, Sir. I'll tell you where I'm coming from. We have it in mind to assist the poorly supported majority in Northern Ireland, against the murderous IRA gangs who are in the minority, using intelligence we have managed to come by. Don't interrupt, Major – wait till I've explained the lot. The secret is getting the killing to stop. I've come up with this. The ethnic cleansing being done against the majority living in the border areas has not been stopped. The loyalist gangs are nowhere, because they have no people, no ideas and no money. That means that they continue to get hit, or their supporters get hit, and they do very little. However, when they do retaliate, what they do is small and gets them plenty of bad publicity, because, unlike the IRA, they are bad at publicity. We'll change that. The IRA have plenty of arms and we know, using satellite surveillance, where they are stored. We want you – and your British major friend – to tell the Loyalist side where the IRA arms and stores are situated. The UVF people – that's the Loyalist side – won't do nothing for nothing. So, we pay them to do it. We pay them not to grab the arms for themselves, but to tell the Brits where they are. The Brits get the arms, the UVF get the credit, and with the arms taken out the killing stops. Any comments?"

Sutton let out a long slow noisy breath.

"You're a backroom, boy, isn't that right, Captain?" Sutton asked quietly.

"Yes, Sir, and proud of it."

"You think up these ideas, and we carry them out – right?"

"Right."

"You get away with it, and we get killed – right?"

MacBride didn't like that. "Don't be nasty, Major. The captain here has the backing of the Pentagon on this one, so just relax and let him hear your comments."

Major Sutton took time to clear his head, and to test his understanding of the project. He started slowly. . .

"Let me check this out. You have satellite pictures of IRA arms dumps, right?" Captain Hunter nodded. "Why not just tell the Brits and save a lot of hassle?"

Hunter came back immediately. "For two reasons. One – the Brits would kick up trouble in Washington if they knew we carried out surveillance over their territory; and two – the Administration would not survive the flack from the Irish-American and Irish National Caucus guys."

"Horse apples," was Sutton's response.

"Not in the Pentagon, Mister," interrupted MacBride.

"Suppose I buy that. What if the UVF people want to keep the guns for themselves?"

"They would get blown away," Hunter retorted, "as the arms dumps are booby-trapped. The Brits could bypass them, they are good at that, but the UVF are not up to it."

"Suppose they want guns?" asked Sutton.

"We could see that they get them, but the risk would be theirs. It's like this. . . if they want them, they organise the purchase and the delivery. All we do is tell them where they are at," Hunter replied smugly.

"The money?"

"Cash. In British notes, not traced to us. You pick up the money in England and transport it to the UVF."

"Just like that, eh? We call at a bank, cash a cheque, put the dough in our pocket, and hand it over to some bloody terrorists? You're mad – mad."

"Not quite like that. There's no cheque. The cash will be waiting for you, all you do is sign a form in front of a solicitor who ensures that it is all legal. By the way, the transaction is done in a place called Carlisle – it's arranged – and you can't transport the money by ferry or air. You will need to arrange for transport under cover. A boat or something with only the two of you – you and Major de Courcy – knowing about it"

"Why?" Sutton was finding the whole idea quite funny, but he managed not to laugh.

"Searches. How would you explain $330,000 to the ferry police or to airport security?" asked Hunter.

"How much?" gasped Sutton.

"Up to one million, the first cut being $330,000, say £220,000 British."

"You guys are serious, aren't you?"

"Just test us out. The money is available in four days – no, say five days after you request it. You request it by phoning the third number on your list using the dish."

"Like recently."

"Yeah, like recently. One final thing, if this gets out of hand, you're on your own. If it comes off, you'll be having lunch with the President. Any more?"

"Only the big one. How do I contact the UVF? Who and where?"

"You don't. Let the Brit – I mean your British major friend make the contact. Details of who will be given to you upstairs, it's some guy called Lacey in Ballycarry near Island Magee. . . Ever heard of it?"

"Yeah. . . I've been through it, it's small place. And it's 'whom', not 'who'." Sutton thought de Courcy and his English teacher would have been proud of him.

During this discussion, Sutton remained seated at the table, head bowed supported by his hands. He didn't care about any of this.

"I take it I can tell the 'Brit', as you call him, all you told me?"

"Sure. One more thing, we must have a weekly call from you – same day, same time. . . usual number. . . the dish, okay?"

"Okay. I'll choose the day and time – any more?"

"Not unless you have."

"The guns for the UVF, where can they get them?" asked Sutton.

"Let's wait," suggested Hunter, "they might not ask for them."

"And if they do?"

"Then contact us for details."

"The money. What if they ask for more?"

"Tough. The budget is fixed. No harm in asking, though, circumstances may change," replied Hunter.

"The surveillance pictures, how many and how do we interpret them?"

"There are twelve known locations in Northern Ireland. They come with map references that are easy to follow. Even you, Major Sutton, could follow them." It wasn't meant as a jibe, Hunter always spoke like that. "Anything else, Major?" asked Hunter.

"Let me out of here, I take it I can get back to Vegas?"

"Sure. Do you want us to arrange it or do it yourself?" asked MacBride.

"Myself, and I need $500, to cover extras. The Brit has expensive tastes."

MacBride pressed the exit button and they left within five minutes.

*

MacBride and Hunter were alone in the canteen with surrounding tables empty.

"Where did you get that rubbish on the arms dumps, Captain Hunter?"

"It's okay, Major. I have a contact in surveillance who told me about it. I know about fifteen locations, but twelve is the maximum he could guarantee me. All I need to do is call him. Let's wait until Sutton – I mean, Major Sutton – and the Brit contact us. We can get surveillance to send the information on the dumps to the solicitor in England. That way we stay out of it."

"If this blows up, son, it's *your* face that gets it," MacBride reminded him.

*

"Las Vegas, old boy, is certainly a night-time venue. I could do with more time here. Did you know that they have a reproduction of a volcano. Imagine it. . . a volcano, complete with noise and lava. . . Did you know that, Elmer?"

"That's quite somethin', eh? What did you make of the shows, Edward?"

"Haven't been to any, old boy, no time."

"We'll get one in tonight before we push off for Brown's Bay. I got an extra $500 for expenses."

"Good for you, old boy. Where are those. . . what did you call them. . . Big Macs? I could risk one of those," and they both ventured into a side street and were engulfed in the crowds of locals and tourists, ending up as nonentities with sticky fingers and gas-filled bellies as they partook of the best that the civilised world of Las Vegas could offer.

*

Airports are much the same the world over, and as part of the capitalist wealth generating system if they don't make money they don't exist. It's not quite a monopoly because there are many airports and many airlines. Should the fees be too high, one airline may threaten to pull out, leaving space for another competing airline, so they stay. So it is virtually a monopoly. The journey home was broken by a long stop in Denver which provided time for Sutton to brief de Courcy on the project. He withheld nothing. They didn't notice the preparation of their Boeing 747 jumbo. The routine had been carried out dozens of times before, with cleaners and their empty plastic bags and machines entering the aircraft, and some thirty minutes later parading out with bags full. How do people on an aeroplane in the air generate so much litter? Separate from this, the catering teams were taking away the used and replenishing with the fresh. Fuel was monitored as tanks were loaded, and engineers having various skills checked the undercarriage, control surfaces and engines. All this was going on while the luggage of those who had arrived was being removed, and in the queue politely waiting their turn were the luggage of those planning to depart. There was a problem with something at the front undercarriage. A gas cylinder was removed from inside the housing and the replacement wouldn't fit. An interested traveller, probably someone who only enjoyed long haul flights once every year or two, was engrossed in the whole exercise and was now a little apprehensive. He saw the engineer take away the cylinder, and wondered whether he would return. How important was the cylinder? As he was due to fly on that plane to London, would it be safe without the cylinder? Perhaps the cylinder should not have been there in the first place. He was deciding whether he should inform someone and if so whom and what he would say, when he saw to his relief the engineer return from the right of the aircraft, standing on one of those low-sided, heavy looking airport machines that moved about at speed. The driver, complete with ear defenders, as was nearly everybody else about the aeroplane, assisted the engineer to lift the replacement cylinder into its home above the wheels. A moving platform was used as a lever. It was similar to, but smaller than, the platforms used to load the luggage. All this detail, all these people, all important for a safe journey.

Understanding the detail of the Dugway project was just as important. Should something be missed or taken up incorrectly, the chances of failure would increase and place them in a very dangerous position. Their discourse helped to shorten the journey, as did the plastic taste of the hygienic dinner. Every other hour, de Courcy took an exercising stroll from the spacious upper deck where they were located, as that was recommended in the passengers' instruction booklet. The cramped tourist section made him appreciate the privileges of first-class travel. Better still was knowing that Uncle Sam had paid for it. It would soon be his turn to contribute, so he decided to make it a priority to discuss part of the project with some of the authorities.

Chapter Eleven

"You're off again then?" her brother-in-law, Joseph Lacy, asked. She needed these breaks away, and he was glad for her to have them. "I leave on Friday, only for a week. Owen says it's big – very big – and I need to know immediately. He can't trust the post, and the phone call would be too long and not safe, so the best way is to see him. You don't mind do you, Joe?"

"You need a break – have you got enough money, Sis?"

"I have it all arranged. Owen arranged the air tickets, and as it's business, expense money should be allocated by Council. That's where I was yesterday. I got £500 – it probably came from that Post Office job they did a year ago."

"Aye – well, don't tell me and I won't know – visiting your brother, that's all I know. See you when you return next week, can you give me a hand with the cattle? The milking is finished and we'll put them in the wee field," as Joe Lacy opened the door.

"Surely," and they went about the farm doing the routine before breakfast.

Susannah Lacy didn't like travelling to Head Office. It was in Belfast, and Belfast wasn't her ideal place. She felt out of it. Her accent didn't fit and she found the people not as friendly as those in Larne. But she needed the money, and it was business. They understood it was business, and in view of her husband's contribution to the cause, and her past help, they granted her an audience. It wasn't a meeting, it was an audience. They didn't use the word meeting. Anyone going to a meeting in that area around Dee Street was going to church or to a gospel hall. She didn't know that Belfast had a different culture, but the cause was the same. Deep down, the cause was the thing, and the cause might be in danger if she had interpreted correctly her brother's request. She didn't know it but the Inner Council needed her. The Inner Council consisted of four people, all of them in their thirties, and all had been successful in front-line operations. That meant killing someone from the other side, not civilians, but hard men on the other side. Hard men of known activity on the front line, who would not be stopped by army or police action, because the Army and police were not interested in stopping them. Their belief in this and in spreading the cause had increased their numbers. They kept quiet about it, of course. No need to let the other side know your strength.

*

The discussion was hard, but they agreed at the end that she was the best they had for the job, so she was going to be offered it. It was fortunate she wanted to see them. They could use the opportunity to ask her. Information gets fed back, sometimes without realising it. The information coming to the Inner Council over the past six months all pointed to her strength. They needed someone to think of strategy. They had managed to date by accident, not by planning. The other side planned, they reacted. That must change. And so they were ready to accept her, and had found her strategy to be good. She would be required to join the Inner Council, but they were prepared for that too and had already sounded out the General and the General Committee, who gave approval.

The guards knew to expect someone, but did not recognise her because they didn't know her. But the man standing at the corner of the bar knew her, and as she arrived, five minutes early, he noticed some of the men giving her the once-over, with approval in their hearts. He moved from the bar, gently spoke in her ear, "Follow me" and, lifting the hinged entrance flap to the bar, ushered her in and up the stairs at the back. One of the guards took up the first man's position, and from his vantage point was able to see anyone enter or leave. The stairs were steep and narrow, not well lit, and appeared to stop at a door marked STORES. Her guide did something to the wall beside the door, and a panel, about three feet wide by four feet high, slid back.

"Mind your head." He ducked down and entered the space behind the panel. More stairs, just as narrow as before were before her, and she climbed them behind the man. The panel closed behind them. She climbed quite a bit which surprised her, as she didn't think it was a tall building. Then she knew why. The roof timbers were just above her head, yet the passage she was now going down was as narrow as the stairs – about two feet wide. It was a long passage, lit by the occasional forty-watt bare bulb. She must have walked over a hundred feet and she was probably nowhere near the building she entered. At the end of the passage there was another door, which the man ignored and waited for her.

"Okay? Got your breath back?"

"I'm fine – go ahead," Mrs Lacy replied.

He again did something – pushed a hidden button, she guessed – and a panel similar to the one she entered earlier opened to allow them to pass. She found herself standing in a small windowless, stuffy and bare six-foot square area that smelt of dusty clothing. The panel closed behind them making a metallic click as it locked. She was surprised to see the wall in front of her, open, as if hinged on the right, offering an entrance into a large room where the Inner Council rose to greet her.

"Welcome, Mrs Lacy. I trust your wee trip here wasn't too bad. It's for your protection – that's all. You don't know where you are, and that's the way it stays." It was the one with the most tattoos who spoke. Pleasant enough, but she wouldn't want to meet him in a dark alley. He was in short sleeves, open collar, as were the others, but he would have been around sixteen stone and less than six foot high. Probably a little older than her. The other two were much slimmer, but that wouldn't be hard. There was a wooden table with a jug of water and a dozen glasses, all clean and tidy, on the right hand side as she looked, and a large union flag on the wall behind. No windows but fans were built into two of the walls to circulate the air, and the place was painted a white that had turned to a creamy yellow and had peeled in many places. A small NO SMOKING instruction was on the table at the left, and there were just enough chairs to go round. The man who brought her moved one of the unused chairs to the corner of the now closed wall and sat down. She noticed doors on each of the walls that were bolted on the inside, top and bottom.

The man continued, "Have a seat," and gestured to the remaining vacant chair opposite him across the table. She sat down, and not knowing how to start found herself saying, "This is some place. I bet it's nowhere near the bar where I came in."

The three men looked at her, each other, then the spokesman smiled one of those smart, smug, self-satisfied grins. "You're right there – and you'll *never* know," and there was some minor noise that came from the man behind her that changed the attitude of those before her.

"My information is," it was the man behind the water jug, "that you have a request. In view of your, and of course your late husband's, achievement for this organisation, on behalf of the Inner Council I am delighted to offer you this audience. Want a drink?" and he offered a glass of water.

"I could use one – please," and she drank a relieving mouthful. Silence.

"I don't know how, where – I mean; this is strange for a country girl like me, and a little daunting." Remembering her brother's words on the phone gave her courage.

"There's big trouble, I don't know how big, but it's coming from the US Government, and I need some money to get there to find out what it is," she said quickly in one breath.

"Slow down a bit, Susannah." It was the man on the left this time. "We are just ordinary people like yourself – except that we are not too good on your accent. Could you say that again – pretend I'm stupid – okay?"

"You are stupid, sure." It was the thin man and the first time he spoke, and it caused the others, including the man behind her, to laugh.

"It's our fault, Susannah, not yours. May I call you Susannah, Mrs Lacy?" She nodded. "What's the big trouble?"

"I don't know yet, but I have a contact who works for the US Army and he has found something that will affect us here."

"Contact? That would be your brother Owen, right?" the spokesman again.

"How did you know. . .?"

The spokesman raised his hands. "Never mind – how much do you want, when do you want it, and how soon are you going?"

She was surprised at that and wasn't prepared for what happened after she answered.

"Say £300 should do – if that's possible? I have the plane tickets but no money to live on. I leave on Friday, so to organise dollars and stuff I would need the money today – is that possible?"

"No sooner said than done – here." The spokesman reached behind him, and from a box that she hadn't seen before he handed her

£300 in used notes and some US dollars. "There's about £500 all told. You can get travel cheques in dollars at the airport – okay?"

She stumbled over a few words of thanks and was interrupted before gaining fluency.

"Fancy a bite to eat? Would a burger and chips do? It's been ordered anyway and will be brought up." He, the spokesman, was doing his best to be nice and making a fair stab at it, so she relaxed a little more.

"Great – I could do with something. You know, I was so worried you might turn me down for the money that I didn't eat much this morning," she responded.

They all laughed now, and the man at the left rose and went to the door at the left, unbolted it, and shouted out, "Bring it up now!"

"That's not too good for security, is it – shouting like that? Why not have a button like that for the panels?" she enquired quite innocently.

They didn't like that. The spokesman was heard to say, "She's right, you know, damn it, she's right," and turning to her, "We have something to ask you, Susannah, we'll talk over the cup of tea – it's about—"

"Here it is now." One of the men went to the door and took a large tray from an unseen delivery person, and slowly set it on the table. Mugs of tea were already poured out, two bottles of sauce – one red and one brown – six plates having a burger, chips, onion rings and a fork – no knife – only forks were removed from the tray and handed round. The man behind her had joined them at the table, where, without announcement, they began to eat.

She moved the plate closer but quickly retracted her hand. "The plate's hot."

"That's okay – the chips are cold," joked the man on the right and then continued, "Would you like a job helping us, Susannah?"

"I might. What is it?"

"Before I tell you – should you say no, you will *never* be allowed to meet us again. It's for safety – nothing else – only safety. The cause must be protected."

"That's fine – I was surprised you granted me an audience in the first place," she uttered rather nervously.

"You've done us proud in the past," the man on the right again said, "and your record and that of your late husband has not been forgotten."

She was quiet now but managed a barely audible "Thanks," and welcomed the burger, which was good, the chips, which were better, and the onion rings, best of all. The others smothered theirs in sauce of both types, but mostly tomato. She didn't use the sauce.

"We are not as well organised as the enemy, and it's our own fault. What we want is someone, like you from the outside, to take a look at how we do things and suggest improvements. How does that grab you?"

"You mean a one-off job? That's not too bad – I think I could do that."

"Initially, yes, then if it works out – for both of us – we could look long term. Say a place on the Inner Council in charge of planning like—"

"On the Council! Do you think I could do it?" she whispered.

"No problem – you have given us ideas without knowing it in the past, this will just put it into a proper form – ah – what's it called? – you know – organised proper, not one-off here and there but ongoing."

"Like a 'think-tank', looking at past, present and future?" she ventured.

"That's it, Susannah, a think-tank. There's a word for it."

"Strategy." It was the man who showed her to the room from the bar. She looked at him with greater interest. He was the oldest there, in his late fifties, and she thought she should know him.

"In charge of strategy – interested?" the spokesman again.

"Interested! – you try and stop me. Oh – there's one thing – or two. Will I be accepted – as a girl on the Council – accepted by the others who are not on the Council, and," pausing to draw courage, "how do I know you are not having me on?"

They laughed.

"If we were not who we are, would we have known of your brother in Dugway?" – That shook her. She thought no one but she knew that – "and of your work with your late husband in Dublin three years ago? The bomb at the enemy's secret hideout near Phoenix Park?" That also shook her. Nobody, nobody, knew that one.

"I see," pausing to gather her thoughts. "When do I start?"

"You just have – welcome, Mrs Lacy, to the Inner Council." It was the man who showed her from the bar. "I'm the General, this is. . ." as he introduced the others by name to her and then instructed her how she might contact them for future meetings.

"Never use the phone, never use the mail – always face to face – okay?"

"What if there's an emergency – how do I—"

"You don't. From now on, one of our surveillance team will always be with you and will know if there's an emergency. That's how it is. You understand, don't you?"

"Yes," was all she could say.

"The next meeting will be – say – two days after you get back from wherever. Are you flying into Belfast International?"

"No – City Airport – I couldn't get a direct flight – I'm flying from London, and the price into City was cheapest."

"City? That's fine – we have people there. We will know when you arrive – so we'll see you two days after that – say 12 noon here – at the bar as usual," instructed the General. "Good luck at Green Bay," he said.

"How did you know that?" Again she was shocked.

It was only a guess, but the General knew that she visited her brother after her husband's funeral and assumed that she would return to the same place. While she was there, she sent a postcard to her brother-in-law with the comment '*Journey good, weather good, all looking after me well*', and the card was in her file. The postmark was 'Green Bay'. The General knew his guess was confirmed.

"You are not the only one with contacts over there. Show her out please, use the usual exit." She left feeling rather bewildered through the door the food came in by. In no time she was in a back street where she was accompanied to her car, which was guarded for her by unseen eyes.

Chapter Twelve

Susannah Lacy liked Canada. It was big and reminded her of home, only on a larger scale. The large towns and cities were so much cleaner than home. The lack of vandalism and graffiti were only noticed when she returned home. Despite that, she preferred home. Home was not perfect, but it was home, and she couldn't envisage circumstances that would entice her to change to a different home. People are like that, unless the whole way of life is threatened and self-preservation requires emigration. Her feelings were not of being threatened, only saddened that a minority were out to try and force the majority to give way. They, the majority, did give way but were forced to do so, and that was wrong. If only they had been allowed to give willingly and gracefully, then force would not have been required, and Willie, her husband, would still be alive. Politicians were to blame. No, that's too simple, she thought, we the people are to blame. We follow the herd instinct to survive, and the leader of the herd is blind. We elected the leader.

The in-flight movie did not interest her and allowed her thoughts to drift into her history.

William Hugh Lacy was a good man. They had enjoyed their short time together – how long was it? Three months, three days and three hours of marriage. Three months, three days and three hours of happiness. No, she was wrong. The time before marriage and up to when they decided to marry was also a good time. Better than good, she was happy then too – four years of happiness and a welling up of joy between them. Her heart ached for a baby. If only we had made different plans, but we were too sensible – the timing had to be right, and it wasn't going to be right for another six months. So she missed out and tried to accept it. She would try and forget by placing her energies into hitting back at the enemy. Perhaps there was a better way than force, perhaps she could think of a different strategy, perhaps. . .

The flight carried her to Montreal, then a connecting flight a few hours later to Chicago, then to Milwaukee, and lastly by car to the cabin between Green Bay and Brussels. Her brother met her at Milwaukee, having flown there the day before to allow him to open up the cabin and get in supplies.

She travelled with one large case and a small holdall as hand luggage.

"Does your wife know?" Susannah asked him.

"She knows I'm at the cabin and she knows you are here, but I told her you wanted away for a few days and fancied the cabin rather than Salt Lake City, so I suppose she knows something's up."

"I've got something for you – guess what?"

"Not soda bread!" She nodded. "Good on you – you don't have any potato bread as well, do you?"

"Don't be greedy," she chided, "as a matter of fact I have."

"Great – guess what's for tea then?" Owen stated.

Croft drove the hired car off the road, down towards the Bay, round the corner, and there it was – The Cabin. Well sheltered, not seen from the road, and sitting in a clearing about one hundred metres from the water's edge. He handed her the key.

"Here – open up while I get the luggage."

"It's quiet, isn't it?" she observed as she took in the scenery.

"Just give it a minute or two – the noise of the car has quietened it. Listen – here it comes."

The birds started up as if being led by an unseen conductor, commencing a new movement in the day-long symphony.

"This is not as heavy as it looks," he said, lifting the case out of the trunk and carrying it into the cabin.

"Tired?" he asked.

"A bit – journeys always make me tired, and the time difference doesn't help."

"We'll not discuss things till tomorrow then," offered Croft. "Another day won't make any difference – let's have a walk around the shore."

They walked about a mile along the rocky shore, sometimes leaving it to pass an obstacle by making a detour inland of a few yards.

"How are you really keeping, Sis?" He called her that years ago when they were growing up on the farm, and it had stuck.

"There are times – you know – difficult – but I get by, Joe helps me to cope – as does the work at the farm. It should be easier now. I have a new job," she smiled as she told him.

"A new job? Tell me."

"I got it before I left – unexpected too. Mind you, it's really unpaid."

"Unpaid? – I see – what is it?"

"You mustn't tell anyone – not even Mary Lou. If it became known, I would become expendable."

He stopped walking, looked around to make sure they were alone – quite silly really, as there was nobody within miles – then grabbed her arms. "You're not into bomb making?"

"No – nothing to do with the killing side," she assured him.

"Thank heavens. This is dangerous enough, this UVF thing – I couldn't help you over there – I need you to be part of it, but not in it."

"I'm in it – and how!" She was now edgy. "We've had this out before – and you'll not change me – I'm staying in – if only for William's sake."

He nearly went too far. It is not possible to be half in. It's all or nothing, he thought.

"What's the job then?"

"Strategy. To help out with strategy."

He said nothing for a while as they stood there in the shade. There were trees round them, and the water could be heard lapping gently on the shore.

"We'll head back," so they turned towards the cabin. "We can go over some information tomorrow. What do you understand by strategy?" he asked.

"Their Intelligence is quite good, but they don't use it property. That's where I come in. They know I'm here, in Green Bay."

"They know?" That worried him. If they know, probably his own people knew. His own people couldn't know the reason. The place, possibly, but the reason – no, he could be secure in his own mind they didn't know the reason.

"How do you know they know?"

"Something said by the General – yes, I met the General."

"You *are* in deep. I hope you know what you're doing."

Conversation died and was not resurrected until they had returned to the cabin.

"I'll start the generator. We'll have something to eat, then see what's what – okay, Sis?"

The generator gave enough power for the cooking, lighting and water heating, but it meant keeping fuel for it, and right now he was low in fuel. He guessed it would last until about noon tomorrow, so decided to go into town now and get some. She prepared the meal, he loaded the car with empty diesel cans and drove to Brussels.

*

"That's good soda, Sis. What is it – Ormo?"

"That's right, but the potato bread is from 'Bread and Butter' in Whitehead."

"I remember them. Do you remember a crowd of us eating potato bread sandwiches with cake, on top of Muldersleigh, and being able to see down Larne Lough one way, and Ailsa Craig and Scotland the other way?"

Memories of childhood. Happy days long ago.

"That's right, but it wasn't cake, it was just lemonade in a big C & C bottle," she recalled.

"I was doing "A" levels, you "O" levels – remember?"

She didn't answer, but the thought was pleasant and brought a tear.

They ate on the porch, which ran the length of the cabin and was wide enough to take the table and chairs. He was concentrating on the bread and didn't notice her wipe her eyes quickly. It was the memory of William that caused it, and try as she might she couldn't fight it.

"Sorry, Owen – excuse me," she said and, entering the cabin, ran to the room at the back holding a paper tissue to her face. She closed the door behind her and from the porch, Owen could hear her sobbing quite heavily. He didn't know what to do. He only knew that he couldn't eat any more. The sight of his poor sister running away like that ruined any appetite he had. He tidied up, poured a mug of tea for her from the pot sitting on the flat stone beside the door, and went inside.

"Tea, Sis?" Knocking the door gently, he ventured, "Can I come in?" and opened the door.

She was quiet now and was sitting on the floor with her head resting on her knees.

"Thanks, Owen. I'm all right now. Silly, isn't it? Something someone says quite innocently and I'm off."

He knew not to say anything, just to wait, to listen, and to be there. He put her tea on the floor beside her and sat on the floor facing her. She picked up the mug of tea and took a sip.

"That's better." After a few moments of silence she explained.

"Sorry, Owen. My first date with William was a walk – we walked up Muldersleigh."

Chapter Thirteen

Breakfast was bacon and eggs cooked on the electric hot plate powered by the generator.

"Is the water hot enough for a shower?" she asked.

"Sure is – go ahead, this will be ready before you're finished."

It was, and out there miles from any room or Inner Council audience, nectar couldn't have tasted better.

"How long can you stay, Owen?"

"Only two more days – but you can stay on if you want. The car is hired for the week."

"No – not on my own – two days will do," she decided.

The cabin was furnished for hard use and evidence of use was everywhere. The floor, bare except for a well worn rug, was in need of renewal, but as the roof was made good last year the floor could wait. The walls had nails hammered in strategic points from which hung the means to survive. A torch on the nail near the front door, the key to the generator house on a nail at the back door. Other nails supported a pair of binoculars, a compass, and a radio. The stone fireplace had not been used since he bought the place a few years ago, but the smoke stains were still there.

"Some day, Owen, you should clean this place. It might look good."

"Some day you'll get a thick ear!" he replied.

"Time for business?" she asked.

"Right – just let me check this place out," as he removed a box of tricks from his large briefcase and gave her a sign to say nothing by bringing his finger to his lips. He switched it on. . . nothing. He walked round the room pointing the gadget in all directions while studying the readings. Satisfied that all was as it should be, Croft left it switched on and placed it on the floor in the middle of the room. The second box of tricks looked similar, but had two short aerials pointing in opposite directions from its top. He switched that one on and repeated the routine. . . nothing.

"Just making sure there's nothing listening, Sis. All clear, but I'll leave them on, in case," and he placed the second box beside the first.

"Some security devices?" she guessed.

"That's right. . . Now. . .," as he settled down in the easy chair, "you first. . . What's this job of yours?"

"Their strategy is weak, their intelligence is quite good, but as I told you, they don't use it properly. My job is to help them use it."

"That's what William did, eh?"

"Yes, but he was only on the fringe of it. They know that now, and yet they want me to take it further. Up to now they have reacted to events with nothing planned to control events. Too much waste, too many deaths. I hope to change their ideas by continuing where William left off. We were starting to do this and getting somewhere too when. . . when. . ."

"Yes, Sis, I know. . . Are you sure you want this?"

"I need it, Owen, I don't know about wanting it."

A minute or so passed before the silence was broken by Croft getting up and checking out the dials on the equipment, and, once satisfied, returning to the chair.

"What do they do?" she asked, nodding at the boxes.

"Just something I put together for work – to warn if anyone is listening to us."

"Out here?"

"Better safe than dead, Sis. Now it's my turn."

He looked straight into her eyes and announced, "How would the UVF react to receiving proof that the US Government. . . – all unofficially, of course – . . .funded terrorism in Northern Ireland?"

She returned his stare, so he continued.

"I have – and they will be made available to you – tapes of secret meetings where strategy for covert work to assist the IRA is discussed, approved, and made ready for action."

"The Americans wouldn't dare send anyone in. It would. . . it would. . ." She was lost for words while her imagination drew up scenarios she found hard to accept. ". . .NATO. . . Europe. . . They couldn't send people in."

"They don't have to." He got up and checked the dials again and, satisfied that all was safe, removed a cassette player from the briefcase and placed it before her on the table.

"Just listen. . . say nothing. . . listen, and wait until you hear it all. You'd better be ready for this – and there's more than one tape."

He switched it on, and in no time she was engrossed. Susannah listened to all the tapes, without a break, that covered the three meetings Croft had recorded. When the last tape had finished, he switched off the recorder.

"The batteries will need to be recharged soon. I suggest you listen to the tapes again after lunch," and set the kit up for a second hearing. She was numbed by it all. It's too much to take in, it's unreal, it's criminal. It's the end of me, she thought, if they know that I know.

"How did you get this on tape? I mean, surely these meetings were held in secure areas that couldn't be taped?"

"Don't ask, Sis, and you can't answer. Just let me say – nobody knows but the two of us."

"You must have set it up yourself," she gasped as the realisation of the danger swept over her. "When this gets out, they could trace it back to you, and then. . ."

"Take it easy, Sis. There is always the other option."

"Option?"

"Destroy the tapes. Let's have lunch."

"Destroy the tapes? Don't you dare! We have evidence here to blow the IRA away! Just think – even the threat to use this would stop the dollars and stop the flow of guns. Well, slow the flow anyway. And the killings. This is better than I first thought."

"Lunch?"

She had not moved from the chair in front of the cassette player. Stretching to relieve the tension, she got up and moved to the door.

"That looks nice – and it's going quite fast," she observed as the small speedboat approached them from across the bay.

Owen noticed what she was looking at and let out a gasp as he moved as fast as he could to the boxes of electronics on the floor. Panic over. The dials had not moved, but just in case he switched them off, picked them up together with the tapes and player and carefully stored them in the briefcase.

"Is it still coming towards us? The boat. . . the boat!" he shouted as she stood in a daze in the sunshine.

"The boat? Yes, it's coming this way. Look. . . they are waving at us. . ."

"Move – Now – Move. Lift your bag – quick – quick – MOVE NOW," he shouted and at the same time switched off the hot plate, checked his pocket for the car keys, and picked up the briefcase.

"To the car, Sis. There's no time to lock up – MOVE. . ." and he forcibly pushed her in the direction of the car while he switched off the generator.

"Are they after us?" She didn't move as fast as Croft had wished.

"Do you want to wait to find out?"

The car started, allowing them to speed away as the boat reached the shore.

"Have you got everything? Your passport and tickets?" and he didn't notice the tree stump he drove into, causing the tyre to burst, and the car to jolt.

"Blast! – are you hurt?" He stopped the vehicle and, not waiting for her reply, jumped out and started to survey the damage.

"I'm okay. . . Do you think they know something?"

Owen Croft could become aggressive at stupid questions, and in his book that *was* a stupid question.

"Don't be daft, woman. . . The stuff on those tapes is enough to kill for. Let's get out of here fast." He got back in and started to drive to the road on the three good tyres.

"I can't change the wheel here – you can help me when we get to the road. What of your passport and tickets?"

She checked her holdall – "Yes, all here. . . Oh! My clothes!"

"Forget your stupid clothes. . . they don't matter."

"Don't *matter*! Some were brand new. I only bought the skirt last week and—"

His aggression was getting worse.

"Do you want to live – or die? Wake up, woman – we could get killed any moment and you worry about clothes?"

She came to realise the danger they might be in after all, and kept quiet while Owen made their way to the road.

"Now. . . Out. . . Quick. . . OUT. . ." and he used whatever resource she could give to help change the wheel. He was too destructive in his current state to do the job in a proper and efficient manner.

"Here – I'll do the jack – you loosen the bolts," she suggested and had the jack in place without trouble while his energy was directed to the blasted wheel bolts. They were always too tight when you didn't want them to be. They started to loosen once he had stood on the spanner a few times. The sweat poured off him as he removed the remains of the tyre and damaged wheel, and with her help he dumped it in the bushes.

"Not exactly honest, but now there's no evidence that we ever had a spare – is there?"

The spare wheel was tightened, again with her help, and once she removed the traces of oil using handcream and tissues from her holdall, they were on their way to the airport.

"I have copies of the tapes, Sis – take this set home with you and do the best you can."

He was thinking while driving and was a lot calmer now.

"How many sets do you have – of the tapes?" she asked.

"Two sets with me – the originals are back home – you should get through airport security all right with tapes, but just in case I'll post the second set to you – how does that sound?"

"Fine – when will you post them? You should do it as soon as possible."

"We'll get the stationery items in the airport – you know, paper, sticky tape, and once they are parcelled up post them from there."

And that's what they did.

"Safe home, Sis – don't send a card or anything – I'll phone to check you got home intact – okay?" And after they had embraced, she entered the departures area.

He waited until the plane had taken off before returning to the car where he sat for half an hour thinking what to do next.

He had his eyes closed, his head resting on his arms over the steering wheel. What a mess, he thought. He had been so careful and couldn't understand how anyone knew. Who were those people in the boat and how did they know?

He had to go back. The cabin was left in a hurry and was not locked up. He must return and lock it up, so he prepared himself for the journey.

Raising his head, something on the floor caught his eye. An envelope. A brown sealed envelope. He stared at it. That's all he could do. Transfixed for a moment, his right hand started to move, without his conscious controlling it, towards the envelope. He turned it over. His name was on it – plus a sentence – he recognised the writing. His sister's! He read – '*Dear Owen, something to defray your expenses – take care – love, Susannah!*'

He ripped it open and counted out $200 in twenty-dollar bills.

His head went back in relief as he crumpled the envelope and pocketed the money. Now for the cabin.

The car was getting low in gas, so he filled up at a service area at Sheboygan, about halfway to Green Bay. He calculated that one tankful would enable him to get to the cabin and back again to Hertz at the airport.

He passed the broken tyre and wheel and slowly started down the track to the cabin. He stopped before the bend and continued on foot. The nervous energy returned causing the sweat to come. His hands were wet, so was his head. He stopped to listen. Anything unusual? Blast it – it was quiet – the birds – he should have stopped earlier. He waited until the birdsong was in full swing, and realised that was all he could hear. Moving further, he could now see the shoreline. There was no sign of the boat, so he took a chance and walked from cover straight to the open door of the cabin.

Chapter Fourteen

The General entered his office, looked at his watch, and noted the time difference. Another hour and he would make the call, which left him enough time to bounce his plans off Jimmy Scott, the intelligence man. Scott had followed him into the office, a small room, and like the Inner Council rooms, it was bare apart from table, chairs, telephone, and fax machine. There were no windows, so the lights were always on, also the fan, so the air was fresh; as fresh as East Belfast air could be, which was not very fresh, but the General and the thousands who lived and worked in the area were used to it.

"Any comments, Jimmy?" asked the General.

"I think she'll do well. Her point of a security button to bring the food in is already being dealt with, but she shouldn't be told too much, not of our active unit side anyway, and definitely nothing of our weapons."

"That's no problem. We can feed her information to help with planning, that's all. William was good at it, but most of his ideas came from her anyway."

"From her?" That surprised Scott.

"Yea – she was checked out – it's for real – she is good on ideas."

"Will she be okay in you-know-where?" Scott was referring to Canada.

"There's no problem with her contact. He's okay. But how about additional protection – would you approve of that?"

"Definitely – but tell them to take it easy and not to go heavy."

"I do have one area of concern," the concern was showing in the General's face, "and to do something could ruin the whole set-up with her."

"Who?"

"Her brother-in-law, Joe Lacy."

Scott nodded in agreement. "That's difficult all right. We can't frighten him off, she would go nuts; and we can't do nothing, she would be in danger. He's decent enough, just can't keep his mouth shut."

"Can I leave you to sort him out? Perhaps a visit, say tomorrow, before she gets back – you know the sort of thing, like 'Do you want her dead or what?' That should wise him up. Who are you putting on surveillance at Ballycarry?"

Scott was going over what the General had said. Some good ideas came from the General – that's why he was the General.

"Billy Milligan will track her in Ballycarry, in fact it would be better to have him with me when I see the brother-in-law."

"I'll leave it in your hands, Jimmy, you are good at that sort of thing."

"Thanks, General – you taught me well," and he left, closing the door behind him.

It was time to make the call, so, unlocking his desk, he took from it a slim notebook and looked up the number in Chicago.

*

"Do you know what time it is, buddy?" The General could clearly hear the yawn.

"I hope you are sober, young man – my dear niece is on her way to see you and we don't want you lifted for drunken driving, do we?"

That woke him up. He knew who it was, and covering the mouthpiece with his free hand, he called out, "Wake up, Matt— we're back on duty."

Matt O'Leary grunted, opened one eye, saw his colleague on the phone and went back to sleep.

"I'm sober all right – don't worry about that. What's this new ah. . ." as he searched his memory for the agreed code word, and managed to say nothing for quite some time until it came to him, "...the – ah – I mean – ah – you know – yes, tell me about the new customer. . . that's it – who's the new customer?" He was careful not to say 'General'. They were told *never* to mention names when on the phone – never. The exception being if the code word was a name.

"My young niece will advise you of the details. Now listen, and listen hard, my young man," – that was code again – "get your butt to the airport. She's getting a flight to Milwaukee from Chicago. Take the same plane if you can get seats, if not go earlier and get to

Milwaukee before her. The agenda is low key, but she's a bit green and could do with your help, okay?"

That means approach at ease and slowly and don't give aggro, but let her know you're her protection if needed. . . "Sure - okay. Is there much baggage?"

"Only the one case, it's an old one, but strong enough." Two of them on the same side working for the same cause, and one is a woman.

"What time?"

"From Montreal to Chicago due in your time tomorrow 0900 hours. Don't mess up - that's an order," and the General hung up.

So, we're babysitting and not allowed to ask questions. Fair enough. The General saved our bacon, and got us out before the heat came. Paul Corbett looked over to the bunk occupied by the sleeping O'Leary and pulled him on to the floor.

"UP - up - you lazy sod - up. That was the General. . . remember him? We owe him, and he wants paid - now."

O'Leary made the groan that sleep-filled people make when they don't want to get up, but know there is no alternative. Like Monday morning after a good weekend, with uninteresting work beckoning.

"Where to this time, Paul?" Paul Corbett was the brighter of the two and was in charge.

"Milwaukee."

"At least it's not too far to drive," remarked O'Leary.

"Drive? We fly, my friend, no driving 'til we get there."

Corbett was more awake and threw some water around his unshaven face, which would do. After all, he had a shower yesterday, so he was reasonably fresh. He dressed while O'Leary showered.

"Fly? That's daft. Sure by the time we get to the airport and hang around and check in and all that, we could be halfway there. It's only seventy miles from here."

"The General said fly, so we fly - okay?"

"What exactly did the General *say*?" The telephone conversation was relayed to him, which gave O'Leary the idea that going by car would be in order and would be easier. There was plenty of time, after all she wasn't due until tomorrow - they agreed to carry out the day's routine as usual. Another day working in the amusement park. They were employed as cleaners. It was the only job they could get.

The next day they motored to the airport in Milwaukee and waited about the place monitoring the arrivals from Chicago that were due after 10 a.m.. They saw her at around 11.30 a.m., and kept their distance. She was welcomed with an embrace from a fit-looking type who resembled her – probably family, thought Corbett – and they saw him guide her out to the car park. Corbett signalled to O'Leary, who also went off to the car park.

"Have we lost them?" asked O'Leary.

"No – no – there they are – about a hundred yards in front – still heading in Green Bay direction – see?"

"Got them – you keep an eye on them, I'll watch the road – I'm driving."

A safe distance was kept, with O'Leary working hard to maintain the distance of one hundred yards or so behind them.

"They are turning off – see? where to now?" asked Corbett.

"Let's find out," as O'Leary followed. "This leads us to where? The map – you have the map," shouted O'Leary.

Corbett lifted the map from the pocket at his right hand and unfolded it. It was some operation, unfolding, then folding it, so that the area of Green Bay and Lake Michigan became prominent.

"Here we are – it could be Sturgeon Bay. The next town is Brussels, and Sturgeon Bay is here – see?" as Corbett held the map over to O'Leary, pointing in the appropriate place. He quickly glanced at it – "Right – that's probably it." Returning his eyes to the road – "Where are they? – they've gone!" shouted O'Leary.

"They couldn't have – quickly – put your foot down." They sped to the outskirts of Brussels without seeing them.

"Stop – stop – they must have turned off one of the tracks back there." The car was turned round, and they retraced their way, stopping at each track to check it out. They were all the same. No evidence that a car or anything else had used the track recently.

"It's getting late and I'm hungry. Let's book in somewhere and work things out," suggested Corbett.

"The General's going to do his nut," advised O'Leary.

"It's not over yet." They found a place, had a meal, freshened up and felt better.

"Hi!" Corbett said to the waiter, "anywhere around here I could hire a boat?"

"Sure – plenty – what size are you looking for?"

"Small – just the two of us – a little sail up to say fifteen miles or so and back."

"Tomorrow would be the earliest – Johnston the boat man has gone home for the day – that's his place over there," as he pointed to a harbour area with a sign on the white wall indicating JOHNSTON BOATS FOR HIRE.

"Thanks."

"You're welcome" and as he lifted the $5 tip, "Have a nice day." He took the empty plates and returned them to the kitchen.

"A boat trip? Are you mad?"

"Take it easy – it could work. The tracks lead down to the water right? So – we take a boat trip and look for the house or whatever. They are bound to be there – happy?"

O'Leary was as sceptical as ever and it showed.

"Look. That's my idea. If you come up with a better one, we'll go with it. Until then, we use the boat – now give over."

They stayed the night there, had a good breakfast, and went to see Mr Johnston about a boat.

*

"You should have picked a slower one – this is too fast for me," moaned O'Leary.

"Stop your moaning – enjoy yourself. This is better than cleaning up after kids with their coke cartons and Big Mac boxes thrown round the place." Corbett was enjoying himself and he enjoyed the speed.

"Let's see what this thing can do," as he opened up the throttle.

"Slow down – slow down. I can't swim!" O'Leary was terrified. "I can't help you look for them if you speed like this – it's too bumpy – too many vibrations."

Corbett laughed. "This is the life – I think I'll steal this boat – it's a great mover."

"Not while it's out on my credit card you won't – slow down," pleaded O'Leary.

He steered the craft about a mile out from the bank and headed towards Sturgeon Bay.

"It's about halfway, I guess, so start keeping an eye out, see if you notice any people or smoke from a hut or house, or open fire," suggested Corbett.

"I told you, I can't see anything at this speed – slow down."

He didn't slow down and O'Leary held on with white knuckle strength to the rail at the side and kept his eye on the lifebelts.

Time passed, one enjoying everything, the other in terror.

"There's something over there – let's turn in and investigate – see?" pointed Corbett.

O'Leary raised his head and saw someone standing in the doorway of a small holiday cabin. They were about a quarter of a mile out, but the air was free from dust and smoke, and vision was good in these conditions.

"She has seen us – look – wave – and see what happens," suggested O'Leary. They waved and noticed the reaction.

"Look at that – they don't want company, do they?" Corbett announced.

'It must be them – wave again. . ." but without effect, and they saw them drive off as Corbett at last slowed down before the boat hit the shore.

"I'm not going back in that thing," declared O'Leary, who got out and looked for the cabin. "You can take the *Titanic* back yourself – I'm staying here – pick me up in the car," and as the door of the cabin was open he went in.

There wasn't a mooring, but it was easy to park the boat by tying the rope to a tree at the edge of the clearing, and that's what Corbett did.

"There's nobody here now. We saw them pull out. Look, they've left their luggage – check the labels."

The satisfied look on O'Leary's face was confirmation enough. The labels, from Belfast to London to Chicago, were all there.

"It's them all right – we've found them."

"You've lost them, you mean."

"They will be back – look – luggage!" Corbett announced.

Corbett looked around, and opened the cool box.

"Well, well – do you fancy a piece of soda bread, Matt? And potato bread?" and he picked the remains of the girl's present to her brother.

"Not half!"

They finished what was there and decided what to do next.

"I'm staying here anyway. Nobody will get me back into that boat," declared O'Leary, who got up from the table. "Let's see where the track comes out," and he went outside. He made his way to the road. It was far enough and took him about ten minutes. Looking around, he noticed the damaged tyre in the bushes and was examining it when Corbett arrived on the scene.

"Some climb that, I'm done." He puffed and fought to gain his breath as he saw O'Leary examining the wheel.

"This hasn't been here too long – no rust." He looked around for something to mark the entrance to the lane, so that when Corbett arrived with the car he would know where to turn off, picked up a piece of the tyre that had separated from the wheel, and jammed it between two branches of a tree.

"There – you can see that easy. Just drive to the rubber marker, and turn down the track. I'll wait in the homestead."

Corbett knew that he meant it and resigned himself to a lonely boat journey back to the car. Before Corbett left, both looked around, and checked out the luggage. There was nothing that shouldn't have been there, nothing out of place.

"Funny how they ran off like that – they must have been expecting trouble, and thought we were it," suggested O'Leary.

"Sure. . . That's it. I hope they turn up. The General will not like it if they don't; and if they do, take it easy. No rough stuff, okay?"

"No sweat," agreed O'Leary.

"I've plenty of sweat. See you later – if I can see that marker."

O'Leary helped him push the boat into clear water and watched him make his way back at a slower pace, to Green Bay. He thought that if only he had sailed down that way, he might have gone back with him. He always was a bit of a show off, was Corbett. That was why they had to get out of Northern Ireland in the first place.

O'Leary made his way into the cabin, picked up an apple, and ate it noisily, throwing the core into the trees when he finished it. Nice here, he thought, and safe. Anyone could hide up here for a while, and nobody would know. Fear must have made them run away – that's right, fear. They were afraid. They thought he was the other side. The other side! Boy, what a mess, as he recalled their famous action. It should have gone as planned, but no, he had to show off. Fancy Corbett shooting into the mirror behind the bar. The glass was everywhere, the largest bit cutting the barman's head off. It looked like that anyway. Three dead when the orders planned for two. Poor innocent barman. Still, they got the targets – the bomber and his sidekick. Neat too. His aim was good – just two shots – one each between the eyes – neat. The General liked it, except for the barman. How was he to know that the barman was one of the General's informers. Imagine it, a barman up the Falls working for the UVF! The order went out for revenge. They didn't wear masks – no need. It showed off our confidence, but we had to get out because we were seen. The General organised it, using the escape route. So two years in Chicago, moving jobs every six months, and after completing only one job for the cause. Now there was this job, and we lost them. Still, if they come back, nothing was lost. If they don't? We'll just tell it as it happened to the General.

Time was passing slowly, so he moved into the back room, lay on the bed and dozed. He woke, not knowing why, then heard it. The silence – no bird song. Why? Then the birds started up again. Again – why? He decided to get up, and sit in the chair beside the bed near a small bookcase. There were some magazines on the bottom shelf, all about six months old. He picked up one of the car magazines and browsed rather than read.

Footsteps – who? Corbett? Or are they back? Better stay quiet just in case. Whoever it was was coming on in. The cabin entrance darkened with a shadow. I'll surprise him – or her – or both, thought O'Leary.

"Who are you?" he asked quietly, putting his head round the door.

"Aaah!. . . Aaah!. . ." Croft jumped into the air and turned ashen.

Chapter Fifteen

Mrs Lacy was observed as she proceeded through the arrivals area, and an unknown soldier informed the General of her safe arrival. The taxi left her at the bus station, from where she telephoned her brother-in-law, who met her at the stop near Whitehead, and she was soon on her way home, holdall on the floor at her feet. Home at last. Her first task was to check that the tapes were undamaged. They travelled well, unlike herself, not knowing whether her brother Owen was safe, allowing her imagination to work overtime and depriving her of sleep. It showed in her every move and her drained appearance. Her brother-in-law said something that wasn't heard, and soon she was asleep in bed, the tapes carefully stowed in a bottom drawer.

The morning was dull, grey and wet, and jet lag filled her mind with listlessness, her ears not yet cleared of the low frequencies from the jet engines.

"Your brother phoned two hours ago. I let you sleep on, you needed it."

"How is he?" The enquiry was half-hearted, purely out of fatigue.

"He's fine. He seemed a bit worried about you. I told him you got here okay."

"Did he say anything?"

"Something happened out there, didn't it? He said to tell you that the people were 'from your people'. Does that make sense?"

She thought for a moment – our people? – the UVF? She would ask the General about it. "Yes. . . Yes. . . that's what I expected to hear. I'm off to get some air. . "

"Here, Sis, what happened? I can't protect you if I don't know. . ."

"Relax, Joe. It's all in hand, and I don't need your protection."

"That's another thing. I had a visitor while you were away. He warned me to keep out of it. Said I could get in the way and could cause you to get hurt"

"You better keep out of it, then," and she left to walk to the Rinkha.

That was worth it, she felt, as she returned home about two hours later. Her head was cleared and her sparkle had returned. Her minder watched every move, and remained unseen, at no more than twenty yards distance. It was easy for the minder to stay hidden, considering the nature of the terrain.

The tapes revealed more the more they were listened to. Susannah spent most of the day following her walk listening to the tapes in her car. All the time she thought 'strategy'. What was done with the information could result in civil war – or peace – maybe. She knew what her husband would have wanted, but persuading the Council to back her ideas now that her husband wasn't around would not be easy. That's enough time in the car, she decided, and gathering the tapes together she returned them to the bottom drawer and sought out her brother-in-law. He was busy repairing the gate to the field leading off the yard to the left.

"Sorry for being sharp with you, Joe. I'm still a bit groggy – It's the jet lag."

He stopped what he was doing and, looking everywhere but at her, displayed his unease by rubbing his elbow, then his head, then returned to his elbow before his courage allowed him to announce. . . "I want out of this mess, Sis. First William got killed, now I've been threatened, and you're up to something that's no good. It worries me, all this terrorist stuff – I want out."

"What exactly worries you?" she asked.

He just had to tell her; he couldn't leave it unsaid.

"There's someone keeping an eye on this place, I know there is. It could be IRA or Army, I don't know, but it's not safe for you here."

She smiled, and by placing her hand over her mouth managed to stop the laugh.

"It's not funny, Sis," he protested.

"Joe – listen. It's not the IRA nor the Army. It's my minder from the UVF."

"Minder? Why do you need such a thing? Sure I'm here."

"Because, dear Joe, you have no nerve and could spoil things, and besides. . ." She looked around, couldn't see anyone, came up to him and declared, speaking softly, ". . .I'm a Council member now working with the General. Now do you understand?"

The relief on Joe's face could have been measured.
"It's definitely one of ours?" She nodded. "Thank heavens for that. I was convinced it was the IRA. Look. . .," feeling more composed, ". . .don't worry about me. Now that I know, it will be all right," and smiling broadly he returned to work on the gate. She wasn't satisfied that she could rely on him. He tended to talk too much.

*

Her car was parked in the same place as before. Entering the pub, she approached the man standing at the end of the bar. She had not seen him before. He looked at his watch, noting that the time was almost noon, and without looking at her he escorted her up the stairs. Her escort didn't speak. Neither did she. The room was as before, with the same people as before rising to greet her. Her escort didn't enter the room, but disappeared when the wall behind her closed.

"Have a good trip?" enquired the General.

"Indeed I did. And do I have something for you! But first, any chance of a coffee?"

Jimmy Scott, sitting at the table end, raised his fist with index finger erect, and in a grand gesture slowly moved it to one of the brass buttons displayed in a row in front of him, and with great ceremony pressed one. "No sooner said than done. Coffee and tea ordered. We put this in since your last visit. Thon was a good idea of yours, so we done it!"

"Good for you T.A." It was Gary McIlroy who spoke.

"T.A.?" queried Mrs Lacy.

"Yes, dear, he's our Telligence Afficer!" They all laughed at the joke, which she had heard before, but she politely joined in.

"First. . .," the General said, stopping the laughter abruptly, ". . .our apologies are due to you. On behalf of the Council, please accept our apology for the frightening tactics our men used in Green Bay, it was—"

"So it *was* your men in the boat," she interrupted.

"That's right. They should have been, shall we say, less dramatic. Your connection in Canada was good about it, and I understand allowed them to finish off the soda bread you had brought him."

"I remember now, he phoned while I was asleep. Accepted – your apology. In fact, it's not necessary. In fact, I apologise for any trouble my brother-in-law may have caused. I think you'll find that he will not be quite so bad from now on. He thought your man at his place was IRA."

The coffee arrived with a plate of biscuits. Nothing fancy, large mugs with a communal spoon having sugar all over it from multiple use.

"I have something that will blow your mind," she announced, "but first, before I go further, I must have your promise for no immediate gut reaction 'in the field'. This one needs careful working out."

"You're part of the team now and are expected to play a team game, Susannah." The General continued, "Your task is strategy, so we're hardly likely to do something in the field, as you put it, without listening to your strategy first, are we? But you'll get no promises."

"Sorry, General. No offence was meant."

She produced the tapes one at a time from a plastic B&Q shopping bag and gently laid them on the table. "This is proof that the glorious US of A Government is planning something against us." They waited, so she continued, "I have listened to these four or five times now and each time it scares me a bit more. I suggest we listen to them twice before any discussion, how does that sound?"

"Where did they originate from?"

"To protect the source, all I'll say is that there is no knowledge outside this room, apart from the source, of these tapes. Do you have a machine we could use to listen to them?"

Each shook their head. "Hold on, there's this wee electric place down the road, let's buy one. Fifty quid should do – eh?" asked Scott.

"Aye – that should do – here," as money was produced from the drawer in the table by McIlroy.

Half an hour later, the first tape was revealing its message. They listened to the tapes twice, and only stopped the machine to change tapes and to take a meal. Comments were made during the exercise indicating their anger, surprise, and bravado. The General allowed them their comments, while maintaining order and seeing that they concentrated on the tapes.

When the machine was switched off at the end of the hearing, Susannah proposed, "Let's each think of what we have heard before making decisions. How about coming back here tomorrow, say, same time and discussing this?"

"I agree, and for security reasons these tapes *don't* exist – okay?" the General ordered. They all nodded ". . .and we will keep the tapes here in the safe. Are there any copies?" the General asked.

"My contact has a copy, and a second set is in the post to me."

"The post? I hope it arrives," said Peter Baker, the first time he had spoken.

She drove home, leaving the others in a mild state of shock.

"She's good, isn't she?" It was Peter Baker's first real contribution that day. "I'm interested to hear her ideas on this one. Should we show her the file, General?" Baker asked.

"Tomorrow. It's time to wise up her brother-in-law. Can you arrange that, Jimmy, while she's here tomorrow?"

"No problem, General.. I suggest Milligan and Rice. I take it, we want him to remain on our side?"

"Just as planned, but no violence. It might put her off, and as you saw, Peter, she's good. Let's keep her happy – and keep her busy."

Chapter Sixteen

Major de Courcy's contact at Thiepval Barracks, Lisburn suggested that the civilian forces, represented by the RUC, should be brought in, as the Army preferred to support the action of the civilian power rather than go in direct. That's how the major met Superintendent Stephen Richards in Castlereagh Belfast, and how the RUC was informed of part of what was going on. The major held back some of the information, only mentioning that there was a possibility of finding out where some of the IRA arms dumps were located, provided his proposed meeting with the UVF was not put in jeopardy by undercover police or army interference. No mention of money was made, nor of arms acquisition in Spain, but he did advise that his American friend would be working with him.

Superintendent Richards confirmed the genuineness of de Courcy and Sutton, before authorising the release of sensitive information to them. Richards was able to confirm to de Courcy, that Joseph Lacy – 'was connected to the UVF, but the only tangible evidence of the connection related to his part in the accidental death of his brother, William. There was a girl who lived and worked on the farm, the widow of the murdered man, and no, she has no children. She doesn't know the details of how her husband died, and no, she doesn't know that her brother-in-law was involved.'

The person with the better information is better placed to get more when negotiating. To give him the edge, de Courcy made it his priority to find out as much as he could about the UVF people he was expected to deal with, as well as those he wouldn't. That meant investing time to prepare, time to understand. Meeting relatives of a dead terrorist, while keeping hidden your own agenda, could be a problem. The case of William and Joseph Lacy was disturbing, and Major de Courcy wondered how he could keep matters away from the girl; Joe Lacy was enough to think about.

Death in any family by terrorists known or unknown is traumatic. The major knew from personal experience, but at least he hadn't caused it. Joe Lacy was directly, albeit accidentally, the cause of his brother's death. How could he sleep at night? The Drugs Squad provided the clues that proved it.

The heat was on the local dealers since the IRA had virtually closed them down, so the suppliers, based in Central America, sent in a team to find out the cause of a sudden downturn in business. With hindsight, it was certain to fail. The team spoke poor English, and were dark and swarthy in complexion. Anyone who saw them knew they were outsiders. They were like a bag of coal on a field of snow. They believed themselves to be in IRA territory when in the UVF/UFF stronghold of Shankill. The UVF sized up what they were about and made secret overtures to the IRA to warn them of the possible drugs explosion. Imagine, six months' supply free, as a goodwill token to start up again, then six months' at half price. There would be enough people interested to start several franchises, and plenty of customers for cheap stuff. The secret meeting took place with information exchanged and verified. It was agreed that the IRA would close down these outsiders, and that the UVF was to bring the South Americans to a neutral area for the exchange. No guns of any kind were to be brought. When the IRA met the South Americans, who were accompanied by William and Joe Lacy, the exchange was ruined by Joe accidentally dropping his gun. The IRA saw the gun and opened up. The only one to get out alive from the UVF side was Joe, who somehow escaped with minor gunshot wounds. The body of William Lacy was retrieved the next day by the Army, with nothing at all of the South Americans. The IRA, for reasons known only to them, were expert in the art of 'hiding' bodies. The major finished reading the Drug Squad material, and left the Castlereagh complex for Brown's Bay.

Sutton and de Courcy couldn't agree about the money. Should they get it first, or arrange and have a meeting with the UVF first? The toss of a coin settled it coming down for the meeting. The advantages and disadvantages were evenly matched, but as they had to wait four or five days before the cash was received, they accepted the decision of the coin. They would set out for Ballycarry tomorrow.

*

"Here's how I see it, General," she started. "We will only know if it's for real if the approach is made. I propose we wait – and let them make their move – then without any commitment to deliver what they want, we work our own agenda to achieve two objectives. One – get the money. Two – get the location of the IRA's arms dumps. They obviously want us to give them the money back by buying arms from them, but I suggest we hang on to the money. The cash could help the Loyalist Prisoners' Association if nothing else. About the arms dumps, in case it's a set up we could use the confidential phone to tell the police, that as a measure of our goodwill we will surrender some of our arms to them, and let the police believe they are ours, not the IRA's." She stopped, took a sip of coffee and went on. ". . all we say to disguise the ownership of the arms is 'some IRA tricks are about, like booby traps and IRA uniforms', but that the Army Bomb Squad should be able to bypass the traps."

More coffee and a bite from a biscuit interrupted her flow, then ". . .should the information prove good, we let the police have details of another dump and demand publicity. That would put us well in with the people, and the IRA wouldn't know what hit them. Any comments so far?"

"Why not pinch the guns for ourselves and forget the Army?"

"The booby traps. I don't know your skills in that area, perhaps you do," she replied.

"They're not bad and getting better, but you're right," stated McIlroy. "What if the dumps are in enemy territory? The Army wouldn't believe they were ours," McIlroy continued.

"Any arms found to date, apart from the small stuff, have been in neutral areas," advised the General.

"That's right," Scott confirmed.

"Hold on – let's not move too far on this." The General's quiet authority brought the gathering back to focus on the basics. "Without the first meeting between these people and our side, nothing will happen. So – let's plan the first meet. There should be the two of them, the Yank and the English. Neither, according to the tapes, knows the full story. Let's go from there."

"I propose, General," it was their new head of strategy who proposed, "we go along with some of what they expect. They expect us to be interested in the money, so we will be. The next is what they think we want to do with the money. Let's just say, 'no decision will be made till we get the money.' The tapes say up to $1 million is available. So, when we talk money, let's go for 50% up front."

"How much is that in real money?" asked Baker, the finance man.

"Half a million dollars? Say £300,000 or even £320,000," she responded quickly, having worked it out. "The reason for asking more than they propose to give is to show that we are not afraid to deal in big amounts. It gives them a chance to trade, of course, but we can come down to their figure of about £220,000 in exchange for, say, the release of some Loyalist prisoners."

"Hey! I like the way you talk, missus, keep going," exclaimed the T.A.

"Thanks," she said quietly. "There's no way they could arrange that, so we might get the half million or £320,000 after all. Lastly, we insist that we get the locations of at least six IRA dumps. If we only get one, it could be a set-up, so if we don't get six or more we say there's no deal. Any comments?"

"I have one," it was Baker, the finance man, again. ". . .make sure the cash delivery is to our trusted people, and that there are no strings attached. I hear what the tapes say, but these guys might add a few nasties of there own, such as a hidden transmitter."

"Good point. There *is* something else." The General thought before he said, ". . .Watch that you don't give yourself away by letting slip the information on the tapes. Don't forget – *you* know more than *they* do."

The plans were discussed and agreed, and gone over many times before she returned to her car. Her minder would contact Council when the meet had taken place and Council reconvened two days later as was the custom. She couldn't help feeling that the money wouldn't be seen by anyone, and wondered if the American would run off with it – or the English, as the General called him, he might steal it. The General's last point, backed by the rest of Council, was the only problem she couldn't answer. "By the way," he ordered – yes, she understood it to be an order, "let your brother-in-law act as chairman for the meet, with you as spokesman – sorry – spokesperson. Don't worry. By now he will be only too willing to do it – my people have had a word with him while you were here. Good luck – and well done. We liked your contribution today. Your ideas are a breath of fresh air." The problem is still Joe Lacy despite what I said, thought the General.

*

Hands in pockets, leaning against the wall beside the door, de Courcy watched Sutton give the final polish to the six-year-old Ford Escort. It was past being adequate for their purpose and had given de Courcy and his son good service over the years, but the English registration was not ideal in their current position. Sutton had done a good job of removing a few years from its appearance. Six years old it might be, but before the wash and polish it looked ten. Now it looked about eight. De Courcy had persuaded the Lisburn people to come up with some funds to change the car. Four thousand pounds might not seem much, but it was better than a kick in the teeth, and cash can produce discounts.

"That's a good job, old boy. Let's go and talk to the car chappie."

Island Magee wouldn't be the first choice for many people to travel to when purchasing a car. From Brown's Bay, they drove down the Low Road, and entered the yard of Busby's Car Sales. The place looked surprisingly well for being off the main highways. The showroom had three new cars on display, the rest (about a dozen) varied from a Marina looking decidedly past it to a one-year-old BMW.

"Just having a look, are you?" The man was rubbing his hands on a rag as he appeared from under the BMW, lying on a car creeper. He gave the usual salesman's glance first at the two men, to assess their worth, then at their vehicle.

"As you say, just having a look. This thing giving you trouble?" enquired de Courcy, nodding to the BMW and the creeper.

"Ah no, not that one. That's a grand motor is that one. The exhaust took a knock over one of those ramps – driven too fast, if you ask me. New rear pipe fitted was too loose, I just tightened it. Are you interested?"

"Too expensive for me. How about that one?" The metallic dark green three-year-old 1.6-litre Honda looked in good order, and had a good name for reliability.

"Sure, that's a good motor – sure, they are *all* good motors here, but that one, now that one is real good," and he moved over to it and rubbed and patted his hand on the bonnet.

"Have a look here," and he opened the boot to reveal a spare wheel that was hardly used. "You couldn't beat that. A dear old lady had it and hardly used it."

"I seem to have heard that one before," commented Sutton.

"You're an American, I hear – fancy that now. Now, it's the truth I'm saying, so it is, as I can show you from the Registration Book if you want." De Courcy moved off to look at the other vehicles but decided to take the Honda, if the price was right. The other motors were fine, but not as good as the Honda. Sutton was satisfied with what he saw of the Honda and, beyond the hearing of the salesman, advised de Courcy, "Edward, there's only one here worth taking," nodding to the Honda. "I'll take a look under the hood," and to the salesman he asked, "All right if I take a look?"

"Surely, surely. Here, I'll open it up for you," and he did so. The engine bay was spotless without any sign of oil leaks or corrosion. Sutton was impressed, and the salesman knew it.

"I keep all my cars in good order. It's good for the car and good for business."

Sutton gave the major his approval, and the deal was on.

"How much for the Escort in exchange, old boy?" The salesman, believing he had a sale, started to examine the Ford.

"Well now, she would be six years old, and a bit rough on it." Taking a quick professional look beneath, inside, under the bonnet, and in the boot, he assessed the machine, shaking his head occasionally.

"The guy's done this before, Edward – just look at him."

"I see that, Elmer – we could write the script for him," smiled de Courcy.

"Well now, gentlemen," rubbing his hands together. "I'll tell you what I'll do, because I like the look of you. . ." De Courcy and Sutton stole a glance at each other, and with difficulty, stifled their mirth. ". . .If it's the Honda, I'll take the Escort and £5,000," and loudly smacked his hands together, and waited for their reply. Silence reigned for the next sixty seconds, the three doing nothing but standing there. I like this chap, thought de Courcy. He survives by giving value for money, and in a place as out of the way as this, he would need to.

"What if it was cash, old boy?" the major ventured in the silence.

"Cash? Well now, I would think about that. How long would you need to get that sort of money in cash?"

"I have it right here, old boy," and de Courcy let him see the bundle of notes he produced from the deep side pocket of his jacket. "Four thousand pounds. That's all I've got. Here, count it," and he offered the money to him. The salesman declined the offer.

"Let's go to the office, gentlemen," and he led them into the showroom. Sutton had an additional £600 in his 'billfold' that was withdrawn from the bank a few days ago, that if necessary would be used to augment the major's funds.

The office consisted of a table at the far corner of the showroom, which was clean and tidy. He offered them a seat, then proceeded to his calculations, making reference to a blue book several times. He put the book down and with open palms advised, "Sorry. The best I can do is your car and £4,500. That's it, but have a look at the Renault. The Renault is a year older than the Honda and is in your price range."

"You say £4,500 for the Honda – and a full tank?"

"Surely."

"Agreed," and de Courcy waited while Sutton made quite a scene producing money from non-existent pockets, deliberately taking time to find the extra £500. The last ten-pound note on the table sealed the deal.

"Are you all right for car insurance, now?"

"Indeed, yes. All I need is the registration number. Can I use your phone, old boy, to set it up? It's to Belfast – I'll pay for the call, of course," and he set fifty pence on the table.

"Surely," and he pointed to the phone.

Chapter Seventeen

They left in the Honda, which drove sweetly and was much quieter and more powerful than the Escort, and made their way to Ballycarry. The farm was to the north of the town and afforded magnificent views over Larne Lough, down the island and over the sea to where the Scottish coast was visible. They were seen by the minder, who alerted Joe Lacy, by throwing a stone, causing him some pain in the small of his back. Joe wasn't expecting that attack and, looking around, he saw nobody about. He was returning to his routine when another stone skimmed along the lane beside him and brought his attention to the minder half hidden in the hedge some thirty yards away, indicating with one hand to keep quiet and with the other he pointed out the two well-dressed men entering the farm yard. Joe understood the meaning of the signal and waited for the visitors to join him. The minder, unseen, alerted Mrs Lacy before returning to his guard duty.

"That's a grand day. What can I do for you?" asked Lacy.

"Mr Lacy, is it?" The major didn't want to be too formal, but needed to satisfy himself that he was talking to the right person.

"That's me."

"I, along with my colleague here," introducing Sutton by looking at him, "may have a proposition to interest you. Could you spare say, half an hour?"

"This place is not for sale," Joe Lacy stated.

"That's understandable – the view alone is magnificent. But, no, what I propose has nothing to do with purchasing your property. It's about helping you in your work with the UVF."

De Courcy would soon know how to proceed. The reaction of the farmer in front of him to the pronouncement 'UVF' was non-existent, which was not what either Sutton or de Courcy expected.

"You want to join, is that it?" Lacy said without feeling or gesture.

"I want to talk over something inside. May we talk in your house, Mr Lacy?"

"No, I think not, but we can talk over here in the outhouse," and he led them to a small whitewashed stone walled, thatched byre. There were no windows and the green door was one of the now rare half-door types, the bottom half usually kept closed and only opened to enter or leave, with the top half open to allow air to circulate.

"Tea? Would you take a cup of tea?" asked Lacy.

"That's very kind of you, old boy, tea would be welcome." Sutton and de Courcy were shown into the byre, then Lacy went off to organise the liquid.

"Tea? Edward, does nobody around here drink anything other than tea? What's wrong with coffee? No wonder there's fighting here – anyone would fight having to drink that stuff."

Sutton was not keen on tea.

"Shhh. . . He's on his way back," as de Courcy caught the sound of Lacy's boots on the concrete yard.

Lacy entered the byre and, seeing that the visitors were still standing, said, "Sit down, sit down. . .," moving dried slurry from a low wooden box with one hand and some months of dust from a chair with the other. It had the smell of a byre, thought de Courcy, so it must have been used recently.

"The girl will be along shortly. Now what's this about? What did you say? UVF?"

"That's right. First some introductions. . . This is Elmer Sutton and I'm Edward de Courcy. We are both majors and work, shall we say, unofficially for the forces against terrorism, and have a proposal that we feel would interest you in your fight against the IRA."

"What's this got to do with me?" ventured Lacy, somewhat sharply.

"We have information that proves you are connected to the UVF. Do you want me to mention a few examples of your past, shall we say, achievements? The death of your brother, for instance?"

"That's enough now, here's the tea, and if you want anything from me, you'll not mention that again. Do you hear?" Lacy, a little red in his face, opened the bottom half of the door, and the girl entered carrying a tray on which were four mugs, a tea pot, a hot water jug, instant coffee, sugar and spoons, and the scones. The smell of fresh scones hit them, scones that had been liberally buttered.

"Here you are now. Help yourself, I'll just get the milk, there wasn't room on the tray," and she set the tray down on the low box where Sutton had just got up from when she entered.

They helped themselves to tea, the American to coffee, and waited until offered a scone before having one. They had to wait until the girl returned before being offered the scones.

"These are sure good cookies, Ma'am," complimented Sutton.

"Thank you. I hear you are an American," Mrs Lacy replied.

"Yes, Ma'am, on duty over here, the major will explain."

They looked an unusual group – two well dressed, one in farmers working clothes, the girl casually dressed in shirt and jeans.

"This is Susannah Lacy, my sister-in-law," Joe Lacy explained. "I suggest she stays and hears what your proposal is. They tell me, Sis, that they know I'm in the UVF, and they want to help us, all unofficial like, against the IRA – is that about it?. . . I forget your name. . ."

"Major Edward de Courcy, and this is Major Elmer Sutton. . . Yes that's about it. I say, I agree with Elmer, these scones are good. Home-made by chance?"

"Just out of the oven," she replied, barely audible, without looking at him.

There was something about her, de Courcy suspected, that showed hurt deep within her. A pleasant attractive girl, enduring suffering that removed the ability or willingness to smile and relax.

"The floor is yours, Major," Joe said, with mouth spitting scone crumbs, "and, Sis, feel free to join in. You don't mind, Major, if she does some of the talking?"

De Courcy was beginning to understand their game plan and suspected that Joe Lacy was the front man rather than being in charge.

"By all means. What we have to say is unofficial and will be denied by the powers that be, should you decide to make enquiries. With that as the backcloth the contents should be of interest." The Lacys waited for more, the girl now studying de Courcy as he spoke. "How would you react to being the party that is credited with the discovery and destruction of a major quantity of IRA weapons, and being paid for it at the same time?" Joe and Susannah didn't react. De Courcy wondered whether he was being understood. Perhaps he should try a little American slang occasionally, or better still let Sutton tell it his way. "Anything you would like to add at this stage, Elmer?"

"Sure, Edward. Like the major said, you guys in the UVF get the publicity and some cash to go with it, and the security guys get the IRA guns off the streets."

"How?" She knew the answer from the tapes, but was making sure that nothing was given away.

"The set-up goes like this," Sutton explained. "The surveillance guys in the States have these satellite pictures showing the location of the arms dumps. There are about a dozen or so. They can't let the Brits have them as that would give away their existence – you know, spying on the allies and all that stuff after the Gulf War? Not good for keeping up the 'special relationship'. At home all hell would break out, what with the Irish American crowd, should the US Government provide help against the IRA."

The Lacys were taking everything in and allowed the visitors to speak without interruption.

"If the fighting is to stop, the means have to be taken out. To do that, we let you know where the arms are. You pass on the info to the guys here who take the arms, and you get paid from a special fund by the US Government and get the publicity for the whole deal. . . Neat, huh?"

"See if I've got it. You give us pictures or maps showing where the arms are?" asked Joe, playing his part well.

"Right?"

"Around a dozen, Major Sutton?" Susannah asked to seek confirmation which Sutton then gave. "How many locations would you give us at a time?"

"That has to be decided. It depends if you're interested in the whole deal," Sutton replied.

"Are we looking at a package here, or can we choose what we sign for?" asked Lacy. Joe Lacy was in good flow, Susannah thought, and was pleasantly surprised with his input.

"What do you think you can accept?" de Courcy enquired.

"The arms locations I like – why not keep the guns for ourselves and the cash, and say nothing?" the girl asked.

"Our information is that the dumps are protected. Your guys don't have the skills to get them without getting blown away. The Brits could do it. If not, they would blow them up so that nobody gets them. Do your guys want arms?" Sutton asked. She waved for her brother-in-law to be quiet, before he answered Sutton's question, ". . .Leave that for now. The money – how much and when?"

"In stages. As a token to show we mean business, the first lot is handed over before you do anything. After that, you get paid by results." De Courcy paused to satisfy himself that they were still with him, then continued, "Major Sutton and I are accountable to ensure value for money is obtained."

"How much?" Joe Lacy repeated the unanswered part of the girl's question.

De Courcy nodded to Sutton, who answered.

"In American, one million dollars in total for the whole deal. Up front, we are looking at $300,000. That's about £200,000 in cash – British notes – used, unmarked notes."

"And the rest, the $700,000?" asked Susannah.

She's a cool one, thought de Courcy, and noticed that she didn't react, neither did Joe, when the million dollars was mentioned.

"After three dumps are taken out, you get another $300,000. After the next three, the balance – $400,000. Our budget is limited to that."

"That's six dumps, Major Sutton, what of the other six? Do we get paid for those?" she asked.

Sutton went on, "We figure that the publicity you guys get over the first six will alert the IRA to move their arms to new locations, so that the best to expect is six."

"What if we get five, and the IRA move seven, do we still get the last $400,000?" Again her brother-in-law. He *is* working well.

"Yea. The deal will stand. Any new location will not be part of this deal," stated Sutton,

"Surely," said Joe in a quiet manner. "Another thing, if for whatever reason you can't get the dump locations for us, or the locations are false, we still get the cash – all of it – right?"

"I'll need confirmation on that one," de Courcy said before Sutton exploded.

Joe Lacy had covered most of the points he was required to, or at least all he had remembered from the rehearsal with the representatives from the Council. It was now over to his sister-in-law to continue.

"What if we wanted to buy guns with the cash?" she asked.

"Whatever you do with the cash is your business," de Courcy said quietly.

"We could contact our people abroad if we had that kind of money, Sis, and have no bother getting stuff." Joe was following the script well. She was pleased with him.

De Courcy and Sutton, however, were taken aback at that remark and waited for their next question.

"We decide on the delivery arrangements for the cash should we accept your plan, gentlemen," she stated.

"Of course, Miss. . . eh. . . Miss Lacy, is it?" de Courcy ventured to test the water.

"It's *Mrs* Lacy, Major," was the cold reply. Yes, she is still hurting, de Courcy diagnosed, and despite her coldness he was full of empathy for her.

"If you want to draw us into this plan of yours, Major, we want something extra from you. There are two of our political prisoners we want released. Do that and you have us with you. What do you say?" she asked.

"Say that again." De Courcy and Sutton were taken by surprise with that one. He heard her clearly and understood her, but needed thinking time. He knew that he couldn't deliver and suspected they knew that. She repeated the request.

"That is outside our control, I'm afraid. There is nothing we can do to have anyone released."

"In that case, we want half up front – that's half now, say £330,000, the rest on the first three dumps, and we want details of all twelve dumps with the first lot of cash."

"I agree with the details of the twelve dumps, but not the cash. My final figure is $330,000, say around £220,000, depending on exchange rates. If you can't agree to that, I shall advise my people to try someone else. I understand the UFF may be interested!"

De Courcy stood up, and, prompted by this, Sutton placed his now empty coffee mug on the tray and shook both real and imaginary dust from his trousers as he stood up.

"Agreed," she said. "How soon do we get the location of the dumps and the cash?"

"Can we, or at least one of us, contact you again, say in two days? We should have the answer to that by then. It's likely to be within

two weeks – how does that sound?" The Lacys gave tacit approval.
"I take it, you have not recorded this meeting?" de Courcy asked.

Joe Lacy smiled, "We might look stupid, Major, but no, we have
not recorded these conversations. Have you?"

"No way," returned Sutton, "and thanks for the coffee, Mrs Lacy,
real good it was."

"Indeed, Mrs Lacy, very good tea and scones. Perhaps you would
allow me to return the compliment sometime," de Courcy added and
meant it. Susannah rather hoped he did.

They returned to their recently acquired mode of transport and
made plans to contact Dugway.

Chapter Eighteen

"Something is wrong, Edward, I can feel it." Sutton was in some discomfort as his head rubbing signified, but his perception of the meeting was clear in his mind. They stopped at the Rinkha, and bought what was locally referred to as a 'slider' and a 'poke'. The ice cream, made on the premises, was delicious.

"Mmm! Real good, Edward, and I've been around. I guess this is as good as any," referring to the 'poke', or cone, he was devouring. De Courcy was enjoying his 'slider', a slab of ice cream set between two crisp wafers.

"Very good indeed," as his tongue circumnavigated the wafer. "It's been years since I had a wafer. It's nearly all cones these days, or rubbish on a stick." He skilfully prevented the melting drops from falling on his shirt as he sat behind the wheel of the car. "Very popular, this. Look at the queue of people, all wanting a poke, no doubt"

"Ha! If you said that back home, you would get booked and end up in court!"

De Courcy understood but chose to ignore the innuendo. "How's the head, old boy? Should you have had the coffee?" he asked.

"Not so bad now – but that barn of theirs, oh boy! If there hadn't been the coffee, I might have passed out." Finishing off the cone, he returned to the events of the meeting.

"They didn't react, Edward – not a thing. Even to the million dollars! Nothing! There's something wrong."

"I noticed, Elmer. She was rather nice, don't you think? He was there to make up the numbers and did his bit rather well, but the girl. . . I bet she was in charge. That one interests me. Her quiet inner strength, probably fuelled by hate, was well controlled. She knows how to make scones too. I could talk to her again without any problem, no problem at all," and he finished the slider, started the car, and headed for Brown's Bay.

"What else did you notice? How about her nice figure, or. . ."

"All right, all right, yank. Point taken. No harm in dreaming. Something wrong, you said, about their reaction to it all? You could be right. We will play our part straight, so if your people want to give them the cash, we'd better arrange it. Nothing happens till they open the bank, and money opens the bank."

They put off contacting Dugway until after eating. Coffee and scones were welcome, but they didn't constitute a meal. Sutton appeared in less pain after meals, and de Courcy didn't want to be left on his own on this one should Sutton be withdrawn due to illness.

*

"You know what we've done, Edward? We have promised those killers in the UVF $330,000! For nothing! What's worse is, if Dugway can't deliver the locations, we have promised them $1 million! The world has gone mad – nuts! – and we are part of it!" De Courcy was standing over the cooker making sure that the steak was not too well done for Sutton, and well done for himself.

"Yes, old boy. It's a stupid gamble, still. . ." remembering his son's death and recalling the details of William Lacy, "if the arms are found and taken out. . . it might. . . just might stop a killing or two. Here – your slab of meat is ready."

*

"I'll show you how to set up the satellite phone. You might have to use it without me. . . just in case, 'old boy'. Tell me, where did you get the 'old boy' routine?"

"An old English Army turn of phrase, I believe. . . maybe not. . . old English, or from the snob element somewhere. Does it annoy you – old boy?"

"Old boy, old boy. Sure it wouldn't be you, Edward, if you were without it. No, it bothers me not, as Shakespeare would say!" The demonstration in Army fashion was given. First Sutton did it, explaining as he went along. Then de Courcy had a go, and errors of omission were corrected. When the major could set it up three times without an error or problem, Sutton prepared to make the call.

"What time is it in Dugway, Edward?"

"About seven hours behind us, I think – that means noon."

"Pity. I wanted to make it about 0300 hours their time. Still, let's see who has turned up for work." He keyed in the third number on the list, making sure that de Courcy saw how simple it was. There was a spare handset, which Sutton gave to de Courcy, ". . .just listen. . don't say nothing."

"Anything, you mean! My English teacher would have been pleased."

Sutton raised his hand to command silence as the connection was made.

"Hi! This is your long-lost nephew in Ireland. . . Yea, that's right, Smarty. Now listen good. Get the cash. The first lot must be $330,000 plus, and get this, all twelve locations, or we have no deal. . . okay?" Sutton waited a second for the message to register, and a few more for the reply.

"That's okay with us," came the reply. "Call at the solicitor in Carlisle as arranged."

The connection was severed, so they hung up and packed the equipment away under the shower tray.

*

Major MacBride listened as Hunter gave him the details. The money would be easy to arrange. All he had to do was make a call to Becker and forget it. The surveillance information was not his problem – Hunter promised it, so Hunter should deliver it.

"No sweat, Sir. You make the call for the capital, I'll make the call for the locations. My guy will deliver – he owes me."

"Just remember, Captain, when the money leaves here it's gone. No comebacks. Any foul up, it's your ass on the line – okay, make your call," and he waved him out of the office.

MacBride contacted the banker in Washington and placed the money authorisation. $330,000! All that dough for nothing. If this comes off, what a way to go into retirement – if it doesn't – oblivion for them both if it got out. MacBride felt safe, after all it was a *Room* job – no records – it couldn't get out.

Hunter made his call and was not too worried at the outcome.

"Hi! Give me Lt Bill Patton in surveillance. . . Yea, that's him. . . Yea, I'll hold. . ."

A few seconds later, then. . . "This is Captain Black Feather, how can I help you?"

"I'm holding for Bill Patton, is he available?"

"On vacation, left yesterday for a week. Can I help?" suggested Black Feather.

"Vacation for a week! okay, leave it, I'll phone back then," and he hung up.

Black Feather logged the call and was advised by Security that it originated from Dugway. Dugway? He thought. . . Didn't they have something to do with 'Ireland 6'? Perhaps not, but just in case he made a point of remembering to monitor the call from them next week. Monitoring – that meant getting Security to record it – that meant getting authorisation. That should be easy, after all Lt Patton was transferred out before he left on vacation as part of the rotation of duties scheme, and Security would want to know why anyone was trying to contact a past member of Surveillance. Black Feather had a good chance of directing the CIA boys away from his own activities, and on to Patton, or Dugway. It was Patton who gave him a hard time when he joined as Lieutenant. Now he was Captain and would arrange for the CIA to give the Lieutenant Patton some of his own medicine. The CIA had muscle.

*

Hunter prepared a short note to be sent by express air cargo to the solicitor in Carlisle, England. He didn't advise MacBride – there was no need to. In one week's time it would all be complete. One week, that should be enough time to advise Liam Magee of the details. After all, Hunter was *required* to advise his IRA contact

Chapter Nineteen

"Can you swim, Elmer?"

De Courcy had worked out how to get the cash safely into Northern Ireland from Carlisle. He sought help from his contacts in Lisburn, and from the Special Boat Service on the Clyde.

"Sure can. I'm no Mark Spitz, but I get by – a few lengths in the pool is no hard shakes."

"What of scuba? Do you have a log book or certificate?" enquired de Courcy.

"Come again?"

"Under water, any experience, old boy?"

"Under water? Scuba? No, Sir. It takes me all I've got to stay on the top."

De Courcy was disappointed at that, and thought again. Perhaps it would work with assistance. He would sound out the SBS on his ideas anyway.

"What are you at, Edward?" Sutton guessed that de Courcy was up to something he wouldn't fancy.

"What am I at, old boy? What does that mean? Have you no idea how to speak properly? I'm at, as you put it, the money. The collection and delivery of cash for our dear team of freedom fighters, that's all!"

"Let's have it," Sutton asked. De Courcy knew that his banter on the use of language had no effect on Sutton and that Sutton enjoyed using 'American' where possible.

"We transfer the cash under water from Scotland to Island Magee – that's what I'm at, old boy."

"Sure! I had to ask! When you come up with the real plan, let me know – I'm off for a jog."

"Wait – I'll join you." They locked up the cottage and, suitably dressed for the event, ran for an hour at a brisk pace, Sutton arriving back at the cottage a full five minutes before de Courcy, as usual.

"Thanks for waiting – old boy," de Courcy puffed.

"No problem – old boy. You have the keys. Any chance of unlocking this place?"

The headache returned, causing Sutton to endure restless and sleepless nights. De Courcy was aware of his friend's suffering; suffering that had worsened over the past three months. He would have one of his contacts arrange a proper medical – the full treatment – not the quick once-over he thought was the norm for the forces in the US of A.

*

It was quiet, it was sunny and warm, and it was Sunday. Sunday morning at eight o'clock, and breakfast was being taken on the porch. Any passer-by would have envied the luxury scene on the table of fresh orange juice, toast, cereal, tea and coffee. It was too hot for a cooked meal. The smell of coffee surrounded the place, and the marmalade attracted the local population of insects. Sometimes the smell was more appetising than the taste. Coffee was better smelt, thought de Courcy, than drunk. The same for strawberries. Tobacco was another smell de Courcy liked, not the smoke, just the tobacco. It reminded him of home, where orange juice and toast was the Sunday morning ritual. His father would be ready early for this, his busy day of the week, as vicar in the parish, with three services plus a short communion to get through. To his father it was clear delight: to him a bore and a waste of time. Now, looking back, there were on occasions good times at the morning services. Someday, he felt he should go to church again. When was the last time? Of course, the funerals. The funerals of both wife and son. No – church did not seem a good idea after all.

"What are you about, Edward?" Sutton didn't want to waste such a good day doing nothing, so he sounded out his partner.

"I don't know yet. I've worked out the money exercise. Tomorrow, one of us should advise the Lacys that it's on. As for today. . .?"

Sutton got up from his chair on the porch and walked to the gate, brushing toast crumbs off him as he went. The gate was just wide enough to allow the car to pass – a car that was getting hot in the morning sun.

"I'll take off in a few hours, if it's okay with you. See you at lunch when I return."

"Where to, old boy?"

"It's Sunday old boy, old boy. I'll go to church," and turning round to face de Courcy, "and no derisory comments."

That surprised de Courcy. How could he have known my thoughts? he wondered He looked at Sutton standing by the gate, and realised that he didn't really know him. There he was, tall, slim, reasonably fit apart from some illness, and wanting, without being forced, to go to church.

"I'll tell you something, Elmer – I was thinking the same thing, then decided against it. But – if you go – I'll go with you. Any objections?"

*

Island Magee Wesleyan Chapel was a small building on the bend of the road, making it dangerous to drive fast in those parts on a Sunday. The minister stationed there also looked after the ministerial duties of Whitehead Methodist Church. The summer visitors expected to swell their numbers hadn't arrived yet. De Courcy and Sutton arrived early and waited in the clearing to the left of the church that served as the car park. The car park was starting to fill with others who were also waiting; waiting for the arrival of the keyholder. Five minutes before the scheduled start at noon, the people left their cars and drifted towards the hundred-year-old stone building. One of their number opened the place. Sutton and de Courcy mixed with the others walking slowly to the narrow door. They were warmly welcomed into the cool interior and told to sit where they liked. The third row from the front was de Courcy's custom as a child, which was continued whenever duty allowed him to join his wife in days past. It was, therefore, natural for him to walk to the front and slip into the third pew.

"What's wrong with the back?" whispered Sutton, who followed de Courcy to the front and sat beside him.

"Sorry, old boy," he whispered back, "habit from my youth. If you want to move, let's do so now."

"We stay where we are – this is fine."

The interior was a welcome respite from the noon sun. The hard pews were not in any way comfortable, and no doubt kept many awake who would otherwise have slept during any boring sermons.

From a door to the right at the far side of the small electronic organ an elderly lady, complete with an equally aged hat perched on the top of her head, entered and placed four hymn numbers on the wooden board displayed for all to see. De Courcy and Sutton automatically looked up the hymns in the book sitting in front of them on the small ledge forming the back of the pew in front of them.

"I know two of the four. How about you?" whispered Sutton.

"I seem to know three, old boy. That comes from a superior education."

The hour passed quickly in the less than half-filled building. De Courcy found himself back to his childhood activities to help pass the time during the sermon. All the preacher had to say was said in ten minutes, with the following fifteen minutes taken up repeating himself. De Courcy, concentrating on the numbers on the hymn board, found that he could remember them top to bottom then bottom to top without looking at them. He would then add them up and carry out various mathematical calculations. Satisfied that there was nothing else about the numbers of interest, the mannerisms of the speaker were next on his list. He stopped counting after six 'In this day and age. . .', four 'As everybody knows. . .', three 'Another point is. . .', and he lost count of the '. . .and emms'. He was quickly brought back to his senses when the words 'What are you really here for today?' hit him. At this point the minister announced the closing hymn, which was well sung by all except de Courcy, who was remembering past times with his father and mother in similar buildings many years ago.

Nobody sat in front of them, so they only saw the minister, the organist, and the two stewards who brought the offering to the altar. It was only when leaving that de Courcy saw Mrs Lacy talking with a small group near the car park, and he realised that she must have been in the congregation. Sutton noticed her and prodded de Courcy to communicate this information.

"I see her. Stay here, I will have a word. Then come and join us."

He shook hands with the minister and stepped out from the shade into the sunlight and smiled at Mrs Lacy, as she caught his eye. She returned his smile and politely waited for him.

"Beautiful morning, Mrs Lacy, I'm sorry I didn't see you earlier. Nice service, don't you think?"

"I didn't know you were interested in such things, Major."

"Yes indeed. My late father was a minister, you know. C. of E., of course, but the Methodists are special to me."

"Special? Why, Major? Short sermons?"

"Ha! That one," pointing discreetly to the minister, who was still standing at the church entrance, "doesn't know when to stop. What!? Ha! No, Mrs Lacy, my late wife and son were Methodists."

Mrs Lacy didn't want to pry but was interested, and she found de Courcy even more to her liking than the day before in the byre.

"I'm sorry, Major. I didn't mean to sound nasty. Your late wife – your son – I didn't know. What? Your son is dead?"

"IRA – killed in Co. Armagh – but no more. Could I possibly ask a big favour, Mrs Lacy? It's simply to invite you round for tea this afternoon. I did say I would like to return the compliment, remember?"

She looked at him. He certainly *is* different, she thought. Perhaps. . . No, that would be stupid.

"I'd love to, Major. What time?"

Chapter Twenty

The Army arranged the transportation to and from Carlisle. The solicitor was expecting them and produced the relevant papers for signature, which he took time to explain before inviting Sutton and de Courcy to sign. A subsequent telephone call to the bank confirmed that the money would be available at 2 p.m. The final task the solicitor felt obliged to carry out was one of warning.

"It is not advisable to have so much cash about. There are people who, if they know, would stop at nothing to rid you of this fortune. It is my duty as your solicitor to advise you against such a transaction in cash."

"We understand your advice, and thanks for your concern, Mr Goodrich. Do you see?" pointing to the Securicor van outside. "We have taken precautions," announced de Courcy.

"Very well. Finally I have to give you this sealed envelope," and handed de Courcy an A4-size white envelope, sealed with tape, and addressed to Mr Sutton. De Courcy thanked the solicitor for his good offices and gave the envelope to Sutton, who examined it quickly, folded it, and put it in his inside pocket.

It was 1.55 p.m. and they, together with their army colleagues, disguised as Securicor officials, drew up to the bank. Sutton took the envelope from his pocket, opened it, and withdrew the single sheet of hand-written paper. He read it and passed it over to de Courcy.

"Locations available in seven days."

"We've only got half of the first transaction. No locations. Will the UVF accept that?"

"Wouldn't you, old boy? Cash for nothing is like money from America!"

Sutton folded the paper and returned it to his pocket, and tore the envelope into pieces, placing them in the waste paper tray inside the bank entrance.

The bank manager's office was typical of its type and gave the impression of solidity, strength, and longevity. The cash was being produced from the vaults somewhere, and the offer of tea or coffee was declined by both Sutton and de Courcy. Sutton made sure that the manager saw the small hand-held radio. For the purpose of this exercise, the radio was marked 'Securicor' in large blue letters.

In unison, they turned to face the door as the official, having knocked, opened it and entered, carrying four large grey bags, which were sealed and could only be opened using scissors. The official produced scissors from his pocket, and from years of practice opened the bags in no time to reveal the contents. There it was, in front of them, £215,000 in Bank of England £50 notes.

"The amount comes to £215,123.85 at the rate of 1.5340. Our commission is included in this rate. There is – let's see. . ." as he counted out the bundles, ". . .£25,000 in each large pile, made up, as you see, of five bands, each of one hundred notes. . ., so. . ." as he counted out loud. " . . that makes £200,000. These three separate ones make up the extra £15,000. I'll get the rest from the cashier," and he left, closing the door behind him.

Sutton and de Courcy just looked at the paper on the manager's desk, wondering if it was always as easy as this. Sutton was first to come out of the trance.

"Can I get the guys in from the van now, Mr – ah —" then, seeing the manager's name displayed on the table beside the cash, ". . .Mr Morrell?"

"Of course – please go ahead."

"Operation 'Muck' – we are ready – over and out," and he placed the radio in his pocket.

The official returned with the remaining £123.85, and having made sure that his paperwork was in order he left as three 'Securicor' men arrived.

Five minutes later they were on their way with £215,000 stored in two watertight plastic containers, to meet up with the Army convoy of two small vehicles, one hundred yards in front of them. The £123.85 was kept separate in de Courcy's pocket.

"That was easy – I wonder if I called at my bank, would I get two hundred grand for nothing?" commented Sutton.

"Your monthly pay, no doubt, old boy."

*

The journey was most uncomfortable inside the armoured Securicor van. Three hours it was – three hours of heat, noise, and every bump on the road. Sutton retrieved the radio and switched it on.

"Hey, you guys, how much longer in here?"

"Nearly there, five minutes say, and that should do it, out."

Anyone who says they enjoy a long drive would change their mind after sitting three hours beside Sutton and de Courcy in that van. It was good to get out of it, and better still they were not getting back into it. Now they would prepare for their trip from Portpatrick to the Isle of Muck. Portpatrick had a lighthouse and, according to de Courcy, that's all. The SBS had everything ready for them, and were making preparations to demonstrate the equipment. Sutton was interested in the mobile home that was to serve as their hotel for the night, de Courcy was interested in the underwater chariot.

"Simplicity itself, Major," explained the commander. "Stop, go, port, starboard, up and down. That's all there is to it."

"I see – yes. Just let me have a try. . ." and he familiarised himself within the roped off area in the sea to the north of Portpatrick. He mastered it quickly, and now needed to understand the navigation.

"Set the compass like – so. . ." as the commander once again instructed, ". . .and keep the heading – so. The compass can be seen from your seated position. This is the depth indicator – no more than twenty feet, Major. I suggest around nine or ten would do. By the way, you're in luck. No wind worth talking about, therefore little swell. Anything else?"

"One little item – the duration of the batteries?"

"We will take you to within two miles of the island on the supply craft. Your batteries should last for eight miles, so there is plenty of margin. Any more?"

"Will you be around to see us off, Commander?"

"All the way, Major."

Sutton had a shower in the mobile home, fixed himself a steak sandwich, and ate it while strolling towards the group of SBS people looking out to sea.

"What's up, Doc?" he spluttered, mouth full of sandwich.

"That's what I call a sandwich," one said, then returning his gaze to sea, "Your major is testing the chariot."

"The what?"

"There – see him? He has got the hang of it. You should have a great trip."

Sutton dropped the remainder of his sandwich and, shaking his head, muttered, "No way, old boy, old boy, and again I say no way." He picked up the steak and bread, and devoured it until the last morsel was gone.

De Courcy had steered the chariot to the water's edge, allowing the commander to show him the stores area.

"Normally this space is for extra batteries, but it can be used for your purposes, Major. I have left you a little something, just in case," and he lifted a sheet of opaque plastic to reveal two light machine-guns, and two loaded magazines. To check for size, the money in its watertight containers was placed into the chariot and the cover closed. There was plenty of spare room for their clothes and towels. During the journey, wet and dry suits would be worn and discarded at their destination.

Sutton peered over the commander's shoulder to look at the black tube shape of the machine referred to as a 'chariot'. The commander had opened and closed the casing a few times to check its ease of movement. When satisfied, he removed the money containers and the guns, closed the cover, and signalled to his team to look after the items while he found a suit for the American.

"For me? That's not funny, Commander, I don't work for you guys. Tell you what. I'll take the car ferry and meet the major at the other side. You can go on that thing. . ." pointing to the chariot, ". . .and keep the major right." That was enough for Sutton for one day. Three hours in a cage, a noisy one at that, and now they want to drown me. Nice try, he thought, and he made his way to the mobile home for a coffee.

His way was blocked by two smiling SBS people, who were shaking their heads. The commander called from behind him. "This way, Major Sutton. You will find this vehicle more interesting."

Sutton turned and allowed the commander to lead him to a dark green high-sided military lorry, where he was assisted into the interior. The inside was lit by two bulbs attached to the sides, revealing all sorts of kit. The commander looked Sutton up and down. "This size, I think," and he selected a blue-black wet suit from a selection displayed on a rail. "Try this on. You will need to strip off first. Here, use these," and he handed Sutton an ordinary swimsuit to use as underwear. Sutton had had it.

"Sorry, Commander. I know nothing of underwater stuff. Breathing – I've never done it – the scuba stuff – all beyond me."

"I see. Never mind, Major, you will learn quickly. Just change. Lt Barnes here will assist you, and we can show you the – ah scuba stuff. Quick now – we need to do this before the tide changes," and he left them to it.

Sutton resigned himself into believing that if de Courcy could do it, so could he. With assistance, he managed to get into the suit and found it to be too warm. He was guided to where the commander had prepared an air supply for him and, trying to disguise his fear, waded in until the water was about chest high. The commander checked the mask and showed Sutton how it should be worn. Next was the mouthpiece.

"Just breathe normally, that's all. Take short shallow breaths to get used to it."

"What about the air supply?" was the apprehensive reply.

"It's all here. . ." as the commander tapped the tank.

"How do I get it into my lungs? Do I bite on something or what?"

"Nothing like that. You breathe as you're breathing now. This is the latest gear here – invented, I understand, by Jacques Cousteau. The special valves in the regulator work with you – you breathe in, the valve lets air in. You stop, the air stops. Breathe out, the air leaves you and goes into the water – simple, old boy."

"Don't you start. One 'old boy' routine is all I can handle."

"Take it slowly at first. Put your head under and breathe. No need to swim off – give it a go – get used to it by standing there." Sutton did so. The first time he breathed, it surprised him. The second time was easier, and that was when he noticed the noise. It was very noisy, not like breathing air as it should be breathed on dry land.

The next hour was spent under the water using all the equipment, including the chariot. De Courcy sat in front, with Sutton behind. It was like two on a motor cycle.

The commander swam alongside and indicated that it was time to end the training session.

The chariot and its passengers were helped ashore.

"I still want to use the ferry – okay?" Sutton began to rub his head again; the pain was returning.

De Courcy and Sutton were led to the lorry as the commander organised the recharging of the chariot's batteries and the air cylinders.

"They did quite well for beginners, don't you think?" the commander asked his team.

"They will not make it without our help, Sir. Should one of us go with them? I am prepared to do it," said Barnes.

"Strict instructions not to. They are expendable, and, for that matter, so is the equipment. We are not to be seen to be involved – remember the brief?"

The weather was as expected as they set out from Portpatrick. Little wind, little cloud, and, according to Barnes, little chance of success. Barnes had gone over his calculations again, and was disturbed to learn that the life of the batteries would only give about four miles travel in the chariot. The commander dismissed his fears with a shrug of his shoulders, saying, "Remember the brief."

The low slung dark green vessel had been *en route* for two hours. De Courcy and Sutton were being helped into their suits while others loaded the chariot. De Courcy cast an occasional glance in the direction of the chariot to satisfy himself that the money was still there.

"How far is it, Limey," asked Sutton of the young officer helping him don the flippers.

"Three miles to go, then you're on your own. Twenty four miles as the crow flies; we do twenty-two, you do the rest. Easy buns, yank. . . How do the flippers feel?. . . and the suit. . . All right?" Sutton looked at him but didn't speak. He was terrified, and no Limey was going to know it, if he could help it.

"Everything to your liking, old boy?" asked de Courcy, who appeared beside him, kitted out as he was.

"No, it is not, old boy, old boy. There is no need for me to travel with you. I could use the ferry," remonstrated Sutton.

"Steady, Elmer. We are nearly there. Take your mind off it by thinking of a good steak, or if that doesn't work try Las Vegas."

Half an hour later, while it was still dark, they entered the water – de Courcy first, then Sutton, and they were relieved at the coolness it brought them. The commander was soon beside them, making sure that all was as it should be. The chariot was launched, and without ceremony de Courcy and Sutton scrambled aboard and were off. The trail of bubbles gave away their position.

"That's the wrong direction, Commander – too far south," shouted Barnes from the mother ship. The commander was about to swim after them, when. . . "Wait – that's better – they have corrected, Sir," as the trail of bubbles turned towards the Isle of Muck.

"They're on their own now. Back to Portpatrick," ordered Commander Owens.

Chapter Twenty-One

It wasn't very long before they were getting cold. The novelty had worn off, and the misery reinforced Sutton's view that the ferry should have been used. Any future trips would not find him doing this again, no matter what.

There was nothing to see. De Courcy had the glow of the instruments to occupy him, Sutton had nothing. The noise of the electric motors could be heard between the noise of breathing. The mouthpiece was not Sutton's idea of comfort. How much longer? – the cold is draining the remains of my energy, thought Sutton. The noise of the motors eased, or was the cold affecting him – he wanted ashore. De Courcy also thought that the motors were not working as well as before. The battery life indicator was low – too low. De Courcy took the chariot to the surface. Good, he thought, land is only a few hundred yards ahead, and he submerged to keep their heads under. I'm right, thought Sutton, the motor is quieter. De Courcy found that the power was nearly gone. What was wrong? The damn thing wasn't moving. He looked behind him at Sutton and saw one terrified cold American. I'd better not worry him, de Courcy thought, just keep it going till the motor stops – that wouldn't be too long. He surfaced again. Only about fifteen yards. He decided to stay as close to the surface as the machine would allow, and removed his mouthpiece. Rocks were about, so he started to zig-zag to miss them.

The motor stopped. De Courcy got off and found that he was waist deep. Sutton followed, and between them they dragged the chariot to dry land, just above the water-line.

Sutton got rid of his air tanks, and started to remove the wet suit.

"The damn batteries, Elmer. We were out of power out there," exclaimed de Courcy.

"Forget it, Edward. This is dry land and I'm staying on it."

With help from de Courcy, Sutton discarded the wet suit, and from the sealed compartment took out a towel, his dry clothes, and proceeded to make himself civilised.

"See where we are, old boy, while I change."

"You don't know!?"

"Afraid not. One thing, this is not the Isle of Muck," declared de Courcy.

The feel of dry land under his feet was sufficient for Sutton, who couldn't care less where he was. It was dry and solid, and that was good enough. Looking around him, now that the morning sun had brought back the feeling to his extremities, nothing was familiar. To the right as he faced the shore, the rock of a cliff face formed an arch, big enough to pass through. Sutton decided to examine it, so, with improved mobility, made his way over the rocky shore to the arch. There was something written there, Sutton realised, as he approached it. I'm right, thought Sutton, there it is, engraved into the rock beside the arch 'THE GOBBINS'. He could not see anyone about, or evidence of anyone being about. Sutton was enjoying his spell on dry land, and made the most of exploring the immediate area, before returning to de Courcy.

"No sign of life anywhere, Edward, but I know where we're at – there's a sign in the rock – actually chiselled into the rock! It says 'The Gobbins'. Ever heard of it?"

"Never heard of it. I don't know about you but I'm still cold."

"Yeah – well, I'm not for more boat trips, old boy, old boy."

"Where is the map?"

"Map? What map?" Sutton hadn't seen a map in the chariot. De Courcy poked around the inside of the chariot's storage compartment and produced a map of Island Magee. The map was removed from its waterproof case and spread out on a flat rock at the shoreline.

"There it is. We must be a few miles off course – about one or one and a half, at most."

"Some navigator you proved to be. Let's get out of here."

"Right – take these," and de Courcy handed the guns and magazines to Sutton, who placed them on the map. De Courcy folded their wet gear and stored it in the chariot, closed the compartment door, and proceeded to push the chariot back into the water. The air tanks were left on the shore.

"What of the money?" asked Sutton.

"It's safe where it is. We'll walk to Portmuck, collect the car, then return for it. Let's go, old boy – the walk will warm us up. Take one of the guns."

*

Terrorism allowed some to prosper, others to fall. Those supplying glass and building materials to effect repairs to bombed property found riches, as did the private suppliers of 'security'. Underground protection was 'offered' and rarely refused. Those who stepped out of line found themselves included in hospital statistics. The suffering of those in the business of tourism, or family retail outlets, was ignored. The fittest would survive, the rest. . .

Norman Stephens operated his small building contractor business from his home in Island Magee, employing his wife as office worker and secretary. Business was tight. He could not compete with the big boys of housing estate fame, who had land banks and planners in their pockets. He was on his own building one-off specifically-designed jobs, or carrying out repairs to farm outbuildings, or extensions. His current job was to repair the chimney of the house down The Gobbins path.

The damaged bricks were removed, new bricks cemented in place, and the pointing completed, when he noticed something most unusual. Something like a torpedo being pulled ashore by two frogmen. The shock of it caused him to drop his hammer as he was finishing off the lead flashing. It got worse. The two men stripped off their frogmen's gear, opened the torpedo, and took out two large machine-guns. After a while, they pushed the torpedo back into the water and started up the path, each with a machine-gun. Guns? Here? In Island Magee? They must be IRA, reasoned Stephens. He scrambled down the ladder as quickly and as silently as he could, and placed the ladder flat on the grass beside the house. It was too late to drive off – he would be seen. He just lay flat beside the ladder, and hoped that he wouldn't be seen by the IRA men.

They walked straight up the path, not twenty yards from him, without seeing him. What relief. Stephens gave them a couple of minutes to get away, then without any precaution whatsoever he jumped up, got into his Land Rover, drove up the lane, turned left at the top, and recklessly drove as fast as he could from that place.

Home – yes, I'll go home, he decided, so he continued past the Rinkha and turned left down the Port Road.

He managed to miss the bank manager and his wife, who were each finishing off a Rinkha poke.

*

"Someone's in a hurry, Pen," commented Martin Richmond, as the noise of a hard driven 4×4 approached. "It looks like Norman. . . It *is* Norman! I wonder what's up. . . Look Out!. . ." and he managed to push his wife Penelope out of the way.

The 4×4 stopped sharply, and Stephens, in a terrible state, jumped out, not aware how close he came to running them over.

"It's terrible – terrible – I tell you, Martin – it's terrible. . . They have guns – mind you – they each have guns! – and a torpedo! Here – in the Island. . . guns and a torpedo!. . ."

Martin and Penelope Richmond, seeing the behaviour of Norman Stephens, forgot the shock of being driven at. There he was, jumping about, hands everywhere as if swatting wasps, repeating the words 'guns' and 'torpedo', his face getting redder and redder by the second.

"Slow down, man, slow down. . ." Richmond said, trying to calm Stephens down to get some sense out of him.

"I'm sorry – very sorry – it's the shock – sorry – those guns and the torpedo – sorry – I don't know."

"Look, Norman, we are here to help," and as they were beside the Richmond bungalow, "Come in for a cup of tea and tell us all about it," offered Martin.

"Good idea," put in Penelope. "I'll put the kettle on to boil." Penelope had the keys in her hand and she opened up the two-roomed holiday home. Martin was guiding Norman into the main room when he started his hand signals again.

"Wait – wait," he shouted with as much agitation as before, ". . .they might be back. I've left my tools down there. . . What should I do?"

"Your tools? Where?"

"Down The Gobbins path – at the house in that clearing. . . What will happen? They have guns!. . . and a torpedo!"

Nothing will help him in his current state, thought Richmond, but to go and get his blasted tools for him.

"I tell you what, Norman," Martin suggested. "You stay here and have a drop of tea, and I'll go and get your tools – okay?"

Before poor Norman could answer, Martin left Norman in Penelope's care, went to the Land Rover and, noticing that the keys were in the ignition, climbed in and managed to turn it round in the narrow space available. Norman was at the door of the bungalow, spluttering, "Thanks, Martin, thanks – leave the ladder – it belongs there," he shouted as Richmond started to move off. Richmond waved to acknowledge the instruction, and was away, leaving Penelope to try and bring him out of shock.

Richmond came upon Stephens' toolbox, beside which was a hammer, and he placed both in the Land Rover. As he was already here, Richmond decided to examine this 'torpedo', or whatever it was that had shocked Norman the builder. All appeared to be normal, so Richmond found his way to the shore, and immediately saw the air tanks. Richmond couldn't see anything that was torpedo shaped, or any other unusual object – just the air tanks.

It was – normal. The sea lapping gently on the stony shore – normal. No people around, normal. The flat stone, he saw – but there were stones on this shore – normal – this was a stony shoreline.

Getting closer to the water's edge, the smooth stone didn't look right somehow. Perhaps. . . Richmond removed his shoes and socks, and waded in towards it. The water was cold, very cold, and he had forgotten to turn up the legs of his trousers, which were getting wet. He reorganised himself before continuing, and when he was ready he made his way to the flat stone. He put out his hand and touched it. That's no stone – it's man-made! He gave it a gentle push – it moved. It was buoyant, not floating, but not acting like a stone either. He reasoned that if it moved out when he pushed it, it should move in when he pulled it. He tried to pull it. It moved again. The shoreline was no more than four feet behind him, so he made up his mind to try and beach the thing. It was quite buoyant, so he managed not to beach it, but to get it into the shallows. That's when he noticed the catches on what appeared to be some sort of door. Without thinking of the consequences, he released the catches and opened the door.

Inside, he saw the wet suits. Those are the frogmen suits, he thought, as he remembered Stephen's frightened words. There were two plastic boxes – like large lunch boxes, Richmond thought – and, reaching past the folded wet suits, he managed to lift one out on to the top of the opened door. The box was grey-white in colour, without marking and reasonably heavy. The airtight lid was of the Tupperware design, but completely opaque. Using both hands, he gently prised open the lid. The sight before him made every muscle in his body go rigid.

He looked around him for signs of human life. Nothing. Focusing his attention on the open box with all that money, he thought it must be forged. That's it, a hoard of forged notes. He managed to prise one of the bundles out of the box and, taking a single note from the paper band, he held it up to examine it. It looked good. Richmond then held it up to the sky. The watermark was there, as was the metal strip. The note certainly felt genuine. Then it hit him – *it was genuine*. All those Bank of England £50 notes were genuine. Used but clean, with serial numbers different – genuine. His thoughts raced. What should he do? Why should he do it? Who were the people that Stephen saw? What did he say? IRA! That thought drove him to act. He returned the note to the bundle and the bundle to the box, then he replaced the lid.

He saw that there was a second box in the space beside where the first box was. He took it out and opened it. More! More Bank of England £50 notes. No wonder the people carried guns. Guns? They might return. Remembering that they could be IRA, Richmond closed the second box and placed it beside the first box on dry land beside his shoes. Then he closed the door of the torpedo and gave it a hard push. It moved about ten feet into the sea and stopped, partly submerged. Richmond left it there, picked up the boxes, his shoes in which his socks were stuffed, and ran as fast as he could in his barefoot condition, back up the track to the Land Rover. He looked around, and seeing nobody, placed the boxes and his shoes on the passenger seat, and drove up the track and back to the bungalow.

Richmond parked the Land Rover behind his own car and checked his pockets. Yes, he had his car keys. He lifted the boxes from the passenger seat, and opening the boot of his car he placed them there. He had just closed the boot and retrieved his shoes from the Land Rover when his wife Penelope opened the bungalow door and waited for him. He took the keys from the ignition of the Land Rover and, holding his shoes in his left hand, entered the bungalow. The pain of walking barefoot on such rough ground hadn't bothered him.

Norman Stephens was sitting there, head bowed, but he turned to see Richmond come over and hand him the keys.

"Your tools are in the back, Norman, and there is something there all right," as he put his socks and shoes on. "I don't think it's a torpedo, but it's something."

"I told you. . . I told you, Martin," Norman kept repeating in a much calmer manner than before. Then, seeing that he was holding the Land Rover keys, "Thanks, Martin – for your help in getting the tools. . . What should we do? The torpedo – what should we do?"

Penelope didn't know how Stephens was managing to stay conscious. He was still agitated, pale, and perspiring quite a lot.

"Let me bring Shirley over to you," suggested Penelope.

"No – no. Don't bring the wife over – I don't want to worry her. If it was IRA, I don't want them near Shirley. . . please. . ." The pathetic figure needed assurance, and Penelope had tried all she could without success. She looked pleadingly at her husband for help, a signal he saw and understood. Richmond stood there for a moment. An idea started to form in his mind.

"Tell you what, Norman," Richmond said as he sat beside him. "How would you feel if I used the public phone at the Rinkha to tip off the police about that torpedo thing? I could use the 'confidential phone' system, where there is no way knowing who phoned. How about it?"

Norman brightened.

"Would you? That sounds a good idea – you don't mind?" he said as he placed an encouraging hand on Richmond's arm. It was for his own assurance – anything to get away from the torpedo.

The telephone booth was vacant and the equipment was working. Richmond made four calls in quick succession, having first written down the telephone numbers. The first call was to the confidential phone, where he knew that his message was recorded. He said, "There is a torpedo near the beach at The Gobbins, Island Magee, and two sets of underwater air tanks. Two men carrying guns were seen at it about an hour ago."

Richmond's second call was to the police at Larne, where he repeated the message. The next two calls were to the BBC and the local TV station 'UTV'.

Chapter Twenty-Two

The journey from Portpatrick had taken its toll. De Courcy was tired, and just sat in the shade of the porch at the cottage rocking back and forth in his chair. Sutton was not only tired, he was drained physically and mentally, and lay down on his bed. They had retrieved the car, discovered that the money was missing, and decided to go home and have a hearty lunch.

"I sure would like to see that Captain Hunter's face when I tell him. Just think of it: 'Send over another $330,000 – we lost the first lot!' He will go nuts, Edward."

Sutton was in no condition to talk to anyone at Dugway, so Dugway would have to wait. De Courcy had arranged for Sutton to go into the military wing of Musgrave Park Hospital for a complete check-up, and would drive Sutton there on Monday. This was Saturday, and they had worked enough for Saturday.

"Hey, Edward old boy – you make the call for me to Dugway – I've had it for the rest of the day."

"Are you sure?"

"Go ahead. Don't give them any chance to shout at you, just give it straight and hang up," Sutton suggested.

"Whom do I ask for? That Captain Hunter fellow?"

There was no reply. De Courcy left his rocking chair and looked in at Sutton. He was asleep on top of the bed with beads of sweat forming all over him. Perhaps the sleep would do him some good, so de Courcy left him and set up the satellite dish.

It would be about seven in the morning at Dugway. De Courcy dialled the third number and waited.

"Yeah?" An American accent.

"Major de Courcy here. I have a message for Captain Hunter from Major Sutton – are you ready?"

"Major who?"

"Here is the message, old boy. 'The money has been lost, believed stolen. Can you get us some more?' End of message," and he hung up and returned the phone to its storage bay under the shower. Give it to them straight, Sutton said, so that's what he did.

MacBride was awake now. He hoped for more sleep, but after that call there was little chance of it. Lost? Stolen? What are they playing at over there? He got up, dressed, and hauled the captain from his bed on to the floor.

"Awake yet, son? Listen up and hear this real good. Your plan is up for second thoughts. Those guys, Major Sutton and the Brit, have lost the capital, that's all! Lost it! And all they want is more money! Work that one out while I get some waffles," and he left Hunter's room for the canteen.

Captain Hunter was slow in the mornings. He was an afternoon person, unless something happened. Now, just now, he became a morning person. He got up from the floor and started to do some thinking. There wasn't enough information, that meant getting some. That meant getting that ass Major Sutton over there, and quick. MacBride was finding it difficult to remain calm. Here was his last chance of promotion before retirement going up in smoke, and the captain was responsible.

The last thing MacBride needed was an interruption during breakfast, and that's what Captain Hunter gave him.

"This is what we do, Sir. We get them. . ."

"Hold it, son. Can't you see I'm busy? Wait 'til I finish – and another thing, it's not 'we'. Remember it's *your* strategy, not mine, that's gone belly-up."

Hunter prudently allowed MacBride to finish his waffles and two mugs of coffee before saying anything.

"Now, Captain. Now is the time to let me hear your sweet tones of excuses and further action. Well?"

"Yes, Sir. We. . . I – have no real facts, so we. . . *I* – need to get Major Sutton over here and talk to him. Until that happens, we. . . I – can't plan for corrective action."

"Okay – you arrange it. When is he due to call in?"

"Blast it. I could be waiting for another week."

"Too bad, son."

*

It was getting late. Sutton was still asleep, so de Courcy turned on the TV, tuned to the local station, and waited for the news bulletin. He was just in time.

". . .*the torpedo is believed to be armed, but an Army spokesperson declined to comment. The Gobbins hasn't been as crowded since the famous walkway was closed in 1961. Local people suspect it was a training session by the Navy that had gone wrong. A spokesperson for the Navy said there were no torpedoes in the area. A man was shot today. . .*" De Courcy turned the set off and reached for the phone.

"Mrs Lacy? It's de Courcy. Have you by any chance seen the local news on TV?"

"The torpedo at The Gobbins? – yes, Major. Anything to do with you?" she asked.

"Can I see you? We could meet at the Rinkha in half an hour, if that is convenient."

She was there before him, looking very beautiful, he thought, standing there holding two ice creams. "Here you are. . ." and she handed him one of the cones, ". . .I bought you a poke." Nodding his gratitude, he felt a little embarrassed as he accepted it.

"Let's walk over here," and he guided her to the rear of the car park where he had parked the Honda. Making sure that they were not being overheard, de Courcy looked around as he licked the poke.

"The 'torpedo', as reported by the TV, was nothing other than the money carrier. The money has gone. Elmer and I haven't a clue what happened. . ." and he told her the story.

"How did the media get to hear about the torpedo? Did anyone see you land at The Gobbins?"

"Can't say. Elmer and I didn't see anyone. It's possible, of course. There may be no chance of getting the Americans to replace it, but I have already asked them to."

"You didn't?" It was more of a statement than a question, but de Courcy's expression told all. "You *did*! I bet that was Elmer's idea. You wouldn't do that sort of thing, would you?"

"He's not well, you know. We worked together in the Gulf War and something – something happened out there, I don't know what." He found himself talking to her about matters he would normally keep secret. He had not intended to talk but she was good company, and. . . "Sorry, Susannah, it is wrong of me to trouble you with my worries. Look – is there any chance of you letting your people know on the quiet about the money? They might hear of something. . . like. . . someone suddenly spending money. . . a new car, a new house – that sort of thing."

"What of your own people? They have the resources, we don't."

"Oh no! If they ever heard of money going to the UVF, never mind it being lost or stolen, there could be big trouble."

She finished her ice cream while de Courcy was talking. "All right, I'll pass it on. What of getting more money?"

"Don't know yet. I should know in a few days, and if I do, I'll arrange to see you again. It will be my turn to buy," and he polished off the remains of his cone. She smiled, returned to her car, and drove off. A second car complete with minder followed her, but the major wasn't looking.

*

Penelope Richmond had taken herself off to bed after having a bath, leaving Martin alone in the sitting-room. The plastic boxes were still in his car. Quietly, he went outside, opened the garage and went to the back wall. He always reversed his car into the garage, so that the boot was against the back wall. The boxes were as he left them. So it wasn't a dream. He brought them into the house, locking all behind him.

Richmond spread newspapers on the floor and placed the boxes on them. He opened the first box. The television was still on but was ignored, except when the late news summary repeated the story of a torpedo at The Gobbins. He listened again then turned the set off. Emptying the contents of the first box, he again noticed the money was all Bank of England £50 notes. He started to count it. Twenty bundles, one hundred notes in each bundle, each note £50. Good heavens! There's £100,000 right in front of me, he thought. And there is a second box! Probably the same. That would make £200,000.

Richmond opened the second box and counted it in bulk. Twenty-three bundles this time – an extra £15,000. That's a full total of £215,000. All that money in front of him spread out on the newspaper. He didn't bother to count each bundle, just a random selection of four, two from each box. Yes, there were one hundred notes in each.

He returned the money to the boxes and sealed them with tape. What to do next? He didn't know. He couldn't leave them there, he couldn't put them back – he couldn't phone the police. And he couldn't keep it. It wasn't his and, being a bank manager, it wouldn't be right – it was plain wrong.

The boxes would do to store the money, but where? Where to put them? Leaving them in the house was too risky. Perhaps not – he was the only person to know about them – the TV said nothing about. . . Of course! How stupid! He would place them in safe-keeping at the bank. There was a supply of strong brown paper in the kitchen which he could use to make two parcels of the boxes, which he would label before taking them to the bank on Monday. Richmond was happy with his plan, and fifteen minutes later he hid two parcels amongst the collection of cardboard boxes and gardening tools in the far corner of the garage.

Chapter Twenty-Three

Sutton slept soundly until 0700. He got up, prepared the breakfast for a change, and decided not to bother with the morning exercise. De Courcy was up and out for his morning jog, and returned as the bacon, eggs, and potato bread was being served.

"How's the head, old boy?" puffed de Courcy as he stood at the door.

"No problem, Edward. In fact I feel like a million. Sorry – I forgot."

"The money? It's not *our* problem. That's the beauty of anything going wrong with this set-up – it's unofficial, Elmer, so it hasn't happened." De Courcy had a shower, leaving the breakfast to get cold. "I can't wait to hear Dugway's reply to our request for more money. Do you think they will send someone over here, old boy?"

"No chance. It makes it too risky. The whole story could get out."

De Courcy was about to mention that he had told the Lacy girl about the missing money, but that comment of Sutton's postponed the message. Too risky? The story getting out? There was no proof, but should the UVF have the money already or find it in due course, the story was likely to get out anyway. De Courcy couldn't keep it from Sutton and he told him of meeting the girl.

"I might have damaged our position, Elmer. While you were sleeping. . ."

Sutton listened to de Courcy and responded, "Like you said, there is no proof, as it's all unofficial. Let's make Dugway wait a few days – that will give Captain Hunter time to worry about it. Your egg, okay? Cold?"

"Fine, thanks. It's about time you did some of the cooking, old boy."

They went to church and mingled with the small crowd in the car park after the service. That was when de Courcy was advised by the girl to spend some time around the Rinkha, where small talk was easily overheard and might produce something.

*

"Fiddle – dee – dee." Penelope was annoyed at something and she used her usual way of expressing it.

"What's wrong, Pen?" shouted Richmond from the bathroom.

"I've left my sun-glasses in the bungalow at Island Magee. I'll go down after church and get them – I'll need them for the holiday."

Richmond offered to go with her and suggested that it would give them the opportunity to call with Norman Stephens and see how he was. Stephens was glad to see Richmond.

"I'm okay. Didn't sleep, mind. I saw the news on the TV and there were plenty of Army and police about last night. But don't tell Shirley, mind – sure you won't?"

"Relax, Norman, it's all over now," Richmond advised as Penelope, having found her sun-glasses, expressed her joy by waving them about. "We only came down to get Pen's sun-glasses. She needs them for the holiday." Richmond waved back to her. "I won't say anything to Shirley if you won't. I suggest you tell her something though. She knows you were working there – at The Gobbins – doesn't she?"

"Aye, surely." Stephens was a worrier – anything outside his building trade world was an intrusion he found hard to deal with. "I'll tell her something. I'll go back to The Gobbins tomorrow. The job's about finished and I need to put the ladder away."

Richmond didn't say anything at that, but thought of the crowds of TV, Police and Army people who had examined The Gobbins since his phone call, and thought it unlikely that the ladder would still be there.

"Have a good holiday anyway. Where are you going, Martin?"

"We're off to tour California, but not for a few days yet."

"California!" Stephens was impressed. "I've not been outside Northern Ireland – don't want to go either. Shirley likes travel, mind. Goes with her sister."

"It's our big holiday, Norman. A tour of the West, mostly in California, to celebrate our wedding anniversary."

Not my idea of a holiday, thought Stephens. There is nothing you can get there that you can't get at home. Stephens waved them off, and went inside.

"Did you hear that, Shirley? The two of them are going to America. California and the like, mind." He shook his head. "They must be daft." Shirley despaired with Norman's attitude. For once, she would like to take Norman abroad and let him see how others lived.

"Not as daft as those who only stay here," she replied softly enough so that Norman wouldn't hear.

The Richmonds stopped off at the general store in the area, the Rinkha, on their way home just to have a browse. Penelope joined the queue for ice cream, while Martin browsed through the car accessories and stationery items. He noticed two well-dressed men wandering about as a team, not bothering with anything but taking great interest in the people. Not locals, thought Richmond, too well dressed for that. They were probably police. He heard the elder-looking one say something. English accent, hardly police then – not with an English accent.

Two men in Army uniform entered the shop, causing the first two to take cover behind a pile of toys. Definitely not police.

Richmond saw that Penelope was being served, so he accidentally bumped into the one that hadn't spoken. "Sorry – my fault," Martin said.

"No problem," came the reply. American accent. I'll remember those two, should I see them again. The American wasn't looking too pleased with life. Richmond had the sentence out before he realised, "Cheer up – you look as if you have found a pound and lost a couple of hundred thousand."

The one with the English accent heard him, and both gave him a look that was unbelievable.

Richmond followed Penelope out of the shop and over to the car and drove off, holding his poke. Looking in his rear-view mirror, he noticed that the two men were looking in his direction. One was taking note of his car's registration number, and a uniformed police officer, noticing this, began to question him.

Stupid! Stupid! Stupid! What a thing to say! Their reaction to his comment meant that they must know about the money. Richmond decided to get rid of the parcelled boxes as planned. When Monday morning arrived, he took them to the bank and had them placed in safekeeping in his and his wife's names.

*

Visiting hospitals was not de Courcy's idea of having a good time. Monday at 10.00 a.m. found Sutton and de Courcy in the military wing of Musgrave Park Hospital in Belfast. It would take three days to complete the tests, so de Courcy left Sutton there and returned to Brown's Bay via Superintendent Stephen Richards' office in Castlereagh, where he checked out the car registration number. Superintendent Richards advised de Courcy that the car was a company vehicle belonging to a bank. That particular car was allocated to a Mr Martin Richmond who, in the eyes of the police, was clean. "Richmond is of good character, married, and is seen about Island Magee taking photographs," advised the superintendent.

Three days later, de Courcy returned to the hospital to collect Sutton.

So far, Professor Withers had drawn a blank. The tests hadn't shown anything unusual, and that in itself was unusual. The medical history provided by Sutton might have been incomplete, suggested Professor Withers, so he decided to interview Sutton again.

"Tell me again about the Gulf War. How were you prepared for it from the medical side?" the professor asked. Sutton was sitting up in bed surrounded by medical equipment and out of date American newspapers.

"The medical side? We all had the usual shots for this and that, like tetanus, typhoid, hepatitis. Then there were the pills. Nobody knew what they were for, for sure. Some said they were in case we got gassed, others said they were to protect us from the smoke coming from the DU shells," Sutton answered.

"The DU shells?"

"Yeah. Depleted Uranium stuff. They went through their tanks like nothing." The professor took notes as Sutton spoke.

"It might be possible, I suppose, for interaction between the drugs to cause your metabolism to react in a way we haven't come across before. The only test result we are still waiting for is the blood analysis." Professor Withers looked at Sutton while he spoke. "Sorry for the delay, Mr Sutton, but there has been a high level of activity since the bomb in town yesterday. Your diet, how much coffee do you drink?"

"All I can get, but I have always taken coffee since I was a kid," said Sutton.

"May I suggest you leave out coffee for, say two weeks, and anything else with a high caffeine or sugar content," ordered Withers.

The thought of getting into herbal tea as a substitute for coffee was not Sutton's idea of a cure, but he would give it two weeks and see. De Courcy, waiting for him to be discharged, used the opportunity to have a discreet word with the professor. He was surprised to find the professor starting to question him about his Gulf War medicines. Yes, he had the usual medical examination, and yes he had the various inoculations, but no, he had taken no pills for gas protection. Yes, there were pills, but he hadn't bothered with them. Gulf War Syndrome wasn't heard of then, but the professor was inclined to go along with the idea that the dust from the DU shells might have caused some sort of radiation sickness that current tests didn't reveal.

*

"Did you ever get toothache, Edward?" An unusual question, out of the blue, as de Courcy drove through Carrickfergus *en route* to Brown's Bay.

"Yes, old boy. Some time ago, mind you."

"Ever notice that it disappears when at the dentist? Like this head of mine; I've had no problems while in hospital, now I'll probably get it before we get to the Rinkha. Some castle, huh?" as they drove past Carrickfergus Castle.

"Quite spectacular," agreed de Courcy. "We must pay a visit some day."

It grew cooler, with rain clouds much in evidence. The roads were sticky from the mixture of petroleum products, tyre rubber and yesterdays showers. The smell was different. Island Magee had taken on an even greener hue than before, and the sweet fragrance of washed and watered hedges with wild flowers was everywhere.

"This sure beats the town smells, Edward. Air quality is good just now. How about giving those guys in Dugway a rude awakening? It will be four in the morning there – just perfect, eh?" The mischievous smile on Sutton's face spelt trouble for Dugway.

De Courcy negotiated the entrance to the cottage, just missing both gate posts.

"Why not, Elmer? You go ahead, I'll have a nice cup of tea ready for you."

"Tea? Well, make it kinda weak, and none of your milk stuff, right?"

Over the past few days, the rain had promoted the growth of daisies, nettles, and thistles in the uncultivated patch others would call a garden. Sutton moved too close to a nettle when setting up the phone, and called it a few names botanists would wonder at.

"Hi, Captain, and how are you this fine morning?. . . Is that so?. . . Fancy that. . . Listen, slug face, we do the work, we decide when to phone. Now – when can the next lot of capital be collected?"

There was silence for a moment as Sutton listened to Hunter making a few passing references to his lack of character, lack of ability, and lack of parents. De Courcy had brewed up and placed a mug of tea on the stone slab beside Sutton that supported the satellite dish.

"That's fine by me. You make sure the Consul has the same amount of cash as before, including the extra $500. Out."

The equipment was made ready for storing away before Sutton picked up the mug and took a sip. He took another, then a third, before advising de Courcy of the news.

"It's vacation time again, Edward. I pick up the tickets and cash from the Consul as before."

"Las Vegas?"

"Yep."

"You off on your travels, old boy, and I'm left to play poker – is that it?"

"Right. Fill me in on that guy at the Rinkha— remember? The missing cash?"

The equipment was stored under the shower tray as de Courcy gave Sutton the details supplied by the superintendent.

". . .Nothing on him at all – clean as a whistle, old boy. He doesn't even have a speeding fine against him." De Courcy surveyed his viewpoint over the bay as the rain started to fall. "He's a bank manager who uses a cottage on the island. Probably a holiday place. I'd say it was coincidence, but the boys in the RUC will check on him now and again."

"Bank manager or no bank manager – watch him, I say. Where does he work?" asked Sutton.

"Belfast, near the Castlereagh Holding Centre. Some of the police use the bank, and the news is that he's straight, easy to deal with, and has a sense of humour. When do we leave for Las Vegas?"

Sutton finished the tea and had a refill. "This stuff can be got used to. Not to my taste like coffee, but better than nothing. I pick up the tickets and cash on Friday – that's tomorrow. We fly out from Aldergrove on Sunday afternoon. It means that you'll miss your chat with that young bird of yours, old boy, old boy!"

De Courcy smiled. "How disappointing for her. I can always take her out on Saturday, old boy, old boy!"

Sutton wasn't sure how the relationship was between the girl and de Courcy, but he was quite certain that both could get hurt, never mind himself.

"Take it easy, Edward. She is a bit on the young side for you and she works for the enemy. No offence, but her people could blow us away."

It was getting cold on the porch, and the wind picking up started to blow the rain into de Courcy's face. He moved inside, closed the door, and agreed with his friend's diagnosis.

"You're right, Elmer. Don't worry, I'll keep my distance. I suppose I'm using her company to fill the vacuum. When this project is over, and that might be now, she will go her way and I mine."

"Back to England?" guessed Sutton.

"Probably. Not the old home town, somewhere north." De Courcy was dreaming again and remembered a touring holiday with his wife and son, somewhere in Scotland. ". . .That would be it. . ." thinking aloud, ". . .Inverness and north to Cromarty Firth. . ."

"Let's get out of here, Edward. What do you say to a drive to the Glens of Antrim and a good hard walk? To keep in shape?"

Chapter Twenty-Four

As usual, Captain Hunter was angry. It was their fault, again. His plans were always workable, provided they were adhered to. Those two assholes in Ireland were trying to break him, and they wouldn't succeed. Hunter would make sure of that. It was bad enough MacBride washing his hands of the whole project; now the two assholes were trying to do it as well! His early call from Sutton had deprived him of much needed sleep, and thinking about Sutton and MacBride would be sure to keep him awake. Hunter was determined to keep out of MacBride's way until he had arranged for the surveillance information to be sent to the English solicitor. He was fully awake now and more angry than ever. The plan was crystal clear to him, and simple too. The changes forced upon him were easy to handle. All that was required was to get that idiot major over here and grill him about the missing money. Once the money was sorted out, the idiot could pick up the surveillance information on his return to Ireland. Simple. The idea that the money was lost or stolen didn't enter into it. Whoever heard of anyone losing $300,000. In cash? No, that ass-hole was having a go at him. He was up and ready for the day by five. Three hours before MacBride would be around, and another three before he could phone the Pentagon. He lay down on his unmade bed, having kicked the wall, the door, and the side of the bed to release his anger. Then he fell asleep.

"Do you work here or what, son?" It was MacBride's emotionless face appearing above him that he saw first. Then he saw the MP and then the dog.

"Nice lie-in, was it, son? It's only 0830 hours after all. Would you like breakfast in bed?"

Captain Hunter woke up with a jolt, confirmed by looking at his watch that the time was indeed 08.30 a.m., and apologised all around him. The MP and the dog? Why?

"Something happen, Sir?" he asked MacBride.

"Nice of you to join us, son. Only some trouble from the Pentagon, that's all. Some guy phoned here at 0800 hours asking for you to say that the deal's off. That's all. What guy and what deal?" shouted MacBride. "Get your ass over to the phone in my office and let's see your superior strategy at work. Move it before the dog gets angry."

"Dog? Angry?"

"Some ass-hole set the alarm off after 0400 hours. Security has found the problem right here," as MacBride pointed directly to him. "After checking it out we find you have broken one of the security wires, that's all. A bit hard on the door, were you, son?" Hunter saw the damage at the door hinge that must have occurred when he kicked it.

"You won't be staying here too long, I fancy. How would you like a transfer to the Antarctic Station, son?"

MacBride turned and marched out, followed by the MP and the dog. Hunter made it to the office in double-quick time.

"Dugway here, Captain Hunter. Get me Lt Patton in Surveillance. . . Yes, I'll hold." The perspiration was forming quite well on just about everywhere it could, especially on his head, as he waited for the connection.

"Captain Black Feather here. You looking for Lt Patton?"

"That's right, is he around?"

"Transferred out last week. He is no longer in this section."

"Transferred out? Where to?"

"Records. Do you want me to put you through?"

"No. . . Wait. . ." Hunter was thinking fast. He needed the locations of the arms dumps, and didn't particularly want to talk to an Indian. "Yes, put me through. I might be back to you later, okay?"

"Sure. Hang on," and the connection was placed on hold. MacBride was staring at him without movement, but his heavy breathing spoke volumes.

"Lt Patton, Records."

"Bill, it's Tom Hunter here. What on earth are you doing in Records?"

"Hi, Tom. Some security flap. We all got shifted around, I ended up here. Look Tom, you can forget about me getting the surveillance info. There's no chance now. My authority in Surveillance is nil."

"Hold on. . ." The perspiration was flowing well now, making pools of various sizes on MacBride's desk. MacBride's heavy breathing was in direct proportion to each drop that fell. ". . .Who could get it?"

"Try the new guy. He's only an Indian, but is supposed to be good."

"An Indian! That's all I need."

"I know what you mean. Captain Black Feather is the guy, okay?"

"Thanks for nothing anyway, Bill, put me back to him."

MacBride had opened the door of his cabinet during this last exchange and placed two towels in front of Hunter.

"Use these. I don't want no wood rot, son." Hunter gratefully wiped his head and the table, and felt the better for it.

"Captain Black Feather, Surveillance."

"Hi, Captain. Captain Hunter of Dugway here. Thanks for getting me Lt Patton, but unfortunately he can't help me. We are in the middle of a project here and need some help from your files. Can you help us?"

"That's what we are here for. What do you want, Captain?"

The relief was immediate. The smile, the punched fist in the air, the stopping of the sweat. MacBride changed to breathing normally. That's better, Hunter thought. Perhaps there *are* good Indians after all.

"I need some surveillance info, and I need it fast. It's under 'Ireland' – to do with IRA arms dumps – can you help?"

"Ireland, you say – what is the project number?"

"'Ireland 7'."

There was silence. Black Feather needed to protect himself on this one and he knew that the call was being monitored. "Hang on, Captain Hunter, just checking." Black Feather used the computer terminal in front of him to check out authorisation. There was no authority to let anything out, so he advised Captain Hunter, "Sorry, Captain – there is no clearance here to let you have access to any Ireland file. Perhaps you could place your request through channels. . ."

". . .Just listen to me, you red-tape-happy red-skin. You get the information I want off to the destination I tell you – do you hear?"

"What destination would that be, Captain?"

"That's better. I knew you would see reason. Send the info, I will give you the details of the exact stuff that's needed, to a solicitor in England. That's England, Europe, okay?"

"I think you should know that this call is being recorded by Security, Captain Hunter. Now, what do you think you should do about authorisation?"

Hunter couldn't believe his ears. What sort of army have we got going here? It's not like it was, and that's a fact.

"Okay, okay. I'll do it by the book. Leave it – I'll get authorisation," and he violently hung up.

"Nice one, son. You sure pulled that one right into the fire. Tell me this, son. Whose side are you on? Are you getting any back hands from the UVF?"

They were alone in MacBride's office, and Hunter had taken all he was going to from MacBride. His temper was at boiling point.

"Back off! Back off! You said that if I go down, you go down too, remember? How about some help around here instead of all the hassle? I might, I just might, save both our hides – and your pension." He wasn't finished with MacBride yet, but took time out to think before he spoke. "The two of us working together will be better than one. Do you want this project to fail – Sir? Because all I get from you these days is nothing but negatives. If you don't trust me on this one, get me transferred out." That should do it. There was nobody listening, no witness to what he said. What could MacBride do? His Irish mate in the Pentagon would be looking for success on this one. Success meant that MacBride *must* back his plan.

MacBride was only thinking of his pension.

"Take it easy, Captain. Sure I trust you – I got the money approved, didn't I? Now settle down and sort this mess out. What do you need?"

'Got him! It was a close thing, but I got him,' guessed Hunter.

"Two things, Sir. First, we decide on what we say to the asshole coming over from Island Mac. . . whatever it is; second – I need you to get authority through channels to access the surveillance info. Can you arrange that – Sir?"

MacBride was observing the strange person in front of him that passed for an intelligence operator, and thought that perhaps there was something to be salvaged after all. He didn't want to get too close to

Hunter, and would divorce himself from the action and planning should there be trouble.

"Let's keep future discussion on this for the *Room* – right?"

"Yes, Sir."

"Okay. Leave the authorisation bit to me. You go and work out how to deal with Major Sutton. The door is over there – okay?"

After Hunter had departed, MacBride decided to contact his Irish friend in the Pentagon, who should be able to pull a few levers and get the authorisation. Authorisation for information to be used for covert operations was tricky. Tricky, because records were kept of who got what and when, and records meant pointing the finger should it go wrong.

How did the world manage before telephones? MacBride used the telephone like anyone else, and took it for granted that requests made and assurances given over the phone would be carried out. It would be different if it was he who was giving the assurance or receiving a request. Nobody expected him to deliver unless it was to repay a favour. His Irish colleague in the Pentagon sometimes delivered on assurances. This time he had to, and MacBride would use every lever he could to effect delivery. The surveillance information was required if only to keep Captain Hunter off his back, and to show again that he could deliver when the captain couldn't. That's why he was only a captain. Yes, he would tell him that.

It took longer than usual before he was put through.

"Is it yourself, Simon? How's that stupid project of yours going?" asked Bishop.

"I hear the Pentagon still throws money at you. How's that young driver of yours?"

"You remember her, do you? She's still the same – why do you ask?"

"Nothing. She has requested a transfer to work with me."

"Nice try, Simon, nice try. Look, there's a bit of a flap on here, can you tell me quickly what you want?" Bishop sounded uptight.

"You have a problem? What problem, Nick?" asked MacBride.

"The CIA are into everything and everybody. Nothing gets done unless it's by the book. It's mad, Paddy, mad – nothing but red tape and interviews. Even the phone calls are taped."

MacBride didn't expect that. This might not work after all.

"What of this call, Nick – are you recording this call?"

"Not yet, Simon boy. These new phones we have here have an extra button. If I think the call should be monitored, all I do is press it. Do you want me to press it, Paddy?"

"Not unless you want some security pen pusher to hear me talk about you and your driver."

"That could be interesting – huh? okay, what do you want, and don't take all day."

"Still as charming as ever. I need authorisation to get some surveillance stuff, and I need it quick. How do I go about it so that it can't be traced back to me?"

"So you *are* in trouble, Simon?" It was a question rather than a statement.

"Not yet. But I could be if I don't get the info, or if having got it, the project goes belly-up."

"Is it to do with the old homeland, Paddy?" enquired Bishop.

"You got it. It's important to make this project work – the authority?"

"Not easy, Simon, not easy. Tell me anyway, what do you want?" MacBride told him and suggested that Hunter's name be used as the source of the enquiry.

"Leave it with me. It could take a day to sort out – I'll phone you back"

That's more like it. That will show the captain what can be done by those with ability.

Chapter Twenty-Five

T. J. Smith of the CIA, York, Laskie, and Black Feather listened to the tape a few times.

"Your opinion, Captain Black Feather?" asked Laskie.

"It seems funny, Sir, that after the rotation of duties and after the 'Ireland 6' file went missing, these people want surveillance details from someone who used to work here. Perhaps they have received stuff in the past and chanced their arm for more."

"Your opinion, Charlie," Laskie asked of his security man.

"That sounds logical. There may be more. The guy that was in Surveillance had nothing to do with the library, which means that the missing file and the surveillance request are not connected."

"So," queried Laskie, "are you saying that we are looking for two people?"

"Yes, Sir. If not, then more."

Laskie didn't want to hear that, but wanted everything out and in the open rather than remain hidden, only to surface later.

"Good work, Henry. Perhaps you would leave us now," and Laskie watched as Black Feather left his office.

"There's another possibility, Gene, one you might not like," T.J. said.

"Not like? Do you think I like any of this, T.J.? It's bad enough thinking of one loose bullet on the team, never mind two – or more. What's your thinking, T.J.?"

"The Indian. It could be him. Nothing points to him for sure. Clean as snow, that one. Our boys found nothing but. . .," he shrugged, ". . .it's a good game plan to get yourself off by pointing the finger at someone else."

"Proof?" asked Laskie.

"None yet, but we are still looking at everybody. This Dugway thing, it could be worth watching. Who's down there, Gene?"

"There's the Irish guy, Major Simon MacBride, and Captain Hunter. Hunter has IRA connections," York replied to T.J.

"It's starting to point to Dugway. I'll get my people on to it, Gene, and it would make it easier if nobody here warned them we were coming."

"You got it, T.J.," agreed Laskie.

"What new projects are you on right now, Gene?"

"Nothing since the fire and the missing files hit us. Nothing except the new one – 'Ireland 7'. Now there is a fact. Guess who's running it?"

"Dugway," T.J., York, and Laskie said in unison.

Chapter Twenty-Six

Las Vegas was as before – a night-time town looking lost in daylight. As they checked into the Alexis Park Hotel, Sutton was handed a sealed envelope by the receptionist. He ripped it open, read the note, then crumpled it and threw it accurately into the bin on the floor beside the flowering cactus.

"They know we are here, Edward. That's to tell me where to be at 20.00 hours, tonight. You better not hang around in case it's a set-up." De Courcy looked at him disbelievingly.

"The whole thing is wrong, Edward. Would you allow strangers to have $300,000 of your cash?" De Courcy nodded.

They made their way to their room and ordered a selection of sandwiches and tea from room service.

"Where is the money for the casino, old boy?" Sutton gave him the lot less $500 that he would use to get out of Dugway fast if there was trouble. "I say," as he started to count the bills, "how much is here, Elmer?"

"$2,000. Don't spend it all – keep, say, $500, in case we need to get out fast. The room is paid for, so all you need is food and booze and women!" De Courcy ignored the comment.

"$2,000. How much could I win, I wonder? Leave me, old boy – I'll see you when you return. When is that likely to be?"

"If I'm not back in three days, Edward, get out fast. Here. . ." handing him the return air ticket, ". . .use it, Edward."

In a similar fashion to last time, Sutton was bundled into a car at the appropriate time and place and found himself heading out of Las Vegas to Nellis Air Force Base. He relaxed as best as he could, knowing that Hunter and MacBride would hang him out to dry and would find the task easier if he was tired. He decided to play it straight and tell all. It would be too late for a meeting today, he hoped, so a good night's sleep should help. His head wasn't right, but cutting down on the coffee and sweet stuff seemed to help. The throbbing energy-sapping pain had gone, leaving a dull ache that was virtually constant.

*

MacBride, Hunter and Sutton entered the *Room*, with Lt Croft on duty in the security section. Sutton had taken his first real look at Captain Hunter, and was surprised how small he looked. Slim and fit, yes – but small in stature compared to MacBride or himself.

"Can this be traced back to us, Major?" asked MacBride.

"No," answered Sutton, his head bowed, supported by his hands using the table to support his elbows. "Not from my end, anyway."

"What do you mean by that?" was Hunter's loud and angry response. Amazing how small people seem to need to compensate by using volume, thought Sutton. "It was you and your end that lost the capital. How can you be sure that this incident won't follow you right to my front door?" Hunter sure can talk loud, thought Sutton. "Well? I'm waiting."

"You talking to me, Captain? Because if you are I'll break your neck."

Hunter knew he shouldn't have talked to a major like that, not when there was a witness. He decided to stay quiet and see if Sutton answered his question. Eventually he heard Sutton's quiet voice declare, "There is nothing from my end that leads here. Nothing. I'm the only lead – along with Major de Courcy – and you made sure nobody followed me here from Vegas – right?" Sutton spat out the last word. Hunter fell for the bait and lost his temper.

"Don't be smart with me. I have connections that can wipe you out without a trace. All it takes is a—"

"Hold it, Captain – there is no need for this." MacBride was feeling embarrassed at the captain's behaviour. "We picked Major Sutton, remember? If he says there is no connection, then there is no connection." That seemed to cool Hunter down. MacBride went on, "Anyway, the problem is not really with Major Sutton, is it? It's your strategy that needs attention."

Hunter, who was sitting beside MacBride, suddenly stood up and started to shout at MacBride.

"Back off, Sir. Back off. My strategy's okay. It's the team on the ground that needs attention."

"Now you back off, Captain." MacBride had enough of Hunter's outbursts. "It's a team game. Always is with us. If one goes down, we all go down. So, let's have some teamwork here, not scoring points off each other. Do you hear, Captain? Remember, you are only a captain."

Hunter sat down with a meek, "Yes, Sir."

"All right now." MacBride turned his attention to Sutton. "Now, Major, perhaps you would tell us again what happened to the money."

"Again?" Sutton still had his head bowed.

"Please, Major - just in case something was missed - by us, of course."

"Missed?" shouted Hunter. "The money is missing, that's what!"

Sutton raised his head, stood up and slowly moved beside Hunter.

"Don't move, Captain - there's a hornet on your shirt."

"A hornet? Where?"

"There. . ." and Sutton hit him hard with his fist just below the heart. Hunter went out like a light. MacBride gave a smirk and helped Sutton get Hunter into a chair.

"You saw the hornet, Major?" asked Sutton.

"Sure did, Major - sure did. And should you see another one, feel free to repeat the remedy. Shall we continue? For my benefit, you understand?"

"Right. The money. We got it to the shore on Island Magee — after that? This is what happened. . ."

Sutton retold the incident, and when he had finished, Hunter came round sufficiently for them to leave the *Room*.

*

Sutton boarded the light twin-prop bound for Las Vegas, and found his seat, as requested, at the rear beside a window, port side. No one sat beside him.

He was tired of all the in-fighting that took place in the *Room*, and of Hunter in particular. Where did Hunter come from, reflected Sutton, and how did such a guy get into the Army? Sutton found out a thing or two about Hunter that wouldn't be in his file, that's for sure. His training was put to good use, as it was in the Gulf where he first met de Courcy. Sutton dozed off thinking of Hunter, as he recalled how he followed him from the Dugway Proving Grounds to a diner in

Vernon, where Hunter, having looked about to see if anyone was looking, removed an envelope of some sort from his inside pocket and slipped it into the mail box. Hunter looked around again, glanced at his watch, then returned to his Ford, and took off towards Interstate 15. It was dry and dusty, the Ford giving evidence of its position from the cloud following it.

Sutton drove up in his hired car and parked near the mail box. Pretending to mail something, he removed the contents, which consisted of four letters – three addressed to the Capital of the State, Salt Lake City, the other to 'L. Magee, Cushendall, Co. Antrim, N. Ireland'. He pocketed the envelope, returned the others to the mail box, and headed for the airport. There was no need to look around as Hunter had; he already checked the place out before getting out of the car.

Sutton returned the hire car to Hertz at Salt Lake City Airport and checked in for Vegas. A visit to the Gents was appropriate and gave him the chance to examine the envelope. Hell, why examine it? – what's in it? It was not very thick, not thick enough for a letter bomb, but he reckoned it had about two or three sheets of folded paper in it. Using his finger, Sutton opened it roughly, withdrew the paper and read, firstly the beginning, then the end. No address – no salutation – no signature. It was handwritten and spaced out over two sheets, written on one side only. He read:

> *'Suggest you leak out to local UVF that you found British £200,000 in sea off The Gobbins then watch out for trouble from the Lacy people.*
>
> *The capital to entice UVF to act has gone missing. Police or Brit. Army likely to have it.*
>
> *Without funds, UVF unlikely to act in accordance with plans, so announcing your 'FIND' could encourage action which will include the death of some of your people.*
>
> *No retaliation is vital.*
>
> *Advise your Political Wing to give media plenty of interviews 12 hours after UVF action.*
>
> *Appropriate reaction from the Irish American/National Caucus to support your media action is ready.*
>
> *White House backing to keep Caucus happy is assured.'*

Sutton moved to the second page:

'Ensure arms are moved to new dumps as soon as possible. Existing (old) dumps to be inspected soon. Only leave unwanted munitions as a carrot. Booby traps still okay.

Watch out for Major de Courcy (a Brit) and Major Sutton (American) who are working with UVF – they are expendable when project is complete.'

Sutton read it three times, then folded it and returned it to its envelope. De Courcy would not like this – he did not like it either. Next time he had the opportunity, he would find out more about Captain Hunter. Hunter was dangerous. Trying to pass the buck to me, and then threatening to wipe me out! Okay, Hunter, okay. If that's the way you want to play, I'll play your ball game. Sutton was a survivor, and Hunter a loser.

"Coffee?" The flight steward's question had awakened him from his doze.

"Tea. No cream – no sugar." It was the usual airline stuff. Okay, but could be better.

De Courcy – what a guy. And a Brit too. De Courcy was the first British major he got to know well. Sutton recalled their first meeting late in 1990 when preparing for action in the Gulf. 'Desert Storm' it was. Boy, what a show – what a guy to work with. A quick thinker and we got on well together, he thought. In his returning doze, vivid pictures of the Gulf War were coming before him. . .

". . .*hold back until.* . ." de Courcy's voice.

". . .*that's good, now let's do this.* . ." de Courcy again.

". . .*how about doing it this way.* . .?" another practical idea from de Courcy.

". . .*I've managed to speed up this end, Major. We're up to Sector 14 now.* . ." Sutton heard himself say.

". . .*Sector 14? Good show, Captain. Our lot will be to your left, repeat, left, about 2,000 yards.* . ."

Sutton was a captain then doing a major's job, but due to his work with de Courcy he was made Major after the war. That was some operation, and no casualties — in our Section anyway. . .

"Welcome to Las Vegas. We shall land in a few minutes so please ensure that the seat back is in its upright position and your seat belt is fastened. . ."

The usual routine of preparing to land had shaken Sutton out of his past life into the present and back to reality.

Chapter Twenty-Seven

The team of three from the CIA arrived at Dugway minutes after Hunter had returned from posting his instructions to Magee of the IRA. For the team, this was a routine matter that had become part of their field of operations since their first success six months ago at sorting out the missing F-15 at Edwards Air Force Base. That incident took them three days, which led on to the week-long case of the missing missile at San Diego, and others less dramatic but equally successful.

T. J. Smith recognised the value of such a team and had them on standby as trouble shooters, fully authorised by the President to carry out their duties.

They had power and were not afraid to use it. Professionals to their fingertips, they reported directly to T. J., who protected them from the consequences of their actions.

MacBride handed over the personnel files and accepted the order that nobody was to leave the base under any circumstances until given the all-clear by the team. He had no option but to comply once he had received confirmation from the Pentagon that these guys were for real and they were in order.

The leader, Guy Adams, took the personnel files and with Stan Hill, who was the computer expert, began to work through them. Their past success had given them the confidence to believe that this case would be over in a day or two.

The objective was simple:

- Check out Dugway for a loose bullet.
- Check out their security.
- Do they know about missing files?

Lance Green was the interrogator, but he preferred to be known as an interviewer. It was the small things that brought success. The piece of information that fell from the lips of an unfortunate who couldn't withstand the pain any further so told all in return for the cessation of the pain. Simple, quick, and as barbaric as they come. The interviewer was clean about it, of course. He didn't resort to drugs but got what he wanted. The subject's pain was not physical – unless. . .

Guy Adams as leader had the ability of drawing together seemingly unconnected pieces of information into a sequence of events. To date, that ability had brought the team their success.

For twelve hours, Adams and Hill dissected the files, cross-checking everything they could before they were ready for Green to join them. While they were doing this, Green used the time to talk to everyone in Dugway to get a feel for the place and a picture of the character and mental attitude of the suspects. To Green, all were suspects – that's how Green worked. Prove to him that you were innocent and you were lucky, otherwise. . .

The next twelve hours found the team in discussion, each participating fully, until they were left with a list of people who appeared more likely to be guilty.

There were only two on the list – Hunter and Croft. Green would take Croft first.

The informal scene of Croft sitting in his usual seat where he monitored people entering and leaving the *Room*, with the CIA team lounging about him, was planned that way. Put him at ease then hit him. Adams was leaning against the wall, Hill sat on the floor, and Green perched himself on the side of the shelf that he had cleared of papers for that purpose. Green introduced the team to Croft, then suggested that Croft might like to 'answer a few questions'.

"I see from your records, Lt Croft, that one of your skills is electronics. This job in Dugway must be a bit of a drag if all you do is monitor the *Room*. What else do you do around here?"

"You're right. It *is* a bit of a drag, but with a family on the way I can get by."

"What are your other jobs here, Lt Croft?" Green quietly persisted. "Other than security?" Green nodded.

"Nothing," Croft answered. "Security covers it – security for the covert section of the Base, the people, the property, and, as you've just mentioned, the *Room*."

Green decided that it was time to hit him.

"Why do you use your position to give information to foreign terrorists?"

In unison, as if prompted by a stage manager, the CIA team moved their attention from looking at nothing in particular to concentrating their eyes directly into the face of Croft.

The shock of the question caused Croft to see previous actions of his in rapid replay. He saw the tapes he had recorded, the secret recording system, the visit to Green Bay. There was nothing he could think of that pointed to him – Croft was sure of it. He was so careful – this *must* be a bluff. He must remember to dismantle the recording system as soon as these three left.

The team were looking for some reaction. There always was some reaction. Usually the suspect would move back in his seat trying to escape, or forward with a quick denial. This one was different. He didn't move at all. It seemed like an age, but only seconds lapsed before the reply came.

"Are you serious? Information to foreign terrorists?" The words came out slowly as he maintained his gaze into Green's eyes. Croft suddenly relaxed, moved back in his chair, and laughingly exclaimed, "I get it! I get it! You guys are trying me out for something – right? See how I react to unusual circumstances. Like a training scenario – right?"

There was no reaction from the team, only the continuing gaze into Croft's eyes. Croft looked at each of them in turn and quickly removed his smile.

"Hold on now. If you are serious in this, just let me think a bit." He paused for a few seconds. "You guys arrived yesterday, and all of a sudden I'm a spy. Is that it?" He paused again. "I would like to know why someone wants me out of the way. I have a lot to lose here – my wife is expecting our first child. So you think I would be mad enough to betray my country and throw it all away?"

Green held up his right hand. "So you need money now that a family is on the way, and got some by selling information. Why did you do it?"

Croft's anger was now pumping adrenalin through his system. His presence of mind, however, guided him to use it in a constructive way, in order to try and steer things his way.

"What proof do you want from me? My bank account details? – you got it. My wife's earnings and her spending details? – you got that too. Anything else? I'll get it. You won't find anything that points to myself or my wife. And when you don't find anything, I want an apology and I want it in writing – okay?" He felt a little better, but knew that there was more to come from these guys. He was right. For two hours he sat through their questions and answered every one. Green did most of the work for the team, backed up by Hill and Adams, who interrupted Green to repeat an earlier question to make sure that the answer given was as before. Croft played it well. The two hours were over and Adams was reasonably satisfied, for now.

"Thank you for your time and co-operation, Lt Croft. Don't talk to anyone until I say so," warned Green, and the team left him for the next interview.

"He's clean," stated Green as they made their way to see Hunter in the main office.

"Maybe he is," commented Adams, "but he stays on the list for now. What do you say, Stan?"

"I go along with Lance – he has no motive and looks clean," stated Hill.

"Looking clean is not enough. He must *be* clean – okay?"

The team took a refreshment break and reminded themselves of the information they had on Captain Hunter before proceeding. Hunter was browsing through back issues of *Time* magazine when the team arrived beside him, and having checked that they were alone with him, he formally arranged their informality.

"Ready for a few questions, Captain?"

"Ready when you are," Hunter replied.

"By the way, congratulations on the 'Ireland 6' job. That was well received in Washington," lied Green. Good news and plenty of praise seems to work with Captain Hunter, the team learnt during their preparation time. They were building him up before the attack.

"You know about that? Yeah, that was a good one."

Hunter was getting to think that perhaps he could teach these guys a thing or two. It wasn't every day that he had an appreciative audience – so, as he was in the presence of people who knew of his work and were prepared to listen, why not tell?

"Indeed," Green went on, "and I dare say the oil fires in Iraq would have been avoided if your strategy was used."

Yes, thought Hunter, these guys know a good thing when they see it. "Too right – but they didn't see it until it was too late."

Hunter was tired and still sore where Sutton had hit him and he spoke while rubbing his eyes.

"Can I get you guys a coffee?" Hunter asked as he stood up and made his way to the flask of coffee by the door.

"Why not – black, no sugar," replied Adams.

"Same for you guys?" asked Hunter of Hill and Green, who nodded their acceptance. Hunter filled four plastic cups and carried them to the table.

Green waited until Hunter had raised his cup to his mouth before pouncing.

"How do you justify working with the enemies of your country, Captain Hunter?"

Three pairs of eyes focused on Hunter, looking to record how he reacted. Hunter did not spill a drop or hesitate in his first sip of coffee. He held the cup between his hands as he set it on the table.

"That's easy. It's my job. To get the project done it becomes necessary to deal with people that others, like you guys. . ." and he left his cup unattended as he swung round to look at them, ". . .wouldn't touch." He returned to his coffee. "Take 'Ireland 6' – see that one," he smiled and shook his head, "you don't want to know whom I dealt with. Just look at what was achieved. And with no harm to the people or the country – right?"

Green saw that Hunter was full of his own importance as he continued with the questions until an opening presented itself during the third hour.

"So, you are saying, Captain Hunter, that you are prepared to place the Government in jeopardy by letting surveillance information get into the hands of terrorists in Northern Ireland?"

The coffee had been cold for some time, and Hunter hadn't got past the first taste of it. Two questions in succession had floored him – he couldn't answer them and the team knew it.

"That means, Captain Hunter, that the Army is paying you to give away State secrets. How would that sound at your court martial?"

Hunter defended himself as best as he could by declaring himself a strategy person, not one who authorises projects – an inside backroom pen pusher not a field man. "And anyway, everything has been done with approval from the Pentagon. How could I operate it on my own, or fund it?" He immediately regretted mentioning the word 'fund'. Did they know of the missing money? How could they? He had only spoken about it to Major Sutton and Major MacBride – in the *Room* too, so they couldn't know. It wasn't possible.

Adams noticed Hunter's change in attitude and coughed. Green heard the signal.

"How much money have you lost recently?" Adams asked.

"Me? Me?" Hunter shouted. "*I* haven't lost a cent. It's those assholes in Ireland who lost it. Now don't try and nail that one on me. I was here, remember. They did it in Ireland," as he violently shook his hands and arms about trying to emphasise his position.

Adams nodded to Green, who took over from where his leader left off, and for two more hours they pumped the captain dry. He had nothing left. He told them everything, including the letter to Magee.

The team left him feeling so alone and down that their departing words barely registered with him. "Thanks for your full co-operation, Captain. Best of luck with your project."

The team left for the Pentagon and would report that although Captain Hunter was probably past his sell-by date and should be considered for early retirement, they had no evidence of a loose bullet; that security was in order; and in their opinion Dugway was clean. Two days later MacBride advised Hunter that he had heard from the Pentagon and that they were okay – clean and able to continue. The captain wasn't impressed.

Captain Croft removed all traces of the recording set-up, and had rewired the room's electrical systems just in case there were tell-tale signs or unauthorised workings. The final tape of the conversation between MacBride, Hunter, and Sutton had been stored in a safe area with a copy already *en route* to his sister.

Chapter Twenty-Eight

It was only 1800. Sutton knew that de Courcy should be at the hotel, and therefore he asked the taxi driver to take him straight there. From the lobby he used the house phone to contact de Courcy.

"I'm downstairs - get your ass down here fast, and bring everything with you - tickets, passports, the lot," and hung up.

This is getting lively again, thought de Courcy, looking forward to more action. He left quickly as requested, bringing all with him. Sutton was waiting for him and guided him to a secluded corner of the entrance mall, looking over his shoulder and about him as he did so.

"Las Vegas is some place, Elmer. All so artificial. Remember the $2,000? Well, it's now $2,850. I won, old boy, imagine it. I won about $1,200, and having spent some on food and what have you, I still have a profit! What's wrong, old boy? Trouble?" As he noticed Sutton making sure they were alone.

"*We* have been had, Edward. The meeting was okay. It was after the meeting - here - read this," and he passed the open letter to him. De Courcy read it and listened to Sutton describe the events that allowed him to acquire it.

"Should we destroy it, or post it?" The possible consequences of both scenarios were discussed.

"I don't much like the 'expendable' bit, Elmer. The IRA are still killing people and this would get us on to their hit list. If we are not already on it."

"So we destroy it - huh?"

"What do you think of this?" and the discussion continued as de Courcy outlined his idea. Anyone watching would have noticed the hand gestures and gentle conversation of ordinary businessmen coming to an agreement. They got up and approached the receptionist.

"Do you have office facilities we could use for, say, ten minutes?" asked Sutton.

"Yes, Sir. The minimum hire is thirty minutes for $50, with use of the paper copier. The first ten copies are free."

"We'll take thirty minutes," said Sutton and he handed over $50 of de Courcy's winnings.

"Stationery? Would you have, say, three plain envelopes and plain writing paper? No hotel name shown?" asked Sutton.

The receptionist nodded and took them to the first of three rooms having a sign BUSINESS SUITE attached to the door. The air-conditioning was working rather too well, de Courcy thought, as he noticed the temperature change on entering.

"The copier is here – and the stationery here. Anything else, Sir?" asked the young man.

"No, that's fine," responded Sutton, who tipped him $10.

They prepared the messages as agreed, made five copies and addressed three envelopes: one to L. Magee, Cushendall, Co. Antrim; one to Mrs Lacy at her Ballycarry address; and one to Supt Richards at RUC, Castlereagh. They placed the copies into the envelopes and set them aside ready for posting. The original, together with the original envelope, was folded and placed in a separate envelope that de Courcy marked with an 'O' in pencil on both front and back. That left two remaining copies on the table.

One each. They took their own copy, folded it, and placed it in their respective pockets.

Sutton checked that there was nothing out of place, then, picking up the three envelopes, they left for a mail box rather than leave them at Reception. Reception sold them the requested value and number of stamps, which equalled the stamps that were on the original envelope prepared by Hunter.

Twenty minutes it took them: twenty minutes that saved their lives.

Returning from the mail box near 'Glitter Gulch', de Courcy noticed someone whom he had seen the previous evening at the poker table. He remembered now. De Courcy won about $1,200, this chap lost $1,200. De Courcy made to acknowledge him, but the man turned away and pretended not to see de Courcy. Odd, thought de Courcy. On returning to the hotel, a party of tourists were leaving for a night's festivities, their courier checking them off against a list as they boarded a coach. Both de Courcy and Sutton saw him simultaneously.

A face at the window, halfway down the coach, wide-eyed, open mouthed, with finger pointed at them. The paralysis that fell upon all three would have appeared to any onlooker as if de Courcy, Sutton, and the face in the coach were waiting for a photographer to take a picture.

"The bank manager!" Sutton and de Courcy gasped in unison.

What is not certain is the exact order of events, but what did happen is that the coach started to move, de Courcy and Sutton also started to move, and a shot rang out. Screaming – then another shot. Instinctively, de Courcy moved left, Sutton moved right, both turning round to face the direction of the shots. There, thirty yards across the street, was the gambler who had lost $1,200.

"Get him," shouted a bystander as de Courcy and Sutton zig-zagged towards him. Sutton was fast, very fast, and the momentum with which he hit the gunman knocked the gun out of his hand and into the air, and the gambler to the ground. A crack was heard when his head hit the road.

De Courcy held the man's legs, Sutton had him round the shoulder, then Sutton knew by looking at him that there would be no more trouble from that source.

"He's had it, Edward," and checked for a pulse. Nothing.

The sirens were heard first, then two patrol cars arrived, stopping sharply, the two officers with guns drawn pointing at de Courcy and Sutton while protecting themselves using their cars as shields.

"They saved us, Officers – those two," was the pained statement of a hotel worker who found himself beside the police cars, holding his side, from which blood oozed. He pointed to de Courcy and Sutton, "They saved us from the gunman." The officer, noticing the blood, bolstered his gun and radioed for medical assistance. The ambulance arrived soon after.

The body of the dead gunman and the injured hotel worker were taken from the site by the ambulance. The police took Sutton and de Courcy to their precinct for questioning, while statements were being freely given at the scene by those who witnessed the incident. The coach was long gone.

*

The lieutenant had satisfied himself that the events were as indicated by the evidence.

"He was always a wild one was B.J. That's the first time he's pulled a gun – too bad. You guys are lucky he missed you – he knew how to shoot"

"Who was he, Lieutenant?" asked Sutton.

"B. J. Smithson, known as B.J. He was the local nutcase – in and out of hospitals like a yo-yo. Sad case, gambled his dough away. Started with a fortune left to him by his pa. You know, pa works hard, the kid blows it – that kind of stuff."

"He could have killed us. The others – the hotel gardener, how's he?" De Courcy was over the shock of the event and remembered the hotel gardener getting the shot meant for him.

"Not too good, I hear. He should live but he might lose a kidney," replied the lieutenant.

De Courcy was drained of all energy and sat back in the chair. Getting shot at is a normal occupational hazard for an Army man, but not in peacetime. He wasn't expecting it in peacetime – not outside Northern Ireland.

Sutton looked just as drained as he sat forward in his chair holding his head. He was quiet and in some pain. The headache had returned, giving up coffee had only postponed it. The pain might have been triggered by the shock of that day's events, but Sutton didn't think so, as in retrospect he found it exhilarating rather than traumatic. Sutton remembered the coach. "A.T.I. on the side," he said in a whisper.

"What's that?" asked the lieutenant.

"A coach filled with tourists moved off just as the first shot rang out. There could be witnesses. It had A.T.I. painted on the side. What's A.T.I.?" enquired Sutton.

"American Tours International. It's a tour company for people on vacation, mostly foreigners. There are a number of them about these parts – we'll check it out" The lieutenant had finished his paperwork on this one and simply said, "You're free to go – okay?" And they left. A life ended, a man in hospital, and they were free to go. Life is cheap in Las Vegas, thought de Courcy as he reflected on the events since posting the unsigned letter. The puzzle of the bank manager remained to be solved. The reflex move towards the coach had saved his life, he was convinced of it. The bank manager had stared and pointed and saved their lives. His life anyway, as B.J. was shooting at him. All for $1,200? Yes, he decided, life *is* cheap in Las Vegas, and it would not be his intention to return. Brown's Bay was decidedly an improvement, and infinitely more civilised.

De Courcy remembered the words on the second page of Hunter's note '. . .they are expendable..' Civilisation is as advanced as the actions of the people. It must be true after all, de Courcy thought, that 'each generation born is equidistant from barbarity'.

Chapter Twenty-Nine

The message just said, 'Contact me – Prof. Withers'. Bad news is not easy to accept when it tears at the heart of relationships. The frailty of humankind is seen in pain and death. The closer to home, the greater the pain. Age enters into it – the younger the person, the greater the loss of a life not yet fulfilled, not yet given the opportunity to contribute to society. Those who promote violence or evil seem to live for ever and enjoy the spoils of their crimes, while the meek and the good die young.

Inheriting the earth in human terms doesn't come to the meek and mild of society. The sleepless nights of the worried parent waiting for the phone call, the knock at the door, or the written message is ever before the imagination, making worse a situation that's already bad.

The professor had bad news, and there was no alternative but to accept it. Nothing could be done in human terms from current knowledge. Knowledge that was increasing daily in all spheres of human endeavour, except the ability to live together as civilised people. New armaments meant new injuries requiring new procedures and medical techniques to be researched and tested before treatment could be given.

De Courcy was not able to contact the professor until the next day, and hear of the DU prognosis. It was too complicated with too many medical references for de Courcy to understand. He found that he wasn't listening to the reasons and explanations being expounded in detail.

"What's the bottom line, Professor?" de Courcy asked.

"His pain will get worse, but we can control that with drugs. The end could be quick. I would say Major Sutton has between six months and three years. Sorry, Major de Courcy, but that is how these things go. . ." The conversation on the phone ended.

De Courcy thought he knew the why and the how but he didn't understand it. The when was the most difficult to accept. He would tell Sutton of course, he had to. Even if only to have him accept the painkilling drugs – yes, he had to tell him.

De Courcy moved to the half-opened door of the cottage and, leaning on it, surveyed the weeds and brambles making their inexorable hold on the property more permanent.

Without a thought or plan of action, time passed in that quiet place, a haven from the trouble that was Las Vegas and Dugway. Sutton returned from his one-hour run around the island, announcing his presence by the loud clatter of gate against post as it was opened then shut behind him.

"I see you are busy, Edward!" as Sutton, getting his breath back, stood in front of the half door.

De Courcy opened the door and stepped back to allow him to enter. Sutton noticed the sign of unease, the head down, the looking at his hands, the movement one way then the other.

"What's on your mind, old boy, old boy?" Sutton said between breaths.

It had to be now. De Courcy couldn't say anything, so he sat down and gestured to Sutton to sit. After a few minutes of silence, punctuated by Sutton's heavy breathing, de Courcy did his best to explain the contents of his conversation with the professor. The great unknown to de Courcy was the medical side, so he left that out, but everything else was there. The room was different somehow. Nothing physical, but the atmosphere and demeanour of both men had changed. A tangible change in the silence. They sat there with everything and nothing happening at the same time. It was Sutton who broke the peace.

"Thanks, Edward. I couldn't take it from anyone else." That was all he said, then went and had a shower. It was nearly too much for de Courcy, who wiped away a tear before going outside for some air.

*

"From six months to three years, you said, Edward – right? Who knows, they may find a treatment." Sutton had digested de Courcy's information and reflected on times now past.

"You know, Edward, those bastards *knew*. They knew about me. Why else transfer me to 'Pensions'?" Sutton recalled others in the Gulf who were sure to be worse than him. "There must be hundreds of us, Edward. Could you do something, old boy, old boy? Use your contacts to find what my current Army status is – huh?"

De Courcy, standing on the porch, heard all, but listened to nothing.

"Sorry, old boy, you said status? Proof that you are still working – officially or otherwise – is that it?"

"Yeah. If I'm not, Dugway can take a running jump."

De Courcy nodded slowly and, entering the cottage, went straight to the phone and had a few words with the appropriate people.

"We'd better find out about the letters we posted, old boy. You contact Superintendent Richards, and I'll go and see what's her name – is that all right with you, Elmer?"

Sutton gave de Courcy one of those knowing looks and smiled. "Sure, Edward. Leave me the dirty bit, as usual."

Sutton made the call and de Courcy took the Honda to Ballycarry. The fuel gauge was registering empty, so a call at the Rinkha was necessary, to replenish with 4 Star. He bought a slider and took a short stroll while he finished it. He was still quite flush with funds, having exchanged the dollars into sterling at the airport, and although he gave Sutton half of it, there was still £900 in his pocket. He returned to the shop and bought a tin of chocolate biscuits before completing the journey over the bridge, across the main Larne–Belfast road, and up the hill to Ballycarry.

Joe Lacy saw the car coming and came to meet him.

"Do you mind me saying something, Major? It's about you and Sis."

The unexpected again, and de Courcy now saw that his position was likely to be misunderstood. The idea of bringing a tin of biscuits seemed rather silly, so he left them on the floor of the passenger's side where he had placed them, and decided that they would do for the cottage.

"Please continue, Mr Lacy."

The pressure was now on Lacy, who, having lost the initiative, struggled for words. "She has changed, Major. I don't know what it is, but she is a lot happier since meeting you."

Perhaps the biscuits would have been acceptable after all. Joe Lacy, provoking no reaction or interruption from de Courcy, continued.

"You don't mind me saying it, do you, but – you are a mite old for her. She is not for getting hurt again. Once was enough. Well, you need to take it easy." There he stopped, turned round, and for the first time looked into de Courcy's eyes. "What exactly is it with you and Sis?"

The last time de Courcy had heard such a line was from his late father-in-law. He couldn't remember what he had said then, and he didn't know what to say now. Thinking that time was what he needed, he bought some the only way he could – by changing the subject.

"I'll answer your questions about Susannah, but first, business. We have been set up and I need to tell Susannah and yourself about it."

"Set up? Here, come into the house," and he pushed de Courcy inside and closed the door. He led de Courcy down the hall and into the kitchen, where Susannah was baking. She looked up, and in that moment of pleasure, followed by embarrassment at being found not properly dressed to meet a visitor, she rubbed her hands on a towel to remove flour and started to tidy up.

"Leave that, Sis – something's wrong. Major, tell her, tell both of us.

"Very sorry, Susannah, I didn't mean to disturb your work – scones by chance?"

Joe Lacy was a little impatient and interrupted the small talk.

"Major, the set-up – you said it's a set-up. Tell us."

"Of course. May I. . .?" and pointed to a kitchen chair.

"Please, Major de Courcy, and yes, they *are* scones. Now, don't fuss, Joe, let the major tell us in his own time."

De Courcy sat down and prepared himself.

"I have posted to you a copy of a document that came into my possession. . ." and apart from the shooting incident, he told it as accurately as he could.

Joe noticed that Susannah had perked up again on seeing de Courcy. It was years since he had seen her looking so well and happy. Perhaps he was wrong in thinking that the major would be bad for her. There was nobody else, so it must be de Courcy. The American was all right, but she didn't react to him, only to the major.

". . .I can only assume that the plan was to anger the UVF, provoking them to do something so bad that the Army would take them on. That's the set-up. I understand Magee is a known IRA man, but I shouldn't have told you that."

"He is, Major. We already know about him," she replied. Looking round, she saw the uncooked mixture and, getting up, suggested that Joe and he look around while she finished off the scones. Say, half an hour, then join us for tea, was her suggestion as Joe and the Major left.

De Courcy went straight to his car, got in and closed the door, wound down the window, and addressed Joe.

"You're right, old boy. I'm too old for her. I'll tell you this, I like her a lot. More than you know, but I'll not cause her any hurt if I can help it." He started the engine and got into first gear. "Tell her I can't stay for tea. If it helps you to accept it, it will not be me who asks her to marry. I give you my word, old boy," and he drove off.

Susannah heard the car drive off as she closed the oven door. Running down the hall, she caught sight of the car as it left.

"What's wrong, Joe? Why did you chase him?"

How did she know that? Joe was feeling bad about events just now, and it showed.

"Sorry, Sis. He couldn't stay."

"Why are you trying to protect me? Can't I have a life of my own?" and she returned to the scones.

She's right, of course. I can't do it anymore. I caused enough trouble for her, now she can have what she wants. He joined her for tea. His thoughts were with de Courcy as he remembered his story.

"Fancy Major de Courcy telling us about the 'set-up'. You will need to tell the Council."

She listened in silence.

"He likes you a lot, you know, Sis. He won't do anything about it, you know." She looked up.

"Why?"

"He says he's too old. Said so before he left. He doesn't want to hurt you, so he just left." Joe looked at her staring into space.

"Did you know that he lost his wife and son on the same day, Joe? It's not me he doesn't want to hurt, it's himself."

Chapter Thirty

"The news is good, Edward. Your Lisburn people telephoned and confirmed that I'm on the retired list. That's not all. I'm on full pension too!" Sutton was pleased with the news that gave him the freedom to tell Dugway whatever he liked. "I'll stay on here, Edward, if you don't mind. We could do some good with this information."

"Stay on? What do you mean?"

"I'm retired, old boy, old boy. I'm plain *Mr* Sutton now. I can go home if I want to. No more Major this, Major that. Hey! What would happen if the US Administration were to hear, accidentally of course, that Dugway was involved with the IRA – huh?"

That sounded like the Elmer Sutton of old.

"Good for you, old boy. Let's work something out. We shall need help on this one, and we also sent Superintendent Richards a copy of that document. Did he say anything about it when you phoned?"

"He sounded interested. He wants to meet us, and I agreed on both our behalves to see him 1000 hours tomorrow. One more thing, the banker – remember?"

The banker indeed. In Las Vegas of all places. A phone call to his branch should sort that out and confirm whether he was on holiday and when he was due back.

"I'll deal with that one, Elmer. Unfortunately, there's the meeting with the professor. It could be beneficial, old boy. Better without the pain than with it."

"Too right, and you never know – I might be back on coffee!"

The phone rang, and as Sutton was nearest he answered it.

"It's the girlfriend, Edward. She's a bit quiet on it," and he handed over the phone.

"Yes?" de Courcy listened while Sutton pretended not to look and noticed the transformation from a hard professional soldier into a soft, warm, granddad-type character in all of fifteen seconds.

"It would be a great pleasure, Susannah. I have some business in the morning. Would, say, 3 p.m. suit?" And after a moment, "Bye."

"Well, well, well. How's the old boy, then?" Sutton joked.

"'Old boy' is right, Elmer, which is why I told her brother-in-law that I would keep my distance. You are right, Elmer, she needs someone younger. This could be it. The end of it. I see her tomorrow in Carrickfergus for tea. It's the 'I'm sorry, I don't mix business with pleasure', etc., etc."

"Where did these come from?" Sutton had lifted the tin of biscuits, turned it over, and examined the label.

"Something for that sweet tooth of yours, old boy. You'll like them."

"Sure, sure. Take it easy, Edward – about the girl, I mean. You two could get on well, so don't spoil it. Nice and easy, I'd say. She's not one for the 'Dear John' treatment by asking you out to tea. All she has to do to give you the brush-off is focus on all business-related matters and ignore you for the rest." Sutton struggled with the seal on the tin before finding the end of the tape, then removed it in one go.

"These look good. Want one, Edward?"

De Courcy took two chocolate-covered biscuits and had one in his mouth before Sutton could move. "I'll phone the bank now – it's just 1600 hours, they should be still in the office."

*

Susannah tidied up after taking the scones out of the oven and, leaving them to cool, went to look for her minder. He saw her looking for him at the gate, and made himself visible once he satisfied himself that nobody was around.

He would arrange it, and she should report at the usual place in the morning.

She took with her the letter that arrived in the post that morning from Las Vegas and met The General in the bar. Together they made their way up the back stairs and along the passages to the safe area where the other council members were waiting. No time was wasted with polite introductions, she just told them what de Courcy had said, and presented them with the letter.

"It's a set-up all right, I can smell it. What's your opinion of the two in Island Magee, Mrs Lacy?" The General asked, quite genuinely seeking her opinion as an equal in the cause of protecting the Union.

"He didn't have to tell me anything," she began. "He must have realised that he was being used by the Americans and came clean about it. He – the English one – is not one for being used. The American? He's sick, and likes the Englishman, and. . . Wait a minute." She stopped. "Of course. . . It was the American who found out about the set-up, then he told the English major, who in turn told me."

They politely waited for her to put it together.

"That's it, they were *both* being used to set us up. That means that – that, whoever thought this one up knew that if anything went wrong, we would take it out on the two at Island Magee."

The General saw it clearly and would explain it to the other members of council later.

"That could have been a problem. Well done, Mrs Lacy. You have probably saved our existence. Just think. If we had taken out those two, which is what the people believed and were hoping for, then we could be on the Army's hit list with pressure from the dear US of A for the Army to act."

"Maybe not, General," replied the girl. "The money and the surveillance information is still just small talk. We would do nothing until we were paid, surely?"

The General accepted that opinion.

"There's more to this American connection than we know," she stated.

Jimmy Scott was shocked at what was said. "We did all right getting you on the Council, Mrs Lacy. You sure work things out fast." Scott turned his attention to the General. "You must have something else – any chance of sharing it, General?"

He saw their worried faces. The IRA was one thing, but the US of A giving support to the IRA was another. Before he gave anything away, he must be sure – very sure of Lacy's intentions. She was in it now, right in it, and letting her know of the newly-acquired intelligence would lock her in. There was no way she could get out, even if she wanted out, but. . . The General must know how she stood in relation to the British major. The minder had noticed a few things about the two of them and passed it on to him.

"Can I be open with you, Susannah? It's personal but vitally important."

"Surely."

"What are your personal feelings towards the two in Island Magee, particularly Major de Courcy?"

The other members of Council gave knowing looks to each other, a point not missed by either the girl or the General.

"I like them. I can work with them, and so far they have acted straight." There was no reaction to this, so she continued. "Major de Courcy is just fine. I don't care what you think, any of you." She started to get annoyed and a little embarrassed. "Since my husband's death there has been no man in my life. Well – now there is – and it's Major de Courcy – and that's all there is to it."

Now it's out. She guessed that there would be nothing but laughter and ridicule – well, let them. She just hoped that de Courcy would understand.

"Thank you, Susannah. That was not easy for you, and I – no, we – appreciate your honesty and frankness."

The General was satisfied.

"Here, here." It was Scott who had piped up in agreement.

"One thing," the General again, "does the major feel the same way about you?"

"No – not yet. But I think he will – soon."

At last, the laughter came, not of ridicule but of comfort and support.

"Well, that's that. Now to business," as the General moved to his big surprise for the day.

"I have proof that the US Government has used their considerable resources to assist the IRA in their violence against us. The question is, what do we do with this information? Any ideas?"

*

Stress can occur when people are forced by circumstances to visit places they would not willingly visit. Such places are regarded as a threat to their privacy, of a change to their way of life that is unacceptable or unavoidable. The dentist's chair would not be most people's ideal way to spend ten minutes. For others, visiting the dentist is a means of solving problems and removing pain. The same could be said for visiting your bank manager, solicitor, or local police station. De Courcy had been to a solicitor and a bank manager in Carlisle, and he was now planning to visit a police station. It didn't worry him in the slightest. Stress for him was in the absence of having something to do. Sutton had a similar outlook.

The visit to the bank would be postponed for a while, as the official who answered de Courcy's request for an appointment confirmed that, "Yes, the manager was on holiday, and yes, he was somewhere in the USA, and no, he was not available until the beginning of next week."

Next on the agenda was the visit to Castlereagh Police Station, where de Courcy and Sutton were 'signed in' by Richards and led to an office on the first floor.

"This is the second floor, Edward, we just left the first," goaded Sutton.

"Not here, old boy – we've just left the ground floor and arrived on the first. We do it differently in the civilised world," replied de Courcy.

"We do it right in the US, old boy, old boy. This is the second floor of a two-floor block – right?" De Courcy ignored the bait.

Richards ordered tea and sat them down. De Courcy and Sutton saw the letter opened on his desk. The letter posted from Las Vegas.

"Arrived today – is this what you talked about?" Richards lifted up, then set down, the paper.

"That's it. I'll let Elmer explain, as he was the first to see it."

Tea came and went as Sutton, punctuated by contributions from de Courcy, related the story, without any reference to the shooting incident.

"What do you think we can do?" The question put by Richards was in a tone that already gave the answer. The tone of 'it's outside my field, my area of responsibility, sorry but I have no resources' kind of response.

"Nothing at all, old boy," suggested de Courcy, "just let the appropriate people in your anti-terrorist section know of its existence – and let us who do the work get on with it. By the way, the original I keep. It could come in handy some day."

"Can I see the original?" asked Richards.

"Sorry, old boy. It's not with me. I have it secured away."
Richards read the note again.

"I don't like this. We are being asked to believe that £200,000 of
US money *en route* to the UVF has gone missing, and that we, or the
Army, have it? I tell you this, it's rubbish! There was nothing in that
torpedo thing except a dead battery and two wet suits. The IRA are
not daft enough to leak out that they have it either. Was there any
money at all?" asked Richards.

"Sure was, Stephen. Edward and I saw it. It was cash, it was
real, and now it's gone."

Richards looked at the paper again. He read aloud, "'White House
backing'. . . That's too political. If we can get proof, we can deal
with it from the top."

"What do you mean – top?" It was Sutton again.

"Get me proof, and I'll get it to the PM, who will have words with
the President. You can't get any higher than that."

This is getting out of our depth, thought de Courcy and Sutton.

"I'd better tell you something else then," de Courcy said quietly.
Richards looked at de Courcy and waited for him to explain.

"You haven't got all the message in front of you. Tell him,
Elmer."

"When we made copies, the second page was not included. It said
that Edward and I were expendable as we were working for the
UVF."

"That sounds like a death sentence," Richards responded.

"It sure does. That's why we left it out."

"We'd better keep this to ourselves – agreed?" asked Richards.

"Are you kidding? No way is anyone seeing the original till this
thing is sorted out, and that Captain idiot Dugway is out of it –
period!"

That was clear enough, thought Richards, and he moved the
subject matter aside. "Anything else?"

"One thing, old boy. We need some background information on a
bank manager, and confirmation of the day and time he is due to
return from his holiday."

Chapter Thirty-One

James William Magee, known as 'Liam' to his friends, examined the envelope and the contents, then passed them to Jarvis McBrien for comment.

Cushendall is a delightful village on the Antrim coast road that extends northwards from Larne to Portrush. History extends way back there with records of a fortress belonging to the MacDonalds being destroyed by Cromwell in 1652. The beauty is not confined to the coast, but extends westerly into the Glens of Antrim, where tourists are rewarded with natural rather than man-made vistas. The village of Cushendall is funded by those in the business of agriculture, and those who commute to work in Ballymena, and is situated some twenty miles north of Larne. The 'general store', that offers customers everything from soap to postage stamps, has been in the Magee family for over one hundred years, and if Liam Magee had his way it would remain that way. There was no Mrs Magee yet, but some day he hoped there would be.

It was five years since he completed his sentence in Long Kesh Prison, where much was learnt in the craft of bomb making and political science. That's where Magee completed his degree course in Political Science, all through correspondence and attending the visiting lecturer's classes, and resulting in a lower second-class degree or a 'Desmond' as his imprisoned mates used to jibe. It proved useful, not in the shop, but in the unpaid political work as a recognised volunteer for the cause.

"It's a copy! Imagine sending a copy, Liam. If it's from Captain Hunter, he has dropped himself in it. Look at the postmark – it's the first one he's sent from Las Vegas. It's his writing, but why a copy? Doesn't he know?" McBrien didn't miss much. McBrien, the shop assistant, also served his time in Long Kesh and was released at the same time as Magee. McBrien was bright, but not the academic type, so instead of a degree he improved himself physically. As fit as anyone could be when leaving prison, McBrien maintained fitness with daily workouts and trips to a fitness centre in Belfast every month, when both he and Magee reported for briefings.

"If it's genuine, we put an end to our contact with Captain Hunter. Does he believe we would go for a few casualties without retaliation? I always said he couldn't be trusted – this proves it, Liam. Just think if a copy of this got into the hands of the Brits! We don't mind the Brits thinking we're stupid, that's easy to achieve – but this! This, if we carry it out, will show we're stupid."

Magee silently agreed with McBrien. It was indeed easy to fool the Brits as it was for any terrorist force facing a government of whatever hue whose support was 50% or less of the voting public.

It was easy to maintain the volunteers' morale now that nearly every month could be celebrated with the anniversary of this death, that victory, or the injustice of the innocent suffering under the gun of the foreign army on Irish soil. The leadership had controlled everything well and, like all good leaders, were pro-active rather than re-active.

Magee knew there had to be a change. So did the others, or at least most of them. It was time to push forward politically in a planned attack on all fronts, even if it meant putting aside the armed struggle to add credibility. It would take time.

"When is the next meeting, Liam?" The note from Captain Hunter was returned to its envelope and pocketed.

"Don't crumple it – here – give," and Magee stretched out his hand to take it, whereupon he flattened it with the base of his fist by punching at it against the wall. There was no room on the counter. "That's better. I'll take it to them now. You stay here and look after the place. I should be back in a few hours."

Clad in leather gear, he took the bike. The van might be stopped and searched – not that there was anything to find, but it was better not to suffer delays, and the security forces rarely stopped motor bikes. He travelled along the back road through Martinstown to Ballymena, then on to Belfast using the M2. Leaving the motorway at the Duncrue Industrial Estate exit, he found his way to the warehouse and offices where he was expected. The appearance of the offices was designed to portray a legitimate business from the framed certificate of incorporation on the wall at reception, to the sales graphs in the back office. Business was good. The 'troubles' had contributed to the company's wealth, as every time a bomb or attack in Nationalist areas resulted in broken glass, then 'Glass Unlimited Limited' were in business.

The political wing had persuaded the owners of the company – a man and wife team who each held 50% of the £100 issued share capital – to provide an area for meetings. In return, the company would get the business of replacing the shattered glass and not suffer attacks on their staff or receive demands for protection money. The arrangement worked, and for the past eleven years some of the leadership used the premises for meetings. Those who met called themselves non-political or non-militant. Those who were political were not militant, while others who were militant were not political. This set-up was required to meet the conditions of the shareholders, who insisted that there were to be no arms about the place, and no military wing in attendance. All were happy, especially the shareholders, who managed to pay £50,000 annually into a pension fund and take out £100,000 annually in directors' salaries and fees.

The meetings were held in a converted twenty-six-foot container that had given good service on the Belfast–Liverpool ferry carrying glass of all types for the company. All evidence of its past use was long gone, with yearly coats of grey paint. The windows were more ornamental than useful, as they faced the warehouse wall, preventing direct sunlight to enter at any time. The steel structure lay on a bed of railway sleepers. The container doors were welded shut on the inside, leaving a door on the side as the only entrance.

Magee made the eighteen-inch step into the office look easy, where he found the familiar layout of table and chairs inside a wooden-lined interior made cold by the strip lighting. Magee remembered to leave his cycle helmet outside on the bike. Not to do so would have made it impossible for him to be identified, and he would have incurred disciplinary action. He had been disciplined in the past, and didn't want to lose another finger. Without ceremony, he closed the outer door before opening the inner door into the smoke-filled office. The smoke made him gasp. He was a non-smoker and they knew it. They smiled at his discomfort and took the envelope from him as he held it out. It was examined and read without comment. They took their time over it. Patsy Campbell, slightly, long-sighted, held the paper at arm's length, while Michael Pearce, short-sighted, squinted as he leaned forward to get as close to the paper as possible. Campbell finished reading it and left Pearce to continue his read.

"Las Vegas postmark, I see. That Yank has gone daft, Patsy," declared Pearce. "What do you think, Liam?"

Both Campbell and Pearce respected Magee's judgement on matters relating to people. They saw during the time they spent together in Long Kesh prison that Magee was able to channel the different strengths of the inmates into a working unit, the working unit that acquired skills enabling some to escape, some to gain self esteem – yes, Magee was good with people. There was a bond between them that was deeper than the rules of discipline that were strictly and rigorously enforced. Campbell would have Magee as leader of any unit at any time, but he knew not to push it onto him. Campbell knew that Magee would decline such an offer, but would continue to offer any other kind of service to the cause. It was his kind of service that was in short supply, and valuable. Pearce was the quiet one whose gift was in asking the right question most of the time and in assessing the validity of the answer. The answer was the thing. Anybody can ask questions, few can understand the consequences of the answers. Both finished their cigarettes at the same time, and both stabbed them out on the floor. There was an extractor fan in the welded door. Campbell switched it on. It was noisy but didn't interrupt the proceedings. Outside, if anyone noticed, smoke could be seen making its way out of the container to join the other pollutants of an industrial city. Magee felt less discomfort as fresh air entered the room.

"He's a liability. We should drop him, and fix it so that he doesn't contact us again." Magee waved his hand as he spoke to emphasise his statement. Gesturing towards the envelope and the paper, he continued, "It's a copy – where's the original? It's posted in Las Vegas, as you said, Michael. What's he doing there? I agree with you, Michael – he has either gone nuts, or. . ." Magee stopped.

"Or what?" Campbell prompted.

"Or it's a forgery to look like it's from him."

"A forgery!? It's his handwriting for sure," replied Campbell.

"What purpose the forgery, Liam?" The right question from Pearce. Pearce put his arm to Campbell's arm to stop him from speaking and interrupting the moment. Magee noticed the movement and took his time to answer. The extractor fan appeared to have increased the noise level as it removed the remaining particles of smoke from that place.

Magee started. "The history of the Yank has been good. The movement has achieved much from him even though we would not want him as a recruit. Up to now he has kept the rules – why suddenly break them? Either he has or he hasn't. Why don't we find out? If he hasn't broken the rules, then someone else has, and if so, then this. . ." pointing to the envelope and paper, ". . .is a forgery."

Magee waited for his speech to sink in. He waited too long.

"You haven't answered my question, Liam." Pearce spoke slowly and quietly. He always spoke that way – he didn't mean anything by it, but it sounded like a threat, and Magee allowed himself to interpret it to be a threat.

"Easy on, Mick. What better way to discredit a good source is there? Here it is – poor information from a good source, with all the rules broken. The purpose? The purpose? To make sure we dump him."

"Calm down, Liam," Pearce said slowly. "Let's talk it over. . ." Magee had won them over this time. Pretending to be hurt by the question had worked.

"Okay, okay," Magee responded in a calmer tone, ". . .just work it out. This letter here – what does it say?" They waited for him to answer his own question. "It tells us to expect some deaths, to accept those deaths, not to defend ourselves, and after that not to react to it! Does that sound like the Yank to you? Then the money! Do you want to tell the UVF anything?"

Campbell nodded and looked at Pearce, who was looking through Magee rather than at him.

"What if it is from him, and not a forgery?" Pearce slowly asked Magee.

"Then I agree with you that he's nuts and must be put aside. But first – it *must* be confirmed." Magee had spelt it out for them. A break in the communication link between Dugway and the unit had to be examined.

They had learned to examine all matters relating to the movement's objective, including the involvement of outsiders and their offers of help. Checking out the validity of the correspondence from Hunter would be easy, as would the action to get rid of him should it be proved to their satisfaction that he had broken the rules. Their system had evolved through time to one that worked well, and they liked a system that worked well. The days of the 70s and 80s, when they proved that they could attack the targets of the foreign invader at will, whether on Irish soil or British mainland, were continuing. Even targets in Europe were reached. Now it was time to move politically with the backing of the military wing when required.

Campbell had spent a few years with Magee and Pearce in the same block at Long Kesh, and each knew the other's thoughts. Not a knowledge full of sentiment or a feeling of welfare, but an understanding that the Movement came first. The people were secondary to the objective. The dead hunger strikers had failed as they had forgotten the main objective and placed secondary demands in its place.

The American wasn't one of them. It was true that he had helped them in the past and had amazed them with the quality and quantity of the information he provided. Nevertheless, rules are rules, and anyone who broke them did not get off. Sending a photocopy was against the rules, against the objective, and must be punished.

Magee left the way he came in, but made his journey to Cushendall via a different route. He wasn't followed.

Pearce had offered to make contact with one of their active units in America to have Hunter checked out, and the offer was accepted. Pearce did it the quick way – by phone. He took his electronic organiser from his pocket, switched it on, keyed in his password, and started scanning the address lists of 'overseas' sympathisers. Having found what he was looking for, he lifted the phone and dialled. As he waited he switched off the organiser and returned it to his pocket.

"Yeah?" It was an American accent.

"Can I speak to Mr Smithson, please?" Pearce asked.

"May I ask who's calling?"

That wasn't Smithson's voice. Pearce didn't want to say who he was, or anything that might frighten the person on the phone, or give his identity.

"I'm just an acquaintance who met him a few years ago, and as I plan to visit there soon I thought I would contact him," Pearce answered.

"You're too late fella – he's dead."

"Dead?" Pearce didn't expect that. He thought quickly and continued, "What happened. . .? Where. . .? I mean. . . Sorry, I'm a bit shaken. . ."

"Take it easy, fella – he deserved it. He took a few shots at some people who went for him, and that was that."

"I see. Who are you, then?"

"Officer Yale, Vegas Police Department. . ." Pearce hung up and hoped that the call could not be traced. He set up his organiser, deleted all reference to B. J. Smithson from it, and searched for an alternative contact. There wasn't one that he deemed suitable, so there was nothing for it but to phone the Yank Hunter directly.

He noted the number as it appeared on the screen of his organiser, and dialled. As before, while waiting for the phone to answer, he switched the machine off and pocketed it.

"Captain Hunter." It was him – that voice couldn't be anyone else. Pearce was ready for him.

"Just listen, Captain Hunter – I said listen."

Hunter was in bed but wide awake at hearing those words. He heard them before and knew the source. He looked at his watch and noted it was 5.30 a.m. according to the luminous dial, and reaching out, he turned on the bedside lamp.

"I'm listening – go ahead."

"Do you know who this is? Careful now – no names."

"Sure I know who you are, and whom you represent."

"Good." Pearce had to be sure that the letter was from Hunter, but he didn't want to ask directly.

"When was the last time you contacted us, Captain?"

"The last. . .? You should have it by now. . . Wait." Hunter realised that perhaps they had received it and were seeking confirmation from him. "Do you have something that suggests – shall I say – no retaliation?"

So it *is* genuine and not a forgery! That settles it, thought Pearce, and he wondered what had happened to the Yank that caused him to make such an error.

"I see. Yes, we have that correspondence, but we don't understand why you found it necessary to break the communication rules. I take it you are aware of the consequences – eh?"

The blood drained from Hunter's face. What broken rules? He had done everything by the book. What's this idiot talking about?

"Hold it, buddy. There is nothing wrong at this end. I can tell you it was properly done as usual, posted in the same place as usual, and no copies taken. So – what's your problem?"

Pearce recalled what Magee had said earlier about the possibility of someone or some organisation trying to trick them into getting rid of a reliable source.

"There is a problem, Captain. What if I was to tell you that the envelope was posted in Las Vegas, and the contents were in the form of a photocopy? Because that is *exactly* what we have." Pearce hung up and the line went dead.

"Hello, hello? Blast you! Why hang up?" Hunter looked again at his watch without seeing it and got up. Sleep had vanished. What's going on here? His thoughts raced to recent events – the missing money – the surveillance information delays – the CIA people, and now this. Something was wrong and he didn't know what. His persecution complex was returning fast. Who is out to get me? First it was those guys in the Pentagon because he was right about the oil fires, but now? Who is after me? He must get out of the building, and fast. He would move into Dugway permanently and to hell with the apartments. He regretted paying the six months' rent in advance, but that couldn't be helped now. The IRA believed him to be a risk, and that was one lot of people who got rid of their risks. He packed his few belongings into the back of his car and left for the base in time for breakfast. He couldn't eat. Hunger had left him, hunger and sleep. Only the adrenalin was left and that fed his fear.

Chapter Thirty-Two

"Go and sit down over there," suggested Susannah pointing in the general direction of the seating area in the coffee shop, "and I'll get the coffee. Sugar?" Susannah handed de Courcy a leaflet from a number that were on display in the rack, to the bottom of which was fastened the notice PLEASE TAKE ONE.

De Courcy chose an empty table by the window, and watched her as she paid the cashier, placed the change in her purse, and carried the tray towards him.

"Back in a minute," she smiled as the tray was set on the table. She was out of his sight as she moved behind one of the pillars that supported the roof.

The leaflet had the usual mixture of pictures, text and art work tastefully produced on white paper, printed in dark green. De Courcy didn't bother with such things normally, but he began to read while he waited for her to return.

> ". . .one of the most impressive Norman Castles in Ireland, Carrickfergus Castle was built by John de Courcy around AD 1180. . ."

John de Courcy! He was hypnotised by the name and couldn't read past it. John de Courcy! Could there be any connection? He remembered his father saying something about having ancient Norman blood in his veins, and now this! He read it again and stopped at "1180 AD".

He hadn't noticed that Susannah had already taken a seat opposite him. He saw nothing but his name – "de Courcy".

"I see you are interested in this place. We could look around if you like." De Courcy didn't hear her for a moment, realising that a family history going back to AD 1180 could give him Irish roots. He awoke to reality.

"Sorry, Susannah. I have just had a bit of a shock." He stared again at the leaflet he found he was holding, with white knuckle strength.

"Are you all right, Edward?"

"Fine, fine, Susannah. Do you know what it says here? This place," he looked over his shoulder and at the castle through the coffee shop window. "Imagine it, this place was built by a John de Courcy in. . ." he referred to the text, ". . .AD 1180. I'm a de Courcy!" His words came out quickly in a hushed whisper that she had to concentrate hard to hear.

"Sure, everybody around here knows that," she mocked and took a mouthful of coffee. "This place has been here quite a while, Edward. If you read on, you will probably see that King William III came here."

De Courcy noticed her smile.

"You knew, didn't you? You knew about de Courcy!"

She nodded and placed her right hand on his left as it held the leaflet.

"Read on a bit further, Edward. There might be more surprises for you."

His gaze moved from the leaflet to her and back to the leaflet. He read on. ". . .de Courcy's kinsman, Hugh de Lacy, assisted with the building. . ." De Lacy! De Courcy stopped and stared at her. He mouthed "de Lacy". She nodded and her smile was bigger than ever.

"That's right, Edward. I'm a Lacy, you're a de Courcy. We both built this place. Now drink up and let's look around."

He did as he was told, and they left together to explore the castle, but not before de Courcy had managed to gather a copy of the different leaflets and pocket them.

For the next two hours de Courcy was enthralled as he was shown round the place, taking time to digest the information on the numerous plaques, glass covered displays, and notices. It was all there, from the beginnings in 1180 right through to the visits of King John in 1210, King William of Orange in 1690, and Queen Elizabeth II in 1961. It was most enjoyable, and her companionship through it all added to the occasion.

She saw him in a different light. Gone was the professional soldier, and in its place a grown-up child, enjoying for the first time new discoveries of life past, as if nothing else in creation was worthy of attention. The spiral staircase was descended from the top-most room in the keep; the portcullis and its machinery examined as were the numerous cannons. De Courcy, his appetite sated for the time being, felt guilty about his attitude towards her. He simply forgot about her. She was there as he mentioned this point and that, but as a person he ignored her. It was now time to remedy that in the most sincere way he could imagine.

"This has been the most enjoyable time I've had for years, Susannah, and it has been all your doing. I don't know what to say." She took him by the arm and they walked out of the castle together, returning to his car smiling and laughing about anything and nothing.

"I bought you something," as she handed him a book bought earlier in the coffee shop. *A History of the Castle* was the title.

He couldn't say anything as he hugged her and kissed her on her cheek. She saw his eyes filling with tears as he broke from her and opened the car door. The drive back to Ballycarry was without conversation. He dropped her off at her request at the farm entrance and managed to extract a promise from her to let him take her out for dinner.

"I would have been disappointed," she said, "if you hadn't asked," and she skipped out of his sight into the house. The book was beside him in the passenger seat. Before driving off, he picked it up and opened it. Inside the front cover she had written, '*To Edward, Love Susannah*'. He then remembered what Sutton said about the two of them. What was it? "Don't spoil it, you two could get on well."

"How right you are, old boy, old boy," he said aloud as he drove off back to the cottage.

Chapter Thirty-Three

Sutton had reasoned that the banker would be tired after his journey, so the best time to tackle him about the money would be as he arrived home. Anytime now they could expect Martin Richmond to arrive from the airport. They waited in their car, about fifty yards from the entrance to Richmond's home in the pleasant surroundings that Supt Richards had described to de Courcy as being a collection of houses of better-than-average design in a well set out area. They would give him the shock treatment and retreat with the knowledge they were sure the banker had, before he knew what had hit him. They had rehearsed their actions and their dialogue carefully, and waited.

De Courcy glanced at his watch for the third time in as many minutes, then realised that he was starting to get edgy.

"Just make sure you don't kill him, old boy," as he looked at Sutton's handgun resting on the floor between his feet. "Into the wall now, remember, shoot into the wall."

"You want to back out, Edward?" Sutton was calm and not in the least worried. "I can handle it so take it easy," assured Sutton. A car passed them.

"That's him. Ready?"

They waited until the banker had stopped his car in the driveway of his home before they moved. Sutton picked up his weapon, took the safety off, and opened the car door. The seat belt hadn't retracted into its inertia reel, causing Sutton to become tangled in it. He lost his balance and accidentally fell against the roof of the car as he stood up. The gun went off – there was a scream – a female voice.

"Idiot!" de Courcy shouted. "Get back in – now – move, man – move," as he started the car and quickly made his escape, out of the cul-de-sac and out of the area.

"Sorry, Edward. I got caught up in this blasted seat belt." Sutton put the safety on and returned the gun to the floor while fastening his seat belt in one move. "Did I hit anyone, Edward?"

"Don't know – there was a scream, but it might have been shock reaction – did they see us?"

"I don't think so – blast it, this damn belt! That puts paid to our well-laid plans. Keep an eye out for the police." De Courcy was driving too fast along the dual carriageway, which worried Sutton.

"Slow down – remember there is a gun here, and we don't want to be stopped for speeding – huh?"

De Courcy nodded, said nothing and eased off the accelerator pedal. What next? The shock treatment plan had back fired, and someone was probably dead.

"Where are we going, Edward?"

Neither of them was concentrating on the direction of travel, only on the quality of the driving, which was as faultless as de Courcy could make it and within the appropriate speed limits.

The miles passed and soon they arrived on the ring road that would take them around Bangor and into the small seaside town of Groomsport, where de Courcy stopped in the free car park at the harbour.

"We must find out what happened, old boy. Any ideas?" They left the car and walked along the picturesque harbour that was home to a mixture of small boats in various states of seaworthiness.

"I guess I should get rid of this thing, Edward." Sutton was patting his right pocket where de Courcy could just see the outline of the offending weapon. "If there's nobody around. . .," he swivelled on his left heel and made a 360-degree turn while looking for evidence of witnesses, ". . .I could drop it off the end of this wall," pointing to the deep water in front of them.

"No, old boy. Let's find out what happened first." De Courcy kicked an imaginary stone into the water while thinking of recent events.

"I could contact Richards, I suppose, and see if he can get me some news. What do you think?"

They had reached the end of the harbour and climbed the few steps that took them to the top of the harbour wall, where they stopped and looked around. Their frame of mind didn't allow them the luxury of taking in the picture postcard scenery, which was beautiful and offered to those who had time to appreciate it the natural coastline of rock, sand, and seaweed.

Sutton couldn't think of anything, as his mind was on the possible innocent party suffering from his stupid action.

They walked slowly along the wall and crossed the road that led to The Stables restaurant. There was a public phone near the entrance, and de Courcy used it while Sutton waited outside. Sutton looked at his watch. An hour had passed since it had happened. In one hour had he become a murderer, a slayer of human flesh, a widow maker, or worse, a widower maker? His imagination was now working overtime. Were there children about? Could he have killed a child? It was too late now, especially as he had only, what was it, three years left? Three years wouldn't allow him to serve a life sentence.

"It's okay, Elmer – it's okay." De Courcy's voice was music to his ears. He hadn't seen him coming at first, but noticed the look of relief on his face.

"A flesh wound only, old boy. A piece of sticking plaster, says Richards, and the banker will be as good as new."

"Nobody else then? The scream?"

"No, nobody else, and, as I suspected, the scream was a shock reaction."

The silence returned, as did the smiles of relief as they returned to the car.

The major gave Sutton all the information Richards had told him, and they agreed that the gun should be disposed of. It made a most satisfactory sound as it hit the deep water beyond the harbour wall, and sank leaving no trace of its existence. After all, Sutton did have another one under the shower tray.

*

A three-week holiday break from the daily routine of the working day together with the effects of jet lag make it difficult to get up to speed on return to a routine, especially when it's a Monday.

When the pile of unopened envelopes, all marked 'To be opened by addressee only' were handed to him by the assistant manager, Richmond knew he was in for a morning filled with the latest news on staff problems, new management procedures, and product and service changes.

"Welcome back, boss. These only arrived last week, so they probably want a reply yesterday."

"Right. Anything else I should know about?" Looking at the desk diary and gratefully noticing no appointments arranged for the day, he invited Hugh Montgomery, his assistant manager, to close the door and sit down.

The office was clean, tidy and bright, although not large enough to hold all the staff, which was why staff meetings were held in the main banking hall, either before or after public opening times.

"Only some rumours, but there are always those," offered Montgomery. "There is talk of a meeting to be held for all managers later this week about possible voluntary redundancies. The details are probably in one of those," and he pointed to the envelopes. There were only three of them, but for a jet-lagged manager on Monday morning three was a pile!

"How are the figures against targets?"

"They're not too bad. We're first in the list for mortgages and for personal loans, and operating profit is 14% ahead of target." That was good news. The assistant manager must have worked well with the mortgage advisor over the past three weeks.

"Well done, Hugh. I take it both Lewis and yourself had a hand in that. This is good news. . . Any more?" and with swift movements of the chrome-plated letter opener, he deftly slit open the three envelopes.

"Just the police looking for you – that's all."

"I see," and without looking up he removed the contents of the now opened envelopes and began to read. "And what do the police want?" The reflex move to rub the shoulder wasn't noticed by Montgomery.

"Unusual request – they were seeking confirmation of your holiday, where you were, and when you were due back."

Richmond heard but continued to read the correspondence.

"Fine. If they want something, they know where to find me. What did you tell them?"

"Little – just that you were 'somewhere in the States' and 'due back today'. That's all."

The letters were read and passed over to Montgomery in confidence.

"Keep that to yourself. You were right about a managers' meeting; on Wednesday, staff restructuring is the topic. The other two cover future training plans, of which more is to follow." It no longer surprised Richmond to read such mundane matters from envelopes that had been stamped TO BE OPENED BY ADDRESSEE ONLY. There were more important and private matters in open circulation than that mentioned here. No doubt it was something to do with empowering the manager to communicate information to his staff to reinforce the management position.

The 'out of order' computer lists were dealt with, and the Monday morning staff meeting was ready to start at 9.45 a.m. The tea was handed round, the telephones manned, and fourteen pairs of eyes awaited the manager's news.

"In my much enjoyed absence," Richmond began, "I find that the profit of this branch has gone up. That means I can look forward to going away again soon in the knowledge that you will continue to improve matters." Montgomery smiled to himself, and was glad to have such an easy person as Richmond to work with. It was the first time in twenty-four years with the bank that anyone had taken time to discuss business matters and staff matters in such an interesting and informative way.

"The meeting is on Wednesday at Regional Office, so I expect I'll have news for you after that. Any questions?"

Open-style management gave encouragement to all for their efforts. No wonder, thought Montgomery, their figures were good. The phone rang at 9.55 a.m., just as the meeting ended. Helen, the general duties clerk, answered it and caught the eye of the manager.

"It's the police, Mr Richmond. Shall I put it through to your office?"

"Yes – okay," and he finished the tepid tea as he closed the door behind him. It was de Courcy, who insisted that he be seen as soon as possible, and yes, in half an hour's time at 10.30 a.m. would be acceptable.

De Courcy, accompanied by Sutton, arrived on time. Both declined the coffee offered by Helen as she introduced them to her manager. Richmond recognised them.

"We meet again, gentlemen," beamed Richmond. "Please – sit down," and he remained standing until the visitors were seated. As Richmond sat and leaned back in his executive chair, he noticed that both de Courcy and Sutton were sitting straight in their chairs, as if awaiting orders from a superior officer. "I saw you both in Las Vegas, didn't I?" ventured Richmond. They were in civilian clothes, but looked every inch full of military breeding.

Richmond had prepared himself for the interview as best as he could from the information he had, by preparing a list of questions on an unruled A4 sheet of paper. As was his habit, the desk was cleared of everything except the list of questions and a pen. Additional paper was to hand if required in the drawer to his right hand, as were the various loan application forms.

"You did. A good holiday, was it?" was the cold monotone reply from de Courcy.

"Great holiday," and the memories of California, Arizona, Utah, and Nevada came back as he stretched and gazed at the ceiling. "My first time in the States. I must say, they look after you well out there, and the food! You know, you can get steaks there of sixteen ounces! And no strange looks when you get it!"

Sutton saw the picture in his mind and was starting to get hungry. "You sure can, buddy, and even bigger – you'd better believe it," as Sutton remembered the time he downed a 24-ounce slab to win a bet.

De Courcy brought them back to reality by first clearing his throat of imaginary mucus, before declaring, "We would like to ask you a few questions about certain matters. First. . ." he paused to give Richmond time to sit upright and face him, ". . .when we met in the Rinkha, you mentioned £200,000. What do you know of a missing £200,000?"

Fifteen minutes later they had left the bank and were travelling to Island Magee.

"I thought *we* were going to interview *him*; I didn't expect that, did you?" Sutton was annoyed with himself.

"It was our own fault. We assumed he would be easy, old boy," de Courcy said.

They journeyed with Richmond's words still fresh in their ears.

First he asked them, "Where is your RUC identity? You made an appointment to see me, saying you were the police." Then he asked for details of the missing £200,000. "You know, there is legislation governing money laundering and such a large amount would require me to consider this legislation."

Thirdly, the phone call to Supt Richards, "How was I to know he knew him?" asked de Courcy.

Sutton had his mind on other matters.

"He has no £200,000. Did you see his suit – and his shoes?" Both had seen better days. "Anyone with £200, never mind £200,000, would dress better than that, old boy, old boy."

De Courcy continued on a different subject. "Blast him anyway. You do realise that he probably saved us in Las Vegas?"

"Yeah – I guess so. And then I shoot him as soon as he gets home. But don't you ever tell him, Major."

"Still, he didn't look like someone who was shot. No evidence of it at all!"

Chapter Thirty-Four

Captain Black Feather had completed two months of duty in the surveillance library before he felt he would be safe to take a look at some of the information held there. He was part of a 'six pack', as they were called, working in twos on an eight-hour shift, 24 hours a day, with no days off. When leave was allocated or sickness occurred, relief personnel from Security were used to maintain the numbers to ensure that nobody worked alone. With two on duty, one would look after the administration while the other would retrieve from, or return files to, the library. In the past six weeks, Black Feather had spent most of his time away from the library at the computer. This enabled him to acquire enough knowledge of the systems to allow him to work out how he could assess material without his shift partner knowing. All he had to do when retrieving files was to take an extra one now and again, which could be returned when he returned the other files.

First, as a trial run, the file he extracted related to surveillance of troop placements and strengths in Iraq. Iraq was an obvious choice as the section in the library allocated for Iraq was beside the section for Ireland. Having pretended to be interested in an Iraqi file, in full view of a disinterested shift partner, he returned it after two days, and moved to the Ireland section. He didn't need to pretend to be interested – he *was* interested. The references contained in the third file marked 'DUMPS – IRA' were unbelievable. There were about twenty-five map references to known dumps covering the whole of the island, with most of the references falling north of a line from Dublin in the east to Galway in the west. Black Feather spent the first day noting the map references with special attention to the fourteen dumps within Northern Ireland. He found this a easy task. Openly and in full view of his shift partner, whose only interest was form filling and completing computer-generated returns, Black Feather entered the map references onto a sheet of paper. Beside the map reference, he recorded the date when the surveillance had been carried out, together with the photograph number. These are up to date, he noted; only a number of weeks old.

To add to his disbelief, he noticed the fact that all map references in Northern Ireland were National Grid references used by the Ordnance Survey of Northern Ireland.

For the next few days, Black Feather decided to take things easy, and ignore all files except those required in accordance with the Authorisations given to him by his shift partner. That gave him time to get the paper on which he had recorded all the references out of the place. The photographs might not be so easy. They were held on the computer, and access was only possible when working on the terminal. He was not on the terminal – his shift partner was.

Never mind, he was prepared to wait until the opportunity arose. He wouldn't say anything, he would leave it to his partner – he would wait – his partner would tire of the terminal. But he must be ready. When the opportunity came, he must be ready. That was why the photograph references were coded onto the wall calendar in full view but unseen. It was easy. Each photograph had a code length between eight and twelve digits. Only Black Feather would know that the small marks beside the dates on the calendar would refer to the references. Two of the months, February and April, had two lots of codes, one in ink the other in pencil. The other months held the codes for the remaining ten photographs.

It shouldn't be too long now. His shift partner didn't like computers much, and was only doing his stint to give Black Feather a break. Black Feather was patient – and waited. All he had to do was enter the code, and when the photograph appeared on the screen, hit the print button. Easy. As easy as taking out those tanks in Iraq in 1991.

*

Sutton was enjoying this one. He was speaking to Hunter on the satellite phone and had just asked him for more money as well as the surveillance information. He smiled at de Courcy, who was making breakfast. Sutton held the handset at arm's length as Hunter's shouts were heard covering topics ranging from the ungodly timing of the call, the stupid demand for more money, to the threat of coming over and sorting it out himself. It was easy to keep Hunter's anger boiling.

"Speak up, man, I can't hear you – did you say the money was coming this week, or next?" More angry unrepeatable comments from Dugway filled the air, to which Sutton replied, "Good man, I knew you would deliver. How much this time?"

After a full two minutes of vitriol, the line went quiet. Sutton brought the handset closer to his ear and made a simple request.

"Don't forget to send the surveillance stuff this time, Captain. The deal is off if there is no surveillance – okay?"

There was a few seconds' pause, during which Sutton could hear Hunter utter despairing groans before coming back.

"Listen good, Major," he started slowly and at normal volume. "I am working on the basis that you and your Limey sidekick have the money and have stashed it some place. Understand? So, if you want to stay alive, just get it and deliver it – okay?"

Sutton smiled and noticed de Courcy signalling that the eggs were ready.

"I hear you real good, fella. Here's the deal. We need the rest of the capital next week with the surveillance stuff, or the whole set-up is off. I repeat – off – finished. By the way, what record do you have of any money arriving here, Captain?" and with that, Sutton switched the phone off, packed it up, and returned it to its home under the shower tray.

The eggs were good, as were the slices of soda bread and rashers of lean bacon.

"I hear you have had words with your Dugway chap, old boy. Bad news?" enquired de Courcy.

"Bad news all right. Bad for him. He'll soon realise that he can't point a finger at anyone but himself."

*

Hunter was afraid for his future. How long ago was it that he could see Washington in his sights? Now he could only see his own execution at the hands of the IRA, due to Sutton's incompetence. Why was everyone ganging up on him like this? What had he done to deserve such treatment? After all, it was he who provided the brains, the strategy, and the success that was 'Ireland 6'.

Hunter noticed that it was almost one o'clock, but he decided that the time of day, or in this case night, didn't matter. He would go now and talk to MacBride. Talking it over might enable him to put things into perspective and come up with a way out. There must be a way out of this one – there had to be a way out.

He left the office and made his way to MacBride's quarters. It was hot, humid, and windless, and his shirt was damp and sticking to his back, arms and chest. What a place, Dugway! One way or another, he would get out even if it meant desertion. He knocked on the door, opened it, and walked in before MacBride had time to register the intrusion.

"There's big trouble, Sir, and I need your advice and help real fast."

MacBride was ready for bed as he sat in his pyjamas in an easy chair in front of the television, watching the closing scenes of an old black-and-white movie, *Casablanca*, his favourite. He knew the dialogue as well as anyone, but enjoyed watching it every time it was transmitted. MacBride glanced at Hunter and returned his attention to the TV as if Hunter didn't exist.

Hunter froze at the reaction to his entrance and prudently waited until Bogart delivered his final words. MacBride sighed with satisfaction as he rose, switched off the set, and stretched.

"Great movie. They don't make them with that kind of dialogue any more – only action stuff." MacBride turned to Hunter and stared at the dishevelled sweaty body standing before him.

"Ever heard of a shower, son? You look like nothing." MacBride sat down again, leaving Hunter to make his mind up whether to stand or sit.

"What's that you said about trouble?"

Hunter stood there, head bowed, with hands in pockets, not able to move. "It looks like this project, 'Ireland 7' has come to an end, Sir."

MacBride didn't react at all. He just closed his eyes and waited. Hunter lifted his head, glanced at his superior, returned his gaze to the floor, and then gave an outline of his phone call with Sutton, in a monotonous disinterested manner. The silence that followed could have been interpreted by Hunter that MacBride had fallen asleep, except for the evil smile that appeared on his face.

MacBride stood up, opened his eyes, and gave Hunter a pat on the shoulder as he left for bed with the comment, "Who cares! Go and get yourself a good night's sleep and see me at breakfast," and closed the door behind him. Hunter didn't sleep too well that night but turned up clean and tidy for breakfast. He placed a glass of pineapple juice on his tray, then a plate that had on it two slices of buttered toast, and a mug of black coffee, before making his way to MacBride, who sat alone at a table for two. MacBride acknowledged his presence by spitting a mixture of toast and coffee as he asked, "Did you get much sleep, son?"

Hunter wiped the fragments of toast from his arm and quietly answered, "No."

"Then you are one stupid captain, Captain."

Hunter looked at him with sad eyes and an empty expression.

"Think, man, think. Who knows about the operation? I'll tell you — you and that's about it." MacBride ate another forkful of egg followed by a bite of toast. "And who knows about the money? Nobody. There are no records, therefore nobody knows!"

Hunter's expression remained unchanged. MacBride stopped eating and took a long look at the specimen before him.

"I don't believe what I'm seeing here. Listen, son. Nobody knows, nobody cares, therefore there is nothing to worry about." A mouthful of coffee vanished with more sound than an Eagle F-15 passing Mach 1, as Hunter changed from a wreck into a wide eyed, smiling ten-years-younger-looking person in ten seconds flat.

"Yes – yes – yes," he shouted. Those around were startled from their half-awake world for a moment, then, noticing that it was Hunter, returned their attention to examining the remains of their breakfast.

"Well done, Captain. I knew you would catch on – eventually." MacBride was amazed at the change in the man.

"Let me tell you something, son, and it's for free." MacBride finished his coffee and pointed to Hunter's untouched mug. "Okay?" Hunter nodded, so MacBride took the coffee and swallowed a bit.

"Remember the famous bomber called 'Valkyrie'? It cost billions to build. Where is it now? It doesn't exist, and nobody cares. 'Star Wars'? The same. The Brits do it too – they had a brilliant plane called 'TSR2' – spent a bomb on it. It doesn't exist either. The money? Nobody cares. Same as for the Brits and their 'Bluestreak'

missile. All the world does it, son – the Russians, the French. . ."
Hunter was taken aback at this flow from MacBride, whom he thought
hadn't a clue of such matters. ". . .So what does it mean? I'll tell
you, son. In our job, we spend the Government's money and forget,
because everybody else forgets. It's all under 'defence' so nobody
asks questions." MacBride had finished his breakfast and rose to
leave.

"Just thank your lucky stars, son, that you don't have to *earn* your
money. We are a protected people – we defend that which doesn't
need defending and get paid for it. I just hope the cuts in defence
don't come 'til I retire," and he was gone.

Hunter was hungry now, so he joined the queue at the self-service
counter and filled his tray with eggs, bacon, toast and waffles. Half
an hour later he was in the deepest sleep he had had for weeks

Chapter Thirty-Five

'The Railway Preservation Society of Ireland announce the running of the steam engine "ANTRIM GLENS" from Belfast to Larne this Saturday, leaving Belfast at 10.00 a.m. Calling at Whitehouse, Carrickfergus, Whitehead, Barrycarry, and Glynn.'

That could be interesting, thought Richmond, as he looked up from the advertisement in the evening paper. This should provide an opportunity for a few photographs, and should any of those be good enough he might win another prize.

"Any plans for tomorrow?" he asked his wife. Penelope sighed long and hard.

"Some day you will listen to me. What did we agree to do when you came home from hospital?"

He couldn't remember, which was the norm, as he often heard his wife speak while managing not to listen. Richmond was particularly good at that when asked to do something that he not want to do. He tried to remember. What was it he didn't want to do at the weekend? That was a reasonable place to start from, and it prompted his reply – "Oh yes – you wanted something done in the garden?"

There was another loud sigh. She picked up the newspaper that he had discarded on the floor, and neatly folded it before placing it on the piano stool. Turning to face him, and with feigned injury, she said, "I don't know why I bother." Richmond looked at her and tried to make up his mind whether she was serious or not.

"I said," she continued, "that a weekend in Island Magee would enable you to get some rest for your shoulder, and you said, 'Good idea' – remember?"

He couldn't remember.

"Good idea is right. I might get some useful photographs," and he unfolded the paper and showed her the steam train advertisement.

"I could try for that place near Glynn – where the rail line has water on both sides – you never know, there might be a winning shot there."

She stopped in her tracks on her way to the kitchen.

"Shot? Shot? Don't say 'shot' – say 'photograph'." He now knew that she was mocking and he spent the next ten minutes checking over his camera gear. The camera had served Richmond well since he acquired it over twelve years ago. Some day he would upgrade it.

The coast road from Larne to Whitehead is interrupted by the charming village of Glynn, once noted for its swans. The railway line hugs the coast, except when entering and leaving Glynn where it takes the shortest route by crossing Larne Lough along the width of a single track viaduct.

Richmond parked his car and made his way on foot across rough terrain towards the track and, having found a suitable position, set up his camera on a tripod and waited. There had been heavy rain during the night, which had cleaned the air from dust and improved the visibility. Richmond looked around the area again to satisfy himself that he was in the best place for his purpose. He had chosen the 135-mm lens which should allow an exposure of f4 at 1/250th second. The conditions were perfect – a clear blue sky supporting a few white clouds, and the sun was in the right quarter. He had ten exposures left, which should be enough, and spare film. Time was a problem. There wouldn't be enough time to take more than seven or eight exposures, less if he found he had to change the lens. He looked at his watch. The train was late. What happened? Was this a wild goose chase? Had the event been cancelled?

Richmond decided to wait for an hour, then he would pack it in. The whistle was loud, shrill, and beautiful. The train was leaving Glynn, and would be making smoke and releasing steam as it gathered speed. Just right for a photograph. Richmond checked everything again – firstly the camera settings, then the composition. The weather – excellent; the light – ideal; the planned picture – well, he would just have to be patient and wait for the results.

Here it came, busy pulling the refurbished carriages behind it, the smoke with a few sparks was poisoning the atmosphere as it left the smoke stack. At the same time, steam from both valves on the top of boiler and from the cylinders on each side of the engine gave evidence of the power being used. Marvellous! The sun, shielded from the camera lens by a branch of the tree acting as a frame, back-lit the scene to complete the composition. He took eight exposures – two, one stop under-exposed, the other six in accordance with the reading of the in-built light meter. The Cannon A1 hadn't let him down in twelve years and surely wouldn't do so now.

It was all over too quickly, but he was satisfied. More than satisfied, he was convinced that he had some great pictures – especially the second and third shots which had the driver waving to him.

He packed up his camera gear and returned in elation to the bungalow in Island Magee, where the builder and his wife were conversing with Penelope.

'Just in time, dear. Norman has bought himself a boat and has invited us for a sail – interested?" Penelope asked, while nodding her head to prompt a positive reply.

"A boat? What sort, Norman?" Richmond enquired.

"It's a clinker hull job – a rowing boat with a Seagull outboard motor." Motor boat, Richmond thought. Better than a yacht. He remembered the last time he sailed on a yacht – it was the only time he was sea sick, and he vowed never again would he—

"Well, Martin? Are you coming with us, or staying here?" Penelope was getting a little impatient.

"Of course I'm coming." Richmond moved to the gate. "Lead on, Long John Silver," and ushered them out. Penelope locked the door of the bungalow, Martin checked that his camera gear was locked away out of sight in the car boot, and the four made their way to the small man-made stone harbour at Cloughfin. The builder's two dogs joined them.

The engine started first time, and they were off at a steady three knots in the direction of Portmuck. It was windless and the noisy journey was made easy by the absence of swell or waves, and only spoilt by the wash from two speedboats that passed them as if they were stationary. They entered the harbour at Portmuck, where Norman managed to find an adequate mooring, and they gratefully left the boat for a walk along the shore. The women led, followed by the men and the dogs. Within minutes, the dogs had taken the lead and managed to destroy a few sand castles on their way to the end of the bay. Small talk was the order of the day.

Returning to the boat, Norman was indicating to Martin to hold back a bit. When the women had moved out of hearing, he found courage to speak.

"How's the shoulder? I hear you were shot."

Richmond involuntarily rubbed the minor wound with his hand. "It's fine thanks, just a scratch."

The apprehensive builder continued, "It hadn't anything to do with the torpedo, had it?" Richmond glanced at the builder and was surprised at his fear.

"Torpedo? Good heavens, no. Nothing about that." The builder was relieved to hear it. They were approaching the harbour and noticed that the tide was further out than when they had arrived.

"You know. . ." the builder was making sure that nobody but the banker could hear him, ". . .I haven't told anybody – not even Shirley."

The return journey was just as uneventful. Passing The Gobbins, the four, as if by signal, looked at the shore then at each other, then towards the lighthouse at Blackhead.

"I wonder how many torpedoes are around these parts?" Richmond asked nobody in particular.

"That's not funny." It was the angry voices of Penelope and Shirley, in unison. Norman and Martin started to laugh, the dogs barked, and the wives' anger disappeared.

After a late tea, when the dishes were washed and put away, Richmond remembered that he had left his camera gear in the car.

He would go and get it now as it would be safer in the bungalow.

"I'll get the camera," he explained as he went outside. Penelope remembered his planned excursion to Glynn and was cross with herself that she hadn't said anything.

"How did the photographs go, dear?" she asked as he returned with the camera bag in one hand and the tripod in the other. His expression told all.

"I have some great shots – just wait until you see them." He opened the camera bag and removed the A1, changed the lens from the 135 mm to the standard 50 mm. "There are only two or three shots left on the film – I'll go somewhere and finish it." He knew not to suggest taking a shot of his wife, as she didn't like being photographed.

Leaving the camera bag behind, he left with the camera swinging round his neck and drove off. Where to? He found himself parked on the Upper Road beside the lane that led to The Gobbins, and minutes later he made his way down to the shore.

The rain that had fallen during the night had made the path wet and slippery. On the basis that if something can go wrong, it will, the banker had no chance. He slipped in the mud and regained his footing, only to lose it again. He fell hard and fast, and slid twenty yards until he was stopped by coming into contact with a crop of stone. He went out like a light. The camera was badly damaged beside him, its back opened, allowing light to enter and ruin the film.

Events that fall into a pattern can either be planned or coincidence. This was coincidence and probably saved the banker's life.

De Courcy decided to examine The Gobbins himself, to satisfy his curiosity to see if there was any evidence of the chariot or its contents ever having been there. De Courcy parked the Honda behind the banker's car. He knew whose it was. The banker here? At the Gobbins? De Courcy made his way down the path and, using his Army skills, proceeded safely until he came upon the mud-coated banker.

"Well, well, well. What have we here?" He saw the blood from the banker's cuts and checked him over for signs of life. The banker was breathing but felt cold. There was a groan. De Courcy supported the banker's head using his forearm, and began to ask a few questions.

"Do you know where you are, old boy?" There was a groan followed by, "I'm in a lot of trouble – that's what." Richmond paused then continued, "I only came to finish off the film – is the camera okay?" he asked.

That sounds good, thought de Courcy, he knows what he is doing here. "Where do you hurt? Arms? Legs? Head?"

The banker looked around him and then saw who his rescuer was. "You!"

De Courcy noticed that the banker was checking out how easily he could move. "Yes, old boy – it's me. How are the arms and legs?" The banker started moving about again. First his left arm, then the right and on to his legs. He shook his head. "No problems so far."

"What about my camera?" Richmond noticed that it was no longer round his neck. He couldn't see it.

"Let us finish looking at you first, old boy, then we'll find out how the camera is. Now. . ." De Courcy slowly moved the patient into a sitting position and removed his supporting arm from behind Richmond's head. ". . .What of the head – is it giving you trouble? Any pain – any dizziness?"

Richmond brought both his hands to his head, made a few movements, up, down, left and right. "No – so far, so good. . . wait. . . the blasted shoulder. . . See if the cut has opened – there were stitches removed recently."

De Courcy recalled the shooting incident and immediately went to the injured shoulder. It was fine – a little grazing, but that was it.

"No problems there, old boy, but you may have internal injuries – best take things easy and have you checked out."

Richmond looked at his watch. What time was it? 6.30 p.m. What time did he arrive? He left the bungalow at – what time was it – 6.10 p.m.? Good, he couldn't have been unconscious for more than say – ten minutes. "Ten minutes, that's all – ten minutes maximum," he announced aloud.

"Ten minutes? What of ten minutes?" asked de Courcy.

"What time is it?" he asked de Courcy, who confirmed it to be just past 6.30 p.m. "I have been here ten minutes in total. My wife will not have missed me yet – that's good news – now, where is the camera?"

De Courcy looked about him and saw the remains of the Cannon A1 in the damp grass.

"What a sorry sight," and, reaching down to his right, he picked it up. "This is unlikely to be of any use to you now. No Oscar-winning material here, old boy," as he showed the evidence to the banker.

Richmond didn't believe it. There it was – damaged lens, body dented, and open with film cassette hanging out. Richmond closed his eyes and groaned.

"No – no – no – not that! Ruined – all ruined!" was the whispered voice of despair. He was shivering now and probably suffering from shock.

De Courcy decided that he must act quickly. The nearest hospital was in Larne, and although the facilities were basic they should be able to check out the patient for problems.

"Thanks, Mr de Courcy. I appreciate your help," and he took the broken camera from him, trying to replace the film before realising that it was not worth the energy. Richmond put the film in his pocket, and closed the back of the camera. He noticed that it was no longer lightproof.

Before de Courcy could stop him, he stood up and swayed a little as he surveyed his appearance.

"She'll kill me - just look at the mud. It's all over me." He looked at de Courcy for comforting words, but de Courcy was concerned about his medical condition.

"What are you doing here, Mr de Courcy?"

"Pure chance, old boy, and it's lucky for you that I turned up." The shivering got worse. "We had better get you home and into something warm - you're getting too cold."

The banker began to move and stretched out his arm for the readily given assistance.

"This place is like tobacco," stated Richmond.

"Tobacco? I don't follow."

"The Gobbins could be dangerous to your health!"

There was no laughter, but de Courcy was now sure that he was not suffering from concussion following a remark like that.

The banker found his car key and made to drive home.

"Sorry, old boy. You are not in a fit state for that. Here, I'll give you a lift." He forcefully took the car keys from Richmond and led him to the Honda. Somehow, Richmond got to the bungalow without further incident and cleaned himself up while de Courcy gently explained to Penelope what had happened, then he left.

"A fine chapter of accidents you turned out to be - are you all right?" she asked.

"I think so," he paused. "I feel so stupid."

He was well wrapped up and feeling better outside a bowl of hot soup. "There's only one real hurt, Penelope, and it won't go away." She was worried now.

"Where? Your shoulder?"

"No. The camera - the photographs of the train - all lost - all that trouble to get it right, and it *was* right - that's what hurts."

She could never understand him when in this sort of mood. There he was, nearly killed, and the only thing that worried him was his blasted camera.

A car drove past the bungalow and stopped, followed by another, which also stopped. A knock at the door was quickly answered by

Penelope, who wasn't sure whether she was glad to see the caller or not.

"I've brought your car around for you – I hope you don't mind." She now was very pleased to see Major de Courcy standing there, dangling the car keys in front of her, and she invited him in to see the patient. He didn't stay long, saying that his American friend was waiting outside, but strongly recommended that Richmond be checked over at a hospital as soon as possible.

"Good idea of yours," said Penelope as she waved de Courcy off. "We shall do that now," she said and proceeded to make ready to leave. De Courcy walked to his car and waited.

"We are going home – no arguments – and we're going up to the Ulster Hospital at Dundonald to get you looked at – and we're going now – all right?"

There was no point in arguing. "All right," he agreed.

The walls of the bungalow were thin, allowing sound to travel. De Courcy heard the conversation and was relieved to hear of the arrangements just made.

"We will follow them home, Elmer, to make sure they make it. You know, that chap had a bad fall and was recovering too fast for my liking."

"Sure," replied Sutton. "I suppose we owe him for Vegas."

They followed the banker and his wife at a discreet distance and managed not to lose them. Coming off the M2 motorway, they took a left which allowed them to pass along the docks area. The road width was restricted in places, due to the civil engineering work being carried out on the new road and rail system that was planned to be ready for late 1994 or early 1995. The one-way system at the rear of the Custom House had traffic from Albert Square joining traffic from Donegall Quay. The road widened at that point. That was when the convoy of three Army Land Rovers appeared alongside the banker's car.

Coincidence or planning? Who knows? The unfortunate banker was in the middle of it and hadn't a chance to escape.

A terrorist sniper, hidden somewhere in the direction of Queen's Square, aimed and fired. The shot missed the people but hit the armoured windscreen of the middle Land Rover. The reaction of the soldiers was fast. The three Army vehicles stopped abruptly and the men, all armed, scattered in different directions, took cover, and pointed their guns in the general direction of the terrorist's shot. The banker's car was trapped behind the third Land Rover, as following traffic prevented escape. De Courcy's car was also trapped three cars further behind as the build-up of vehicles became solid.

A second shot rang out which hit the leading Land Rover's front offside tyre and burst it.

"I see him," shouted one of the armed soldiers.

"I have him also, can I shoot?" shouted a second.

"Yes, yes – take him out," a third voice replied.

The next two shots were in quick succession. First, the second soldier lying face down on the ground in front of the leading Land Rover fired, followed by a third round from the sniper.

"He's down," shouted the second soldier, which prompted a team of four soldiers to run, with weapons on safety, in the direction of the sniper.

"That last shot – anybody hurt," shouted the leader.

There was no reply.

Penelope was shocked into silence during the minute or so that passed and she hadn't noticed Martin's wide-eyed stare at his right leg.

"I can't believe this," he gasped. "That last shot hit me – look," and he pointed to the red patch growing larger by the second.

That was when Penelope screamed and attracted the attention of the lieutenant in charge. De Courcy and Sutton also heard the scream and both left the car and ran to give assistance. Sutton opened the passenger door of Richmond's car while de Courcy and the lieutenant looked in.

De Courcy produced his ID card and showed it to the lieutenant, suggesting, "You could use your radio to warn the nearest hospital that a gunshot wound is about to come in."

Penelope was still screaming, but not hysterically so. She was in no state to think clearly or to drive anywhere. The lieutenant nodded and spoke into his radio. Richmond looked around him, aware of what was happening, and he put in his penny's worth.

"Make it Dundonald – or the Ulster as it is called. It's handy for my wife to visit – okay?"

The lieutenant nodded and continued to relay his message. One of the other soldiers arrived and, pushing past Sutton and de Courcy, said, "First Aid, here – make way please – make way," and used a knife to cut open the bloodied trousers from the ankle to the thigh. Having done that, he noticed that the wound was only a flesh wound and applied a field dressing to stem the bleeding. Lifting the banker's hand, he instructed, "Hold this here – that's right – now don't move," and turning to the lieutenant continued, "He's okay, it's clean, Sir. In one side and out the other. I suppose we had better look for the bullet?"

"Yes – usual search pattern. The police are on their way."

Returning his attention to de Courcy, the lieutenant asked, "Any chance of you driving this chap off to the Ulster? By the time the ambulance gets here you could be there."

"Of course, old boy," de Courcy was only too glad to help. The procession moved off. De Courcy drove the banker's car with Penelope in the back leaning over to give comfort to her husband, followed by Sutton in the Honda. The lieutenant's radio announced, "We have him, Sir, and the weapon. He's hit and needs attention. . ." The message was heard by the occupants in Richmond's car before they were out of earshot and *en route* to Dundonald.

Richmond started to look down at the side of the car. First right, then left.

"What's wrong, what's wrong?" asked Penelope, doing her best to remain in control.

"I was just looking for bullet holes. The bullet entered the car somewhere and then exited somewhere else – I wonder. . ."

"For heaven's sake. . . you have been shot!. . . forget about silly things like that. . . you mind your leg."

De Courcy smiled. He thought, now I know he isn't suffering from concussion. He stole a glance at the banker and saw Penelope's hands move restlessly on top of Richmond's shoulders. He caught the banker's eye that winked at him before he returned his attention to the road, and decided that he might be a good banker but he certainly would have made a good soldier.

Chapter Thirty-Six

The General convened the Council to grant someone an audience, and demanded full attendance. That was why Susannah apologised to de Courcy for postponing their planned outing to Portrush. There were double the guards on duty for the meeting, a point noticed by Susannah as she arrived and made her way to the usual venue. Extra tables were made available, which would be used to examine the evidence.

It was unusual to meet on a Saturday. In fact, it was the first time they had called a meeting for Saturday since the bomb on the Shankill Road on 23 October 1993. Innocent people died that day because the IRA believed a meeting of loyalist extremists was taking place in a room above the fish shop.

That was on a Saturday. It was a long time before the people on the Shankill Road were able to relax on a Saturday after that atrocity. Like all terrorist incidents, the relatives and friends of the bereaved never forget. It is the pain that diminishes over time, only to be resurrected at each anniversary.

The information made available by an overseas well-wisher to the General reinforced his position as leader for the time being. The other members of Council accepted him as leader and would continue to do so for as long as he produced the goods, and maintained the cause.

"It will take some time for all of you to get the whole picture," the General said after the preamble, "so I have copies of the documents for each of you."

He handed each of them a blue folder containing copies of 'Ireland 6' and suggested that they each use a table to make examination of the contents easier. He also suggested that he would go over the information with them so that their understanding of what was before them would be uniform and accepted.

The General's earlier meeting with Susannah had paid off. She had taken time to understand the information and had formed the skeleton of a strategy based upon it. Two hours had passed before the General was satisfied that the blue folder was understood by all present. They stopped for twenty minutes to polish off the lunch that was provided. A lunch of chips, beef burgers, and ice cream, followed by tea and biscuits.

The second folder handed out by the General was red. There were no green folders used by the UVF. Nobody, apart from the General, had seen the contents of the red folder until now. It didn't take them too long to understand the contents of the red folders.

There were maps, reference numbers that the General explained were grid references, and photographs with dates when they were taken.

The facial expressions on those gathered in that place ranged from delight to fear and anger, depending on the thought that arose within each mind. Should anyone have managed to look in on the meeting, they would have seen and heard the delight of terrorists having information on the enemy's arms dumps, the fear that perhaps their own arms dumps were available to others on photographs, with details of grid references, and the anger that the American Government hadn't passed on this information to the British. Just thinking of the lives that might have been saved had these arms been taken out of circulation would make any sane person angry.

Susannah again looked over the information in the red folder, and compared it to her brief notes on the strategy that she had formulated based on the information in the blue folder. The General noticed that Susannah was studying the papers before her and totally ignoring the conversations going on around her. The General made his way from the top table to hers at the back of the room.

"Something wrong, Susannah?" he enquired as he stood in front of her.

She continued to cross-reference her notes. Without glancing up, she closed her red folder and pointed to it. "That's damning evidence of a government that doesn't care about the lives of ordinary people." She looked up at him. "I have the bones of a strategy based on the blue folder and was wondering if this new intelligence. . ." again she pointed to the closed red folder, ". . .made me want to think again."

"Does it?" the General probed.

"No. I think I will stick to what I have."

"Hmmm. . ." was the reply as he returned to the top table.

The General brought them to his attention by clapping his hands a few times and suggested that now was the time to discuss their reaction to the papers before them. Rather than a free-for-all, which would produce nothing constructive, he asked each in turn to give their comments. He kept Susannah until the end and started with Jimmy Scott, whom he knew would keep on the right track. Scott kept his seat and supported his head with his left hand, with elbow on the table, and used his right hand to wave the air while speaking.

"It's like this, General," he began. "We represent the majority population even though they don't know it. If we had some information on, say, the Libyans and their planned attack on the US Navy in the Mediterranean and kept quiet about it, *I* would resign from the organisation." He paused to change his position as he was getting uncomfortable supporting his head with one hand. Scott decided to stand and managed to do so without knocking any of the papers off the table. "The Americans have this stuff on the IRA weapons and have kept quiet. Worse than that. . ." he lifted the blue folder, ". . .they have approved the killing of our people, and have assisted the IRA to do it. We must do something to let the people know about all this, and," he gestured violently with his fist, hitting the blue folder, "if it spoils the so called 'special relationship' between us and them – so be it." He sat down. Before anyone reacted to Scott's comments, the General moved on to the next person.

The words expressed by all, including Susannah, were similar in their condemnation of the great democracy that was America.

" Okay – now let's move to the next stage." The General had allowed them to talk, now they would listen. "You all know that we appointed Mrs Lacy here, to help us plan things."

They all turned and gave her approving nods and smiles.

"Perhaps, Susannah, you would join me at my table here, and let us hear of your plans so far – would that be acceptable?"

There was approval to that statement expressed by a few 'Sure thing' and 'sticking out' and 'here, here', together with polite applause while Susannah gathered the papers in front of her, placed them in the appropriate folder, and moved to the top table.

"Is it all right if I sit and talk, General? I find it a little daunting to—"

"Of course, of course. Sit here," and the General offered her his chair as he took up a new position at the end of the table where he could see both her facial expression and those who were about to hear her.

"I take it," she looked at them as she spoke, "that you agree that the Americans have played dirty here – right?"

She received the answer she expected and their full attention.

"I suggest giving them some of their own medicine, and see how they like it."

Scott liked what he was hearing, and let the General know of his approval by giving him the thumbs-up, which the General acknowledged.

Susannah continued. "There are two different sets of material in front of you – the blue and the red. I want to take them separately. I'm not suggesting we act separately, only to give you my ideas in an organised manner." She lifted up the blue file. "This accounts for the death of over fifty people – some Army, some Police, some civilian, and some of us. How do you think the British and American Governments would react to the following?" and she outlined her proposals.

When she had finished with the blue file, she turned her attention to the red one, and simply said, "We could get some powerful media backing here, and at the same time remove these weapons from the IRA stocks for good. Do you want to hear more?"

*

The guards were being changed for the second time outside the building, around the car park and in the surrounding streets. Sammy the Smoke, a reliable look-out for the UVF since 1980, relieved one of his tired colleagues at the car park.

"Some meeting – eh? Over five hours and they're still at it. It must be something big." He stamped out the cigarette butt after lighting his fifty-third of the day.

"You should cut down on those, Sammy," his colleague suggested.

"I have, mate," and he inhaled deeply. "I used to be on eighty a day, now I'm down to seventy." He looked around to satisfy himself that there was nothing or nobody out of place. "Double guards, too. We might get an attack – keep your eyes and ears open – and don't forget to come back in a couple of hours. Don't be late." His colleague departed for a welcome break, and left Sammy the Smoke patrolling the car park with three others. In a few minutes, he would be on his fifty-fourth, but he wasn't worried. He collected his money from the organisation's welfare fund every Friday, and had enough to keep him in smokes for the next four days.

An hour had passed and Sammy the Smoke was out of cigarettes, just as the signal was given to indicate that the meeting had ended. As usual, the guards made themselves scarce, and from unseen vantage points watched as the three Council members, who had arrived by car almost six and a half hours ago, left and made their way to unknown destinations.

Susannah didn't go directly home. She was tired, but felt she had to call on de Courcy and see for herself that he wasn't too annoyed with her for postponing their Portrush trip.

The small cottage above Brown's Bay had seen better days and was due some decorative maintenance. De Courcy's car wasn't there, but the front door was open, and looking in she saw Sutton making himself some coffee.

"Hullo, Elmer. May I come in?" she asked as she closed the gate behind her.

"Hi, Susannah. Come in, come in. Want a coffee?" and without waiting for her reply, he took down a clean mug from the shelf and handed it to her. "Hold that while I get the coffee. It's instant – is that okay?"

"Surely. Should you be drinking coffee? What about your head?"

"Ach – now, don't you start on me. Sure, it's only one cup. You won't tell Edward now – right?" as he poured hot water into the mug.

She looked around, and moved the *Belfast Telegraph* newspaper that was spread out over one of the easy chairs, and sat down. "Your secret is safe with me. Tell me, where is he – Edward? Is he about?"

Sutton took a look at her and admitted to himself that she was a good looker, or could be if she dressed up properly. "Hospital," and he sipped his coffee. "Ahh – beats tea every time, this."

"Hospital? Is he all right?"

"Sure is. He's visiting a poor civilian who was shot earlier today. Here. . ." he showed her the paper, ". . .you can read all about it. Well, not all about it. They got some of the story, but not all."

She picked up the paper and silently read the two paragraphs of the event.

"There's no mention of Edward here, Elmer. Was he involved?"

"Don't worry about it, Susannah. His name was kept out of the paper, as was mine. We were both there 'by accident', and did what we could to help the banker and his wife – that's all."

Sutton didn't miss her interest in de Courcy, and took the opportunity to sound her out.

"He could be back in half and hour – want to wait?"

She looked up. "You don't mind, do you?" she said pleadingly.

"Mind? No way, Susannah, I don't mind." He finished his coffee and went straight in. "I tell you this, Susannah, you have done the major a lot of good."

She looked up at Sutton and put the paper on the floor. Sutton found it hard to talk to her, especially as she was looking at him. He looked away and placed his mug in the sink. "I've known him some time, and since he met you he's changed. A new lease of life you have given him, so thank you. You don't mind me talking like this, do you – huh?"

This was the first time Susannah had the opportunity to be alone with Sutton, and it wasn't as daunting as she had imagined.

"No, Elmer, I like Edward, and I think he likes me."

Sutton was now able to look at her. "You *think*? Man, dear, he's smitten," he shouted. "Sorry, Susannah, I didn't mean to come on that heavy. It's just that he feels he is too old, and he's afraid to get in too deep with someone your age."

The conversation died, the silence broken by the sound of a dog barking in the distance.

"Can I tell you something, Elmer?"

Sutton found that it was now her turn to look away while speaking. "I haven't felt for anybody like I do about Edward since my husband died. If I can't have him, then I'll have nobody." She looked at her watch without seeing it.

"Look, Susannah – let's walk down to the bay. By the time we get back, the major may have returned. What do you say – huh?"

This brought her back to life.

"Surely – let's go." Leaving the place unlocked, they started to walk down to the shore.

"Shouldn't you lock up, Elmer?"

"Lock up? Sure there is nothing worth taking – come on," and he took her arm and led the way.

"This part of the world is beautiful – isn't it?"

"Indeed it is," she agreed. "It's the people that cause the problems."

They walked on down the hill and found that there were few people about.

"He's afraid, you know, Susannah. Afraid of hurting you and of getting hurt."

There was silence again. Eventually she replied, "I know. I never thought. . . Never mind. We'd better start back now," and she pulled him round, realising that they were continuing to walk arm in arm.

"He'll not ask you, you know. Never. Sorry, Susannah, but that's how it is."

"Ask what?"

"To marry you. He will never do it. Even if it hurts him to death, he'll not do it." Sutton stopped walking and looked her straight in the eye. She was smiling, and her eyes were wet with joy.

"I know," she whispered, "and it doesn't matter, believe me – it doesn't matter."

In such a short time, she had come to know the American a little better. She never thought of Americans as a caring people, but Sutton *was* a caring person if nothing else. Here he was, looking after the interests of the major while at the same time suffering from some illness that would kill him. All that mattered to him was not allowing Susannah to hurt the major and not allowing the major to hurt her.

She saw de Courcy first, and waved. Sutton looked up and, holding on to Susannah as he had done since leaving the house, made to salute, but changed it to a wave at the last moment. De Courcy was standing beside the car, looking at them walking up the hill towards him, arm in arm. She broke away from Sutton and ran the remaining few yards that separated them and threw her arms around him. Nibbling his ear, she asked, "How's the patient, then?"

"Oh, the banker chap? He'll recover."

She waited until Sutton joined them before advising them that she had some news that might be of interest to them. She went to her car and retrieved a blue and a red folder, then all three went inside closing the door behind them.

*

Richmond was discharged from hospital two days later and arrived home at 4 p.m. on Monday, thus avoiding the evening rush hour. Two days later, he gratefully received the insurance claim form from the assistant manager whom he had telephoned at the bank that morning with the details of his damaged camera. The assistant manager was accompanied by Richmond's secretary, Helen, who, on behalf of the staff and customers, presented Penelope with a large bouquet of flowers, with a note attached offering sympathy at having to cope with such an impatient patient.

"How long will you be off, Martin? All week? asked the assistant manager.

Richmond, with injured leg supported on a cushion placed on top of a stool, sat in his favourite chair in front of the TV, which had been switched off as soon as the visitors arrived.

"I haven't taught you much, have I? You have just asked me a question and then answered it."

"Don't be so nasty, Martin," interrupted Penelope. "That's no way to treat your visitors." Then, turning to Hugh Montgomery, "he has a sick line for one week, Hugh, so he could be back next Monday – if he lives that long!"

Montgomery prodded Helen, who produced an envelope from her handbag and gave it to Richmond.

"This is especially for you."

He looked at the plain envelope. There was nothing on the front or the back, so he opened it and read the contents.

> STAFF PHOTOGRAPHIC COMPETITION. Please have your entries in by 30 September. There will be no further reminders. If you're not in – you can't win!!"

Richmond heaved in silent laughter and, crumpling the note into a ball, threw it at Mongomery, who caught it, uncrumpled it, and gave it to Penelope.

'The Gobbins,' thought Richmond. 'The blasted Gobbins. Why did I go there? I had a brilliant photograph and lost it at The Gobbins!'

Chapter Thirty-Seven

Captain Sands of the Bomb Disposal Unit had received the latest reports from the Parachute Regiment stationed in Co. Tyrone and Co. Fermanagh, and from an SAS unit in South Armagh. That dealt with seven of the fourteen arms dumps. The other seven dumps were in Co. Antrim (two), Co. Down (two), Co. Londonderry (two), and in West Belfast (one). The Bomb Squad, as they called themselves, did their own reporting on the seven assisted by the Ulster Defence Regiment. Manpower was not going to let them tackle all fourteen dumps at the same time, which had to be done to achieve surprise and to comply with the order.

Captain Sands accepted the order, which in his opinion was unusual but not against his terms of engagement or against the Geneva Convention. Put simply, the order was, take out as many arms dumps as you can simultaneously, without loss of life, without publicity, by retrieving the arms and weapons, or by destroying them so that they cannot be used. The 'no publicity' was the unusual bit. Captain Sands shunned publicity as part of his routine, so to have it in the order was unusual.

The experienced team of bomb disposal experts could manage ten locations simultaneously. They would prefer to limit it to eight to allow for maximum cover should something go wrong, but ten was possible.

The locations were the known element of the operation. The unknown was the contents of each dump, its size, and of course, what type of booby traps would be in force. The locations gave Captain Sands his first set of problems. Of the fourteen; four were near to, or formed part of, buildings that were inhabited; two were close to water; two beside electric power lines. The remaining six in open but hilly countryside were easy. The second problem was one of logistics. How to retrieve an unknown quantity of arms and have them transported out of the area; how many and what type of transporter would be needed for each location.

If there was an easy option that would achieve the objective, Captain Sands decided that he would take it. He worked on the plan with his four lieutenants before the rest of the team was brought in and briefed. The input from the team would be incorporated into the final plan, which allowed added flexibility with alternatives depending on the circumstances at the time. It would be assumed that all the dumps were booby-trapped.

The agreed plan was to destroy, using high explosive, the six dumps in open country, and to try and retrieve arms from the four dumps located at:

1) North of Ballyrowan at Lough Neagh   near water
2) North of Martinstown on the A43   near water
3) West of Larne on the A36   near electricity pylon
4) East of Newry on the B8   near electricity pylon

The others were either too dangerous to achieve without guaranteeing no loss of life should the booby traps go off, or made it impossible logistically to retrieve the weapons without publicity. That was especially true of the dump in West Belfast.

The operation was timed for 0200 hours on Monday, which gave them five days to organise the ancillary teams responsible for transport, communication, diversion, and protection, and briefing them properly.

The six dumps that were to be destroyed would not need transport, apart from that required for the disposal teams and the protection teams. The other four would need a full transport team. During these five days, others would carry out covert surveillance on the ten locations. Those involved were carefully selected. There were no locals on any of the teams, only full-time regulars from the British mainland. The involvement of locals from the Department of the Environment – Roads Service was not due to breakdowns or accidents, as believed by the Department, but to the actions of the diversion teams. The Department erected road diversion signs and carried out repairs near Ballyrowan and Newry, making the covert surveillance an easy task. The other locals were from the electric company. The Emergency Maintenance Unit from Northern Ireland Electricity were surprised on finding the damage to two pylons that had been advised to them anonymously. They apologised to their customers and advised them that to keep the interruption of supply to a minimum, power loss would be limited to four hours, commencing at 0200 Monday morning. During that time, the pylons at Gardiner's Corner and Mayobridge would be repaired and tested before power was restored at or before 0600.

Captain Sands was happy with that, as he expected the operation to take two hours – one hour to clear traps, one hour to move the arms. This was to prove too optimistic.

They were short of the tracked robots needed to check for booby traps, and arrangements were made for the Transport Corps to bring an additional three from military bases in Gibraltar and Cyprus. That brought the number of tracked robots to eight – one for each of the four locations, plus a back-up. The laser-guided rockets were brought in by helicopter along with their operators, from their base at Aldershot. Their kit consisted of three high explosive warheads and two incendiary warheads for each of the six dumps to be destroyed, together with two high explosive and one incendiary warheads for the others should it prove impossible to retrieve the arms.

The bomb disposal teams, complete with their back-up, assembled at their positions at 0100 hours. Transport for the four locations was timed to arrive at 0300. Captain Sands led the team for the job near Ballyrowan and used his radio to confirm that the other teams were ready.

In around an hour and a half's time, the six dumps in the country areas should be destroyed, and the booby-traps made safe on the other four. Radio communication was to be kept to a minimum and using their recognised code would keep Captain Sands briefed of each location's progress.

It was now 0155. The teams on the A36 and the B8 announced 'power off'. Five minutes early! The electricity was switched off five minutes early! They would wait until 0210 before sending the robots in, as would the other teams. The teams in the country should have it easy. All they had to do was line up the laser, shoot a few rockets, then retreat as fast as they could. The noise could be a problem, as could the vibration, especially if it travelled to one of the sites being examined for booby traps and placed the disposal expert into an irretrievable situation. That was why the rockets were not to be used until 0330.

Captain Sands checked the time. In twenty seconds it would be 0210, and four tracked robots would start to move into their respective dumps and send live high-definition TV pictures to a 20-inch monitor.

The dump near the A36 had no traps, and was pronounced 'clear' at 0230.

Off the B8, Lieutenant Fox found and disarmed two booby traps, and pronounced it 'clear' at 0245.

Captain Sands found himself knee-deep in swampy ground on the shore of Lough Neagh, and lost the robot as it sank before it had travelled ten yards. For the next hour, Sands and his team waited for the engineers to arrive from Ballymena and construct a floating platform to give the spare robot a suitable surface to travel upon. During this time, he was advised that the team near Martinstown had lost the dump. Sands knew that either the robot had set off a trap which destroyed the dump, or the IRA had their own surveillance in operation and, seeing what was happening, had set it off themselves.

At 0355, news came through that the six country dumps had been 'burnt out'. The noise from the two dumps in South Armagh were heard by the team on the B8, and by a few thousand others whose sleep was interrupted.

At 0420 Captain Sands sent in the second robot. The TV picture was clear and bright, and showed two trip wires each connected to a box of tricks that could blow up everything. It was made safe.

The time was now 0422. The pressure plate, hidden under a matted square of air bubble plastic packing material, was discovered by accident. The second robot started to sink, so was reversed. The camera was tilted down and the remotely controlled arm was used to grab the loose material on the floor of the dump when it picked up the edge of the plastic. It required careful manoeuvres until 0520 before it was disarmed.

The radio messages had ceased long ago, and the teams had returned to quarters – all except Captain Sands and his team, who were commencing the retrieval process at 0525. Fortunately, it was the smallest of the four retrieved dumps, and by 0605 had been emptied completely of its stock of ten Armalites, two hundred kilos of Semtex, 1,000 rounds of assorted ammunition, and one heavy machine-gun complete with four cases of magazines.

By 0632 the objective had been achieved, and by 0714 the helicopters had taken off to return the rocket launchers and their operators to Aldershot.

The local news broadcast at 0655 made a passing comment to a series of explosions heard at various locations in the early hours.

> 'A spokesman from the security forces confirmed that explosions were heard, but that their examination to date failed to find any damage to property or injury to people, but they would continue in their search and would encourage the public to give any information they had to any Police Station, or use the Confidential Telephone'.

*

Magee was summoned to attend an urgent meeting of IRA/SINN FEIN without fail in the West Belfast office on Tuesday at 8 a.m. Word began to filter back that something was wrong. First, it was about explosions in South Armagh that had destroyed two arms dumps. Then another dump was reported destroyed in Co. Derry, then another in Co. Antrim. By 1400 on Monday, when the number increased to five, with another reported empty, the decision was taken to check out all dumps and report back to the Executive. That was yesterday.

Today, Magee listened to the Chief of Staff of the military wing giving an account of the review exercise.

Magee couldn't take it in at first. What he heard smelt of dirty tricks. The last to speak summarised the position. "In total, we have lost about one third of our arsenal. Most of it has been destroyed, but three stores have been removed. Our people didn't hear or see a thing. Oh, some heard the explosions, but apart from that, nothing. Is that about it?" he asked nobody in particular.

"What do we do about the remaining dumps? Remove them?" The question came from one of the political wing people.

"Any ideas?" asked the Chief of Staff. "Liam, you usually come up with suggestions in difficult times – what do you say?"

Magee was still digesting the enormity of the loss, and was thinking along different lines.

"Hang on a minute." He took time to work out what to say, then began. "Before we do anything, let's try and find out who is behind this, because. . ." there was a murmuring building up which Magee interrupted, ". . .BECAUSE – I said because – if it's the Brits, they may have guys planted at the other dumps waiting for us; if it's the INLA or Loyalists, they may have left fresh booby traps." The murmuring grew again, and subsided when the Chief of Staff raised his hands. "The dumps that remain – four old, two new – are okay. We checked them out last night, and there is no sign of Army, INLA or loyalist people. We can move them if we need to move them."

The Chief of Staff handed control of the meeting over to the Chairman of Sinn Fein, who gave comfort by saying, "We can leave the matter of the dumps to the military wing with our full confidence, just as they leave political matters to us." There was applause and all heads nodded agreement to that remark.

"Thank you, Chairman," replied the Chief. "However, I would welcome comments from you, Liam."

Magee was still going over in his mind all that had been reported on the dumps. They waited for him to speak.

"Don't move them – use them."

They didn't understand the remark and began to question each other.

"Quiet please – quiet," the Chairman again. "Let's hear it from Liam." When they had settled down, Magee explained.

"Parties unknown to us have taken out some of our weapons. Let's not let them think we are worried about it. Instead of taking time to restock or to move to new dumps, why not use the stuff we have to show the world we are still here. That's why I say, don't move them – use them. Blow up a few things – a few town centres, a police station, an Army unit. Use the weapons – that's what they are for – right?"

The militants loved it and cheered. The rest smiled and waited until the noise died down. The Chief of Staff noticed that Magee wasn't smiling but still held a deadly serious expression. That fact was also noted by the Chairman.

"He's not usually wrong," whispered the Chairman to the Chief. "We will leave it to the military people to decide – all right?" said the Chairman to the meeting.

"That's fine by me," the Chief replied and left within two minutes.

Once again, the peoples of Belfast, Dungannon, Bangor, and Portadown suffered death and damage to relatives, friends, and property in the name of freedom at the hands of the oppressed minority, to demonstrate their ability to kill and destroy rather than build up and create a free civilised society.

*

Washington DC was hot, both politically and climatically. The President was losing out on Capitol Hill as the Republicans managed to run things their way by out-voting the Democrats, and the Police announced record crime levels in the areas known as the black ghettos.

The President's advisors had the ear of the Irish National Caucus, who made much of the strength of the Irish-American vote, and were pressing the advisors to encourage the President to do more on the Irish issue. The advisors had passed on this message to the President. The President wasn't deaf to the Irish issue and could see the benefit of keeping the Irish-American vote in his pocket. But the President had more than one problem. The value of the dollar had fallen, especially against the Japanese Yen; employment was a worry in the defence industry; the drain on resources to give aid to the former USSR and other Eastern Block countries; the drug problem being supplied by South America; the British and their help in the Gulf and the 'special relationship'; famine and strife in Africa; China and the 'favoured nation' status. Yes, the President had more than the Irish problem to deal with in matters of foreign policy. That's why he passed it on to the Pentagon to come up with something.

The Pentagon looked at it and gave it to General Laskie. General Laskie had other problems, not least of which was the letter from 'The Central Council, Ulster Volunteer Force' addressed to him personally. That letter was the reason Captain Hunter from Dugway found himself with orders to report to Laskie. Laskie wanted Hunter to explain his contribution to the 'great American way' over recent months.

Captain Hunter, in his best uniform, was ushered into the presence of General Laskie, Colonel York, and Captain Hudson, who closed the door and took his arranged seat directly behind Hunter.

"Well, well, well – look what has arrived from Utah."

General Laskie pointed to the straight-backed office chair in front of his desk and ordered, "Sit."

Captain Hunter sat.

"I have here. . ." Laskie opened the drawer to the right of his desk and withdrew a genuine 1858 Colt 45 loaded revolver, which he placed on the top of the desk close to his right hand, ". . .a magnificent piece of good ol' American machinery, and what you do and say here today, Captain, will determine whether I use it to blow your brains out or not."

There were no smiles on anybody's face, except Hunter's, who thought this a bit of a joke.

Laskie noticed Hunter's smile. He picked up the Colt and, aiming it at a sand bag put there for this purpose, fired once and gently put the gun down again.

The noise was terrible. They all jumped with ringing in their ears – all except Laskie. The staff outside the office were told in advance what might happen, so they didn't react to the noise. Laskie noticed that Hunter's smile had gone.

"Guess where the next bullet goes, Captain? Now. . ." and Laskie produced the UVF letter from the drawer that a few moments ago held the Colt, ". . .take time out to read this before I ask you a few questions," and he threw the letter on the desk. It landed top down and out of Hunter's reach, forcing him to stretch to get it. He read:

> 'Dear General Laskie,
>
> I am commanded to convey the thanks of the grateful loyalist people in Northern Ireland to you for your assistance in enabling us to destroy, and in some cases acquire, arms from arms dumps formerly under the control of the murdering terrorists – IRA/SINN FEIN.
>
> Your locations of the fourteen arms dumps proved to be accurate. I'm sure that the British Government would be surprised to know the source of our intelligence.
>
> This organisation is proud to be associated with the USA intelligence service, and would welcome the continuation of this association. I understand that your people in Dugway were involved, and I would ask that you pass on our thanks to them.
>
> However, we still await receipt of the promised $330,000. Please send by return.

To push matters along, I am also commanded to ask for the locations of IRA/SINN FEIN arms dumps in Eire (Republic of Ireland), which I understand you have. We shall endeavour to render these 'out of use' as soon as possible.

Your confidence in this organisation is well placed, and shall remain secret unless it comes to our notice that you change your allegiance to IRA/SINN FEIN. In that event, the surveillance information you sent will be published internationally along with a number of other sensitive documents.

Remember – Ulster still says NO.

Yours sincerely

Captain Black (Signed)"

As he was reading the letter, Hunter became rigid and found himself standing and shaking as he came to the end of it. He looked up at Laskie, then returned his eyes to the letter and read it again.

"It's genuine, boy. We checked it out," said Laskie, who then pointed to the blanked out address marked 'Censored' and added, "We did that so you wouldn't see it."

Hunter collapsed into the chair as he reached out and returned the letter to the desk.

"Now – Captain. Listen real good – ready?"

"Sir," was the word that followed. It was barely heard, but it was there.

"What damn information have *you* given to the UVF?"

"The UVF?" was the even fainter reply from Hunter. He keeled over and hit the carpet before York could reach him.

"Leave him – if he's fainted, he'll come round; if it's a heart attack, it will save you a bullet, General," was Becker's contribution.

"Heart attack? He can't do that here. Quick, Hudson, get a medic in here fast," and they formed a ring around the heap on the floor.

Laskie, seeing the Colt and the letter on the table, moved them to the drawer and locked it.

Two medics, complete with trolley, arrived in double time and made their way to Captain Hunter, who was sweating profusely.

"Looks bad," said the one with sergeant's stripes. "We'll take him to sick bay."

They put him on the trolley and wheeled him away.

Laskie, still standing with the others where the captain once was, was lost for words. Becker was thinking of budgets and was the first to speak. "It would be difficult if he died on us – I mean, he is the only one with connections to the UVF and the money."

"Yeah, yeah – I know. Let me sit down and think," and Laskie took his place behind the desk and sat down. "How about some coffee huh? Hudson, coffee all round, and phone sick bay for the latest."

Hudson lifted the phone and dialled sick bay, while York, with nothing to do, got the coffees. Laskie was looking at and listening to the secretary as the telephone conversation proceeded.

"Yes?. . . yes?. . . How bad?. . . Good. . . I see. . . Can he be moved?. . . Can he come here?. . . I see. . . Yes. . . Look, phone me immediately of any change – okay? And I mean *immediately*." Hudson made his way from the phone back to Laskie's desk before advising the others of the prognosis. "Mild heart attack confirmed, General. No sign of damage, but he can't be moved for a few days. We can go and see him in a few hours' time when they have stabilised him – that's it, Sir."

"I'll put a guard on him, Sir," ventured York. "We don't want him to take off."

Outside the office, a sergeant managed to attract Hudson's attention.

"Excuse me, Sir," Hudson said to Laskie and went to see what was so important. "Yes, Sergeant? This had better be important." The sergeant was covering the telephone with both hands as he spoke.

"It's some Major Sutton, from Ireland, using the sat. phone. He is looking for Captain Hunter at Dugway, and Dugway patched it through here, Sir."

The secretary's eyes opened wide. "Ireland? Just hold," and he opened the door to Laskie's office. "Excuse me, Sir. A Major Sutton in Ireland on a satellite phone link. Do you want to take it?"

Major Sutton," interrupted Becker, "it's the guy Captain Hunter was working with on 'Ireland 7', Sir."

Laskie assimilated the information from Hudson and Becker fast, and nodded.

"Put it through to the general's phone, Sergeant," ordered Hudson.

Laskie lifted the phone, and switched on the speaker so that all could hear.

"This is General Laskie – what can I do for you, Major Sutton?"

Chapter Thirty-Eight

De Courcy had returned from the Rinkha with enough supplies to keep them going for a week, and he began to unload the shopping from the Honda's boot. Sutton heard the car arrive and gave assistance by opening the gate.

"How's the head, old boy?"

"Just fine, Edward. The pills are working just fine," he lied. There was no point in worrying de Courcy any more than was necessary. It was true that the painkillers worked, but their effect was short-lived and he was already taking the maximum daily dose, and then some.

"Your young lady has some ideas! Do you think they will work, Edward?"

"We'll know when you phone Captain what's his name – But yes, she and her friends have some ideas! Just think – if this was to get out!"

"Yeah! Well, we're okay. We are retired, remember? We have no power or authority, so we are out of it!"

"True enough, old boy," and de Courcy took a bite from a large apple and threw another to Sutton, who caught it and did the same. "As long as the IRA don't know about us, old boy. Remember the message? The implied instruction to kill us?"

Sutton stopped eating for a moment. "Too right I remember, Edward. I'll say something about that in the call. It's nearly time to make it. I'll set up the dish," and continuing with the apple, he set about erecting the satellite phone.

It was 1900 local time.

"This should be interesting – want to listen in, Edward?"

"As you would say, too right!" De Courcy took the spare earpiece and held it to his ear.

*

"Hi, General. I was expecting Captain Hunter. Something wrong at your end, General? What's up with the captain?"

"Never mind that, Major – what do you want?"

Sutton pulled a face for de Courcy's benefit and continued. "I want that two-timer Captain Hunter strung up – that's what. First he arranges for me and my buddy Major de Courcy to get on the IRA hit list, then he let's the UVF know about the IRA arms dumps. That leaves us out in the cold. Is Captain Hunter with you?"

"You are talking rubbish, Major. I said, what do you want?"

" Okay – okay, General. Get a load of this. One – the UVF are pushing hard for money – the money that was promised. Two – they have got their hands on some IRA arms using surveillance stuff they got from you guys. Three – they also have some file called 'Ireland 6' which they—"

"What??. . ." The general and his team jumped at Sutton's remark. "Say that again, Major – the UVF have what?"

"Easy on, General – you nearly deafened me. I said, they have some file called 'Ireland 6', which they will publish if they don't get the cash. Something about $330,000 for them, and something about the US funding the IRA in the files. Does that answer your question?"

The general and his team were thinking fast. Captain Becker was working out how to get the money organised if it was authorised, Captain York was working out how 'Ireland 6' and the surveillance information got into UVF hands, and Laskie was waiting for someone to speak.

"Oh – another minor thing, General. Captain Hunter is talking to both the IRA and the UVF – the IRA direct, the UVF through us. This will look good when the President gets to hear it – and that's the last thing. The UVF will contact the President of the US of A and the British Prime Minister by sending them copies of the stuff. Have a nice day, General. Now, what of Captain Hunter?"

"Hold a minute, Major – just hold," Laskie ran his hand over his head.

"Sure, General. I'm not going anywhere," replied Sutton and gave de Courcy a wink. De Courcy was enjoying the performance with a large chunk of disbelief.

York broke the silent tension in Laskie's office. "Let's get him over here, and we can sort it out between them, Sir. Between Hunter and Sutton."

"That's if Captain Hunter is still alive," said Laskie. The conversation was heard in Island Magee.

"What's that, General? Is Hunter in a bad way? I'm glad to hear it," was the interrupting sound from Sutton.

"I said hold it, Major." Laskie looked from York to Becker. Becker nodded, saying, "Money is okay if you authorise it. I agree, get him over here." Laskie knew that Sutton could hear what was said. De Courcy couldn't believe he was hearing such conversations. *More* money? How stupid could they get?

" Okay, Major," Laskie began, "get yourself over here fast. By Concorde – make it over here tomorrow – okay?"

"Sure is okay by me. Hold on and I'll ask Major de Courcy," and, pretending that de Courcy hadn't heard anything, he shouted out, "Hey, Edward – fancy a few days in Washington? You could look at the museums and all."

"Hold it, Major – it's you we want here, not your Limey sidekick. okay? You – ALONE," shouted Laskie.

"A return ticket – maximum stay four days – plus spending money, say $1,000 – have it waiting at the Consulate in Belfast. I'll pick it up tomorrow – okay?" Sutton instructed.

Laskie was about to blow a blood vessel. Becker indicated to him to agree and 'mouthed' that it was okay. Becker scribbled on a piece of scrap paper – '*Play it his way – when he arrives you have him*' and pushed it in front of Laskie.

"All right, Major – have it your way – a return ticket and $1000."

"Two tickets, General. I want my partner with me – okay?"

" Okay," resigned Laskie. "Anything else, Major?"

"Just one. I'm not a major anymore. I'm a civilian, so you'll not be giving me any orders – out," and the line went dead.

"What's that? He's retired? Is that right, Charlie?"

York checked through the personnel files using the computer terminal in the corner of Laskie's office. It was taking a bit of time and allowed Laskie and Becker to crowd around the screen.

"There it is, General," and York pointed to the screen. "Major Lee Elmer Sutton retired— no longer on active service – since September 1993."

"Look at that date. That's before the 'Ireland 7' thing was set up. Who authorised that – huh? Was it me?" Laskie asked.

"Captain Hunter, Sir?" suggested York.

"Yeah! Make it Hunter!"

*

"Another nice trip to look forward to, old boy. What's Washington like?"

"You'll like it just fine, Edward." Sutton was making sure that the shower tray was back in its proper place. "There is no way we'll make it to Washington tomorrow. The tickets will not be organised 'til then, and we need to get organised ourselves."

De Courcy remembered reading a bit about the National Air and Space Museum and the Smithsonian Institution, and believed them to be in Washington. Yes, he would enjoy his few days, but first he would have a word with a certain young lady – today.

"We travel in civilian clothes, Edward. We don't want some top brass coming down on us – okay? We'll take our ID but no uniform."

*

The hospital was like any other, and smelt like any other. Being the Pentagon, the hospital wing was thought necessary in case things went wrong at the wrong time. They usually did. Nobody liked to work for the military so close to a hospital, so they called it the sick bay. That didn't sound as bad; therefore it wasn't as bad, and everybody was happy – everybody, except the patients and those who were obliged to visit. Wanting to visit is different, a point missed by a few padres who took it upon themselves to visit by adhering to an organised visiting rota, or shift; not because they wanted to, but because they were obliged to. Laskie didn't want to visit the sick bay either, but he did so to get some information from Hunter, before Major Sutton arrived. York was towed along by Laskie to the sick bay.

Captain Becker, who was already organising the air tickets for Sutton and de Courcy, had been authorised to get the $1,000 ready, but not to have any of it released by the Consulate until Laskie had spoken to him.

The doctor on duty acknowledged the seniority of Laskie, but, as was the accepted practice, didn't salute. It could prove fatal if, during a delicate operation or procedure, a doctor or nurse happened to see a senior officer pass and stopped to salute. So it wasn't required in the sick bay.

"How is the bastard?" asked Laskie.

"Captain Hunter? He'll live. He was lucky - more of a faint than a heart attack after all, it seems. He's clear of any heart problems that we know of, and his circulation is okay too. He should be up by tomorrow, I guess. Just a precaution - that's why he stays in bed."

Laskie nodded and took a step forward and stopped when he saw the MP. "You're the guard - right?"

"Yes, Sir," the guard replied.

"Good. Don't let him move without you knowing it, and if he tries to get up to run away - shoot him. That's a direct order, soldier - okay?" Laskie shouted.

"Yes, Sir," the guard shouted in return.

"I see you look after your men well, General," the doctor commented quietly and then moved quickly to another patient before Laskie nabbed him.

"This isn't a hospital, Charlie, it's a funny farm," Laskie said to York.

"Let's see this Captain Hunter," and they moved past the guard and took up their position at the foot of Hunter's bed. Captain Hunter straightened up a little when they entered, with the loud order to the guard to shoot him still ringing in his mind. He was, therefore, somewhat surprised at Laskie's opening words.

"How are you feeling now, Captain? Any better?"

"I'm fine, thank you, Sir. I should be back on duty tomorrow."

"That's good, Captain - real good. Any. . ." Laskie paused and looked Hunter up and down, ". . .broken bones, bruises or anything - huh?"

"No, Sir. Nothing like that, I just fainted, Sir."

"I see." Laskie looked at York and shook his head. "I don't know what this Army is coming to, I really don't, Charlie. Here we have an up-and-coming soldier who makes Captain, and he faints after reading a letter." Laskie turned to Hunter in disgust. "Just answer me this, Captain – yes or no. Okay? Yes or no – that's all I need for now. If I get you a phone, can you contact the IRA people? Yes or no?"

Captain Hunter began to sweat again and wasn't sure what this was about. "Yes, Sir."

"Good boy, Captain. Have a good night's rest – I'll see you in the morning," and he turned and left, bringing York with him. As he left, Laskie made sure the Captain heard him address the guard, "Remember, soldier, that patient is a traitor, so if he starts to run, shoot him."

Hunter was not in the best of condition to sleep and wouldn't have done if the doctor hadn't given him a shot that put him out for eight hours.

*

Friday morning at 0700 saw Sutton and de Courcy jogging down to Brown's Bay, along the bay and back by 0745. Showered and breakfasted by 0815, they started to arrange their packing for a few days in Washington. Each managed to put what they deemed adequate into a holdall small enough to qualify as hand luggage. By 0840 the task was complete, apart from the tickets and cash.

"I'll get some travel funds at the airport, old boy. Friday is a bad day to call at a bank in this country – some people still get paid weekly, I hear, and the queues will be long."

"Too right, Edward – I get paid weakly myself – huh? Forget the travel funds – the $1,000 should do."

Sutton picked up the *Yellow Pages* and started looking through the solicitors section. He telephoned, arranged an appointment for 0930, and then passed the receiver to de Courcy who rang Susannah.

Sutton was driven into the centre of Belfast by de Courcy, where he was dropped off in Donegall Square North. De Courcy returned alone to Island Magee.

Sutton called at the solicitors as arranged, completed his business, paid the amount due in cash, and left for the US Consulate Office in Queen Street.

The Consul saw him immediately and offered him coffee, which Sutton refused.

"I'll take a glass of water, if that's okay."

"Water? No problem," he replied and poured him a glass from the drinking water globe in the office. Sutton took two pills from the box in his pocket and swallowed them with the water. "Indigestion," he explained to the Consul.

"Mmm," sounded the Consul. "Now to business." The Consul pushed a button or two on the telephone that sat on his desk and waited. A young girl's voice, American accent, answered. "Yes, Sir?"

"I have our traveller with me, bring in the tickets, please," and he released the buttons. "Off to Washington, I see. Lucky for you. With all these bombs going off, you are well out of it."

The door opened and a young girl of about twenty entered, carrying a plain brown envelope, and she handed it to the Consul.

"Thanks, dear," he said. She left a surprised major as she closed the door behind her.

"I take it you know her," said Sutton.

"I hope so – she's my daughter. Now," the surprised look on Sutton's face remained, but the attitude changed. The Consul opened the envelope, which was not sealed, and allowed the contents to fall onto the newspaper in front of him. ". . . here is the money. . ." and he placed the bundle of US notes, complete with rubber band, in front of Sutton. "Please count it. Here are the tickets. Let me see. . ." The Consul examined them before handing them over. ". . .Belfast to London tomorrow, leaving at 0700. That's early. Then from London to Washington at 1100. Good heavens – by *Concorde*!"

He looked up at Sutton, who was expressionless and in the middle of counting the money. "That's right – Concorde," Sutton confirmed, without interrupting his count.

"Very nice, Major, very nice. I see you are returning in four days' time, also by Concorde. Here are the tickets. Now, sign here please – it's our usual form of receipt. . ."

"Hold it. There's something wrong." Sutton was examining the tickets.

"The money is not okay?" asked the Consul.

Sutton shook his head. "The tickets are for one. There are two of us travelling, or the deal is off. Do you want to phone someone about it, or what?" asked Sutton as he returned the money and tickets to the table and stood up as if to leave.

"I'm only the messenger, Major. Don't take it out on me," said the Consul calmly, which made Sutton feel quite small. "Allow me to make a few enquiries." The Consul stood up and, lifting the newspaper, he folded it and handed it to Sutton. "Something to read while I find out what is what – okay?"

The paper was today's edition of the *Financial Times*, complete with supplements. Sutton thought to himself, 'who but the Limeys would put out a paper on pink paper! The editor must be gay.' In the side office, the Consul had made direct contact with Laskie, as instructed, and told Laskie of Sutton's reaction to the single ticket.

"Are you certain he won't travel alone, Consul?"

"Yes, General, quite certain. He refused to take the cash and was about to leave."

Sutton put the paper down and moved to the door. Standing with his ear close to the door, with his foot jammed against it in case someone suddenly opened it, he listened. Nothing. He opened the door an inch and listened again. Still nothing. That's it, he decided, I'll go. He pocketed the money and the tickets that were still on the table, and left the room. He heard someone talking in the room to the right – probably the Consul, he thought. Sutton turned left and walked at normal pace down the corridor. There was a turn to the right, which he knew led to the reception area, which would be manned. Without changing pace, he turned the corner and saw the surprised look of the Consul's daughter as he approached.

"Sit tight, kid – all is okay. Just give me the other tickets. . ." he stretched out his hand and firmly said, ". . .NOW."

The unexpected produces the unexpected. The firm action of Sutton towering over the girl was unexpected. She lifted a brown envelope that was in front of her and handed it to Sutton.

"Don't move, kid – don't move," and he flashed his gleaming teeth complete with broad smile as he looked her straight in the eye. Sutton withdrew two tickets from the envelope and quickly examined them, noting that one was a return Belfast to London, the other a return London to Washington on *Concorde*. Sutton returned the tickets to the envelope and put the envelope in his pocket.

"That appears to be in order, kid. Tell your pa, I have what I need and – thanks."

There was a sound of running feet behind him. Sutton turned and saw the Consul running towards him.

"A minute please, Major – we have sorted this matter out."

"So have I, Consul." Sutton patted his pocket holding the tickets. "Your daughter here has given me what I need. I guess you should phone Laskie again and tell him his dirty plan didn't work."

"Sorry. I don't understand, Major."

"Is that so, now – is that so? Well, let me spell it out. Tell General Laskie next time you speak to him that should anything happen to me, or to Major de Courcy, a certain juicy piece of information will be released by a certain solicitor to the press – okay?" and he turned and left.

"Did you sign the receipt, Major?" Sutton heard the pleading Consul ask as he left the building, mingling with the shoppers in Queen Street, and made his way to Oxford Street Bus Station.

"Blast it!" was all the Consul could say. He returned the puzzled look his daughter gave him, and made his way back to his office. Laskie was on the line in seconds and listened to the Consul's remarks in silence.

Chapter Thirty-Nine

De Courcy met Susannah at the Rinkha as she requested, where she bought him a honeycomb cone of ice cream. He always felt good in her presence and made up his mind to enjoy these times while the relationship lasted.

The quiet in the car, while they both enjoyed the ice cream, was pleasant, comfortable and relaxing. There was no need for conversation - being in each other's company was enough. De Courcy remembered days long ago of similar bliss and happiness with a family now gone.

"Penny for them, Edward," she asked as she finished off the last piece of cone.

"Worth more than a penny. Old memories of days past, of eating ice cream in Cyprus. Nearly as good as this, it was," and he finished his poke.

His pensive mood remained as Washington came into his mind. He was looking at her looking at him.

"You will never know how much you have helped me, Susannah, but I mustn't get you worried." De Courcy sat up straight. "Some news for you. Listening?"

"Yes, of course." She dared not believe it was what she hoped for.

"Elmer and I have been asked - no, stronger than that, ordered - to go to Washington DC. We go tomorrow."

"Tomorrow!" Hopes dashed, but not for ever, surely.

"Your ideas must have hit them hard in the Pentagon. Even the White House - who knows, even the President may have heard. Anyway," he clapped his hands together and rubbed them hard, "it has produced a free trip for three or four days to Washington." He leaned over to her. "Unfortunately, I will be travelling with Elmer and not you - but," he straightened up again, "you wouldn't want to come anyway."

"Why do you say that? Of course I would go with you." De Courcy glanced at her with raised eyebrows and saw that she was serious.

"I know you would, my dear." His voice was softer and full of emotion. "If only I were ten years younger – or you were ten years older." She was still looking at him and saw his impish grin as he said, "Of course, you look ten years older, so I suppose it could be arranged!" She hit him quite hard while laughing. He breathed in sharply, surprised at the blow, and just caught her reply at the end of her laugh, "You look younger than your 'four score years and ten', you know!" The satisfying silence returned.

"Where to, Susannah? De Courcy Castle?"

"Wrong – it's Lacy Castle. Yes – why not."

De Courcy drove to Carrickfergus and parked in the free car park beside the castle.

"It's my turn – coffee or tea?" he asked.

"Coffee please – no sugar, and no buns, just coffee," she added.

She looked around the coffee shop and chose a table on its own near the window.

"Here we are, old girl – sorry, young thing!" and spilt some coffee as he sat down.

She lifted the coffee mugs from the tray that de Courcy had placed on the centre of the table, and put the tray on the floor against the table leg.

"What a beautiful country this is. You know. . ." de Courcy was really thinking aloud as he sat forward, the coffee mug cupped in his hands, ". . .all this trouble will not stop because of us, or what we – the Army do. It will only stop when the people, enough of them, want it to stop." He took a sip and sighed. "A great pity and a great waste. . ."

"It might stop sooner than you think, Edward." She glanced around.

"You think so?"

"There are meetings going on – all unofficial – between the churches – or at any rate, people representing the churches – and the paramilitaries. Did you know that, Edward?"

"Only what's in the papers. Unofficial, you say?"

"Don't downgrade it. It's the only positive thing going on behind the scenes. I have backed it every chance I could, and will continue to back it at UVF meetings." The silence was short this time. "If there is anything I can do – for the peace process – I will give it my best, as long as it's legal."

"Legal? Don't you mean lawful?" he answered.

"Perhaps I mean not unlawful or not illegal." They were playing with words and with each other, the coffee being ignored.

"Clever boy – what's the difference between unlawful and illegal? Do you know?"

"Of course. Do you?"

She thought for a moment. "Same thing – isn't it?"

"Try again." He was enjoying this, and couldn't wait to deliver the punch line.

"All right, Smarty – what *is* the difference?"

He looked directly at her and, with eyebrows raised and the forefinger of his right hand pointing heavenward, pronounced, "One of them is a sick bird!"

He caught her left hand as it was about to hit him and, bringing it to his lips, kissed it. "I do hope you're right. It's about time meetings took place to stop the killings," he said.

She brought her right hand round and held his, holding her left hand. "Do we do any good with our secret plans?"

"Not really, my dear. All we do is prolong it and justify the need for the legal arms on the streets. The police, in a civilised society, shouldn't need to be going about armed."

"And what of freedom?" she ventured.

"Freedom for the minority at the expense of the majority is no freedom. It's the lack of responsibility that gives birth to freedom fighters, or terrorists if you will. Responsible peoples keep to the law, and if they don't like the law, then they change it – but not by force." They finished their coffee. "It starts in the home. The example of parents and their standards are passed on to their children, and so on. Still. . . we can't order parents to bring up their offspring properly. Some do a good job, mind you, some do – but. . . the prisons are full of. . . Never mind – shall we go?"

They toured the castle again, but this time de Courcy paid more attention to Mrs Lacy than to the castle.

"How is Elmer?" she enquired as they crossed to the car park.

"He is bearing up well. Taking too many painkillers, poor chap?"

Her head was bowed. "Has he any family?"

256

"Just me, I suppose," and he unlocked the car door and opened it for her to get in.

*

Sutton made it to the bus station and sat down before he fell down. His head was both spinning and hurting, and he didn't know how he was going to keep going. He had to get back to Island Magee. He must get back. He managed to focus his eyes on the sign TELEPHONE, and saw two public phones – one in use, the other empty. They were less than two bus lengths away. He struggled to his feet and somehow got to the free phone and lifted the receiver. It was broken – out of order. Person or persons unknown had rendered it useless.

He had had it. That's it, he thought, what a way to go. Adrenalin kept him going as he saw a man walk away from the other phone. He was at it, and dialled. The ringing tone started and went on and on. "Blast you, Edward – pick up the phone," he groaned. No reply. He took the plastic pill bottle from his pocket and looked at it. On it was the professor's phone number. He dialled – the ringing tone. No answer. "Come on, Professor – now. . ."

"Hullo?" Sutton perked up a little.

"Is that you, Professor? It's Elmer Sutton."

"Who?"

"Sutton – you know – the DU fella with the painkillers?"

"What? Of course – yes. How are—"

"Oxford Street Bus Station – phone box – I'm about to pass out. okay? Oxford St—" Sutton hit the ground letting the pill box fall and roll away.

Two twelve-year-olds died later that day from an overdose of unusually strong painkillers, a chemical derivative of MST, source unknown. The bottle was never found.

*

This was Captain Hunter's second good night's sleep in months. He woke up seeing the multitude of monitoring equipment around his bed and the dozen or so electrodes leading from the sockets in the machines to various parts of his body. Plenty of equipment, but no people. Of course, the guard would be there, but he was out of sight, probably talking to one of the few female members of the medical staff in the corridor. The corridor – the only means of escape. Hunter sat himself up in bed as best he could, being careful not to dislodge any of the connections. He didn't know if to do so would set off an alarm.

"Hey, you guys – anybody around?" he shouted. The nurse and the guard heard him.

"I'd better go," the nurse said to the guard as she went to the patient. "Good morning, Captain – sleep well?" and as a matter of routine glanced at each monitor and found that all was normal.

"What time is it, Nurse?"

"Just after eight. Want any breakfast?"

"After eight – huh? I must have slept well." Hunter found himself rather uncomfortable and was moving restlessly to try and relieve the discomfort.

"Here – let me. . ." and the nurse removed the electrodes from him. "There you are. Why not get out of bed and sit here," as she tapped the back of a visitor's chair.

It must be in order if the nurse says so, so he got out of bed and took the seating position as offered.

"Coffee and toast okay, Captain?"

"Is it all right?"

"Sure. You are as right as rain – that's what they told me anyway."

He didn't know what he wanted.

"The bathroom is over there," she pointed, "and the guard is over here," and she left him to fix some breakfast. The guard. I wonder if he would have shot me? He decided not to risk it, and made his way to the bathroom.

Shaved and showered, and in his own clothes, he felt better after finishing the toast and coffee. The doctor had gone over him again and pronounced him fit for duty, waving him away with, "The guard will escort you to the General's office. Have a nice day, Captain."

Laskie was ready for him but kept him waiting outside as he concluded another matter with Hudson. Captain Becker was in attendance, as was Colonel York and a new face from the CIA that Laskie had arranged on the quiet.

The plan to grab Major Sutton as he left the plane in Washington was scrapped. They thought that Sutton was bluffing about the arrangements to have material released if he didn't return, but it was too big a risk. The word had gone out from the White House that the Irish situation was receiving some Presidential interest following the Irish American lobby getting themselves on prime time TV news bulletins. Too risky to have Sutton taken out.

York asked about Dugway – so did Becker.

"We could cut a few million off our budget, General, if it didn't exist," advised Becker.

"The consequences are – what?" asked Laskie.

"Next to nothing. All we have is six officers and a couple of dozen others. The files show. . .," York referred to papers in front of him, ". . .the officer in charge retires soon. He could be retired early. The others – the electronics guy looks good – transfer him. The others – let me see – yes, transfer them too." York looked up from his papers. "It would tidy it all up, General. Dugway wouldn't exist as far as covert operations were concerned. No comebacks if there were leaks."

Laskie glanced at Luke Stanton, the visitor from the CIA. "We could use a good electronics guy if you don't want him. It's a 'him', is it?" Stanton asked.

"Yes – lives with his wife in Midvale – near Salt Lake City," York confirmed.

"What rank is he?" asked Stanton.

"Lieutenant," volunteered York.

"Promote him to Captain and get him a company house. That will sweeten the move for him – okay?" prompted Laskie.

" Okay with us, General," nodded Stanton.

"That's it then – agreed. Close the place down now, Charlie." York didn't move. "What's your problem, Charlie?" asked Laskie.

"What of Captain Hunter?"

"Forget him. After today he is out. Retired on medical grounds – okay?"

"In that case, I'd better get off to sick bay and have the captain's records sorted out. Do you need me to stay for your meeting with the captain?" asked York.

"All I need is this baby," as Laskie unlocked the drawer and placed his .45 on the desk. They all laughed – all except Stanton, whose hidden agenda was coming along nicely.

Laskie moved his Colt close to the edge of his desk, easy for his right hand to reach, and he checked to confirm that the sand bag was still in place.

"Charlie, before you go, is there some paper the captain needs to sign? To keep records in order, if you know what I mean?"

"I got you, Sir. I'll check it out and get back to you."

"Fine. As you leave, get Hudson to wheel him in," and, turning to Stanton, "This you won't believe." Laskie began to reread the UVF letter.

Captain Hunter marched in smartly, stood to attention and saluted. Laskie acknowledged the salute without looking up.

"Please be seated, Captain – and take it easy. I don't want you to have another heart attack." Hunter was about to say that it was only a faint, but was prevented from saying anything as Laskie was quick to continue. "Tell me, Captain, did they treat you well in sick bay? Good night's sleep and all that stuff?"

"Sir."

"Good — good," and, arriving at the bottom of the letter, he raised his eyes to look at Hunter. "Say — you sure look a lot better. Now, just let's remind ourselves of a few things — okay?"

Hunter was about to give his acknowledgement when the general placed the letter in front of him and picked up the gun and pointed it directly at the captain's head. After a moment, Laskie lowered his arm and returned the weapon to the drawer and locked it.

"We won't need this today, Captain, in view of your remarks yesterday. Just use this phone here. . ." and he pushed the phone towards Hunter, ". . .to call your IRA contact – okay? Now – Captain – let's be sure what we are trying to achieve. All I want to find out is this. This letter says the UVF have. . ." Laskie quoted, ". . .'destroyed and in some cases acquired arms from arms dumps.' Now – see if your contact confirms it – okay?"

"Sir."

"Good man, good man. Then using your skills as an intelligence officer, try and find out if they know who gave the UVF help — okay?"

"Sir."

"Any questions, Captain?"

"Yes, Sir. Just one – can I take a few minutes to work out what to say – and – can I see the letter, Sir?"

Laskie pushed the letter towards him and looked at his watch.

"You got ten minutes. Will that be enough for you, Captain?"

"I think so, Sir." and Hunter started to study the letter. Hunter knew that the gun stunt was only that — a stunt. He wouldn't get shot here – too many witnesses. That gave him enough comfort to concentrate on the letter. Hunter could read and assess what he read very quickly, a point that was noted in his file and known by Laskie and the others now present.

Eight minutes later, York returned from sick bay holding a few sheets of paper. He waved them at Laskie from the other side of the glass door, and entered the office when Laskie beckoned him to do so. The captain's concentration on the UVF letter and his planned phone call precluded him from seeing York hand Laskie the papers. York took his place between Stanton and Becker just behind Hunter.

"This should suit our purposes very well, Charlie. In triplicate, I see. One for records, one for Personnel, and one for the captain – right?"

York didn't speak in case he disturbed the captain, he just gave the general a thumbs up.

"Ten minutes about gone, Captain. Are you ready?"

Hunter leant forward to get closer to the desk and the phone, and, placing the letter in front of him, lifted the handset. "Yes, Sir. I think I have it. Can I go ahead?"

"You know the number, Captain?" asked Laskie in a most unbelieving manner.

"Yes, Sir."

Laskie stole a quick glance at those in the room, Stanton raised and lowered his head, Becker didn't move, and York pointed to his ear with one hand and to the phone with the other. Laskie understood.

"We'll have the speaker on, so we can all hear. That means you will be doing all the talking, Captain – okay? The rest of you, keep your noises in your belly."

Hunter started to dial.

"Wait." Laskie reached out and stopped Hunter getting any further. "Charlie, tell Hudson there are to be no interruptions," and pointed to the door. Laskie noticed the uncertain look on Hunter's face as he studied the letter again.

"Problem, Tommy?" It was the first time that Laskie had not addressed Hunter by rank.

"The 'other documents' that they say they will publish – any idea what they are, Sir?"

"Something called 'Ireland 6'."

"'Ireland 6'! How do you work that out, Sir?"

"A phone call from your friend Major Sutton, that's how. Anything else, Captain?" The general had reverted back to his rank.

"No, Sir."

Laskie looked at the others. "Okay?" They were ready, so Hunter began to dial for the second time.

"It's possible, Sir," Hunter suggested as he entered the number, "that there will be nobody there."

"In that case, Captain, we stay here until someone is in."

York concentrated hard on the captain's movement by the phone, and was able to see the digits being dialled. He took a note of the number, as no records would be available from Security, as the general's phone was a 'safe' line.

The CIA man cleared his throat as a precaution against a possible cough at a wrong moment

The connection was made, and the ringing of the phone in Ireland was heard through the speaker.

"Hullo?"

"Can I speak with Mr Magee, please? It's Captain Hunter speaking from the States."

There were a few seconds of silence.

"Captain Hunter, you say?"

"That's right. Is that you, Magee?"

"It depends. What do you want?" That was Magee's voice – Hunter recognised it.

"I have vital information that updates the earlier communication. It would take too long to send it the usual way – in fact it's possibly too late by now. Do you want it?"

There was another period of silence before Magee answered.

"Where are you phoning from, Captain Hunter? The phone sounds different."

"Different is right. I'm using a safe phone in the Pentagon, Washington – don't hang up. I've been ordered here following a big leak of information. Look – I could be interrupted – someone might come in – are you interested?"

There was less of a pause this time. "Surely – go ahead."

"Some guy called Captain Black of the UVF has claimed that the UVF have knocked out some IRA arms dumps and captured others – is that right?"

The silence returned, then, "How did you hear that?" The voice was firmer now and had an air of mild surprise.

"My superior in Washington got a damn letter from a Captain Black – that's how. I need to tell him it's a hoax, but I need confirmation that it *is* a hoax. Can you help me?"

"Help you!? You're the *cause* of it, Captain Hunter. Who else but you gave them the locations? I'll not be helping you."

So it's true! The UVF have not been bluffing, and the contents of the letter can be accepted. "There's more, Magee – there's more. It's possible, but not confirmed, that our earlier successes – I mean, earlier – those good times – well, the UVF have details of what happened. Can your people get confirmation on this?"

"You're in it now, all right. What's past is past, Captain Hunter. You can consider our business relationship at an end."

"I understand your anger, Magee – but who is trying to break this up? Someone or some group of people is putting a wedge between us. Who?"

"You must be stupid, Captain Hunter. I'll say this, and then it's goodbye. Have a look under your own table. The UVF are not big enough for this without getting help from your Government and the Brits." Magee hung up, leaving Hunter and the others looking at the emptiness that was their future. Only the CIA man appeared content.

Hunter was drained of whatever energy he had. He was breathing hard, leaning back in his chair, arms towards the floor, eyes closed, head back, and beaten. His IRA connection severed, his military career at an all-time low, and nothing to look forward to but a life at Dugway.

Becker, seeing the state he was in, went to the coffee jug and fixed five coffees, placing them on a tray and carrying them to the general's desk. "Try some of this – you look like you need it," he said and placed one of the cups in front of Hunter.

York went to the coffee table and brought the plate of four chocolate cookies to the table.

"Thanks, David," said Laskie as he took a cup from the tray, and urged the others to take a cookie. Laskie did without. The break was welcome and passed without interruption.

"Well. . . That's that," announced Laskie when he had finished. He looked at the empty cookie plate, not even a crumb. Very clean eaters here, he thought.

"Credit where credit is due, so – thanks, Captain," said Laskie. "You got what we were looking for." Laskie looked at Hunter, who appeared surprised at the unexpected praise. "It's okay, Captain. The information wasn't what we hoped for, but at least you got it." Laskie stood up, stretched, and sat down again.

"The next item for you to contemplate, Captain Hunter, is Major Sutton." Laskie phoned for Hudson and asked him to bring in the tape machine, which he did.

"Major Sutton called us, Captain, just after your heart attack. This is what he said."

The tape machine was switched on and the conversation between Laskie and Sutton, with muted asides from York and Becker, occupied Hunter's mind for its duration. Hunter sprang back from the desk at the sound of Major Sutton wanting his demise. Something not right – odd even. No, not odd – *wrong*. Hunter wasn't listening to the recording now, he was trying to remember. . .

"You got that, Captain?" asked Laskie as he examined the ceiling.

Hunter was thinking hard and didn't move. The silence brought Laskie from the ceiling back to Hunter. "Got something?"

"It's wrong, Sir – something not right. The conversation from Major Sutton is not right. Can I hear it again?"

Laskie shrugged his shoulders and waved at York, who ran the tape again. Hunter concentrated again.

Major Sutton's voice hit him again when he heard, "I want that two-timer Captain Hunter strung up – that's what. First he arranges for me and my buddy Major de Courcy to get on the IRA hit list, then he—"

"That's it, Sir! I have him – I have him!" The others were showing an interest in the captain's ability. Perhaps he could come up with something to save the day.

"Don't keep it a secret, Captain, let us all know how you have him," goaded Laskie. He had just about had enough of Captain Hunter and couldn't take him for much longer.

Hunter was quite excited at his discovery and began to move about the room in short fast steps, stopping occasionally to check his thoughts. This went on for a minute or two before he ventured to his seat and invited them to listen.

"Here it is, gentlemen. The sequence of events that I believe prove that Major Sutton is the leak to the IRA." His confidence had returned. He knew that Sutton had tried to get him, but he was too good for Major Sutton and would now show these people how real intelligence people worked. "Major Sutton was briefed in Dugway and left for Ireland at the same time that I sent a communication to Magee. Magee received the communication, but it was compromised. Major Sutton intercepted the communication in Dugway, read it, and posted it on to Magee. That's how he knows he was on the IRA hit list! Magee didn't tell him, *so how did he know*? He knew because he read the communication! Proof? The communication was posted by me in Dugway – Magee received it from Las Vegas. The connection? Major Sutton left here for Las Vegas before returning to Ireland. It fits – it fits!"

Hunter looked at the dark faces round the desk. What's wrong with them, he thought – can't they understand it?

The CIA man was having no more of this. From the time when the captain entered Laskie's office until now, he had kept quiet. He could keep quiet no longer.

"Captain Hunter," Stanton began, "are you telling me that as a serving officer in the US Army you gave instructions to a foreign terrorist organisation to eliminate one of your fellow officers?"

Hunter saw the trap he had fallen into. How could he get out of it? It was the major, he was convinced of it. The major was the only connection between Dugway and Las Vegas. Sutton was the bad egg.

"The major's the leak, Sir," Hunter responded to the CIA man, "I can prove it. It was the major who set this up to discredit the US with the help he got from the Loyalist terrorists – who else?"

"Why ask to have Major Sutton eliminated, Captain?" Stanton asked.

"It was – it was. . ." Hunter needed to move fast on this, ". . .a security measure to check out the reliability of the major. That's all –

a security check - and it worked!" Hunter looked at those conspiring to trap him, and didn't find a single friendly face.

"I think we have heard enough here - OK?" as Laskie took over the proceedings. "You have a choice, Captain." Laskie lifted the papers that York had produced earlier, and separated them before placing them in front of Hunter. "Sign these now and retire from the Army now, due to mental problems - or face getting kicked out with nothing." Laskie took a pen from an unlocked drawer and placed it on the paper.

"Retire, Sir?" Hunter was now the person who failed to understand. "Mental problems?"

"You get a pension, Captain. With a dismissal you get nothing."

Hunter wasn't going to go down without a fight. "Where's your proof of mental problems, Sir?"

"Are you kidding? For one, having Major Sutton put on a hit list, and two. . .," Laskie lifted one of the papers, ". . .I just fill in a few forms and sign them. Next question, Captain?"

York added to the captain's misery by giving backing to Laskie's remarks. "The surveillance information, Captain. There was no way Major Sutton could get it, but we do have records of you trying to get it. We have taped phone calls - remember your call to Captain Black Feather?"

Hunter picked up the pen and signed the forms, which Laskie had witnessed by York and Becker. Laskie retrieved the pen and returned it to the drawer, then he held out his hand, rubbing forefinger and thumb together, "I'll take your ID card, MISTER - please."

Hunter fumbled a while before finding a leather billfold; he opened it and withdrew his Army ID Card. Laskie noticed the Dugway Pass in the billfold. "I'll take that too, MISTER. Just regard yourself as being on a long vacation - thanks," and he took the plastic cards and ceremoniously dumped them in the waste basket. As soon as Hunter had left, he would shred them.

Laskie phoned for Hudson and had the civilian shown out with the words, "Enjoy your vacation - MISTER," ringing in his ears.

Chapter Forty

They walked arm in arm along the bay, stopping occasionally to see the Larne ferries make their way to Cairnryan or Stranraer. They had grown to be more than friends, and each knew it. Being in each other's company was sufficient as they returned to the cottage. No conversation, no strain, no small talk, but the attraction of being there in this beautiful place enjoying the pollution-free atmosphere and each other's presence.

The phone was ringing as they came to the cottage. De Courcy opened the door and stood aside to let Susannah enter, then he followed and answered the phone.

"Thank heavens I caught you, Major. It's Withers here – your American friend collapsed in town earlier today and we have him here. Can you come over?"

"Of course, Professor – same place?"

"Yes – the military wing."

Susannah heard the word 'professor' and waited until de Courcy had finished the call.

"It's Elmer. He's in hospital – I must go to see him, Susannah. I'm sorry about this – can I drop you off on the way?"

"Don't be sorry, Edward – of course you must go. I'll come with you, in fact I'll drive. You will not be in a proper state to drive. Car keys?"

"No, my dear – you would not be the most ideal of persons to be seen where I'm going. I'll drive you home – let's go."

*

"He will be all right. We got him in time," advised the professor. "You had better take these," and he handed de Courcy two envelopes.

"They were in his pocket – some US money and air tickets. He's in no state to fly, I'm afraid – not for a while anyway."

De Courcy took the envelopes and without checking the contents slipped them out of sight. The story of how Sutton was found in Oxford Street and brought to the hospital was relayed by the professor, who brought de Courcy up to date on the medical condition. De Courcy wasn't well enough informed to understand the professor's talk on the reaction of the human body to different types and strengths of drugs, but the professor told him anyway.

"We will vary the type of drugs for a while and see if they help him. It's still something of an unknown, you know. The latest from the hospitals in Texas and Aldershot suggest the Depleted Uranium cases do better on a variety of painkillers. However, I'm afraid the end result will be the same."

The end result, thought de Courcy, is the same for all of us, sooner or later. "Can I see him?"

"I don't see why not. This way," and he led de Courcy past one of the military guards into a room where they saw Sutton reading a newspaper.

"Hi, guys! Real nice to see you, Edward," was Sutton's welcome. "Sorry about this – I just passed out. Still, I got it arranged – we leave for Washington tomorrow. Did the doc give you the tickets, Edward?"

"Yes, old boy, I have the envelopes, but we need to talk about the trip. You are in no state to travel."

"Listen, Edward, the trip to Washington stands. We just postpone it a couple of days – okay?"

"We will see, old boy."

"We'll see about it now. I'll stay here tonight and tomorrow. You arrange to change the flights. Don't go near the Consul, phone the airline – okay?"

"And what of General Laskie?"

"Sure it will give him time to think we ain't coming! No. Use the you-know-what – and phone him. The third number is probably no use – remember the last time? They put us through from Dugway? Well, use the second number on the list for Washington. By the way, how is Susannah?"

"She wanted to come with me to see you – she is just fine, old boy."

"She sure is, old boy, old boy. Don't forget to pick me up, say midday tomorrow – right?"

The professor had left them to visit the pharmacy, where he arranged for a supply of painkillers for Sutton to be withdrawn, but had returned to hear the implied talk of leaving tomorrow. "What is this about midday tomorrow?"

"Our trip to Washington, Professor. He suggests putting it off for a couple of days – what do you think?"

"Not a good idea." The professor saw the resistance from Sutton. "I can't keep you here but I don't recommend you leave so soon."

"Thanks, Professor – thanks. I'll bring you back a souvenir.. We will only be away for four days. That's all – four days. Can you keep me in pills till I get back?"

The professor shook his head at de Courcy. "What's wrong with Americans, Edward? They always do what is bad for them."

Professor Withers reluctantly agreed to organising a supply of drugs that should keep the pain in abeyance for eight or nine days. He would also organise a note that should satisfy any drug enforcement checks at the airport.

*

De Courcy drove back to Island Magee and set up the satellite phone. "He's sick, you say, Major? When can he get here?" asked Laskie.

"We shall be delayed two days before he is fit enough to travel, but we shall return as planned, General."

Blast it. That means he'll only be here for two days. That will have to do. It must do, thought Laskie, as I can't force a retired officer to stay if he doesn't want to. "Right, Major. Okay, we will arrange to meet you on your arrival. Anything else?"

"He is a sick man, General, and he doesn't want you to know it."

"How sick?"

De Courcy told him.

Chapter Forty-One

De Courcy looked well in his plain light blue shirt with navy red polka dot tie, over which he wore a navy jacket. Light grey cotton crease-resistant trousers and black Barker shoes completed his outfit, which complemented Sutton's attire of white shirt with light blue jacket and navy trousers, and black leather sandals. They travelled with cabin baggage only, which enabled them to get round the inconvenience of waiting for luggage, allowing them to pass through Immigration near the front of the queue.

They had agreed to separate when leaving the aircraft, and to meet up at the Howard Johnson Hotel, where de Courcy had booked two rooms the day before through a travel agent in Larne. The hotel was 'middle of the road' in price, but the travel agent advised that it was comfortable, central, and therefore convenient to the best tourist spots – and was good value.

De Courcy had no problems passing through Immigration and Passport Control, and made his way to the exit, passing as he did so two US Army Officers keeping an eye out for someone. Once outside the building, de Courcy took a taxi and checked in to the hotel, advising the receptionist that Mr Sutton would not be arriving until later. He then made his way to the National Air and Space Museum, where the hours simply flew by.

Sutton deliberately took his time getting through Passport Control and, seeing the Army officers, waved and called them over.

"You guys looking for me?"

"Major Sutton?" the captain enquired.

"Yeah – that's right, except call me MISTER."

The officers were still looking around. "Where's the other one – Major de Courcy?"

"Oh – Mr de Courcy, you mean? He's gone on ahead – there's only me, okay?"

The captain shrugged and motioned to the other to accept the situation.

"This all you got?" the captain asked, looking at the small bag that Sutton had slung over his shoulder.

"That's it. Just the bag and a few papers here that General Laskie will want to see." Sutton patted his jacket pocket that bulged slightly.

The officers led him off to a waiting stretched limousine, where a sergeant opened the door and closed it behind them.

"Ah!" was the satisfying sigh from Sutton. "Good old Washington."

He looked around, taking in the familiar landmarks as the car transported them to the Pentagon. The car was stopped at the entrance where ID badges were shown, including Sutton's. The captain used the opportunity to take a look at Sutton's ID just to confirm that the passenger was who it was supposed to be. I should have done that earlier, the captain thought.

There was no preamble when he entered Laskie's office, apart from, "Coffee, Major? Try a chocolate cookie – they're good."

The coffee was tempting but, following a lecture from the professor on what not to eat or drink, Sutton asked for a glass of water and a tomato sandwich.

"A sandwich, Major?" Laskie found this funny but arranged for Hudson to fix it.

"Now, Major," as Laskie made sure that he was alone with Sutton. "Sit here and tell me that this is all a hoax – eh?"

Sutton sat where requested, still carrying his cabin bag. Without saying anything, Sutton opened the bag and removed two folders – one blue, the other red – and placed them on the desk in front of Laskie. Again, without a word, he took an envelope from his pocket and placed it on the desk.

"You might want to look at these, General. Start with the envelope, and then examine these babies," as Sutton hit the folders with his fists. "This should take you an hour, so I'll make my way to the canteen and get something while you and your boys check it out – okay?" and he got up and made his way to the door.

"Wait," Laskie said firmly as he gave Sutton a frown. He picked up the phone and asked York and Becker to join him, and arranged for a guard to accompany Sutton to the canteen with the order, "Bring him back here in one hour, Lieutenant, and don't let him wander around or leave."

Sutton gave Laskie a grin. "Don't worry, General – you'll not get rid of me until I see Captain Hunter. Just have him here when I return."

Hudson arrived with a plate of tomato sandwiches at the same time as York and Becker, and as the guard escorted Sutton to the canteen.

"Come in, boys, and take a look at this." Laskie showed them the folders and envelope still where Sutton had left them. Seeing Hudson and the sandwiches, "Leave those here, we might use them."

"Was that Major Sutton?" asked York. "Where is the other one?"

Laskie, holding his head in his hands, moaned, "He's around somewhere"

Laskie took up the envelope and withdrew the contents, inviting them to examine the evidence. The first of three pieces of paper showed a list of names, titles, and addresses of high-up people in the military and government in Washington. The sixth name on the military list was Laskie's. The second sheet was a copy of the UVF letter addressed to Laskie, and the third sheet was a copy of Hunter's letter to Magee that included the second page. York was able to confirm that the writing was Hunter's.

The folders had copies of what was later proved to be the missing 'Ireland 6' file, and the surveillance information that originated from themselves.

York had made out a list of questions to be put to Sutton, to try and fill the known gaps and to have Hunter's story confirmed or denied.

Properly fed and watered, Major Sutton returned to Laskie's office, where Laskie dismissed the guard and introduced Sutton to Becker and York.

"I see that you guys have had a good look at the stuff – right?" jibed Sutton as he saw the desk covered in the papers. "Do you consider these to be a hoax, General?"

"Well, Major Sutton – they are only copies. We would need to see the originals to check authenticity," as Laskie tried to outdo him.

"Is that so? Tell you what, General – you put your request in writing to the UVF and I'll deliver it for you."

"You don't mean," queried York, "that the UVF have the originals? Have you seen them?"

"Some of them, yes – I've seen them," lied Sutton.

"Damn!" General Laskie was somewhat displeased and banged the desk in time with his outburst. "This is dangerous stuff, Major. We must know how they got it."

"That can wait, General. I want to ask Captain Hunter why he put me and de Courcy on the IRA hit list. Where is he?"

"Forget him, Major. He's finished."

"Forget? No way, General. I want that guy, and I want him now."

They were getting nowhere and Laskie knew it. He would have to get Sutton off the Hunter track. "You're too late, Major. He was 'retired' – bad health – and he is no longer in the Army."

"You let him go?" shouted Sutton.

"He let himself go, Major. Suicide – killed himself yesterday."

York and Becker looked up smartly at that while Sutton was shocked into silence. The opportunity Laskie was waiting for had now presented itself to him, so he used it. "Captain Hunter was wrong, Major. He realised what he had done to you and couldn't take it. Now," Laskie cleared his throat, "let's see if we can put this to bed. Charlie, you have a question for the major?"

"Yes, Sir." York referred to his list of questions. Sutton saw the list, reached over and snatched it from him, saying, "Excuse me."

Sutton smiled back at the angry York, saying, "This will save you time, Colonel. I'll read the questions, and if I know the answer, I'll write it down for you – okay?" Sutton began to read the questions, but gave up as soon as he started. "Your writing is lousy, Colonel – here," and gave the list back to him.

Becker laughed but stopped when Laskie and York both gave him a rebuking glance.

"Major," began York, "the letter to the IRA from Captain Hunter – how did you get it?"

"The UVF have people everywhere," he answered as suggested by Susannah when she discussed how he should handle this meeting, "including the post office in Belfast. The letter was intercepted by them before being delivered."

"How did they know to stop *this* particular letter?"

"They didn't. They know Magee and look at everything addressed to him. This one they kept and sent him a copy."

"Did you not intercept it yourself at Dugway and wait until you were in Vegas, then posted it there?"

"I knew nothing about the letter 'til the UVF showed it to me," Sutton replied.

"Maybe," retorted York, "maybe not. I'll come back to that. Now, Major. What about the 'Ireland 6' file and the surveillance info. How did they get that?"

"I asked that one too, Colonel. You know what they said?"

Laskie was trying to retain his composure by rocking back and forward in his chair. "Oh, please, Major. Stop the games and give it to us straight," Laskie shouted.

"They said, 'The IRA have their friends in NORAID, National Caucus, and in the Irish American crowd, while we have ours in Washington,' and please stop calling me Major. Mister will do," Sutton teased.

York didn't like that. "Washington, you say. Where? Here in the Pentagon?"

"All they said was Washington. I asked for more, but didn't get it."

York looked at the list of questions on the list. There was nothing left to ask - except the money. "Who has the money, Major?"

Sutton noticed that Becker hadn't asked anything and had not participated in the proceedings. "He has it," and Sutton pointed to Becker. Before anyone reacted to his flippant remark, he continued, "The police don't have it, neither do the British Army nor the UVF. Neither do I or Mr de Courcy. So you are left with the IRA, or perhaps some unknown local farmer or fisherman - I don't know."

"The police? That's the RUC?" asked Laskie.

"Right," confirmed Sutton.

"How do you know they don't have it?" asked Becker.

"Oh," was the surprised tone from Sutton, "so you can speak. And I thought you were only here to eat my sandwiches." Sutton waved his hands in apology before Laskie had a chance to rebuke him. "The Army contacts we have, using Mr de Courcy, got us the information from the cops - okay?"

"Are you saying that the Brits know about the money?" Laskie asked, realising it was getting worse.

"Sure do. It was the Brits that helped us get the money from the bank in Carlisle, England over to Ireland. If you remember, you didn't want us to use a perfectly safe car ferry."

Laskie, York, and Becker ignored Sutton for a time while they discussed the information they had just received. Sutton listened as the discussion went from Dugway to the White House and included damage limitation and the possibility of bringing down the Administration. It was listening to them that gave Sutton the knowledge that they had closed down the Dugway operation and, more important to him, had accepted his answers as being the truth. That was good news. There was a good chance that if they asked him for his views, he would be able to give them the rest of the plan worked out by Susannah, and pass it off as his idea. Sutton interrupted their deliberations.

"Look, guys, I don't want to spoil your fun, but I would like to look around while I'm here. Tell you what – I'll push off and take in the Smithsonian or something, and see you tomorrow. Say 10.00 hours – okay?"

Laskie knew he couldn't retain him, and besides, there was more to discuss. "Tomorrow 10.00 hours will be fine, Major Sutton. Before you go, have you anything to add that might get us out of this mess?"

What an opportunity! It wouldn't come again, so he had to use it now and hoped he wouldn't put his foot in it.

"I sure can, General, but you won't like it. Do you want to hear me?"

Laskie nodded, "We'll take all the help we can get – shoot."

Sutton pulled his chair closer to the desk, and with his right hand moved the papers aside to find a clear spot to lean on. "The UVF are small compared to the IRA, but they are not that small that they can't cause trouble. Get some of your people, General, to look up the history. They are not good propagandists like the IRA, they are mostly thugs. Thugs with the Ulster Protestant ethic. That means, they stick to an agreement but expect you to stick to it too. Captain Hunter promised them money if they took out IRA arms dumps. They did it, but have yet to be paid. So," Sutton looked at the tired faces, "all you have to do is pay them."

Laskie shook his head. "It's not as easy as that. What's to prevent them publishing the stuff anyway, and that's for starters. Two

- they want the locations of the IRA dumps in what they call Eire. We can't do that."

Sutton let them wait for his next piece of advice, which allowed York to bring in, "Blackmail! We pay once, we will be paying for ever"

Sutton continued. "I did say you wouldn't like it, General - but just check out their history. They keep their word. There has never been any kind of blackmail in the past. All you need say is that any surveillance information they received was by theft, as proper authority was not and would not be, given for it. That means that no more information of this kind is available." Sutton stopped to gather his thoughts, and was pleased that he managed to recall all that was rehearsed with de Courcy and Susannah. "See you tomorrow, General - okay?" and he got up and moved to the door.

"Right, Major - tomorrow at 10.00," Laskie acknowledged and nodded to Hudson through the glass partition to let Sutton go.

In the silence that followed, Laskie gathered up the papers into a single pile.

"Well, Charlie - what do you think? Is it a bluff?"

"It's no bluff, Sir. This stuff is real, and the major came up with answers that fit."

"And you?" as Laskie looked at Becker.

"I agree, Sir. There's nothing that can't be pointed to anyone except Captain Hunter. The missing capital?" He shook his head. "That looks a lost cause - no sign of it - I'm inclined to accept the major's line on it."

There was another silence, broken by Laskie calling for a break. "What a mess. Let's stop for an hour, have something to eat, and maybe we can arrive at some decisions."

They left for the canteen with Becker saying, "That was a surprise about Hunter killing himself, General. Any throwback to us?"

"Say nothing. He's still around, but I don't want Sutton to know."

Chapter Forty-Two

De Courcy was comfortably tired as he entered the hotel carrying two quite heavy plastic carrier bags. Souvenirs of books on the history of space flight, and three high-quality glass mugs, each engraved with pictures of aircraft long assigned into recycling.

The receptionist confirmed that Mr Sutton had checked in, so de Courcy called him from the lobby. "How did you get on, old boy? Any problems?"

"So far so good, Edward. I go back tomorrow to finish it. How about dinner?"

Half an hour later saw each showered and shaved and in the main restaurant of the hotel exchanging experiences. De Courcy noticed a display of 'What's on' leaflets when he entered the restaurant, and he took one, folded it, and stuffed it in his pocket. Over their second cup of coffee, de Courcy produced the leaflet and wondered if there was anything that would interest them.

"Go easy on the coffee, old boy – what would you suggest," de Courcy handed him the leaflet "provided the head is up to it?"

"It's fine right now. The new pills are doing their job – let me see," and he examined the leaflet. Sutton noticed an item for 'I-Max' and read of a large-screened cinema, with multi-channel sound. Duration about seventy minutes. He showed it to de Courcy, who agreed to give it a go.

They travelled by taxi to the I-Max cinema, joined the queue of a hundred or so, and waited for fifteen minutes before managing to get two of the best seats. They found themselves halfway up and in the centre. The seats were functional rather than comfortable, and the screen was a curtainless curved white wall stretching for what seemed like miles in all directions. It was so big that they had to turn their head from left to right and up and down to take it all in.

"If the picture is this big, we could have watched it in our hotel!" Sutton remarked.

The auditorium filled quickly; most were tourists like themselves, and making the usual noises of expectant punters seeking their money's worth.

The lights dimmed, the sound began, making a few cracks, and then the picture. De Courcy was disappointed when the first scene was an old film showing early attempts at flight, filling no more than a fraction of the screen. The change was dramatic. The screen was suddenly filled, the sound full and clear, and space shuttle flight became a reality to those sitting there.

*

An all-day guided tour of Washington was gratefully accepted by de Courcy while Sutton returned to the Pentagon for 'Part two' of his encounter with General Laskie.

The meeting began with sandwiches – egg and watercress this time – and a choice of coffee, fruit juice, beer, or tea.

"Tea? I've had enough tea to do me, General. Make mine a fruit juice," answered Sutton to the request from Laskie. Hudson fixed the drinks and was asked to join them in the elevated position as waiter. "Mind you, tea can be a better thirst quencher than coffee at times," added Sutton.

"You gone off coffee, Major?" asked York.

"Yeah – it gives me migraine which eases when I knock off the coffee."

When all had finished, Hudson cleared up and left the four of them to their business.

"We have been working at this, Major," started Laskie, "and here's the deal. As I see it, we are running a 'damage limitation' exercise. Charlie, you give him the run-down."

York sat up. "Yes, Sir." York always had paper in front of him to refer to, and this occasion was no different. Referring to the sheet on the top, he announced the security angle, starting with the shut-down of Dugway, and finished with the demand for the return of the satellite phone together with any arms and unused rounds of ammunition. Sutton agreed to the return of the equipment, as long as it was collected. Neither he nor de Courcy were delivery boys, he said.

York finished his party piece announcing that any connection between the US Government or any of its military with the UVF would be strongly denied, and would prove to be false if the UVF decided to publish. Sutton listened, but wasn't interested in York's party piece. Sutton thought that Becker and York had probably worked on this mess most of the night. They were certainly looking tired and were trying hard to impress Laskie and pass the buck elsewhere, or at least keep themselves clean.

It was now Becker's turn. Sutton glanced at his watch in a manner that conveyed urgency. Becker noticed and went straight in. "The money is not from the US Government, or the military. We know nothing about it. Where it comes from is not traceable, and not, I repeat, *not* to be repeated. I don't care how you chose to word it, but it's NOT money from America," he emphasised.

"How much are you talking about, Captain?" asked Sutton.

"The agreed amount: $330,000."

"What's in it for me?" asked Sutton innocently.

"What the hell does that mean?" yelled Laskie.

Sutton wasn't expecting such a reaction. Surely they had thought about his share during their discussions? It didn't seem so if the body language now displayed was anything to go by. "Take it easy, General." Sutton had raised both hands to head height with palms open. "Captain Hunter implied that I wouldn't lose out on this. Well, so far I've got nothing. Neither has Mr de Courcy."

Laskie was having none of it. He wanted this whole project closed down, not turned into a pay-day for the boys.

"Forget it, Major. Like me, you'll make do with your salary – okay?" responded Laskie with a few grunts, a shake of the head and, "I don't believe the US Army has such people, I really don't."

"They don't, General," came back Sutton's reply. "I'm not on salary, remember? I get nothing for this. I'm retired."

Laskie, Becker and York had somehow overlooked that angle, a point that Sutton himself now realised from their appearance. None talked, moved, or made any sign of life for a few seconds, then Becker came in to save the day. "What had you in mind, Major, or should I say, Mister Sutton?"

"Mister, will do just fine, along with a minimum of $50,000 each. And no funny business. Just credit my bank account like it was an additional pension. I don't need to mess around with cash like the last time! And no tax deductions either! The same for Mr de Courcy, and," he produced a small piece of white card from an inside pocket and let it fall on the desk, "Here are Mr de Courcy's bank account details – okay? You already know mine."

Laskie looked at the card, then at Sutton and back to the card again. Then he moved on to Becker; surely he could find a way out? There was no response.

Sutton offered them the opportunity to talk it over while he stretched his legs and visited the bathroom, and they agreed.

"Something to think about before I go, gentlemen," suggested Sutton, "I said a *minimum* of $50,000. There *is* such a thing as 'goodwill'," and he left the room for twenty minutes.

*

De Courcy and Sutton were met at the check-in desk by Becker, who handed Sutton a sealed envelope and departed without saying anything.

"Friend of yours, old boy?"

"Not any more, old boy, old boy," Sutton replied as he felt the envelope trying to guess its contents. He was told to expect a package at the airport, but wasn't expecting such a thin one. The meeting the previous day ended quickly with Laskie waiting for him alone when he returned from his twenty-minute break. He recalled the conversation again as he had when briefing de Courcy at dinner.

"Well, Mr Sutton," Laskie had said, "it's a permanent goodbye, and I trust we never meet again. Captain Becker will deliver a package to you at the airport tomorrow when you leave, and that's it. If you don't like it, too bad." Laskie then showed Sutton out of his office and ordered Hudson to, "Show him what the outside of the door looks like, and don't let him back in."

Sutton cut open the envelope using a pen he borrowed from the check-in clerk, and quickly examined the contents. Without reading it, he saw the contents were two or three folded sheets of paper. No bomb or incendiary to be seen. Satisfied for the time being, he pocketed it and saw the check-in clerk waiting for something.

"Yeah?"

"My pen, Sir?"

"Sorry. I get all my pens that way," and he returned it.

They entered the departure lounge, having gone through the usual checks of baggage and passport examination, and waited for the flight to be called.

When they had reached Mach 2, Sutton recovered the envelope and started to read the papers. His muffled laughter was infectious, causing de Courcy to join in, not knowing why. He handed the top sheet to de Courcy and started on the second sheet. It was de Courcy's turn to laugh. He read:

> "1. Use the same solicitor and bank as before. Delay one week to give us time to set it up.
>
> 2. This is the end of it – there will be no more.
>
> 3. As a goodwill gesture, each of your bank accounts will be credited $75,000 within five days.
>
> 4. For your own protection, destroy this paper."

They enjoyed the moment and acknowledged that the success of their mission was entirely Mrs Lacy's. They had followed her ideas and they came off. The laughter continued on and off during their Concorde dinner, which was surprisingly good for aircraft catering.

The second sheet gave the bearer access to the funds that would be obtained through the solicitor in Carlisle.

"Tell me, old boy, does this sort of thing go on often within your Army? Because I could do with another free trip to Washington!" De Courcy nearly spilt his drink as he started to laugh again. What a mess, he thought. Probably due to the size of the US military, making it difficult to audit and monitor what goes on.

"One and only, Edward. There is only one outfit like the one run by General Laskie." Sutton managed to stop himself laughing for a moment to add, "I think we should ask for a transfer to Laskie's outfit – think of the vacations!"

They enjoyed the journey to London and managed to catch their connecting flight to Belfast within two hours of landing.

"Let's not say anything, Elmer, until it's completed," warned de Courcy. "No point in letting the UVF know we managed it until the chicken has hatched."

"Good idea, Edward. I tell you this for free – no way am I using one of your underwater chariot things again – right?"

They were over Liverpool now, and heading out to the Irish Sea.

"Don't worry, old boy – we will do it our way this time. No cash, just a paper transaction. Let me work on it. How's the head, old boy?"

Surprisingly, he had no trouble with it over the past three days, and managed to keep to the dose recommended by the professor. "Just fine, Edward, just fine. What will you say to Susannah?"

"I don't know. I'll wait until the money has arrived."

*

She met them at the airport and drove them home. She was finding their silence confusing. "What happened, then?"

"We will not know for another week. I think it went according to plan, but. . . We shall wait and see. Any news while we were away?" de Courcy asked.

"The usual. This side blames that side, who in turn blames everybody else, while more people get killed. Another bomb yesterday. I forget where – there are too many to remember each one." She thought of the sad state of affairs, where the extreme left or right with access to explosives show how powerful they are by killing people, that in turn destroys relationships and damages society. Was it always thus? Did it exist in the minds of people and lie dormant until technology and the criminal mind combined to release the hate on to society? Freedom is fragile and requires constant vigilance for it to survive.

The cloud cover was low on their journey to Carrickfergus from Ballynure, and it was damp, cold, and not at all like Washington. But it was home.

They arrived at the cottage and soon had tea and toast, while sharing in the events of recent days.

"Something for you, my dear," as de Courcy produced one of the glass mugs and presented it to her. "I haven't forgotten you, Elmer," and presented him with the second mug. Neither expected it, which made it all the more welcome. Susannah was already treasuring it – his first gift to her bought with his own money. She didn't know about the cash from the Consul.

*

The following week saw the rain continue at a slow drizzle, broken by a few bright spells when the clouds had given up its contents. A couple of phone calls confirmed that they were each the richer by about £50,000 – a fact that was celebrated in style by having a sausage soda at the Larne Market, complete with onion rings and tomato sauce.

Susannah confirmed that if the money came through, de Courcy's plan would be acceptable to the Council. So arrangements were made to visit the solicitor and bank in Carlisle.

Chapter Forty-Three

Mr Hunter made his mind up to destroy that which had destroyed him. His worldly possessions were few and easy to turn into cash. He sold the contents of the apartment to the landlord, and his vehicle to the first garage he came across, and converted most of the cash into American Express travellers cheques and got out of America.

His officer training had equipped him with the art of travelling light and fast, and, having disposed of his army clothes, he arrived in London travelling economy on a Boeing 747. He spent a week in London, in a bed and breakfast, in what he considered a dump in Norfolk Square near Paddington Railway Station, and took in the tourist sights without enthusiasm. He didn't particularly like London. In fact, he didn't particularly like anywhere, but it was better than Dugway and it was away from Washington. He wanted to be sure within himself that he wanted to do this thing. Take time to make sure, he thought. Stay a week in London. If he felt the same, then he would go ahead.

He did feel the same, so he went ahead.

He didn't know anybody in Ireland except Magee and Sutton, but he knew Magee's address so would start from there. Hunter purchased a map of Northern Ireland in a large book store and began to study it, to familiarise himself in a general way where places were. He found Belfast and Cushendall on the map, and guessed that once he was in Cushendall and had explained his plan to Magee, he would be able with Magee's assistance to find Sutton and his Brit friend, de Courcy.

Hunter left the dump in Norfolk Square and made his way to Heathrow, finding it quite easy to understand the colour-coded Underground system.

British Midland was a pound or two cheaper than British Airways, so he purchased a one-way ticket on the next available flight to Belfast, and checked in.

Arriving at Belfast International Airport at Aldergrove, he was surprised how clean and pleasant it looked. Certainly not what an airport in this savage underdeveloped part of the world should look like. After all, he was in Northern Ireland, the land of the IRA gun and the British invader.

The small shuttle bus took him to the centre of Belfast, where he soon found himself in a clean and tidy bus station, and minutes later he was on the only bus that day going through Cushendall. It was cooler than he expected, and the rain seeped into everything.

He sat near the back and felt every stone and pothole that the driver purposely drove over until, an eternity later, heard the driver's voice announce, "Your stop, Mister – this is Cushendall." In no time he was standing alone in that town, and followed the bus with his eye as it travelled round the corner and out of sight, splashing anyone unfortunate enough to be out in such weather.

"Come in out of the rain, man – you'll catch your death," was the voice behind him of a man standing in the shop doorway.

Hunter swung round to see the smiling face of a baker, complete with floury hands, beckon him.

"Thanks. I will be glad to," and he entered the shop, carefully trying not to wet anything.

"I hear you're not from these parts, then," the baker continued in an accent that Hunter found was hard to understand. It was similar to Magee's, but had differences.

"That's right. I've arrived from the States and thought I would look up a guy I met some time ago." Hunter looked at the place, which had the smell of sweetness – dough and sugar. There were a number of framed certificates on the wall behind the counter, giving credence to the proprietor's skill in his art.

"I see," the baker went on, "and who would that be, then?"

"Magee. A Mr Liam Magee. Do you know where he's at?"

"Magee? Surely," and he pointed to the dark building across the street. "That's Magee's place over there."

That close? Hunter felt better about the place and, expressing his appreciation, left the baker's shop with the man talking to himself saying, "Watch yourself with that one. . ." and he crossed the road. Hunter entered Magee's shop without hesitation and made sure that the door closed behind him. There was a grill at the far end of the shop, behind which the figure of a man could be seen. Hunter summed up the shop as rather like a hovel and of little value.

"Hang on there, I'll be right with you." It was Magee's voice – the man behind the grill was Magee. That was easy. Now the rest should also be easy, provided he played it right. Magee came into the customer area of the shop from behind the grill that served to segregate and secure the post office part of his business. Magee examined the rain-soaked stranger before him. His expression managed to ask the customer what he wanted without having to say anything, a skill that countless shop assistants have mastered over the centuries.

"Hi! Mr Magee? I'm Tom Hunter, formerly a captain in the US Army – remember me? I'm here to ask a favour."

Magee moved quickly to the door of the shop, opened it, and looked up and down the street – saw nobody, closed the door, and turned to face Hunter. "Are you alone? Quick – are you alone?"

"Sure I'm alone. What's the problem?"

Magee stole a further look outside, saw nobody, and briskly pushed Hunter into the rear of the premises.

"Jarvis – are you there?" Magee shouted.

"What do you want?" was a reply from outside somewhere.

"Look after the shop – something has come up," Magee replied.

"All right," was the disdainful reply of the reluctant shop assistant; a door opened, and Jarvis McBrien entered from a store area into the rear of the shop.

"Look who's here, Jarvis," Magee said softly. "It's Captain Hunter from Dugway."

McBrien stopped in his tracks and stared at the damp looking specimen standing beside Magee. "So, you're the smart one that sends us messages – eh? And now you come here to die, and that's a fact," stated McBrien in a manner in which he would address a wasp before killing it.

"Shop, Jarvis. Leave this to me," and Magee sat down while McBrien went into the shop. "Now," Magee cleared his throat," any chance of you telling me what you are doing here, Captain Hunter?"

Hunter took off his wet jacket, placed it over the back of a wooden chair, and told Magee of his plans. ". . .so I know that Major Sutton is behind it all – I know it. The stupid fools in the Pentagon couldn't see it. You know what they did? They threw me out of the Army,"

Hunter nodded to emphasise the point. "They threw me out. It was either that or a court martial and, Liam – it's all Major's Sutton's doing. So I'm here on my own to kill him."

Magee now knew that Hunter was mad. He had thought so before, and now it had been confirmed. Magee believed Hunter to be dangerous, he might even be armed. All right then, he thought, I'll play along with him for now.

"You look a mite tired, Captain Hunter. How about a hot bath and something to eat, then we can discuss it?"

At last Hunter could relax, and accepted the offer. "Just call me Tom. I'm no longer a captain."

"Where is your luggage, Tom?" enquired Magee.

"This is it," as Hunter lifted his bag and put it on the chair. "I travel light."

Magee saw that it was small, but big enough to hide a decent weapon or two,

"Say, Liam – any chance of getting these clothes dried off? Where's the bath?"

Magee noticed the gain in confidence, but played along, and took him to the bathroom upstairs.

"You'll be needing something to wear 'til your clothes are dried – try these," and a pair of not too clean jeans, a shirt, and sweater were taken out of a wardrobe and handed to Hunter.

"Yeah – thanks, Liam. Wait." Hunter ran the water into the bath, checked the temperature, and started to undress. "Here, take my clothes – okay?" and gave the bundle to Magee, who took them and returned to the back of the shop, and threw the bundle into a tumble-drier. Magee had already checked them for items of value, or interest, and apart from a few coins there was nothing. Magee decided let McBrien do the rest, so went into the shop and waited until the customer McBrien was serving had left.

"He's in the bath," Magee advised, "so take the opportunity to search his bag and jacket. Use the sideboard."

That's more like it, thought McBrien, and right up my street. McBrien knew how to search and set out items of interest from the training days in prison. He didn't take long to lay out the contents of Hunter's jacket on a tray. Then he placed the tray on top of the tumble-drier that was still removing the damp from not very clean clothes. The tray held a US passport, some US dollars, a map of

London, a map of Northern Ireland, two handkerchiefs, some American Express travel cheques, a pen, and the remains of two airline boarding passes and air tickets. The bag contained a change of clothes, a pair of good quality Reebok trainers that would cover foot and ankle, and a pair of Leica 10×42 binoculars inside a protective case.

"Look at these, Liam," said McBrien, showing off the binoculars by looking through them to the other side of the street. "Boy, these are good," he commented as a clear picture of the baker opposite came into view. "These must cost a pound or two, they—"

"Any weapons?" Magee interrupted.

"No. Nothing."

"Probably hidden somewhere before he came here."

Magee looked at the clock above the grill of the post office area and, noticing that the collection van would be due anytime, suggested to McBrien that he kept Hunter company – and quiet – until the van left. Then he would close the shop and have their prisoner interrogated before killing him.

"Now you're talking," replied McBrien. "Just leave him to me," and he returned to the display of items on the sideboard.

Hunter's footsteps were heard on the bare wooden stairs, and then they stopped as he reached the worn carpet of the floor. Hunter opened the door to the back room and saw McBrien examining his passport.

"Hey – what's the big idea—?"

"Just shut your trap and sit here." McBrien indicated the chair that had Hunter's jacket over it.

"Give me that passport," Hunter demanded, and made a grab for it. That was a mistake. McBrien stepped back and, using Hunter's momentum, threw the off-balanced body over his shoulder. Hunter landed painfully on the floor in a heap, dazed and winded.

"You deaf? I said shut up – remember? Now, stay where you are – don't even think of moving." McBrien had his right foot placed on Hunter's chest, pinning him to the floor. As he relaxed the pressure, Hunter used his left arm to force the leg away, whereupon McBrien pivoted full circle and kicked Hunter in the back. Hunter groaned and raised a hand in surrender. McBrien smiled at his handiwork and placed the passport back on the tray.

"Where is your gun, Mr Hunter?" asked McBrien.

"Are you nuts? You can't get a gun past airport security, you should know that."

"Of course you can. We do it all the time," McBrien retorted and smiled at the heap trying to ease the pain in his back by moving about.

Traces of a faint conversation were heard coming from the shop, and McBrien brought his finger to his mouth to indicate silence. The Post Office van had arrived to take away the two parcels and the single registered letter to the sorting office in Ballymena. The conversation ended, and Magee was heard closing up the shop.

"What's happened to him?" as if Magee couldn't guess as he saw Hunter continue to ease the back pain.

"He fell," smiled McBrien, "and he says he has no gun."

"Too right I've no gun – that's the favour I need from you guys." Hunter struggled to his feet, still feeling the force of McBrien's kick, and decided to sit down. "You sure have a way of hurting people, Jarvis." Hunter remembered how Magee had addressed him, and used his name.

"Before you get anything from us, Mr Hunter, we want some information," Magee stated calmly. He went over to the tray of items that were still on the tumble-drier, and moved the tray to the sideboard, beside Hunter. The drier had just completed its task and the damp smell stopped.

"First – how did you get here? I want all the details, then second, why?"

Hunter tried to relax. "That's not a problem, Liam. First – I flew here, stopping off in London for a while, then on to Belfast. I know your address, so took a bus." Hunter stopped rubbing his back, which wasn't so bad now. He looked at Magee, then at McBrien, who looked away from him.

"Second – the reason I'm here is to settle, permanently, my score with Major Sutton – I already told you – and the Brit sidekick. That's why I need a gun. The favour I mentioned. Just get me a gun, any sort will do, and I'll get rid of them – okay?"

Magee sneered at Hunter's remarks. "Tell me, Mr Hunter, how many people have you yourself killed with a gun? And you call me Mr Magee."

"What do you mean?" Hunter didn't see the problem. All they had to do was to go to one of their arsenals and get him a gun and a few rounds.

"Just answer – how many people have you killed over the past ten years?" Magee pressed.

"How many? None. But what's the big deal?" pleaded Hunter with open hands.

"You have no idea, have you?" Magee turned to McBrien, "Imagine giving him a gun! Not only would he get himself killed – which doesn't matter – but he could lead the Brits to our door, and he wants to know what's the big deal!"

McBrien smirked at Hunter, spitting out at him, "Americans! You're more trouble than you're worth, Mr Hunter."

"You guys owe me," shouted Hunter. "You owe me. I delivered good for you guys, and you know it. All I want in return is a gun to put away an American. If you hate Americans, give me a chance to get rid of one for you – eh?"

The memories of the past began to flood back. McBrien remembered how amazed he was at the information coming from some unknown in America called Captain Hunter, and how impressed he was at the success that flowed from putting Hunter's plans into operation. Yes, it was good, and yes, they enjoyed the success. But that was it – now it was over. History was history and it would be too dangerous to set him loose with a gun. Getting their own people properly trained and disciplined to use a gun was hard enough, but this foreigner?

There might be a way, but Magee would have to agree.

"Have you ever shot a gun – at any time?" McBrien asked.

"Are you nuts? Of course I have! Every year at firearms refresher course – and I'm good too. Just try me," Hunter pleaded.

"I might consider it. What do you think, Liam? Do we owe him that much?"

Magee remembered past successes just as vividly as McBrien.

"We appreciate what you did, Mr Hunter, but we don't owe you a thing. What you did, you did because you wanted to, not to make us owe you," and Magee emphasised the point by stabbing him with his finger.

"I know, I know, Mr Magee," agreed Hunter, "but I can't give you guys any more stuff now. That Major Sutton put paid to that." Hunter stood up and shrugged his shoulders, ignoring the back pain. "But I could at least stop him from ruining any future plans. If you think that's a good idea?"

Magee latched on to the word 'future'. "What could happen in the future that needs your help, Mr Hunter?"

"Me? Not me – I'm out of it thanks to Sutton – but there are others still in the Pentagon who can continue the job."

That interested Magee sufficiently to allow Hunter to continue. Hunter span them a believable yarn saying that he couldn't have achieved his success without others knowing what he was doing, those others included top brass in Washington who were still in place. "Of course, should they get to hear that you guys turn round and bumped me off after the successes I got you, then. . ." he shrugged again, ". . .they could decide to forget it, if that's how you show your thanks."

Far fetched, but just possible, thought Magee. Just believable enough, perhaps, to reconsider letting him show us what he could do with a gun. "Leave it with me, Mr Hunter. I'll need to speak to some people. In the meantime, you had better stay here and out of sight for a few days. Jarvis, put his passport away – for safe keeping – okay?"

McBrien lifted the passport and pocketed it.

Chapter Forty-Four

The solicitor had the paperwork prepared, and compared the authorisation sheet that Sutton had with that received from Washington. All was in order, and the visit to the bank arranged. The bank manager invited them into his office, and within minutes handed over a bank draft drawn on London for £216,316.06, saying, "The rate is 1.5252 less our commission charges of £50, gentlemen. I trust you find everything in order?"

They returned to Larne, using the ferry from Cairnryan, and made their way to Ballycarry. During the short journey, de Courcy saw Sutton swallow a pill or two from his pill box. "Head giving you bother?" That's all de Courcy could think of saying.

"Yeah."

Ballycarry was not as inviting as before. The rain changed the town's appearance as it usually does, and the temperature had fallen, making it necessary to turn on the car's heater to demist the windscreen.

The Honda was seen by Mrs Lacy's minder, who went to the house, knocked on the door, then vanished into the dampness.

Susannah came to the door as the car stopped in the drive. De Courcy returned her wave and allowed Sutton to enter the house before him.

"His pain has returned, poor chap," de Courcy advised Susannah quietly. "A glass of water would be welcomed, I'm sure."

Knowing that they were coming, Susannah set before them a meal of home-made Irish stew, home-made scones with strawberry jam, and tea. Joe Lacy joined in the small talk and wasn't misinterpreting the body language between his sister-in-law and de Courcy.

"That was a meal to remember, Susannah," began Sutton. "I'll probably have another belly ache!" Pain in the head or not, Sutton's sense of humour was as sharp as any round the table. She feigned injury as the others laughed.

De Courcy concluded the main business of the day by handing over the envelope containing the bank draft. "As the Americans would say, 'What do you think of these potatoes?'"

"Apples, Edward – it's apples," corrected Sutton.

She opened the envelope and withdrew the document.

*

The Secretary of State for Defense, Melvin Avery III, had emerged from the meeting to talk to T. J. Smith, the Director of the CIA, at the request of the President. The President had made a disturbing comment at the meeting that required immediate attention. The President was understandably angry.

"It's bad enough," the President said to T.J., "having to fight Congress, but when some subordinates in the Pentagon are doing things behind my back, like an 'Oliver North' job, I wonder what sort of a country we are changing into. Here's some information I got from Prime Minister Major, T.J. Will you and Melvin sort this out? I suggest you both go now. This meeting is nearly over anyway."

The information was on paper. The world survives on paper and fast food, and would starve without them.

"What's he on about, T.J? He's using every trick he can to get votes and then some – what's this on the Prime Minister? Is it hot?" Avery asked.

T.J. was reading over the papers while walking down the corridor in the White House. He stopped.

"Holy—!" T.J. moved at double time, past Avery and towards the exit to his car.

"Hey! What's bitten you?"

"Hot it is. Quick – get to my office fast – follow me," and shouted over his shoulder as he ran to his car, "Get your Chief of Staff there as well."

Secretary of Defence Avery caught up with T. J. Smith and managed to stop him before he got into his car. "I'm blind so far, T.J. Tell me what's on. Let me read the blasted paper!"

"I'll tell you this much," T.J. moved closer to the Secretary, "the British Prime Minister accuses the Pentagon of funding the IRA and the UVF in Northern Ireland, and has proof. We have a few loose bullets to sort out. See you in my office," and was driven off, leaving Avery standing there.

The Chief of Staff, Colin Travis-Whiting, together with the Assistant Director of the CIA, called unannounced on General Laskie, and were ready to hit the place hard.

Laskie was relaxing over coffee and a chocolate cookie when they arrived.

"This is a surprise," Laskie began.   "Have a seat, you guys, and—"

"What explanation do you have for this, General?" shouted Chief of Staff Travis-Whiting, throwing the evidence in front of him. Laskie wasn't in the best frame of mind to be shouted at by the number one military man in the country. Not in front of a civilian like the Assistant Director of the CIA, anyway.

"Explanation, Sir?" as he took his first look at the evidence. He recognised it immediately. The papers included a copy of the UVF letter, and a document from 'Ireland 6'.

"Where did you get this?" Laskie asked, open-eyed, pale and shaking in anger.

"From the President."

"The Pre—"

"Who got it from the British Prime Minister. Now – TALK!"

*

The cuts in government spending exceeded their expectations with a few early retirements and closures of certain covert intelligence sections deemed no longer necessary. All due to the end of the Cold War and the better relationship between East and West. The President gained a few votes from the left of the Government, and assured the British Prime Minister that those trying to forge a wedge in the 'special relationship', by devious means, would not succeed. The President extended an invitation to the Prime Minister to visit Washington, which was accepted, and he also assured him that he would do all he could to get the IRA to hand over its arms.

The reorganisation within the Pentagon saw a Major Black Feather being appointed to be in charge of covert intelligence and within the CIA, Captain Croft heading up the electronic surveillance research unit.

*

Sam the Smoke was on duty that Friday. The General had convened the Council to give audience and allow everyone to voice their opinion on recent IRA bombings. It was extremely dull hearing the condemnations from people who would carry out the same actions against the enemy, if only they had the resources.

Susannah didn't participate in the vitriol, and wasn't really listening. When it came to 'Any Other Business', she would wake them up. The agenda was not in written form, neither were minutes recorded. Should there ever be a raid, there would be nothing to condemn them, except what their memories held, and no court had managed to achieve much with that.

As usual, the General was controlling the gathering with a professionalism that showed he had experience chairing meetings. Susannah wondered what he did for a living. The General was not from the working class society.

"Any other business? Has anybody a contribution to make on matters not covered?"

Was it that time already? Susannah removed the envelope from her hand bag and got the General's attention.

"Yes, Susannah?"

She remained seated. "The Council may be interested to know that the strategy adopted over the surveillance information has produced results." She held up the envelope. "I have here a contribution to the Loyalist Prisoners Welfare Fund, amounting to £216,316.06." Calmly and slowly, she separated the bank draft from the envelope and placed it on the table in front of the General.

There was pandemonium that must have lasted a full five minutes. The laughter and smiles were infectious, and she couldn't help but join in. Susannah could ask for anything now, and they would grant it. Or at least would give her a fair hearing, and that's all she wanted. They gave a respect that was based on her results, not because she was the widow of a former member. In her own right, she was an equal.

They promised to talk to the commanders in the field and report back their reaction to her suggestion. Her suggestion of a ceasefire. It was not even considered before, but she had proved herself and they were willing to listen. It would certainly swing the publicity machine of the media away from the IRA and towards the UVF if they were first to bring about a ceasefire.

The members leaving the hidden chamber were subdued and thoughtful. Not the noisy band that were celebrating the receipt of money, the noise of which Sam the Smoke heard in the car park. Sam the Smoke couldn't help but notice the mood of those walking back to their cars, and commented to his guard partner, "Something big must have happened."

*

The training ground was well disguised in the hills south of Lough Melvin in Co. Leitrim, and was used on a well planned basis by various Commands of the IRA. The shooting range was cleared for operation, and four potentials were being given instruction, and one, a Mr Hunter, being assessed.

The all-clear was given and live rounds handed out. Hunter expertly checked out the ageing AK-47 rifle and the Browning 9mm handgun. The first set of targets were at 300 metres, and Hunter made himself ready. He would show them – he had to. This was old hat, and although the rifle was not one he would have chosen, it would do.

His first shot missed, but he expected that. So did McBrien, who was watching his every move. The margin for error at 300 metres is next to nothing, but Hunter knew how to correct the sight to take account of the first shot. His second shot was good. McBrien was impressed. The rest of Hunter's rounds found their mark, which was more than McBrien would have achieved, and McBrien knew it. The rifle was handed over to the weapon's supervisor, and the handgun taken up.

The Browning was quite new and had the high capacity 13-round magazine filled. The target this time was at 30-metres distance. As before, Hunter's first shot wasn't important, but he managed to hit the outer edge of the target. Hunter made the necessary adjustment and quickly let off the rest of the magazine. It was a most credible performance, forming a respectable group around the bull. McBrien nodded his acknowledgement that the American could shoot. But shooting a target is not the same as shooting people.

Hunter used the journey time from the training camp to Cushendall to try and improve McBrien's attitude towards him. Hunter tried all he could from commenting on how impressed he was on the Movement's selection and state of weapons, to how professional the shooting range was run. Through small talk, Hunter learnt that McBrien would have liked to be one of the top shooters, but wasn't good enough. Hunter offered his services, suggesting that the arms training that he received could be passed on to McBrien. That was the beginning of the improving relationship between them.

They travelled in a small van, the back of which was empty. It was too dangerous to transport the weapons that way, but the weapons were needed. It was no use Hunter showing that he could shoot accurately with a particular rifle, and then providing him with a different rifle to carry out the job. The same rifle had to be used. The logistics section would have the weapon transported to Cushendall in due course, using the network of legitimate carriers, such as Post Office vans, and electricity and telephone maintenance vehicles. It was quite a set-up, even though the number of vehicles they could use was small.

McBrien briefed Magee most favourably on Hunter's performance and was of the opinion that perhaps Hunter could carry out the job on Sutton after all.

"Whereabouts is that Major Sutton? You can't do the job if you don't know where he is," stated Magee.

"You are absolutely right, Mr Magee," agreed Hunter. Hunter had, for the time being, won over McBrien. Now he must try and get Magee on to his team. "I have a general area only to work from. It's not much, but I'll show you the map," and he set the map of Northern Ireland that he had purchased in London on the floor.

"Sutton and the Brit are somewhere here," pointing to an area covering Larne, Glynn, Whitehead, and all of Island Magee. McBrien and Magee stepped away from the map.

"What's wrong, guys?" asked Hunter.

"That's all strong loyalist territory you are looking at. How do you know your target is there?"

"He has used a satellite phone to contact us at Dugway. I was able to see part of the trace of his position – which was here," as he pointed to the map again. "I couldn't get the full references."

"A satellite phone? Where did he get that? US Army, by chance?" Magee asked.

"Too right he did. If I was only able to get my contacts to deliver, I would pinpoint his transmission spot. As it is, all I have is this. . ." and again Hunter traced out the area around Island Magee.

"What do you think, Jarvis? Too risky?"

McBrien nodded to his superior. "It's risky all right. No friendly faces in those parts at all. Let me see the map," and he began to examine the area. "It's likely to be in Island Magee – that's bad."

"Bad? What's bad about it?" a slightly annoyed Hunter asked.

"Look," replied McBrien. "There is only one way in and out," as he indicated the road at Ballycarry Station and the road to Whitehead. "The only other way out is by sea."

"Out? What's the deal about the way out?" Hunter retorted sharply.

"You've never done this before, have you? You need to work out your escape routes in advance. You don't want to be trapped in a Loyalist area after killing someone with an IRA gun, do you?" Magee answered.

"Of course, of course," acknowledged Hunter. Hunter was beginning to see these people in a different light. "You guys sure think of everything. I would be lost without you."

"Not lost, dead!" McBrien warned.

Hunter returned his attention to the map, and tried to picture the layout of the island from it. The high ground called Muldersleigh Hill was a possible starting point, he thought. If visibility was good enough, his binoculars should afford him a good view from that hill. He didn't want to push it too hard though, as Magee and McBrien would move at their pace, not his.

"What would you guys suggest?" he asked. Get their ideas out first, Hunter thought, and see what opportunities they present him.

"You could always forget it," suggested Magee.

"Aye," McBrien added, "unless you didn't mind getting killed doing it."

"Come on, guys, that's not what I came here for. I need your help," he pleaded. "I know I can't do this on my own, but I can do it – I can do it."

McBrien raised his eyebrows and took another look at the map. He pointed at two areas without saying anything. "We need a larger scale of map than this. I suppose we could take a trip to Larne and check out the maps in the library."

"Say – I like that idea. How about we go there now?" Hunter enthused.

Chapter Forty-Five

Susannah drove too quickly for the car to negotiate the corner without incident. The damage was slight but could not be hidden, and fortunately nobody was hurt. She must get there, and quickly, and hitting the parked car was nothing but nuisance value. But she didn't stop, and as she was seen there would be trouble. Trouble about a damaged car she could handle, trouble about her new love being killed was too much.

She ran from the car to the cottage and banged on the locked door. Her breathlessness caused by fear did not help her composure. There was no reply. Her imagination was working overtime. Perhaps she was already too late – perhaps they had already killed him – perhaps. . . She wasn't thinking straight and returned to her car to wait. Then she remembered that they habitually jogged down the hill to Brown's Bay, so she started the car and drove down the hill. There was nobody around. Within minutes she had returned to the cottage, and in case they had come back since she was last there, she tried banging on time door again. How silly of me, she thought. Of course they are not back yet – their car is not here.

It seemed like a lifetime, but eventually their car returned complete with passengers and a fresh stock of food. They had been to the Rinkha to get supplies of fresh fruit and vegetables, and of course an ice cream each.

De Courcy perceived her unease, as did Sutton, who commented, "Something's up, Mac."

"Quickly," she called, "get in here quickly," as she hurried them inside the cottage as soon as Sutton unlocked it. "Leave your shopping, this is important."

De Courcy had the shopping bag in his hand anyway, so he brought it into the cottage.

"Calm down, kid – calm down," coaxed Sutton, "now tell us – where's the fire?"

She blurted out her information in short bursts between quick breaths. "You know a Liam Magee? He's IRA. Have you heard of him?"

"Yes, dear, we know of him," replied de Courcy.

"He's been seen. With someone in the library. In Larne, examining the maps of Island Magee – well?"

They looked at her, faces blank.

"This is not IRA territory. There is no reason for the IRA to bother with Island Magee unless – they are looking for someone. YOU!"

"Are you sure, Susannah?" de Courcy enquired.

"Oh yes! I'm very sure. Our contact in the library heard them discuss possible surveillance points and something about a satellite phone."

Sutton and de Courcy began to put two and two together. De Courcy brought his hands together with a loud slap. "The sat. phone can give away our position – is that right, Elmer? Do you think the IRA could get our position from sources in the States?"

"Another thing," she interrupted, "the man with Magee had an American accent."

"That means they don't know where we are," stated de Courcy. "How do you know that?" Susannah replied.

"If they did, they wouldn't need to look for us on a map. You said they were discussing possible surveillance areas – so they think we – if they *are* looking for us – are in the area. That's all."

"I buy that, Edward," Sutton's first comment on the affair. "If they knew where we were, they wouldn't risk it by openly looking up maps in a public library. Say, kid," as Sutton turned to her, "you say this is not IRA territory. Does that mean they have no support here?"

"As far as we know, that's right. They have no support here – but," she was trying hard to get over the seriousness of it, ". . .but, please take no chances. Are you allowed to carry a gun?" They looked at her. "Legally, I mean. Do you hold a certificate or whatever is needed to carry a gun?"

"Sure do, kid. We both do," Sutton assured her.

"Good," she sighed with relief, "then do so. Everywhere you go, make sure you each carry one – and have it loaded. Please. Promise me, Edward – you will?"

She wasn't normally as assertive as this, a factor that persuaded them to give her their promise.

"We can look after ourselves, kid – we did okay in the Gulf and we will do okay here," Sutton confidently announced. "As soon as you go, we shall arm ourselves."

"Promise?"

"Promise," confirmed de Courcy. "Now let's see you off. I saw a bit of a dent in your car, what caused that?" De Courcy and Sutton went with her to her car and heard the explanation of how she sustained the damage. In return for the promise to carry a gun, she promised to go directly and report the accident to the police station. "In fact, do it now from here – use this phone, dear, please."

While she was advising the police, Sutton extracted two handguns from their secret hide, together with two full magazines and shoulder holsters. Sutton returned to the main room as she completed her call. He let her see him put on the holster, load the gun, check that the safety was on and holstered it.

" Okay, kid? Happy? This one is for lover boy here," and de Courcy took the weapon and put it on.

"Thanks, boys," she smiled, "and be careful. I've to go now to the police station."

It was fortunate that the desk sergeant at the RUC Station knew her and her late husband. She got away with paying the cost to repair the parked car and a £50 fine for careless driving.

*

McBrien and Hunter spent two fruitless days on Black Hill overlooking Larne Lough and Island Magee, taking it in turns to spy out the land using the Leitz binoculars. McBrien wasn't really doing any good to their cause, as he didn't know what Sutton looked like. But he liked using the binoculars, and to maintain the sweetness Hunter allowed him to do so. They had the guns with them. It was an argument that Hunter won based on his scenario that if they didn't have them and they came across Sutton, they couldn't do anything. Worse, stated Hunter, they would lose the element of surprise if Sutton saw him, and as Sutton would most likely be armed, it would be he and McBrien who would get it, not Sutton.

Hunter kept the discipline tight. McBrien was glad that he did, especially keeping the weapons out of sight.

Their next viewpoint was about one mile north west of Ballycarry, some 574 feet above sea level. They approached the spot overland from Glenoe, and parked the van on a side road. Where it was possible, they kept away from known loyalist towns and villages, unless there was no alternative.

They brought their food and drink with them, using flasks to keep the tea, coffee, and soup warm. Hunter would have made do with less, but McBrien liked his comforts when in the field. McBrien also believed that it would add credibility to their cover story of being bird-watchers should they be asked what they were doing. That day produced nothing of note, except that Hunter did spy a couple of flying swans.

There was nothing for it but to move their surveillance spot to the island itself. They knew that the risks were high, but anything planned by terrorists, using open countryside to track down and kill somebody, was risky.

The next day would be Saturday, and preparations were made to climb Muldersleigh Hill at 8 a.m. from a disused quarry, close to the golf course. Saturday would mean people. People who would be free from the Monday-to-Friday grind, taking a change of scene for the weekend, or at least for a few hours, on Saturday.

McBrien parked the van in a side road leading to the quarry. Hunter carried the rifle, disguised — if it is possible to disguise such an article, as an artist's easel, complete with tripod. He also carried the binoculars. That left McBrien to look after the backpack containing the food. Leaving the car close to a tree that grew out from a break in a thorn hedge, they proceeded up the quarry lane until they arrived at the barbed wire fence, with a corroded DANGER – KEEP OUT sign in large red paint, riveted to one of the fence posts. The fence was old and weathered, and, to the right, a break in the fence gave evidence that maintenance had not been carried out for some time. Good, thought Hunter - no regular traffic here. Hunter climbed through the break in the fence, followed by McBrien. They saw nobody.

The climb up Muldersleigh wasn't hard, just difficult getting through the brambles and gorse bushes. They came across a second barbed wire fence and saw the golf course to their right, and the island spreading out to their left

The view was good, allowing them to see over the island and down Larne Lough without hindrance. At the top of the hill, they sat down on the rough ground that gave little cover but enough to make it virtually impossible for anyone to see them. McBrien removed one of the flasks from the backpack, and two plastic mugs, and a packet of shortbread biscuits. They had coffee and biscuits as they sat on the damp ground. To the left, the train from Belfast *en route* to Larne made its way past Ballycarry Station.

*

The Canon A1 and the 50mm lens were not worth repairing, so Richmond used the insurance money and some of the £2,000 Criminal Injury money to buy a new camera and a selection of lenses. The new toy was carefully handled, with every function tested, using each lens, to familiarise himself of its operation. It was the first time that Richmond had come into contact with an automatic-focus facility, and he was surprised at how fast it worked.

The car bodywork was repaired, leaving no trace of the bullet hole in the door. The driver's window was open that day, which was assumed to be the entry point of the sniper's round that had passed through his leg. His staff at the bank had made a joke of it and were toying with the idea of organising a competition to see who could guess where and when he would be shot again.

The manager at Tecno had thrown in a couple of free films in view of the large sale, and Richmond had already used one of the thirty-six exposure films as a dummy run, to satisfy himself that all was as it should be. It was slide film, and it was already in the mail to the processing laboratory.

Penelope suggested that Major de Courcy and his American friend be invited for tea on Saturday, to thank them for their assistance when they drove Martin to the hospital. That's why the bungalow in Island Magee was being used that weekend. Richmond didn't bother to bring his camera, as he didn't want to use it until the first film proved that it was working properly.

304

De Courcy and Sutton accepted the invitation, and arrived at 3.30 p.m. Each were armed, a fact that was not noticed by Richmond or his wife at the time of their arrival.

*

Hunter was not tired of the job in hand, just fed up that success was slow in coming. Hunter and McBrien had watched a farm worker clear out a ditch, a couple of cyclists repair a puncture, a few families with noisy children walk down the lane to the shore, and when scanning the sea saw numerous small fishing boats pass. But no sign of anyone that looked like Sutton.

The morning passed by, and they had lunch. During lunch, they heard a swish followed by the thud of something land on the rough ground beside the backpack, and the breaking of glass. A golf ball. Someone had miss hit and broken one of McBrien's flasks – it was the empty one. Hunter stood up and looked over the fence and examined the green beyond. Nobody. He picked up the ball and threw it onto the rough at the far side of the green.

"We don't want them coming around here looking for it," explained Hunter, and he and McBrien lay down until the golfers passed. That was their only excitement for an hour or so. A few cars drove down the lane and parked. Others drove down, turned and drove out again. McBrien was enjoying the relaxing time, and compared the sitting on Muldersleigh with his time in prison.

"Real nice here, don't you think, Mr Hunter?" McBrien asked. He maintained the formality to emphasise that he was in charge. Hunter put his binoculars down beside the backpack and looked about him. "How does this compare to your Dugway? Is this as good?"

Dugway! A million miles away was Dugway. The hot dusty home of covert operations that was Dugway couldn't compare with this. The weather here, he thought, could be warmer – and drier. But then there wouldn't be so much green about. No wonder they call it the Emerald Isle.

"Dugway is a dump, Mr McBrien. You don't want to go to Dugway, not for nothing. This place is cooler, but wins hands down in everything else."

McBrien liked County Antrim. County Down was for the snobs, the real people are from County Antrim.

A man was setting up a barbecue in the small space behind the cottage at the foot of the hill they were on. Hunter looked at the efforts taken to light it, and smiled. "He doesn't know what he's at, that guy. Look down there, Mr McBrien," and Hunter gave him the binoculars.

"I thought you were never going to let me take a look," commented McBrien. It was over an hour since he had looked through them. McBrien focused on the man, who by now had succeeded in lighting the firelighters and had surrounded them with charcoal.

"He's got it going now – yes, it's starting to smoke a bit. It will be an hour or two before he can cook on it, mind." McBrien lifted the binoculars a few degrees and swung over to the left were he saw much activity. "I see the Rinkha is doing a good trade. Just look at the car park – full it is. Do you want to see?" Hunter hadn't forgotten the comment about never letting him use the binoculars.

"I'll look later. Do you see people? Say, two guys on their own?"

McBrien knew what he meant. "No. Just families or couples getting sliders and pokes."

"Come again? Sliders and pokes?" quizzed Hunter.

"Ice cream – local talk for ice cream," explained McBrien.

These were the best binoculars he had ever used. It wasn't too clear today, with a misty haze interfering with what would have been a clear view of the fields beyond Portpatrick in Scotland.

"What are your plans when this is over, Mr Hunter?" McBrien was examining the area over the North Channel towards Ailsa Craig rock.

"Nothing."

The word didn't register with McBrien for a moment. He lowered the binoculars to chin height and turned his head to face Hunter. "Nothing? Did you say nothing?"

Hunter nodded as he stared into space. Returning the binoculars to his eyes, McBrien swept across the island and, without thinking, sarcastically offered, "You'll probably be good at that."

Chapter Forty-Six

"What would you like, Edward? We have steak, chops, and sausages," asked Richmond.

This was more than they expected. Coming round for tea was, in their mind, just that, with perhaps a few sandwiches.

"Would a chop and a sausage be in order?" de Courcy responded.

"A chop and a sausage? How about two of each – and if you want more we can throw another one on – all right?" asked Richmond.

"Of course he will," Sutton answered for him, "and I'll go for a steak. How big are they?"

"Come and see for yourself," and Richmond and Sutton went into the small kitchen to examine the meat stock in the fridge, while Penelope and de Courcy continued the small talk. Richmond returned with Sutton and announced that Sutton had offered to do the cooking, as he often did that sort of thing for the congregation of his church back home when Father O'Malley asked him.

"I didn't know you were a Catholic, Elmer," commented Penelope.

"He's a bit of everything now," de Courcy piped in. "Even been going to the Methodist Chapel here on Sundays – haven't you, old boy?"

"Sure have, Edward. I enjoy the good sing there. How about getting this show on the road? Is the fire ready, Martin?"

The four of them, complete with plates, knives, forks, and raw meat went round to the back of the bungalow and organised themselves by erecting a folding table for the plates and food, and four camping chairs. Sutton confirmed that the charcoal was ready – hot and white. The sizzle was appetising and mouth-watering, as steaks, chops and sausages were changing colour over the heat.

Penelope had forgotten the condiments, which were still on the kitchen table, as was the bread and butter, so she brought them out and placed them on the table.

Not for the first time had the young heifers in the field next to the bungalow congregated close to the fence to take notice of what was going on.

"There they are again – look!" as Penelope pointed the audience out to de Courcy and Sutton. Penelope laughed. "They always do that, you know. Every time we have a barbecue, they come round to see what we are doing. You'd think they would run away. After all, we might be eating their brother!"

They enjoyed their meal of steak, chop and sausage butties, washed down with mugs of tea.

*

"The lucky people. They are making me hungry." McBrien put down the binoculars. "Let's have something to eat," and he opened the backpack and removed the last of the sandwiches and the remaining flask. Coffee and cheese sandwiches followed by a chocolate biscuit and a banana.

Hunter saw that the four people below them were starting to tidy up, so with plastic cup of coffee in one hand, and binoculars in the other, he glanced down at them. The scene was one of contentment, with the lady stacking up the dishes and taking them inside, one man putting the chairs away, the other man folding up a table, and the third man – Major Sutton!

Hunter dropped his cup, spilling the coffee over McBrien, who yelled out.

"Shut up. It's him – he's there – Major Sutton!" Hunter moved left to where the rifle was hidden in the rough, removed it from its disguised wrapping, and loaded up.

McBrien had taken the binoculars from Hunter, and was looking down at the picnic party. "Which one is your man?" McBrien asked.

"The one at the barbecue, that's Sutton. He's the one working with the UVF. One of the others must be the Brit."

Hunter was ready now, and settled himself into a shooting position. "Now, where are you, you American traitor? Where are. . . I see you — say goodbye," and he fired.

*

The shot missed Sutton by inches and hit the leg of the barbecue, causing it to fall over. The charcoal was still burning and smoke filled the small garden when it hit the grass. Sutton recognised the sound for what it was, as did de Courcy.

"Get back, Martin – get back," Sutton shouted and waved Richmond to get behind him.

De Courcy had his gun ready now and was scouring the hill for signs of the gunman. Sutton quickly took his gun from the holster, and moved right, his back to the bungalow. De Courcy moved left towards Richmond, who just stood there. "This way, old boy," he said to Richmond. "Someone has taken a shot at us."

*

"Blast! Blast! Blast! The sight must have moved," raged Hunter as he got ready to shoot again. "You'd better get ready to move out, McBrien, those guys down there are armed. Handguns, two of them. Of course! The other guy will be the Brit!"

McBrien gathered the bits and pieces around him and stuffed them into the backpack as Hunter fired again.

*

"I see him," shouted Sutton as he let off three rounds in the direction of movement at the top of the hill. Sutton saw de Courcy and Richmond fall over. Richmond had tripped over the leg of the barbecue and had fallen against de Courcy, pushing him out of the way of Hunter's second round.

That had my name on it, thought de Courcy. The round found Richmond instead, who let out a yell as he fell on top of de Courcy.

"Don't move, Martin," ordered de Courcy as he moved from under Richmond and joined Sutton. "Where is he, old boy?"

He pointed with his handgun to the left of the quarry, "There, against the skyline – see – someone moved to the right – see – again," And Sutton fired again. De Courcy saw and, taking aim at the source of movement, fired twice.

"What's all this noise?" Penelope asked as she came round the side of the bungalow. She noticed Sutton and de Courcy pointing their guns at Muldersleigh, and her husband with blood on his hands. She didn't scream, or say anything, she just fainted.

"There's a second one moving just below the skyline – see him?"

"Got him," replied de Courcy. "Out of range for a chance of a hit, old boy. You start climbing going left, I'll go right – ready?"

"Sure."

"Go," signalled de Courcy. They jumped the fence, entered the field, scattering the heifers, and started to climb.

*

"I think I got the Brit. No – blast it. He's moving – okay. . . You'd better have your gun ready, McBrien – okay?" There was no answer. The shots from the bungalow were too close for comfort. "McBrien – where are you?" as Hunter looked for him. He saw him, face down at the edge of the quarry. There was no movement. Hunter, with rifle in one hand, moved, keeping low, in the direction of McBrien. He turned him over and stared at the open eyes looking heavenward. "Get up, McBrien – get up." He was dead. Hunter noticed a trickle of blood coming from behind his right ear, then saw the bullet hole. What a lucky shot, he thought, and was about to kick the body into the quarry when he remembered the van. The keys of the van? They must be in McBrien's pocket. He started to search for them. Where are they. . . Wait – what's this? Good heavens, it's my passport! Hunter pocketed his passport then found the van keys and took them along with McBrien's handgun and wallet. Hunter put the wallet beside his billfold in his inside pocket, and the handgun in the right outside pocket, and took off towards the van. The van was easy to find, and, opening the door, he put the rifle on the floor under the passenger's seat, and hid it as best he could under the mat. He then got in, started it up and drove off. Where to? Hunter didn't know, but drove off anyway. As long as it was off the island – he must get off the island.

*

Sutton heard the noise of the van driving off, and stopped to bring de Courcy's attention to that fact. "Looks like one has got away, Edward – the other one's here, look."

De Courcy met up with Sutton, and together they examined McBrien's body.

"Some shot, old boy."

There was little to indicate who the dead person in front of them was. There was nothing of importance in McBrien's pockets.

"I'll go back, old boy, and call the police. You know, I believe our banker friend has stopped a bullet again. I'll check him out."

"How is he? Is it bad?"

"Looks like shoulder again – flesh wound hopefully. And he's done it again – I can't believe it. You know, he tripped over the barbecue and pushed me out of the way – that's the second time he saved me from a bullet."

They saw the smoke rising from the rear of the bungalow.

"I'd better put that out before the whole thing goes up."

Returning to the bungalow, de Courcy checked up on Richmond while Sutton helped Penelope to her feet.

"What's going on?" she asked.

"It's all okay now, take it easy. It looks as if the IRA tried to take us out," Sutton announced. She fainted again.

De Courcy, using his mobile phone, had telephoned his contact number in Lisburn, and requested police and ambulance facilities, while Sutton had filled a basin with water and put the fire out. A large area of the lawn had been damaged by the barbecue coals.

"Don't worry about the lawn," Sutton said to Richmond. "You will not be cutting grass for a while till your shoulder gets a chance to heal."

*

Magee heard of McBrien's death from Hunter, who telephoned him from a public phone box in Larne.

"How did it happen?" Magee asked calmly. He and McBrien had come a long way together, and his death was a painful loss. He tried to listen to the explanation from Hunter, but he imagined that blame could well be attributed to some foolhardy action of Hunter's, giving McBrien no chance to defend himself. Another death, another wasted talent, and most of all the loss and support of a close friend. Magee felt empty. The void didn't evoke anger or the need for revenge. That might come later, but now he wanted to be alone.

". . .I'll leave the van in the car park by the Fire Station – okay Magee?"

"What's that? The van?"

"Yeah, at the Fire Station car park in Larne, and I'll hide up some place. Once I've finished the job, I'll go back to the States. Sorry about McBrien – he was all right," and Hunter left the area on foot and proceeded to the outskirts of the town to pick up the hidden weapons. The rifle was too risky – too easily seen, so he left it there and relied on McBrien's handgun to finish the job.

Hunter made his way to the harbour and went into a pub where he ordered fish with french fries and a pint. He was tired and starting to feel weary of the day's activities. The States didn't seem so bad right now, and perhaps he could arrange a flight from the airport near the centre of Belfast.

The bar TV was on and the local channel was broadcasting the end of a commercial break. The news followed, and led with a bombing in some place he had never heard of called Bessbrook. Then there was story of a shooting in Island Magee. The locals took interest in the story, as did Hunter, and the noise level dropped allowing the newsreader to be heard. . . *'Police have recovered the body of a man, believed to be in his forties, who was shot in Island Magee this afternoon, and would like to speak to anyone who saw or heard gunfire on the island around six o'clock. Another person was slightly hurt in the incident.'*

Slightly hurt? Is that all? Perhaps it is a bluff to smoke me out, thought Hunter. They must be somewhere on the island, and if so I'll find them.

He paid the barman for a second beer, and casually asked if there was a way to get over to the island, apart from the road near Ballycarry. The barman mentioned the ferry, that wouldn't sail until Monday morning.

"Is there a motel or some place I can stay a couple of nights?" Hunter asked.

"Surely. Do you want it cheap or fancy?" replied the barman.

"Cheap will be fine," he replied, and was offered bed and breakfast for £10 per night in the guest room upstairs. Hunter took out McBrien's wallet and handed over a £20 note. The barman examined it carefully before accepting it, and then gave Hunter a receipt and the key to the room.

"What's with the note routine?" asked Hunter.

"There have been some forgeries about – I check all the notes as part of the job. What time do you want breakfast?"

Hunter asked about the times of the ferries to the island, and hearing that there was one every half hour or so from eight in the morning, but none tomorrow (being Sunday), arranged breakfast for 8.30 a.m.

Chapter Forty-Seven

De Courcy was firm in his belief that the danger was far from over. Whoever was attempting to kill them had failed, and would probably try again. Now that there was an important person in his life, she must be protected, so that night after returning from the hospital at Dundonald, where Richmond was once again stitched up and sent home, he paid a visit to Ballycarry.

Susannah was unaware of the events on the island. Her day was spent looking after the farm, while her brother-in-law drove to Ballyclare to pick up some new fence posts and cement. When he returned to the farm, she assisted in mixing cement and erecting posts along one side of a field, where the hedge had long since disappeared.

She was delighted to see de Courcy, even though he was not in the best frame of mind.

"Turn on your television to the local station," he suggested, and asked them both to listen for some news of the island. The item was brief.

"Who was killed, Edward, and who was injured? Elmer?"

"Elmer is fine. I don't know who the dead person is – he may be IRA, one of those you warned us about. But that's not why I'm here." De Courcy found it hard to talk to her. Would she understand why he was going to insist that she do it? The brother-in-law made himself scarce, a move that Susannah appreciated.

"Who was injured, Edward?"

"Injured indeed. The unfortunate civilian, that's who. The bank manager chap who was shot before. It's not so bad – he was lucky and is home with a flesh wound."

"As long as you weren't hurt," she added and gave a sigh of relief. He would just have to tell her. No – stronger than that – order her.

"It's not over, you know. Whoever they are will be back, and they know what we look like – we didn't get a look at them, except the dead one. Tell me, would it have been your UVF people?"

She was surprised at that and it showed. "No, none of our people would touch you, or Elmer. Not after the money thing was achieved. No – my belief is that it's Magee and his connection. He has a close friend who acts as guard and gun-hand called McBrien. Now McBrien would do that sort of thing,."

"I'll mention that name to the police." It must be now. "There is something I must ask of you, Susannah. It's vital – No – don't interrupt – please," as she was ready to do so. "Until this is settled in Island Magee, I am putting your life at risk. I must not be seen with you, and you must not be seen with me. That is the easy part. The difficult part is this." De Courcy found his hands were damp, as was his face, so he dried them on his pocket tissue. ". . .If the IRA can find me, they can find you. For your own protection, and our future relationship – if we are to have one – you must break your connection with the UVF, and that break must be permanent. You must resign – get out – now – please," he pleaded.

Susannah stared at the tired man in front of her. How he had aged over the past day- or so, she thought – yet he was such a wonderful person in her eyes. She reasoned that de Courcy's request was not logical, and would not achieve anything. "You're wrong, Edward. By staying in, I have their protection. Nobody in the IRA will touch me, because if they did there would be such bloody reprisals, and they know it. Don't worry about me – I'm safer in the UVF than out of it."

De Courcy thought she would say something like that, which left him with no alternative. "You are totally wrong. In a civilised society, there is no room for secret armies or terror groups. If you put your trust in them and not in the forces of law and order of the state, what future has the state? I must insist that you resign from the UVF." He found himself speaking quite loudly, and she was becoming angry, upset, and tearful.

"You have no right to insist anything," she shouted, crying as she spoke. De Courcy raised his hands in surrender.

"This, then, is the end between us, Susannah." He was speaking quietly now. He noticed that she was sobbing her heart out, a sight he couldn't bear, so he turned away from her. "Goodbye," he said quietly as he left the house and returned to the car. De Courcy got in and started the engine. She ran after him, tears flowing freely down her face. They faced each other – she standing beside the car, he sitting in it with opened window.

"What right," she demanded, "do you have to insist of me this thing?"

"None," he sighed as he spoke, "except the right of an old man who has fallen in love with you." He closed the window and drove off, leaving her standing there alone, miserable and broken.

Susannah ran to the kitchen, sat in one of the wooden chairs, and cried her eyes out.

Joe Lacy heard the major's car depart and he left the barn where he was passing time. He was shocked at the sight before him.

"What's wrong, Sis? Can I help?"

"He's gone, Joe. It's for ever – he's gone. I've lost him – the only good thing since William, and he's gone." The tears started up again.

Joe sat beside her heaving body and held her close to him. "Tell me what happened, Sis."

The story came out in between the crying, which was now a little hysterical. Once her story was told, she composed herself and became quiet and withdrawn. Joe made her a cup of tea and suggested that she take a hot bath and wash her hair.

"It all depends on what you want, Sis. It's simple. Do you want him or the organisation? You can't have both, and you have done more than your fair share for the cause."

She looked up from the table she was leaning over. "Would they let me leave? They usually don't, because of their rules and all."

"Why not ask the General on the quiet. You can't keep fighting for both the UVF and your major. I've seen you, you know – you and de Courcy. You are made for each other."

She smiled. "Thanks, Joe. Maybe I will do that," and she went upstairs, had a bath, and washed her hair.

*

"Say, Edward – I've an idea," said Sutton. "Why not ask Richmond and his wife down here for tea or something? Sort of a way to say 'cheer up' and all, and to thank them for the barbecue."

It was Sunday morning, and de Courcy had risen early, mainly because he hadn't slept well but also he felt that he must keep in shape if only to ward off unknown assassins. He had had an hour's run before breakfast, and felt the better for it. If they were coming back to try again, the fitter he was, the greater the chance of survival.

Sutton was still asleep when de Courcy left for his run, but now Sutton was preparing breakfast on his return.

The previous evening de Courcy had advised the police that the body might have the name of McBrien.

He couldn't get her out of his mind. The unhappy face he saw through the car window as he drove off made him feel guilty. Better, he thought, to appear cruel. She would get over it more quickly.

"What do you say, old boy, old boy?" asked Sutton as he set up a plate before him of two eggs, sunny side up, and three rashers of lean bacon.

"Sorry, old boy. I wasn't listening – what did you say?" De Courcy began to toy with one of the eggs while Sutton repeated his suggestion.

"That sounds fine to me. Have we enough supplies to cope with two extra?"

"Sure we have." Sutton saw that de Courcy hadn't eaten anything yet. "What's hit you? Had your first fight with Susannah?" and he gave a little chuckle.

"Something along those lines. It is for her own safety, you know. I asked her to resign from the UVF," he said without emotion in his voice.

"Good for you, Edward. She would be better out of that crowd of terrorists."

De Courcy changed his attention from the egg to one of the bacon rashers. "That's what I said, old boy. She didn't say it, but she implied that I should mind my own business," was the quiet response as he continued to mix egg with bacon. "What has been said is said. I, a retired Army Officer, can't be part of a terrorist group – agreed?" and he put the first forkful into his mouth.

"Agreed," replied Sutton. "Shall I give Martin an invitation, then? We could suggest tea today – okay?"

"You have the number?" de Courcy asked as egg and bacon vanished.

"Sure. I noted it from the hospital records when I went there with him and his wife yesterday." With coffee mug in one hand, he telephoned Richmond and appeared to find him still in bed.

"Hi! Martin – how's the shoulder?" Sutton sipped the coffee while listening to the banker. The invitation was made, discussed with Penelope, and accepted. Directions were given, and arrangements finalised for their arrival at around 4 p.m. Sutton replaced the handset and finished his coffee, then cleared up.

"It's Sunday, Edward – are you for church?"

Church attendance was the last thing on de Courcy's mind, especially if there was a chance that she might be there.

"I don't know, old boy. Are you going?"

"Yeah – why not? You sure get a good sing in that place, not like back home. Let's go – okay?"

What if she was there? It didn't matter, he supposed, as his decision to keep his distance was already made, and church didn't count. If she was there, he would be polite but distant. There was the chance, he supposed, that she might reconsider her position. She had every right to be angry with him for expecting her to accept his order, but he was sure that she was wrong in staying in the organisation.

"All right, we'll go. Walk or drive, Elmer?"

"Drive, of course. We need to prepare for our visitors, remember?"

*

Hunter had breakfast, and returned to his room to work on his strategy. Waiting for Monday was one option. The other was to go for it today. He unfolded his map and, placing it on the bed, started to study it.

His eyes focused upon the hill where it happened, Muldersleigh. He would make a few enquiries. What was it McBrien said? He remembered. A shop where people bought sliders and pokes. He would go there first and ask around.

Looking at the map, he guessed that the shop was on the road that led right down the middle of the island. Hunter packed the map into his jacket pocket, slung the binoculars round his neck, checked that McBrien's gun was loaded, then pocketed it before leaving the room. Halfway down the stairs, he stopped to make sure that he had his passport. Yes, it was there. If necessary, he could leave after the job was done and catch a plane to London that day.

Entering the empty bar where much earlier he had eaten a huge breakfast, he advised the barman that he might be late as he was taking in a few sights. He left the key on the top of the bar counter.

"What's the bus service like around here?" he asked.

"Sunday service is not too frequent, now. There are a few leaving for Belfast, now, taking the coast road," the barman answered, gesturing with his hand. "The best place is down that way to the bus station, now. You'll get all the times there too, now."

Hunter left. The time was approaching ten thirty, and he got to the bus station by eleven. The next bus for Belfast would leave in ten minutes, and would stop in every hole in the hedge, including Ballycarry. Hunter bought a ticket to Ballycarry and climbed aboard the bus, where he sat at the rear, having asked the driver to let him know when he had arrived. The driver gave him a strange look.

"I'm on a tour, just taking a look around – never been here before, but my people came from these parts over a hundred years ago," he lied.

The driver shouted, 'Ballycarry' on their arrival in the town, and waited for Hunter to get off.

Hunter saw Island Magee clearly. There it was – down the hill and across the main Larne-Belfast road. Hunter began his walk. There were not too many about, which suited him as he was able to journey without interruption. He crossed the road at the bottom of the hill and saw the road sign to his left, pointing to Island Magee. He was soon passing the Ballycarry railway station. He remembered the train passing there yesterday.

Hunter continued, over the curved stone bridge, where two boys were optimistically trying to catch fish. The bridge curved anticlockwise as a sweep in the road rather than a hump, and afforded a good view down Larne Lough towards the open sea. Hunter found himself at the crossroads, and although there were shops, he couldn't see the hill. He took out the map and found his position, so continued straight over the crossroads, where he now saw the hill, and before long, he found himself at a shop called 'Rinkha'.

There were plenty of people at the shop, and the car park was full. He decided to risk asking for a 'poke' to see what would happen. At the shop's entrance, one of the assistants was tidying up some spilt litter. Hunter went up to her and got her attention by asking, "Excuse me, ma'am. I'm on a tour of your beautiful country and I believe one of my American mates from back home is living in these parts. You don't know, by chance, where he's at?"

The girl stopped brushing and declared, "You are an American, now – is that right?"

"Yes, ma'am, I sure am," Hunter smarmed.

"Fancy that, now. And you must be a friend of the other one at Brown's Bay, is that right?"

"I don't know Brown's Bay," he replied as he got out the map and showed it to her.

"Ach, you don't need a map, now. Just drive to the end of that road," and she pointed down to her right, "and when you come to the sea, sure you're at it."

He pocketed the map and expressed his thanks. "Which place is it at Brown's Bay?"

"That would be Mr de Courcy's house, just before the road goes down the hill to the sea. You can't miss it – it's the only house there is, now."

Hunter's eyes lit up. "Mr de Courcy. That's him. Thanks, lady." Now I've got him. A second chance that would not be wasted. "Say, ma'am – where do I go for a big poke?"

"Just join the queue inside and one of the girls will get you one."

He returned her smile and entered the shop. The queue for ice cream was longer than he expected, running from the ice cream counter by the entrance, to the toy and china department a good ten yards back. The place was larger than he imagined, and it appeared to be a converted barn or old dance hall. People were milling around everywhere – the children examining the toys, the parents grabbing a free read at the newspapers and magazines. Hunter joined the queue, and turned round to see three men in Army uniform, fully armed, and two police enter the shop. They didn't seem to be looking for anyone in particular. Hunter noticed their relaxed and smiling manner. He tried to be natural by not looking at them, but he didn't want to be trapped. Turning round, he saw at the rear of the shop a sign indicating EMERGENCY EXIT. He walked slowly towards it, glancing at the fancy goods on display on each side of the centre aisle. One of the policemen joined the queue where seconds before he had been standing, while the others waited patiently at the entrance. Ice cream was what they wanted – not him!

Hunter waited until the armed group had departed the shop and had driven off in their armoured Land Rovers before he rejoined the queue. He purchased his poke and a plastic bottle of orange juice, and left. He made his way past the football ground on the left and the new houses on the right, licking his cone of ice cream as he went.

An hour later, he stood at a fork in the road with a sign announcing PORTMUCK. What a name, he thought and, noticing that the road was clear of people and traffic, made his way to investigate this place called Portmuck. The road led him to a very steep decline where an oncoming car, full of elderly ladies, managed to negotiate the hill by staying in first gear. He watched the car struggle, exhaust oils filling the air, finally making it to the top, where the engine noise increased before the driver engaged second gear. Heaven help the guy who buys that heap, Hunter thought aloud, it's already past it. He carried on down to where the road bent to the right and levelled out, before arriving at the harbour and small sandy shore. Very pretty, but nothing here worth the journey, was his negative feel of the place. You can keep your Portmuck – I'd even prefer Dugway.

The climb back up the hill made him breathless, a reminder that he was not as fit as he used to be. Fit enough for a fight with a couple of retired soldiers, especially at close range with a handgun at the ready and surprise in his corner.

Retracing his steps to the main road, he continued his journey to Brown's Bay.

Chapter Forty-Eight

Martin and Penelope Richmond arrived at de Courcy's cottage just after 4 p.m. and were warmly welcomed by the inhabitants. The four stood talking beside the open gate in the sunshine; the first time the sun had broken through the clouds that day.

"Why don't we walk down to the bay?" suggested Penelope. "Now that the sun is out, it is warm enough."

The suggestion was taken up, and four walkers made their way down the hill after de Courcy had closed the windows and locked the door.

Hunter had the four of them in view through his binoculars. Earlier, Hunter had stopped sharply as the car approached him then overtook him and stopped beside the cottage. He watched from his position in the ditch. The knowledge that Sutton was one of the men who came out of the cottage to meet the car travellers made his heart beat faster. There he was – Sutton – the trouble he caused me. . .

Hunter used his time in the ditch to survey the surrounding area. Two cars parked there – one that had just arrived, the other parked in front of it. A choice of two get-away vehicles! Things were looking up!

The four had their backs to him now and were walking down the hill. Matters were certainly better still! He could let them have it as soon as he was in comfortable range. He could see that the cars would give him cover – they would be dead before they knew it. Hunter reasoned that the two others were likely to be UVF people, so it didn't matter if he managed to get them all. Cool down, cool down – the American, Sutton, was number-one target – the others could wait. But Sutton? He must die – must, must, must.

Hunter had to get closer to ensure that he didn't miss. His record in training with small arms was good, but he needed to get to within twenty metres of the target to be sure of success.

They were well down the hill now, and soon they would be out of sight round the comer that led to the public car parks that flanked both sides of the road, parallel to the sandy shore.

The place was clean and quiet. No sign of litter or graffiti or noisy children. There should have been people there. What had happened?

Was it a trap? If he looked about him properly, could he see guns pointing at him, in his direction? No. His imagination was taking over. He must be ready, there was no trap, and by looking in the direction of the sandy bay, he could see families playing with their children. Ready now – no foul-ups this time. I have one go at this – only one.

Hunter kept his distance behind them to about two hundred metres. He left the cars behind him and arrived at the bend in the road. He heard and saw the children now. His breathing was getting deeper and he was starting to perspire. He took the bottle of orange juice and drank deeply – that's better. It was carbonated, but his thirst demanded that he swallow it fast. Another deep drink and he finished it. Hunter threw the empty bottle to the side of the road, where it landed at the foot of a TAKE YOUR LITTER HOME sign, and he began to jog towards the targets.

He was now a hundred metres from them and gaining on them fast. They had stopped walking and were looking out to sea. A small rowing boat was passing and attracted their attention.

It won't be a boat they will be stopping, it will be lead, thought Hunter as he came within fifty metres. He slowed down a little, as he withdrew the weapon and removed the safety.

Now thirty metres. He could do it from here. No, get closer. His slow jog continued. A few more steps and it would be done. Hunter stopped, took aim, and the carbonated drink caused him to burp loudly.

Sutton turned to see what the noise was, saw the man with the gun pointing at him, and shouted.

Sutton moved to his left and brought his automatic to his hand, released the safety and fired. Too late.

Hunter had already shot twice. His first shot was meant for Sutton, but missed him. Where Sutton was standing, there was now de Courcy. De Courcy stopped Hunter's first bullet. The second from Hunter also struck home, but who got it?

They moved about too fast. Hunter wasn't shooting at stationary targets: these targets moved. Taking better aim, Hunter was ready for his third shot. It was not to be.

Sutton fired again, and again. Hunter crumpled on the spot and fell forward on to McBrien's gun, which became buried beneath him.

The scene was unreal. Three people down, not moving, another with gun in hand, walking towards one of the three, and one screaming silently before fainting.

Sutton reached down at the body of the person who seconds ago took shots at him, and kicked him over on to his back.

"Hunter!" he gasped. Sutton checked for a pulse – nothing. He took the gun from the dead hand, removed the magazine, taking care not to destroy Hunter's fingerprints, and wrapping it in his jacket, carried it under his arm. To the left of the car park, a man with a mobile phone in his hand came to assist the injured.

"I'm a doctor," he said, "stand back. I've called for an ambulance and for the police. I suggest you stay here," addressing Sutton, who was still holding his gun in his free hand. The doctor pocketed the mobile and made a quick examination of Richmond. "Looks worse than it is – you will be fine. A bit of pain, but nothing serious. Don't move." The doctor pulled a clean handkerchief from somewhere and stuffed it into the leg wound. "Hold this here. That's right, keep your thumb here and your finger there – good."

The doctor moved to de Courcy and shook his head.

"Is it bad, Doc?' asked Sutton.

"Difficult to say. Any bullet to the head is bad." The doctor checked the pulse – strong and regular – good. Breathing steady too – good. "Don't leave him. I will check out the lady."

There was a deep throbbing sound filling the air. It was coming from somewhere. It was getting a little louder, but nothing was seen. Sutton knew exactly what it was – a helicopter – an Army helicopter.

"Doctor, your phone – quick – please." The doctor had satisfied himself that Penelope was in any medical danger, so he handed the mobile to the man with the gun. Sutton dialled the Lisburn number, and while he waited for the connection he moved to Hunter's body. Sutton gave it a quick search and removed a passport, a billfold, and a wallet.

324

"Hi! Major Sutton here. There is a helicopter over Larne – I guess a Wessex. Can you patch me through to it? Quick – there has been a shooting and I need to get two people to hospital fast."

The doctor had heard Sutton's side of the call as he examined Hunter for signs of life.

"Captain Young? Major Sutton here. I'm at Brown's Bay, Island Magee. Two people shot, one a British major. I need to get them to hospital fast – can you get here? I'll clear the car park for you to land – okay?" Sutton nodded into the phone then returned it to the doctor.

The people had left the sandy shore and were gathered beside their cars. Parents were making sure their siblings were all accounted for.

"Listen, people," Sutton shouted as loud as he could. "Move your cars out of here," gesturing to the car park on the sea side of the road, "and park them over here," pointing to the car park on the land side of the road. "MOVE IT – NOW – Come on, now – MOVE."

Slowly at first, then with conviction, the cars moved as requested, leaving a landing space away from overhead power cables, large enough for a couple of Wessex's to land.

It was a Wessex, and it was noisy, and it was coming. It came over the hill from Mill Bay direction, made a wide circle, and approached the beach of Brown's Bay from the sea.

Sutton, standing in the middle of the now vacant car park, was signalling to the helicopter by waving his hands above his head, and then pointing to the ground around him. The Wessex moved towards him and reduced height.

I had better get out of here, Sutton said to himself, and went back to the doctor, who was taking care of his jacket and of de Courcy's head.

The noise was worse now, and the size of the beast dwarfed all around it. The Wessex hovered at about twenty feet, while a helmeted soldier swung out from the body of the beast and abseiled to the ground. Landing on his feet, he let the wire go, undid his harness, and made his way to Sutton, who in turn brought him to the doctor.

"Get these two to hospital fast. Try Dundonald – there is space to land there," suggested Sutton to the soldier. "The doc here will let you know how they are." Sutton left the doctor and the soldier to sort it out.

Penelope had recovered and was comforting her injured husband. The noise of the engine and the rotors didn't seem to matter.

Penelope didn't notice it. She didn't notice the soldier speak to the pilot either. The machine was guided in to a smooth landing after the area was checked for obstacles. Two more men left the helicopter carrying a stretcher, and with help from the doctor they got de Courcy strapped onto the stretcher and into the helicopter. The banker was next.

"I'll look after his wife," offered Sutton. "Come with me, Penelope. I'll drive you to the hospital. By the time we get there, Martin will have been treated." Sutton guided her away from the noise. "Doctor," Sutton called out. "Get confirmation that it's Dundonald they going to."

The doctor nodded and spoke to the first soldier, who was now beside Hunter's body.

"Soldier," shouted Sutton. "Leave him for the ambulance," pointing to the lifeless body on the ground. "You get the hell out of here fast." The soldier waved and said something to the doctor. The soldier lifted the harness from the ground and roughly threw it into the helicopter, climbed aboard, and they were off.

The doctor confirmed that they were off to Dundonald, as the noise subsided and silence returned. The silence was shortly broken by sirens, which were heard coming down the hill as ambulance and police arrived in convoy.

"Come on, Penelope, back to the cottage – okay?" The walk to the car didn't seem to register with her, but she produced the car keys, which Sutton took, opened the car, and helped her into it. "Hang on a minute," and he went to the cottage. It was locked, and de Courcy had the key. Sutton went round the back, smashed open a window and climbed in. He lifted his mobile phone, deposited his gun and holster in the secret place, climbed out through the broken window and returned to Penelope.

The layout of the car's controls were unfamiliar to him. Sutton started up and proceeded, gingerly at first, on the journey to Dundonald.

In the waiting area of the hospital, they comforted each other, and felt helpless at the same time. The worst was uppermost in their minds, the best a hope sustained by not accepting the worst. Over an hour had passed before a surgeon, accompanied by a theatre nurse, came out to see them.

"Mrs Richmond? Your husband is going to be all right. A couple of torn muscles, a chip in one bone, and some loss of blood – but that's about it," he declared.

"Can I see him?" Penelope asked.

"Of course, but he is suffering from shock, as you understandably are – and some pain, so. . . try and keep him quiet – no talking. Nurse – take Mrs Richmond in, thanks. I'll see you later, Mrs Richmond." The surgeon waited until the nurse and Mrs Richmond had left the waiting area before turning to Sutton.

Sutton wasn't exactly in good humour.

"You sure know how to cheer a person up. What she's seen and suffered, and you tell her she is in shock!"

"Sorry, Mr Ah. . . I'm so tired. On the go for – what is it – twenty hours now. Please forgive me!" The surgeon sat down wearily on the bench seat beside Sutton. "There have been quite a few in here today – following the bomb, and – Never mind. Your friend, Mr de – what is it?"

"De Courcy," volunteered Sutton. The tired surgeon nodded.

"Yes. Mr de Courcy. I don't know, I really don't. Head wound – his scull cracked just here," and he pointed to his high forehead, "and here," pointing to a spot above his left ear. "He's a tough one, in good condition, so he could pull through, but. . ." he closed his eyes and took a deep breath, ". . .right now he's in a coma."

Nothing more was said, to allow the dreadful news to sink in.

"What are his chances?" Sutton's quiet words were spoken with real concern.

"If he has a good night and comes out of the coma tomorrow, I say he has a fair chance. That's the best I've got. Does he have any family?"

"You're looking at it. Can I hang around here? I got no place to go!

"Of course. You are probably hungry – I'll see if there is anything I can get. Sandwiches all right?"

"Thanks, Doc – sure sounds good. And something for Mrs Richmond – okay?"

Another hour passed. Sutton and Penelope finished the selection of sandwiches and tea, and felt the better for it.

"Let me drive you home, Penelope. There is nothing we can do here but wait, and you wait easier at home – okay?"

"I want to thank you, Elmer. You have been a great help to me."
She stood up and gave Sutton a tired smile. "Thank God he is not
badly hurt. How is Edward?"

"Not too good," was all he could say. "Come on – let's get out of
here. You can visit Martin in the morning – okay?"

They left that place and took their worries and cares with them,
leaving behind the only people they really cared for.

Sutton left Penelope and the family car, and returned to the
hospital by taxi, asking the staff on duty to keep him informed of de
Courcy's progress.

It was a long sleepless night, with much walking up and down the
waiting area, with frequent brisk walks around the almost full car
park. There were others besides him, all looking worried, all
wondering how their loved ones were progressing following traumatic
injuries from bombs that once again had destroyed innocent lives in
the name of freedom.

Somehow, Sutton managed to sleep a little on the bench seat which
had become vacant at 3 a.m. He was dreaming of recent times, the
shooting at Brown's Bay and earlier at Muldersleigh.

". . .Mr Sutton. . . Mr Sutton. . ." Someone was shaking him.
He put the dream aside and focused on a white coat standing beside
him. "Mr Sutton – are you awake? I have news for you." A lady's
voice. He sat up, stretched and looked into the smiling face of a
young nurse. "Mr de Courcy- has come round. He is no longer in a
coma, only sleeping. The doctor asked me to tell you. Is that all
right?"

"All right? Sure is all right. Thanks, kid! Can I see him?"

"Better not. Leave him to sleep in peace for a few hours."

" Okay, I'll wait," and he resumed his position on the bench.

"Would you like to lie down in one of our side rooms, Mr Sutton?
We have one that is free just now."

Sutton stood up at a speed that surprised the nurse. "Just show me
the way, kid."

"Oh!" She was not expecting to be called a 'kid'. "If we need the
bed for a patient, I'll have to move you out," and she led the way
down the corridor and into a side room, where he gratefully lay down
and slept.

Sutton was rudely awakened by a person dressed in black, who
shook him rather violently. He woke with a start and was on his feet

before the policeman knew what happened. There were two of them, the uniform branch of the RUC, and it was dark green not black that they were wearing.

"I have a few questions, Sir, if you don't mind." It was the one who awakened him. "You left the scene of an accident in Brown's Bay before the police had a chance to talk to you," he stated. He was waiting for a reply, but Sutton just stared at him. "Well, Sir?" asked the interrogator.

Sutton raised one eyebrow and retorted, "Well what, Sir?"

"It's a serious offence to leave the scene of an accident, Sir."

Sutton couldn't believe this idiot. An accident indeed! Some accident. "Let me tell you something, kid," he started, and came to within inches of his face. The policeman couldn't back away, as he was already against the wall of the small side room. Sutton removed his ID card from a back pocket without taking his eyes off the man, and held it up. "I'm Army – see? And the patient is Army. I'm Major Sutton, the patient is Major de Courcy. Now back off and have a word with Superintendent Richards, who will confirm my story, before I throw you out."

Before the policemen reacted, Sutton lifted one of the clean towels beside the bed, took Hunter's gun from his jacket and, wrapping it in the towel, held it out. "Take this to your guys in Head Office. It's the dead man's gun. Watch it – there are prints on it. And here," Sutton withdrew the billfold and wallet, "These were also on him – okay? Give me a receipt – now."

The shock tactics worked wonders. The policemen looked at each other in bewilderment, as one accepted the wrapped gun and the billfold and wallet, while the other produced some sort of notebook and wrote something before tearing out the page and giving it to Sutton. Sutton read what was written.

"Thanks," he said. "Now – you sign it as well," and he handed the paper to the officer who was holding the gun and wallets.

Sutton stole a glance at his watch – it couldn't be! "What time is it, you guys?"

"6.35, Sir." That confirmed it.

"You guys came in here and got me up at 0635? Are you nuts? Go on – get out of here," and he followed them out of the side room, where he saw the nurse giving him a furtive look as he pocketed the signed receipt. "I suppose you put them up to waking me up at this hour – huh?" She felt trapped. "Don't worry, kid. I owe you for the bed – thanks. Tell me – how is Mr de Courcy?"

The police left them to it and approached their car, where a radio message was made to the superintendent's office, who confirmed that there existed such people as Major Sutton and Major de Courcy, and yes, they were on their side.

"I'll find out for you. Would you mind waiting in the waiting area, please? I need to make the side room ready." The nurse left him to find his own way as she went to make enquiries in Intensive Care.

She didn't return, but the doctor on duty, a different one from before, entered the waiting area. The habit of the white coat brigade walking around wearing their gear unbuttoned, and hands stuck deep inside deep pockets, was practised by this one. Sutton thought it must be part of their training to be able to walk looking tired yet still awake.

"Mr Sutton?"

"Yeah?"

"I can tell you that Mr de Courcy is still on the danger list, but progressing as well as can be expected. All the signs are good, but it's still too early to be sure. You know, we were told that it was a bullet that did it. We didn't find a bullet, and the X-ray is clear. Tell me, do you know the other one?"

"Mr Richmond? I know him – I brought his wife here yesterday. What's the news?"

"You know, that's the fourth time he's been here for bullet wounds. Not a lucky person – is he?"

"He's alive. That's lucky in my book, Doc. When can I see Mr de Courcy?"

"Leave it until eight. I'll still be on duty, so you can phone and ask for me – I'm Dr Eric Chalmers."

"No need. I'm staying till I see him. I'll hang around here," and he gestured about the place including the car park.

Sutton was jogging in the car park at about eight, when he heard his name being called. "Elmer. . . Elmer. . ." Mrs Richmond was waving to him from across the car park. He returned her wave and jogged towards her.

"Hi, Penelope, you're here early."

"So are you. My, you look in a bad state," as she noticed his unshaven, unkempt look. "Have you been home at all?"

"I've been here all night. No point in going to the cottage until I know how Edward is. Your man is okay – he is fine. Edward is another story."

"I'm sorry, Elmer. Look – let me see how Martin is, then I'll give you a lift home." Sutton was about to protest against such an offer. "No argument, now. Let's see how the wounded are getting on – coming?"

Richmond was in a little pain, but fine, de Courcy was no worse and looked peaceful in his bandaged state. Sutton was advised to leave and wait for a further twenty-four hours before a visit could be recommended.

Penelope drove Sutton to Brown's Bay, where he made coffee and set out the tin of chocolate biscuits on the table. A little rough and ready, but friendly.

"What does the bank make of your man getting shot for the fourth time?"

"The bank! I forgot to tell them. Can I use your phone, Elmer? I'd better contact them." Rather embarrassed at her memory lapse, she telephoned the branch and asked for the Assistant Manager. "Sorry I'm late but I forgot! Martin has been shot again. Yes – again! He's in Dundonald – again! Yes – the fourth time. I don't know how long he'll be off, but you're probably getting used to it. Oh yes – not too serious – thank you – bye." Penelope noticed how weary Sutton appeared and didn't see him take a couple of pills when she was on the phone. "Look – I'd better go. And thanks for everything you did yesterday, Elmer."

He saw her out and waited until the car was out of sight before having a shave and shower, then caught up on some sleep. What did he do yesterday that warranted thanks? He killed someone! Why thanks? Hunter was a bad one – but he didn't need to die. He struggled in his sleep over Hunter, and the image of his death — nasty, unnecessary. . . He was interrupted – a banging sound – more shooting? No, the door was on the receiving end of an agitated fist.

"Coming," he said in a voice loud enough to stop the banging. It was 3.30 p.m. Sutton opened the door to find Susannah standing in front of him.

"I must speak to him, Elmer – can I come in?"

He stepped aside to let her enter and closed the door behind her.

Sutton looked again at his watch – the last time he looked, he hadn't seen it. Mental calculation told him that he could take two more pills, which he did using some water to assist their journey.

"Let me think for a minute, Susannah – don't say anything," and with head bowed and eyes closed, he sat on his easy chair. She sat in de Courcy's chair. He remembered – and started slowly, "Are you – going to – get out of – the UVF? Because if you don't – I won't let you see him. Not that it matters anyway, not after yesterday."

"I don't know – I really don't know. I'm going to see someone tomorrow and I'll know then. Where is he?"

"He's not here." Sutton relaxed as the painkillers started to work. "And he won't be back here, unless things turn out good. Did you hear what happened here yesterday?"

"I heard nothing – what are you talking about? Look, I've been out of my mind since I last spoke with him – I must see him. Please."

Sutton raised his head and looked at the sad face in front of him.

"Do you want it straight?"

"What do you mean? I want to *see* him."

"You can't. He might be dead."

Chapter Forty-Nine

Whatever colour she had, vanished. The pale sickly look of one on the verge of death was upon her. It was cruel, Sutton realised, but she asked for it. She can't be hurting him now, he reasoned, he needs all his strength to recover, not be knocked down again by someone whose loyalties are opposed to his.

"Dead?" she whispered. "Might be *dead*?"

"All he wanted he saw in you, Susannah, but it was torturing him. He is an Army man and can't be having close relationships with terrorists. We were in the business of working together on one job. The problem was, he fell for you." He was feeling a little better now. He stood up. "Look, kid. It was all business then, you and he overstepped the boundaries of business, and. . . well. . . Now it's happened!"

"What happened?" She found that she could only talk in a whisper.

"Another shooting – here – in Brown's Bay. One dead – two injured." She was paralysed at the news. "Edward received a bullet wound to the head. He's in intensive care. If he was to see you, the strain of it could kill him. That's why I'm not telling you where he is. And if you find where he is and go to him," he was trying to frighten her – to keep her away, "the armed guard is likely to shoot you as a known UVF terrorist. So – stay away."

She was fixed to the chair as if part of the upholstery. "How bad is he?" Another whisper. She imagined someone with head wounds, perhaps brain damage, requiring full-time nursing attention. Perhaps confined to wheel chair – Perhaps. . . Her imagination was uncontrolled. She would look after him, no matter what.

"I will not know for another day. If you like, call here again tomorrow – after you have seen whom you need to see – okay? I'll let you know what I know." She didn't move. "I can't give you false hopes, kid. I guess you will be praying for him – I have."

She remained seated for fifteen minutes before managing to get to her feet and speak. "Tomorrow then. I'll be here at four in the afternoon, if that's all right, Elmer."

Sutton saw the pathetic figure leave and drive off slowly.

*

Sutton nailed a piece of hardboard over the broken window, and cleared away the glass fragments. Sometime he would get it repaired – but not now. Now, he needed something to eat something substantial, something that would satisfy the appetite. He locked up and pocketed the spare key, remembering that de Courcy still had the other key, and made his way to the 'Coffee & Cream' restaurant in Whitehead, where a simple meal of fish and chips, followed by apple pie with custard and a pot of tea, did wonders.

He called at the filling station on the corner of the road that leaves Whitehead to join the main Larne-Carrickfergus route, and filled the tank. Then he bought an early evening paper before returning to the cottage for the night.

The Brown's Bay shooting incident was reported as front page headlines. The names of the victims were not given, only a passing reference to, 'believed to be an American', and 'wounded Army personnel and civilian'. There was the expected, 'Dramatic helicopter dash to hospital' and 'Anyone not interviewed by police who saw the incident is asked to contact. . .' In a separate article on an inside page it was reported that an Armalite rifle in good condition was found by the police near Larne.

Professor Withers was satisfied with Sutton's condition and he arranged for the pharmacy to supply him with the pills on a monthly basis. As long as the dose was maintained at the current level, Sutton was told, the side effects should be minimal. Good – he could accept that.

Sutton left the professor to journey across town to the Ulster at Dundonald. He spent a few hours there, not seeing de Courcy, but feeling the better from having been there, before returning to Brown's Bay. He gave himself enough time to get back before four. She was there before four – it was 3.40. She looked much better, and Sutton told her so.

"You look better, yourself, Elmer. What's the news?"

"You first – have you any news?" He didn't need to listen. Her news was written all over her.

She told him how she had read yesterday's evening paper and heard the news of the Brown's Bay shooting on radio and TV. She had worked out a plan where they couldn't refuse to let her resign; the details she kept from him. She did tell him, ". . .as from 2 p.m. today, that's two hours ago, I'm no longer connected in any way with the UVF. You know, I had a minder! He was always around – well, he's gone. The funny thing is, I feel better now that I'm out of it." Sutton enjoyed the telling. She had regained her youthful energy and colour. She was no longer the pathetic figure in the chair who couldn't talk.

"When I left them and walked to my car – they even had a guard on my car! Well, it had been damaged!" She said it as if she wanted the car to be damaged. "The guard was taken off, so someone kicked in the lights! Proof in my mind that I'm not considered one of them. Good – eh?"

Yes – she was a changed person. That was no act. "Now it's your turn – how's Edward?"

He didn't want to hurt her, but couldn't keep the truth from her. It was all about how you allowed the truth to be expressed and perceived. That had been the problem in Northern Ireland for generations. One side believing things about the other side because they always believed it, and always would. To prove their belief, some well-meaning but loud-mouthed politician would put his or her foot in it, the Government spokesman saying, 'We are winning the war against the IRA', only to find that that encouraged the IRA to increase the bombing and shooting more than ever.

"The good news is, he is out of the coma. The bad news – it will be another day before they can test for brain damage. The other good news – all the signs are right for recovery. But recovery is not certain."

She seemed to accept the news as good news. He was alive, and that was all she needed right now.

"Can I see him? Tell me where he is," she pleaded.

"First, let me tell him about your departure from the UVF. Then I will take you to visit him – okay?"

"But why? What's the harm in visiting him?"

It was probably illogical, but Sutton told her anyway. "Until they have completed their tests, it would not be in his - and your - best interest for him to see you thinking that you are still a terrorist. Let me tell him your news, and let him have time to work on it before he sees you."

"That's stupid." She was walking around the floor trying to keep her composure. "All right, all right, I accept that - provided you let me send him something. I would like to send him some flowers - is that all right?"

"Sure, kid. Flowers with a hand-written message could do wonders. I'll buy the flowers, you start writing." He took the thirty pounds she offered, and read the note she wanted to accompany the flowers, then saw her to the damaged car.

"You could take that heap to the garage on the island. He would fix the lights for you."

"No thanks, Elmer. And it's not a heap. I know people in Larne who will do it for me. They are not UVF, in case you are worried," and she climbed into the heap. The window was open, allowing her to ask, "When will you phone me about Edward?"

"Tomorrow - at noon. Will you be home at that time or at another UVF meeting?" She stuck out her tongue, closed the window and drove off. That's better, Sutton decided, more like it. He lifted his mobile phone and called the hospital. The news was promising, so he made ready to visit the hospital that evening. It was a wasted journey - there was no change, and no visitors were allowed.

He returned to the hospital at ten the next morning, and was advised that de Courcy was moved from intensive care into the wards. There he saw him. He was lying down, his head heavily bandaged and raised on pillows to allow him to see more than the ceiling. The eyes were closed, surrounded with bruises, all black and red and distorted. He could be asleep.

"It's all right - you can talk to him."

"Who can talk?" enquired de Courcy.

"Boy, am I glad to see you, old boy, old boy. You have been in the wars - huh?"

"Elmer. It's good of you to call." De Courcy remained motionless with eyes closed. "How are things? They tell me nothing in here. Sorry I can't take a look at you, old boy - the eyes are a bit tired."

"Yeah. They look worse than tired, Edward." Sutton sat on the chair beside the bed, pulling it close to de Courcy. "Tell me if I'm tiring you or speaking too loud – right?"

"That's – just fine – Elmer, no louder. Tell me – are we alone?" Sutton looked around. The side ward had a capacity for four beds – three were empty. Sutton saw how de Courcy was wired to monitoring equipment that probably had connections to other monitors in an adjacent room.

"Yeah – just the two of us. Why do you ask?"

"Get closer, Elmer. Now tell me, what happened? I remember seeing a chap pointing a gun – then – nothing."

"You were told nothing? Nothing at all?"

"I was told not to move or exert myself, and to press this button," he held out the plastic box he was holding in his hand, "if I needed anything – that's all."

" Okay. First, the guy who shot you is dead. It was Captain Hunter from the States – he's the guy from Dugway." Sutton stopped to take notice of de Courcy's reaction.

"Go on."

"Right." Sutton looked around the ward – still nobody- about "The banker stopped one, again. He's okay and in the next ward. You are in the Ulster Hospital in Dundonald. I'm okay and so is Penelope. There was a doctor at Brown's Bay who gave you first aid – that's about it. I'll give you the details later – okay?"

De Courcy was digesting the information. He didn't remember any of it, only a faint recollection of noise. "Was there much noise? I seem to think of noise of some sort."

He's not as bad as he looks, thought Sutton, so he told him of the helicopter. De Courcy took it all in, and asked sensible questions to have his understanding of the events made clear.

"What time of day is it – and what day is it, old boy?"

"It's Tuesday."

"Tuesday. That *is* news. Whatever happened to Monday?"

"And it's 1030 hours, or it will be in five minutes or so. Do you need anything?"

"I'll tell you what I don't need – visitors! Apart from yourself, old boy, I don't want to see anyone for a few days. Not until I can get up and walk anyway." That's not the de Courcy of the Gulf War days. He must be feeling it. "How's your head, old boy? Still on the professor's pills?"

"Yeah. The head is real good now. Yesterday it was rough – real bad."

The conversation stopped for a while. The silence wasn't a problem, and gave each time for their separate thoughts – de Courcy, to go over the events as described by Sutton, Sutton to go over what he should say about Susannah.

"I've some other news for you. Good news from Susannah."

"NO." The 'no' was painfully loud, so loud that Sutton wondered whether it related to his head. Was he in pain? "I don't want to see her. I don't want her to come here and see me." De Courcy was still hurting from the last meeting with her, and couldn't face meeting her again.

"She resigned from the organisation – she's out of it. I said – she is out of it." Sutton spoke the words slowly, softly, and gently. "And she told me yesterday afternoon that she feels better for being away from it."

The silence came again, and Sutton witnessed tears fall down de Courcy's face.

"Blast it!" de Courcy whispered. "I love that blasted girl, Elmer, and I don't know what to do." Sutton lifted a tissue from the box on the bed cabinet and gently wiped away the tears.

"You are a lucky man, Edward. Lucky. She's going nuts over you and she doesn't know what to do either. Tell you what. Let me bring her here on, say – Friday – okay? By Friday you should be a little better." De Courcy remained quiet. "She needs to see you. She doesn't know the extent of your injuries and is demanding to see you. I haven't told her where you are, but she will find out soon. Friday?"

"Yes – please, and thanks – old boy."

Sutton reached over to the cabinet and lifted the glass of water to allow two pills to be swallowed before returning to the island. He stopped off at a large supermarket called Abbeycentre, and stocked up with fresh vegetables, fruit, and a few steaks that he would store in the freezer.

On his arrival at the cottage, he telephoned Susannah and managed to extract a promise from her that she would not contact or visit de Courcy until he would take her on Friday. In return, Sutton advised her of his improving condition and that de Courcy seemed pleased of her resignation from the organisation. No, he hadn't got the flowers yet, but would do so on Thursday. To get them earlier would be pointless as de Courcy couldn't see them.

Chapter Fifty

It was the day after the shootings at Brown's Bay that saw Willis Chapman, reporter with the *Belfast Telegraph*, enter the proceedings. It had been raining earlier in the day but had brightened sufficiently for Chapman to decide to play a round of golf. It was some time since he had played – about two months – so he wasn't expecting to do well. He was a member of Scrabo Golf Club and presented himself ready to make up a four. If he found himself alone, he would go round alone.

Chapman was in luck. Three other members invited him to join them. He was right not to expect to do well – he didn't. Entering the club house afterwards, the conversation was taken up by one of the four.

"You'll find this interesting, Willis. There may be a story in it for you, but I can't give you names – interested?"

"Don't stop now, Eric – what's your news?"

"It concerns a patient we have in the hospital. A civilian with no terrorist or military connection who gets himself shot."

"Is that it?" Chapman was disappointed.

"There is more. He has been shot four separate times in as many months. Interesting, don't you think?" suggested Dr Chalmers.

"Come on, you two," interrupted the victorious pair of Pat O'Connor and John Small. "It's your turn to buy!"

Shot four times? A man not connected to terrorist groups or to the security forces? Yes, it *was* interesting – and demanded investigation. Chapman had good contacts within the RUC and was not slow to use them. He would use them on this. Face to face was better than the telephone, so Chapman called at the RUC Station in Castlereagh and, being known, was allowed in to one of the offices. Superintendent Richards, expecting some news item that would once again stop some unnecessary loss of life, gave Chapman an audience.

"Nothing for you this time, Stephen. This time I want something from you. A name of a person and the history – if there is one."

Superintendent Richards provided Chapman with the information on the basis that the source would not be disclosed.

Later that day, Chapman entered Dundonald Hospital to visit Martin Richmond. He knew Richmond. He hadn't seen him for years, but he knew him. They were at school together. How small Northern Ireland was. That would be his opening gambit, Chapman decided, and he approached the ward.

Richmond, sitting up in bed, was listening to a performance of Bruckner's 5th Symphony by way of a personal CD player and some ageing Sony MDR7 headphones. He was engrossed, motionless, and oblivious to the surroundings. It was over – the end of the great orchestral masterpiece. Richmond removed the headphones, leant over to his left, switched off the Discman and returned the CD to its plastic case.

"Hi, Martin! Remember me?" That was as good an opening remark as any, thought Chapman.

Richmond looked towards the blurred figure before him, took up his glasses that were beside the Discman, and put them on. Then he recognised Chapman.

"Good heavens! Willis Chapman! King of the hacks! What brings you here?"

"Just passing. You know how it is – looking for a story that might be worth investing some time on."

Chapman steered the conversation to their schooldays, bringing back memories of teachers and fellow pupils. It wasn't long before the subsequent years of starting employment, getting married and rearing families were included.

"What happened to you, Martin, that finds you in hospital?" Nothing like going in to the heart of it.

"I wish I knew, Willis. You tell me, you're the journalist."

Chapman could never accept the title 'journalist' to describe the work he did. "No, not a journalist – a reporter," he replied.

"Touched a nerve, have I?" as Richmond registered the changed tone in Chapman's voice.

"It's only me and my dislike for journalists," responded Chapman.

Richmond wasn't in pain; more a discomfort that hindered movement. Being shot twice in the same leg wasn't his idea of fun.

He caught the reporter's views on journalists and found that he could agree with Chapman's explanation of the differences between the terms.

"So, Willis, as a reporter, you stick to the facts without moralising, but journalists forget the facts to put forward their own agenda. Is that it?"

"Near enough. Now tell me how you managed to get shot for the fourth time." That was neat, thought Chapman. Now, let's see if there is a story here.

"What protection do I have, should I tell you, Willis? You have nothing to lose but I could get shot again. I need your agreement that you won't print or tell anyone else without my prior approval."

Chapman didn't like working with his hands tied. More and more of his contacts were looking for this type of arrangement, particularly the criminal and terrorist elements of society. This made life complicated for him, and impossible for his editor. Fortunately he had good contacts, and his work had helped cement the trust between them. This trust worked both ways and Chapman did his best not to abuse it. Superintendent Stephen Richards had benefited from the reporter's information, in return for which Chapman had scooped the dailies numerous times. But Martin Richmond wasn't much of a catch. What could he know? "What sort of agreement do you have in mind?"

"As simple as possible, Willis. Whatever I tell you is not to be published or discussed with others without my authority – I'll accept that. That's all."

That's all! Another person protecting their own interests, never mind the public good. "What information could you have that would require such an arrangement?"

Richmond's leg was annoying him just now, which didn't help him in his thinking. He didn't mean to give so much away at this stage. "What purpose is served by a British and an American Army officer working together here and in America? Would that do for starters? And the authority to call up helicopter support using a mobile phone. Interested yet?" Richmond moved his leg a little to the right – that was better – yes, it had eased up a bit. Chapman was interested now and asked for an explanation. Richmond shook his head and, reaching out, picked up his headphones and took off his glasses.

"If I were to agree to your arrangement, it has to be two way. I need something from you. You, in turn, should agree to tell no other reporter, or journalist, unless I authorise it. Will you agree?" Chapman asked.

"That sounds fair. We agree to keep the information between us, confidential. I tell you what I feel I can tell you, and you will not tell anyone else without an authorisation from me. That includes publishing in any form, such as TV and the papers."

"I can go with that. Agreed – I agree. Now, what can you tell me?"

Richmond didn't know where to start. The torpedo at the Gobbins seemed the best point to start, so he started and told Chapman everything. Everything, except the examination of the torpedo, and the money. No, he left out everything to do with finding and 'storing' the money. Richmond probably left a few other things out, but not deliberately. Time would bring back other incidents. . .

"Let me check on this. You said that an American Major Elmer Sutton and a British Major de Courcy are involved. Where can I find them?"

Richmond pointed to the end of the ward. "Try the Sister on duty. Major de Courcy got shot at the same time as me. In fact, he has been around me on three of the times I got shot – remember, I already told you."

"You mean he's *here*? In Dundonald Hospital?" Chapman expressed in surprise.

Richmond put on the headphones, and inserted a CD into the player. "Got it in one. See you later – that's enough for one day," and pressed 'play'.

The Sister confirmed that de Courcy was a patient, and no, Chapman couldn't see him as he was too ill. That brought Chapman to decide to leave the hospital and pay a return visit to RUC Castlereagh, and talk to Superintendent Richards. Richards, persuaded by Chapman that there was the possibility of a big story, let the reporter see the confidential file on Major de Courcy.

"The usual agreement, Willis? You take nothing and publish nothing without my clearance. Is that understood?" asked Richards.

Not another one in the same day! "The usual agreement – all right," resigned the reporter.

"I want that back in an hour, Willis, and it's not to leave this room," ordered the superintendent as he left Chapman alone in an interview room with the material.

Chapman had done this before on other cases and was aware of the privileged position that his fellow hacks would kill for – if they knew. He started to inform himself about Major de Courcy. He was impressed with what he read, and memorised the salient points. ". . .served with distinction in Aden, Cyprus, and with NATO. Worked with the Americans in the Gulf War (Desert Storm), and lately with the Army and RUC in Northern Ireland, where he assisted in the gathering of intelligence. The prevention of numerous incidents not recorded here for security reasons are known to the Americans, who consider him responsible for the successful outcome of many NATO problems. Lost his wife in a motoring accident in Cyprus while he was on NATO duty in Italy. His only son, James de Courcy, was killed in S. Armagh while serving with the Royal Green Jackets. Both deaths occurred on the same day and caused Major de Courcy to have a minor breakdown. NATO chiefs for whom he worked appointed a minder to look after him; a Major Lee Elmer Sutton accepted the task. The two officers have worked well together on undercover work against terrorism in Northern Ireland since then. . ."

Chapman read the file, skipping past the boyhood history of him being the son of a Church of England canon, and concentrated on current activities. There wasn't much to read on current activities.

Chapman closed the file and reviewed in his mind what he had just learnt. Perhaps de Courcy would be a better bet than Richmond, the bank manager. Chapman wondered how soon he could talk to him.

The file was returned to the superintendent, allowing Chapman to leave to discuss matters with his editor.

"There might be a big story, Temple, but I'm locked into the usual terms – authorisation before I can publish," Chapman advised Temple Spooner, his editor.

"Are you likely to get the authority? You have in the past," encouraged Spooner.

"I think so. But there is a problem – not only do the police need to clear some of it, but there is the chance I'll need clearance from two Army people. One English, the other American – Oh, and a civilian bank manager!" Chapman added.

"How much time do you want?"

"Say, two weeks? I can't see it being done in less."

Spooner wasn't about to spoil his best man's chances of another scoop. The last story was sold to the big boys in London; and who knows - if there was an American Army officer involved. . . "Fine. See me again in two weeks. Anything else?" asked Spooner.

Chapter Fifty-One

Captain Owen Croft and his wife Mary Lou, settled into the company house in Washington, which was formerly the residence of a major recently moved to NATO. It was considered most unusual for a captain to live in quarters deemed good enough for a major, a point that other captains and majors in the CIA were only too quick to make. Croft concentrated on his job in the Electronics Surveillance – Research unit and kept out of the in-fighting. This philosophy produced it's reward, as Croft's paper to his boss, T. J. Smith, on how to improve the monitoring of people entering and leaving sensitive areas won approval from both the Secretary of Defence and the Chief of Staff. It was to be implemented immediately. To celebrate this success so soon after his arrival in the Pentagon, Croft invited his sister to stay for a few days.

Susannah didn't know what to do. She was torn between family and matters of the heart. She phoned Sutton but there was no answer. She wrote him a note saying that she would be away for a few days, so she would not be back in time for their Friday visit to de Courcy. Family problems, she gave as the reason.

"I'm off to see Owen for a few days, Joe. Do you mind?"

*

"You must destroy all the tapes, Sis – it's vital! I've destroyed all the originals and the spare copies I had. Can you destroy your copies?" Susannah had one set, the other she gave to the General. There was no chance that the General would return his copy of the tapes – not now. She couldn't even get an audience. How was she to explain that to Owen? The copies she held could be destroyed, and she gave Owen word on that – yes, she would burn them, not just erase them. . .

"I can't, Owen. I've left the organisation – I'm no longer part of it."

Owen noticed the change in her since they last met in Green Bay, and guessed that she had at last met someone. Over dinner in the company house, Susannah talked to Owen and Mary Lou of how she had met de Courcy, and how she had taken him to Carrickfergus Castle. ". . .You should have seen his face," she laughed, "when he saw his name in print – imagine it – de Courcy the castle builder!"

She answered Owen's questions on de Courcy's history as best she could. Thinking of him made her regret the journey to Washington – she realised that she did miss him. Was he all right? Would he recover? "I thought you were in trouble, Owen, that's why I came. I would not have come just for your celebration." Oh yes, she was pleased to hear of his move, his promotion and his success, and of course of their forthcoming family, but she was making a new life for herself. Would he live? Susannah told Owen of the trouble in Island Magee, and how Sutton had supported her.

After dinner, Mary Lou insisted on clearing up by herself to allow brother and sister some time together. Owen used the time to go into the matter of the tapes again.

"If the tapes get out, I'm finished – finished!" resigned Croft. "The only chance I had was getting your copies destroyed."

"Calm down, Owen. How can they be traced back to you? Surely the only way that can happen is if the people on the tapes give the details to someone, and they don't know of the tapes."

Croft wasn't convinced. "As long as the tapes don't surface, we will be safe. But if they are not destroyed. . . well, remember the UVF people in Green Bay?"

"What of it, Owen?"

"What of it? Wake up, Susannah! If the UVF can find us in Green Bay, how much easier is it for the US Army to find the source of the tapes? I'll tell you – very easy. And when they do – I'm finished." Croft remembered Susannah mentioning Sutton by name. "Major Sutton is mentioned on the tapes, along with your de Courcy, you know. Did you know that?"

She didn't respond, just regretted all the more her decision to leave de Courcy for this wasted journey. There was nothing that could be done about the tapes, and Croft knew it. Croft changed his attention to de Courcy. "Will you marry him, Sis?"

She didn't respond to that either. How could she? Sutton's latest news was promising, but not definite enough to allow her to plan the future. Softly, as if dreaming, she thought aloud. "If he lives, he would probably want to leave Island Magee and return to England. There are too many bad memories there. I don't think I could live in England." She pictured the cottage in Brown's Bay. "I suppose we could keep the cottage as a holiday place and spend the summers there."

Croft forgot his problem and put his contribution on the table. "You can come here anytime, Sis. With or without de Courcy."

"And the tapes?" she goaded.

"To hell with the tapes!"

*

Sutton left de Courcy's bedside just as Superintendent Richards pulled up in the car park. They missed each other, which was unfortunate as it would have allowed Richards to get, first hand, the Brown's Bay story.

Richards didn't stay too long with de Courcy, not because he felt de Courcy wanted him to go but because Richards saw Chapman enter the ward and thought that Chapman could get more information than him. Richards gestured to Chapman not to come any closer. The reporter understood and retreated to the visitors' waiting area outside the ward.

Ten minutes later, Richards passed Chapman on his way back to the car.

"Take it easy, Willis – he has had it rough. Don't stay too long. Try and get something on his UVF contacts for me," and he was gone.

Chapman approached de Courcy and stood at the foot of the bed. De Courcy sensed that someone was there, but kept his eyes closed.

"Yes?"

"It's all right, Mr de Courcy – I'm only visiting and called to say 'hullo'. I'm Willis Chapman from the *Belfast Telegraph*."

De Courcy remembered the name from somewhere. The files in the RUC and in the Army HQ Lisburn often mentioned a Willis Chapman. "You are a journalist, then," pronounced de Courcy.

"No. I don't like journalists – I'm a reporter."

Now I remember him, thought de Courcy. Not being able to see yet makes it difficult to confirm his identity, so de Courcy wasn't going to say much.

"I've just visited a fellow patient of yours, a chap called Martin Richmond. A bank manager." Courcy understood but remained silent. "He is in some pain, but should be all right. Are you all right, Mr de Courcy?"

"Fine. They don't tell me much, so I must be fine."

Chapman decided to leave "Look – you're in no mood for company. I'll leave what I want for another day," and he began to walk away.

"Wait." Chapman returned to the foot of the bed. "Right now, company is welcome. I just don't want to talk much, but if you don't mind the silence, I would appreciate your company – Mr Reporter."

"Reporter? Thanks, Mr de Courcy. You are one of the few who compliments me."

"I know some of your work, Mr Chapman."

Chapman didn't want to push his luck too far. "I'll take that as a positive remark. Your injuries, Mr de Courcy, how did you sustain them?"

"All in the line of duty, old boy. Not in a position to say more."

Too soon. Chapman tried another tack. "What do you think of Northern Ireland, Mr de Courcy?"

De Courcy gave a slight smile. He began to voice his opinions in a slow and quiet monotone. "Northern Ireland – what a beautiful place. The Mournes. Great walks in the Mournes – and the lakes in Fermanagh – the boats, the fishing. Good food and plenty of it. For something to eat, 'reporter', try the Coffee and Cream – Whitehead. Cheap too. . ." De Courcy continued mentioning places he had visited with Sutton, or his son. The memories flooded back, slowing his speaking but not his thinking. "I'll probably retire here. I am retired! Can't make my mind up – probably County Antrim." De Courcy raised his hand to his head. It felt damp. Chapman noticed the red patch getting larger.

"Ring for a nurse, old boy. . ." He had forgotten about the call button. Chapman pushed the button, and waited until Sister and nurse arrived, then he left.

*

Sutton called with de Courcy on Wednesday morning, and for the first time since the shooting he noticed de Courcy looking at him. The eyes were still black, but open. The swelling was not as pronounced, and the wounds had received fresh dressings.

"Hi, Edward. You still look like nothing. How's the head?"

De Courcy raised his hand in acknowledgement but said nothing.

"I have some pills here, Edward. Great for sore heads! Do you want a couple?" The silent de Courcy smiled. "Friday's okay. She will be here on Friday. I'll bring her with me – okay?"

This time, he spoke. "Fine, old boy. I gather your head is not troubling you."

Superintendent Richards joined them, and as usually happens with hospital visitors after the expected 'How are you' to the patient, they ignored him and carried out their business amongst themselves. In this case, the business was with Sutton. Sutton answered Richards' questions concerning the gun, the billfold, and the wallet. It didn't take long.

"See you later, Edward – okay?" and Sutton was gone.

Richards and de Courcy, exchanged pleasantries rather than business before Richards left for another meeting. "Go and see Martin Richmond as soon as you can," suggested Richards as he departed. De Courcy watched him leave and speak to someone in the waiting area. De Courcy recognised him – Chapman. The reporter had turned up again. Richards and Chapman talked for some time. Why? What was going on between them? De Courcy would ask Chapman should he pass that way. The opportunity arrived when Chapman, now alone, approached de Courcy's bed.

"I saw you talking to Richards. What business have you with Richards?"

"Just enquiring after your health. You were not in great condition yesterday," Chapman answered. De Courcy grunted.

"Do you mind my company?" Chapman didn't want to force matters.

"Sit down, please – and then tell me what you know of Superintendent Richards." Chapman sat beside the bed.

"*I* was planning to interview *you*, not the other way around."

"Interview me, indeed," de Courcy voiced without colour. "And what do you intend to do with anything I may say?"

Not another one. First the banker in the next ward, and now this one. The story would not come easily. "That depends. I can't do anything without approval," Chapman offered.

"Whose approval? Your editor's?"

Chapman knew that de Courcy was mentally quick, head wound or no head wound. "I will certainly need my editor's approval, but that's not it. I have information from the superintendent and can't use it without his authority."

De Courcy recalled to his mind some of the RUC files that confirmed a history of how Chapman kept quiet until being given the 'all clear' to publish. Yes, Chapman could be trusted. "Keep going," prodded de Courcy.

"There is also Mr Richmond, the banker."

De Courcy was surprised at that and hoped he didn't show it. He was a good poker player in his day and believed that he gave little away. Chapman was no fool and he did notice de Courcy's reaction, slight though it was.

That's it, thought Chapman, an entry into his thoughts.

"The banker was with you when he was shot, and was able to tell me a few things."

De Courcy didn't expect that and moved back against the pillow.

Got him again, thought Chapman, so he continued. "Interesting, isn't it? An ordinary bank manager being shot four times, and you were around at the time. . ."

"Hold it right there – just hold it, Mr Chapman." De Courcy moved his position.

"It's all right, Mr de Courcy. I told you that I can't publish without authority – the banker's authority in this case."

"What?!" A quiet astonished whisper of disbelief followed by a gasp from de Courcy let Chapman open the door into his side of the story.

"That's right. I promised the banker that I would not publish or discuss his story without his approval."

De Courcy tried to reach for the glass of water, but it was too awkward for him. Chapman stood up and got it for him, waited until de Courcy had taken a couple of sips, then set the glass down before sitting down.

"What if I were to give you the same assurance, Mr de Courcy? Would that make it easier for you to tell me your story?"

De Courcy thought over the proposal. Usually if someone wanted an answer now, it would be 'no', but if he was permitted to think it over, then the answer could be 'may be'. What had he to lose?

"Drop the 'Mr de Courcy', old boy – Edward is the name. Let me think this through." Chapman's record was good – de Courcy accepted that fact, and was prepared to work under the offered conditions. He might regret it, but. . . being part of the old school, Edward offered his hand to seal their agreement. Willis accepted the hand and welcomed the firm grip.

"Where shall I start from?" asked de Courcy.

"Tell me about the banker. Start with Martin Richmond," suggested Chapman.

De Courcy pointed to the glass and held out his hand for Chapman to pass it to him. Holding the glass without drinking from it, de Courcy began.

"He saved my life – that's all. Imagine it! A middle-aged unfit bank manager saved my life, and I feel troubled about it." De Courcy paused – Chapman waited. "And that's not all – he did it twice. Twice! Once in Las Vegas, and once here in Brown's Bay, and he doesn't know it."

"Why do you feel troubled, Edward?" Chapman decided to use de Courcy's first name now that he was invited to.

"Why? Think, old boy, think. Twice, and he doesn't know, and ends up getting shot himself. That's the element that troubles me. I can't face him – he wouldn't want to know me. By the way, how is he, old boy?"

Chapman was surprised at de Courcy's attitude towards the banker. "He's in some pain, but coming along. He was shot in the same leg as before. You should go and see him when you can. He would cheer you up."

"Not you as well. You are the second person to say that today," and de Courcy guessed that Superintendent Richards had told Chapman to say that.

Chapman wanted to move the story along – to take it away from the hospital. "For a person who is retired, you seem to be pretty busy. How did you get into this job, a job that gets you shot?"

De Courcy needed some time on that one. "It's a long story. Look, old boy – leave it for now. Call again tomorrow and we will see." Getting slowly out of bed, he steadied himself, and with assistance from Chapman he put on his dressing gown.

"Should you be doing this?"

De Courcy nodded his head once and immediately regretted moving it at all. "Of course, old boy. I'm paying a visit to the bathroom," and, lifting a newspaper, he put on his slippers and made his way to the door marked 'Patients Only', leaving Chapman on his own looking around at nobody.

De Courcy waited about thirty seconds behind the door, then slowly opened it an inch or so and looked out to satisfy himself that Chapman had gone. No sign of him, so de Courcy shuffled to the public phone box at the side of the ward and telephoned Superintendent Richards. A coin from the pocket of the dressing gown paid for the call.

"Listen to me, old boy. Get back here PDQ. I want you to tell me what is going on between you and Chapman over our current situation."

"Calm down, Edward – you're not out of the woods yet. Just calm down," Richards said.

"Calm down? Listen, old boy. . ." De Courcy was speaking too loudly and might be overheard, so he reduced the volume. ". . .get over here in twenty minutes – no excuses," and he violently hung up. De Courcy noted the time, added twenty minutes to it, and mentally started to prepare himself to meet Richards as he returned to his bed.

How did he get into this job, indeed? The reporter had asked him that earlier. De Courcy was somewhat calmer now and feeling tired following his exertions. Must be getting old, he thought. Perhaps the doctor was right, and he should take it easy for a while. There were things to do, so he would make enquiries. That's it, he would make enquiries.

He dozed off and remembered another time, another voice. . . 'We would like you to make enquiries, Major. That's all. You would still be retired, but on full pay, of course, and have authority to use the contacts in the RUC and the resources in Lisburn. How does that sound?' It was as clear as hearing it for the first time. His reply was just as clear.

'Who is the RUC contact', de Courcy had asked the general in charge, who was accompanied by a senior civil servant from the

Home Office and another from the Northern Ireland Office. 'One thing at a time, Major. Will you take the job?'

It was some job. All he had to do was make contact with the UVF in County Antrim, gain their confidence, and find out what they knew, how strong they were, and what their plans were. That's all.

'I'll take the job.' Thinking of his dead son made the decision for him, but he found it difficult to believe that he had taken the job. It worked out well. The RUC contact was good, and Sutton was on board with him. He liked working with the Americans. De Courcy found them to be well trained and organised. Not quite as good as our own, but good enough. The team of three worked well and found that their work had diversified dramatically from Northern Ireland to include the USA. The three of them – Sutton, Richards and himself.

He remembered the other team of three – now there was only one. His wife and son were long gone. He was sad and strangely happy at the same time. Happy that his wife did not have to hear of their son's death – it would have destroyed her. Happy too for his memories. It was a good marriage that lasted and grew in strength despite the separation of duty. The memories came back again. They usually did when in the twilight world of half sleep.

'. . .Congratulations, you have a boy!' He would never forget that day. The first time he saw his son. So small, so helpless, so perfect. He remembered holding him for the first time. 'He won't break – here,' said the nurse as she handed him over into his arms from the metal cage that was a National Health cot. 'Your wife is getting tidied up, you can come in in a moment,' and the nurse went behind the screen. Alone with his son, James, for the first time. 'You can come in now,' offered the nurse as she held open the screen to let him pass, then left the three of them to start living.

He was by himself now – the other two. . .

"Having a nice wee sleep, are we?" It was Superintendent Richards quietly rousing him from his dreams.

Coming round, de Courcy recognised his visitor. "I must have dozed off. What time is it?" and he glanced at his watch. He didn't see the watch, or hear Richards reply, but used the time to gather his thoughts. "Yes, old boy, of course. I want to talk to you about Chapman."

Richards sat down, as de Courcy pulled himself up to a sitting position.

"Chapman's good. I owe him for his assistance – you've seen the files, Edward, you know his work."

"Whose side are you on, Stephen?" That hurt Richards. "Allow me to remind you, old boy," de Courcy declared, "that the team does not include the hack. He could be a liability to us. What if he gets shot? How would you explain that?"

Richards allowed de Courcy to state his case before responding. Richards stood up and simply said, "If you don't want me on your team anymore, just say so and I'll get out. I have plenty to do outside our little sphere of operation, you know. There are many things that 'the hack', as you call him, is working on, and his information is good, is regular, and as far as I'm concerned is continuing."

"Sit down," ordered de Courcy. "Let me think." He silently cursed to himself, 'Blast this head of mine'. It was taking too much time to get these matters sorted out. If only he hadn't been shot. It could be weeks before he was considered well enough to leave hospital. Perhaps Richards was right. Perhaps an extra person on the team would be beneficial.

"I suppose he does have contacts that could be useful. What has Chapman been doing for you recently?"

"Nothing much. Making a few enquiries, trying to get a story. I've told him a few things about this case, and he has agreed not to publish anything unless I first clear it. He has also been speaking to the banker with the same restriction."

"The banker! It keeps coming back to the banker. Why? How is he? He is in the next ward, you know."

"Go and see him. He would enjoy your company, and you his. He can't move about yet, but he's mending."

De Courcy looked at Richards, then laughed a little. "Stay on the team, Stephen. Who knows, the team might grow to five! Just think! A banker and a reporter on the team. What a mess that would be, old boy!"

Chapter Fifty-Two

De Courcy couldn't put it off any longer. The sooner he started the move, the sooner he would finish. He wanted to talk to Richmond before settling down for the night, especially as Chapman was due to see him in the morning. To get the meeting with the banker out of the way would leave him free to prepare for Chapman. Preparation was always the key to success. The person who was better prepared had the edge. What was it the text books said? 'Fail to prepare equals prepare to fail'. Text books were usually right, and as de Courcy had taken no time to prepare for his meeting with the banker, he would probably fail. So what? De Courcy was here to recover not to plan strategy. What would he say? Just come straight out with – 'Thanks, old boy, for saving my life. It was a real good show. Anything I can do for you, old boy, just ask'. He must be tired to think of such rubbish. Well, here goes.

The next ward was only about twenty yards down the main corridor. He would take something with him – a newspaper. That's it – buy the evening's paper from the hospital shop, and before giving it to Richmond, read a few of the stories. That would give him something to say. Something like —'I see the local team has performed well' or 'Sad about old so-and-so' or 'I see there is still trouble in Israel'. Rubbish again, decided de Courcy, and he shuffled his way to the shop that sold anything from indigestion tablets to shoe laces, where he purchased the *Belfast Telegraph*, folded it, placed it in his dressing gown pocket, and journeyed to the banker's bedside.

He recognised Richmond immediately. Good – his eyes must be improving. Richmond was near the window on the left and seemed asleep. Asleep at this hour? Perhaps he's worse than I thought. No, he's not asleep – he's listening to something. Earphones were the give-away. Some tape, no doubt.

Here goes; de Courcy slowly made his way to the bed. Richmond was totally absorbed in whatever it was, his head nodding in time to something. Not a constant nod, just now and again. Suddenly the scene changed. Richmond's arms moved violently as if conducting the proceedings, then stopped as he let out a sigh and opened his eyes.

Richmond saw the blurred outline of de Courcy in front of him, so he removed the headphones and put on his glasses.

"Edward! Good to see you – sit down, sit down. Here, let me switch this thing off," and he pressed the appropriate button on the Discman.

"Good, was it – the music?" enquired de Courcy.

"Wonderful, Edward. Most rewarding."

"Fiddle-dee-dee, I assume? The Chieftains?"

"Good heavens, no. Bruckner – Symphony No 5, very exhilarating. Fiddle-dee-dee! What a good one! I must remember that," laughed Richmond. "Well now, Edward – let me guess," played Richmond as he looked de Courcy up and down. "No, you'll have to tell me. Where were you shot?"

They both laughed at that simple remark. De Courcy felt better already, and reflected how easy it might be after all to talk to this bank manager.

"How is the head, Edward? Hangover again, was it?"

The smiles remained. "Fine, Martin," as de Courcy handed over the paper. "Something to read, old boy – and how are you? Progressing well, I trust?"

"I suppose so. Yes, progressing would be a good way to describe it. I find that it takes me all my time to move to the bathroom. Still, it's better than using the bottle – eh?" and laughed again. "By the way, Edward, have you talked to a certain reporter recently?"

This man, like myself, may be injured, and a fool of a banker, but he's not stupid to come out with that one. Or perhaps he is stupid and doesn't know what he has asked. "What reporter do you mean?" de Courcy asked to gain thinking time.

"I see," Richmond quickly responded. "You don't want to talk. Fair enough, I'll change the subject. What brings you to see me? Still looking for money?"

No, he's not stupid, thought de Courcy, and he decided to come clean.

"Sorry, Martin – I'm not at full power yet. The reporter – Willis Chapman?" The banker nodded. "I have spoken to him, yes. I suggested he gives me time to gather my thoughts. He's due back again in the morning, and has promised not to publish unless I give him the 'all clear'."

"Same with me, Edward."

"Good. I. . ." De Courcy held on to the chair. ". . .I'm about to pass out. . ." and he keeled over onto Richmond's bed.

"Nurse – Nurse – here – over here." No reply, no answer, no nurse, so Richmond reached over and pressed the 'call' button while holding onto de Courcy to prevent him falling to the floor. De Courcy started to come round as two nurses arrived.

"Who has been a silly boy, then?" the first nurse said patronisingly.

"Yes, indeed, Nurse – my own fault. Sorry Martin, old boy," de Courcy- responded.

"Have a drink of this, Edward." Richmond offered him water poured into a glass from the jug beside the Discman.

"Slowly, now, Mr de Courcy – that's it." The nurse assisted him to his feet after he had sipped some water. "Sit here for now," the nurse suggested.

"I'm all right now, thank you," de Courcy declared as he recovered quickly. "I'll take another drink, please – thanks," and he downed another few sips. "That's better. I'll just sit here a while – with your permission, of course, old boy – and yours too, Nurse."

The nurses were giving him the once-over – pulse, temperature and blood pressure – as de Courcy sat looking and feeling embarrassed.

"All in order," announced the senior nurse, then she addressed her colleague, "but get the wheelchair while I stay here, and we'll get Mr de Courcy back to his bed."

De Courcy looked at Richmond, raised his eyes to heaven as a sign that he had resigned himself to the situation. "See you tomorrow, Edward, and don't forget about Chapman," reminded Richmond. Within minutes, he was wheeled away, leaving Richmond to read the paper in peace.

"No more of this behaviour, now, Mr de Courcy," as the nurse waited for him to get into bed. "You do want to get out of here, don't you? Well, relax, and give yourself time to heal – please," pleaded the nurse who stood there, she sighed, turned, and left him for the night.

*

Sutton was surprised at the information given by Joe Lacy. He was wanting to speak to Susannah, but was advised that she was in Washington to visit her brother. She didn't leave a note, or even telephone – strange. Still, he had other matters to attend to, and he prepared to journey to the hospital.

Sutton was at de Courcy's bedside at the usual time of 0800 hours. Being Army had its privileges when visiting time was the topic. Sutton told de Courcy that Susannah had gone at short notice to visit her brother without saying anything.

"Her brother-in-law, Joe Lacy, told me. He says that she is due back next week, so don't expect her on Friday – okay?"

De Courcy made a movement with his lips, drawing them in to his teeth and out again. "It's the end, I suppose. The 'nice to know you, but' sort of thing. What do you think, old boy?"

"Don't you believe it, Edward, old boy, old boy. She is for getting back, and getting back to you. Her brother must be in trouble or something. Tell you what – I'll call Joe now and ask him. Back in a minute," as Sutton made off in the direction of the phone.

"Joe? Listen, Joe. About Susannah's brother in Washington. What's he at in Washington?"

"Owen Croft? He's something in the US Army over there. He's an American citizen – has been for years. Look, it's all right. Sis often goes to see Owen when she feels down, or he is in trouble. They help each other out, that's all."

"How long has Owen Croft been in Washington, Joe?"

"Not long – moved there a month ago or thereabouts. Some new job following his old place being closed down."

"What old place?" asked Sutton.

"Now you have me. Sis didn't say much about it. Some place called Dugway."

Dugway! That name again. Sutton couldn't speak or move for thinking of Hunter. Croft? Sutton hadn't heard of a Croft when he was at Dugway.

"Dugway, you said?"

"Something like that, yes," confirmed Lacy.

"What did he do at Dugway?"

"You have me again. He was only a lieutenant there – now he is a captain. That's all I know. Is there anything wrong?"

"Thanks, Joe. I just wanted to know if she had gone for good, or is—"

"For good? Man dear, not Sis. Not now she's met your man Edward de Courcy. She'll be back, surely she will."

" Okay, Joe, thanks."

Now Sutton had another problem to deal with. The girl's brother at Dugway! That's no coincidence. There's more to this yet, and Mrs Susannah Lacy knows more than she's saying.

De Courcy watched Sutton standing by the phone. He saw Sutton rub his head. Poor chap, thought de Courcy, the pain must have returned. He would have a glass of water ready for him – he would need to take a pill or two – and he got out of bed to prepare the glass. Sutton saw him out of bed and walked up to him.

"Head bad, Elmer? Here, take your pill with this," and he held out the water. Sutton declined the offer and sat down in the chair.

"My head's okay, Edward. Look, you had better get back to bed. You're not going to like what I have to tell you."

Susannah, thought de Courcy, she's gone for good. De Courcy got into bed still holding onto the glass of water.

"Give me the water, Edward, before you spill it over the place," and Sutton took it from him. "She will be back all right, she will be back. It's her brother I want to talk about. A brother who is a captain in the US Army in Washington. Now, get this. Until the place was closed down, Owen Croft, Susannah's brother, worked in Dugway!"

De Courcy closed his eyes and slowly he lay down.

"Leave it with me, Edward. I'll find out from Personnel Records what he does before we jump to conclusions – okay? It sure looks bad at first hearing." added Sutton. Seeing de Courcy lying there, he added, "Are you okay?"

De Courcy raised his hand to his head. "Do something for me, old boy. Contact that reporter chap, Chapman, and postpone our meeting for twenty-four hours. He was due to see me today – I couldn't face him."

"That's the guy we read about in Lisburn, right?" De Courcy nodded. "No problem. Are you okay? You look bushed."

"I'll be okay, as you put it."

Sutton stayed a while until reminded by de Courcy to phone Chapman before he arrived. He left de Courcy to make the call, then contacted Personnel Records. Sutton learnt that Captain Croft was an electronics buff working for the CIA. Past history at Dugway wasn't available. No, they were not holding anything from him; there was nothing on file for Captain Croft relating to Dugway, nothing at all.

*

The rest of the day dragged by. De Courcy dozed. He didn't mean to, but it just happened, and it would probably mean that he wouldn't sleep well that night. The memories flooded back again. This time it was different. Memories not of years past, or of his late wife and son, but of more recent events and people he found he was forced to meet. The UVF people. Strange occurrences. It was as if they knew it all, and expected he and Sutton to say what they said. The set-up wasn't known then.

De Courcy dreamed about the girl. In his eyes, beautiful. Hers was not the beauty of the glamorous pin-up or of the catwalk model, more of the classical heroine who had to work with her hands. The physical hard work around the farm, not the office administrator or retail counter. He saw that clearly now, and the image of the first meeting between them was before him. Time stood still that day in the byre as she appeared with tea and scones.

Short hair, no make-up, jeans not too tight for show, but just right for work and comfort, as was the dark blue – not quite navy – long-sleeved high neck sweater. She wore trainers that had seen better days. The man, de Courcy recalled, wore hobnailed boots. But it was the girl who attracted him. What was her name? He couldn't recall it in his twilight world. She was too young anyway, and he dismissed the foolish thoughts. Except in his dreams. In dreams, *all* is possible.

De Courcy woke with a start. Stupid, he said to himself. This was not reality. In reality, he was there, a reporter coming to see him tomorrow, and Susannah – her name was easily recalled now – yes, Susannah – was in Washington.

Looking at his watch, he guessed that he must have dozed for an hour, or perhaps a little longer. He waved to the person moving slowly towards him, noticing a newspaper under his arm.

"Thanks for the paper yesterday, Edward. I thought I might chance it and visit you. It's my turn," and Richmond, with some discomfort, made it to the chair and thankfully sat down, puffing his lips into a whistle of relief. "Here," he said, giving de Courcy the paper. "I see old what's-his-name is dead, there's an obituary, and the Middle East is still boiling over."

De Courcy remembered that that was the type of comment he intended to use when visiting Richmond, and he gave a wry smile. Richmond moved to ease the discomfort.

"The leg giving you some trouble, old boy? I take it, you shouldn't be here." Richmond's body language confirmed the last statement.

"I don't like this place much, do you?" the banker said. "It's not exactly user friendly. Just look at it. For one – the phones. Why not have an extension by each bed? Each call could be monitored centrally and paid for, say, weekly. Or even daily if they didn't trust us. And secondly – the food. Why not a menu? They ask you what you want then write it down – so why not put it down on a menu?" Richmond rubbed his leg again.

"It's your turn to faint. Do you want a wheelchair, old boy?"

Richmond pretended to keel over onto de Courcy's bed, and he whispered, "I could do with a blonde nurse now – only one – can you arrange it?" and he received a smile for his trouble.

The ice broken, communication channels opened – humour did it. De Courcy had never met such a bank manager like this one before. The nurse said something yesterday about the pain he was in.

"How is that leg of yours, old boy?" He had asked that before without getting an answer.

"Giving me some jip. I have painkillers, but the after-effects are not too pleasant. It's like indigestion, so I only use them to get some sleep." Richmond had stopped rubbing his leg. "And sleep is not great either."

"Have some of my liquid refreshment, Martin, old boy. Orange? Apple? Poteen? Which?"

"Poteen? Say, the shop must have improved its stock! Apple would do. Say – is that grape juice you have?" asked Richmond, pointing to a carton.

"Indeed. Pure alcohol-free grape juice. Dreadful stuff. Want some?"

"The one carton will do," and the carton was opened and a glass filled and slowly drunk. "Thanks, Edward. That's quite good." Richmond put the glass down. "Say, Edward, I've not been sleeping too well, as I've said earlier – so I've used the time to think over events, and I have an idea. I would like to bounce this idea off you. Do you mind?"

De Courcy couldn't really refuse to listen to the man who saved his life. "Delighted, old boy. It would give us something to think about."

They were interrupted by the sound of the tea trolley. "Tea, gentlemen? Do you want yours here, Mr Richmond, or by your own bed? You do know that you should be in your own bed."

That time already. It seemed no time since dinner. Tea was a tray for each patient on which was placed a pot of tea, a pot of hot water, a small milk jug, some packets of sugar, and a plate. The plate was filled with two sandwiches, a large slice of wheaten bread thinly buttered with a generous slice of cheese on top, and a slice of cake. All the trays were the same, unless, due to circumstances, there were patients on a special or restricted diet.

"Have your tea here, Martin. We can dine in each other's company. That's all right, isn't it?" de Courcy asked the caterer.

"I suppose so. This isn't a hotel, you know," and she set out two trays on the wheeled table that went over the bed.

"I ordered fish and chips! Is it coming later?" asked Richmond. She ignored the remark and went on her way.

"You are wasting your time there, old boy, there's no humour there." She heard de Courcy's remark and, turning partly to face them, responded, "Your fish hasn't been defrosted yet. Maybe tomorrow," and she was gone.

"Not bad. The wheaten's good, Edward." They ate mostly in silence. The plates were emptied and two trays pushed to the end of the bed.

"What's your idea, old boy?"

"Yes – right. Let's say that, between us, we have different experiences and skills. I'm talking about you, Elmer, and the reporter, Chapman. You have your contacts and knowledge, as has Chapman, and of course there is myself. All this is going to waste. My idea is, why not get together? Have, say, a pooling of ideas and knowledge – what's the word? – synergy. That's it – synergy. The objective is, say, finding out what's going on, or what has gone on. I mean. . ." Richmond took a long time to say little, but de Courcy didn't mind letting him talk himself out. Richmond finished by closing with, ". . .This is the fourth time I've been shot, so it's now beyond coincidence. What do you think?"

De Courcy had listened to Richmond, but was thinking of a girl in Washington. He was sure now that Richmond knew more than he was saying.

There was silence now. Richmond had stated his case and stopped. The pressure now was on de Courcy to respond.

"Work together as an unofficial team, you mean?"

"Only if you think there is value in it." The banker decided to have another cup of tea and he poured himself one. "Want one, Edward?" De Courcy declined.

"It could prove interesting, I suppose. Information not known becoming known."

"Like, where the money came from?" asked Richmond.

Or where it went to, thought de Courcy. "You are in the wrong job, old boy. To think like that shows a devious mind that could be put to better use than banking. I always knew you had something to do with the money," de Courcy responded.

"So you admit it. There is the money question to sort out."

Blast it! He's got me on that one, de Courcy realised. Getting too tired again. Looking for a way out, he noticed that evening visiting time would soon be upon them, so he changed the subject.

"Anyone visiting you this evening, old boy?"

"I expect so. My wife will probably call, so I should not be here when she does. And you?"

"Not this evening, old boy. Unless Elmer shows up." He was more tired than he thought and was answering as if controlled by the drugs.

"Any family, Edward?"

"Nobody around now, old boy." The words came without emotion or feeling. "Once there were two of them, both killed – the good lady and the boy. Your idea might work – do you mind if we call it a day, old boy?" and he put his head back and slept. Richmond made his painful journey to his bed just as the visitors arrived, increasing the noise level to that of opening time at the bank on the last Friday of the month. Penelope called, as did two members of his staff, and they passed the time like other visitors talking of everything except gunshot wounds. Politely, the staff left, leaving Martin and Penelope alone. He told Penelope of de Courcy's loss of family, she told him of a phone call from the bank's head of personnel, Mike Woods, who might call sometime.

Speaking of the devil, Mike Woods arrived with some magazines and a beaming smile. Woods suggested that Richmond might want to consider early retirement – just to think it over, and leave the decision until he returned to work.

De Courcy had no visitors, but received a delivery of a large bunch of flowers with a card saying, '*Best wishes, get well soon, love Susannah.*' He didn't see them, he was asleep.

Chapter Fifty-Three

"Good afternoon, Edward. I've brought you this morning's papers. The contents out of date by now, but it's something to look at – *The Times* and *Daily Telegraph*, I hope you don't mind."

Afternoon already, and Chapman standing in front of him. De Courcy had forgotten he was coming, then he remembered the purpose of his visit.

"Thank you, old boy – very kind of you. Bribes always accepted."

"Your head – any better?"

"Fine, Willis, just fine. I've been sleeping a lot since you were last here and it must have done me some good."

Chapman noticed the flowers and surreptitiously glanced at the card. "Would you mind if I started on a few questions? If you feel you are up to it, of course."

"Back to business – eh? We have an agreement – yes?"

"Of course. Nothing published without your permission," Chapman confirmed.

"Good. But I still reserve the right not to answer you, should I feel I shouldn't."

"I can accept that."

De Courcy looked around at the selection of fruit juices beside him. "Here, old boy, have some of that," and he handed over the opened carton of grape juice. "The only person in these parts who drinks this awful stuff is the banker fellow."

"You have seen him?"

"Yes. Twice. Decent chap, you know – and easy to talk to after all."

The time was passing, but nothing new was forthcoming. Chapman had to move it along. The editor wouldn't give him for ever on the story.

"Edward, there is something big going on, or perhaps it has already happened. What do you know of the UVF and the connection between the Army and the UVF?"

De Courcy quickly glanced at the flowers, then fixed his eyes on the reporter. Before saying anything he looked around. Nobody was there, but he was taking no chances.

"There are lives at stake, old boy." The whisper had a tremble in it. "Not least one very dear to me." De Courcy put up his hand to stop Chapman interrupting him. "Let me tell you a story. It will take some time, and may not be complete, or in the proper sequence." De Courcy paused. "See what you make of this. . ."

The major's story, slowly at first, unravelled without a break for an hour. Chapman was finding the information fascinating. Chapman knew from experience that information from one source reflected the perception of that source, and was coloured by culture, circumstances and politics. Receiving information was not easy. What people meant was not always said, and what's said was usually misunderstood. The information from de Courcy would be no different but was likely to be close to the facts, the facts as understood by de Courcy.

There was much to hear and to remember in that hour, some of which Chapman would forget unless it could be repeated. That was why the tape machine was invaluable. Nothing was covert here. De Courcy saw the machine and was happy to hold the microphone as he spoke. De Courcy had finished for now and he handed the microphone back to Chapman, who took it, turned the pocket-sized recorder off, and put both in his pocket.

"Don't lose that thing, old boy." De Courcy turned back the sheet and made to get up. "Time for walkies. Let's go and see old Martin Richmond – coming?"

During the time it took them to walk to Richmond's bed, de Courcy had, in a concise manner, explained to Chapman how some UVF people thought of the Northern Ireland situation. ". . .violence by the minority on the majority under the guise of change by force," de Courcy explained, "the repression suffered under the majority, is supported by outsiders who traditionally support all minorities. This has brought about success for the minority. Result? The democratic majority is forced to give way to the violent minority. So? So the UVF regard it as their right to use the same tactics against the minority to protect the majority. Why? Because the legal forces of law and order won't do it. What do you think of that, Mr Reporter?"

Chapman had heard such drivel before. "You certainly know how to talk rubbish, don't you?"

"But, which is the rubbish, old boy? The tape in your pocket, or this conversation?"

They saw Richmond, headphones in place, transported to another world: the occasional twitches, nod and conducting movement, as he was listening with ears, mind and soul. Chapman and de Courcy stood looking at him. Richmond was returning their gaze but didn't see them.

"It's the poteen, you know – he can't take it," commented de Courcy and motioned Chapman to sit.

"Fiddle-dee-dee music, I suppose? The Brook Boys, is it?" De Courcy made sure that Richmond could hear him. In fact, de Courcy was so loud that Chapman thought the whole hospital would hear him.

Richmond removed the headphones and switched off the Discman.

"Ruined – ruined. If only you had waited a few more minutes. . . Still. . . Nice to see you. The two of you?"

"What was that you said, Edward? Fiddle-dee-dee what?" asked Chapman.

"Our musical money man here listens to the Brook Boys. That's right, isn't it, old boy?" jibed de Courcy.

"Such uncultured and uneducated remarks. You're not English, by any chance?" Chapman was surprised at the banter between them. "It's Bruckner – B.R.U.C.K.N.E.R. . . The Brook Boys, indeed! I see I have two half wits today for company, what's the latest?" Richmond put his Discman aside, and with hands together as if in prayer asked the question again. "What's the latest?"

De Courcy started the ball rolling. "Tell the journalist here – sorry, reporter. We must call him a 'reporter'. Tell the reporter, old boy, of your idea, remember? Synergy?" prompted de Courcy. Richmond enthusiastically repeated his idea to Chapman and saw him nod a few times, not necessarily in agreement but to indicate understanding.

There's mischief about those three, decided the girl with the tea trolley. "We have 'three stooges' in full flow, have we? I suppose you all want tea? The poor hospital budget – no wonder we get paid badly."

*

It was some time since Chapman had seen his editor, and now was as good a time as any. Chapman had left the hospital with sufficient information to advise Temple Spooner of progress without betraying confidences. His desk was as he left it – nothing there but the computer terminal.

Chapman 'booted up', logged on, and accessed the messages left for him. They were read and electronically receipted to the sender, thankfully there were not too many. Some messages were repeated – those were from Spooner, his editor, who had the knack of making anyone feel guilty should his messages be ignored. Chapman read: '. . .It grieves me to find it necessary to ask again. . .' and another, '. . .Lessons on how to send replies are available at night school. . ." and again, '. . .What the **** are you doing about the situation of your forthcoming dismissal. . .?'

Chapman closed down and ventured in the direction of Spooner's office.

"Have a good holiday, Willis? You didn't send a card," someone said as he passed a colleague. Another jibe, ". . .I thought you were dead!"

Spooner was in conference with the Sports Desk people, but nodded for him to enter the glass house that was Spooner's office.

Chapman heard some comments on various sporting activities and the plans to interview this or that personality, which continued as Chapman entered. The conference ended, and the Sports Desk people left.

Now alone with Spooner in the glass house, he was now going to try and keep the editor on his side. Chapman needn't have worried, but he didn't know the editor's mind. Spooner had been advised from separate sources that Chapman had been seen talking to Superintendent Richards in Dundonald Hospital, and that was good enough.

Chapman told Spooner as much as he dared, in a few sentences, limiting the story to a probable this and a possible that, and awaiting proof to confirm help to terrorists from outside the country. Spooner was satisfied and gave Chapman more time. In half an hour, Chapman left with the editor's blessing, and went home.

He took time out to get away from it all and parked the car in Crawfordsburn Country Park. The walk to Bangor along the coastal path from Crawfordsburn was used by many. Chapman was amazed at the NO CYCLING signs being ignored by those who cycled, NO CAMPING by those who camped, and the NO LITTER by everyone else. It was not as peaceful or as environmentally friendly as it used to be. Much work had been carried out over recent years at Bangor harbour, which now supported a marina. Chapman didn't see anyone on the fleet of yachts, dinghies or runabouts, all moored in neat rows, and he cynically wondered about the invisible sailors who flaunted their wealth on boats permanently fixed in cattle-stall fashion. Why imprison themselves with these trappings of wealth?

He found himself in the small café attached to the church in Queen's Parade, and had a bowl of hot soup. 'Profits for Mission Work' was on top of the menu, so he felt a little guilty when he left tenpence as a tip, and departed before the waitress came. He returned to his car at Crawfordsburn taking the same route, thinking about synergy. All working together to produce a fuller picture. De Courcy would be good, so would Sutton and the superintendent. The new man – Richmond? Perhaps not, but it was his idea, so. . . Chapman would have a word with Superintendent Richards and see if the police would work with the idea and provide a place for them to meet.

*

"Where did these come from?" Superintendent Richards asked of the Duty Sergeant.

"Anonymous package left in at the gate, Sir. Security checked it out thinking it was a bomb. There's nothing traceable. The 'lab' boys say it's clean."

"Have you listened to them yet?" asked Richards.

"No, Sir – all we did was make copies, the usual routine."

Richards looked at the cassette tapes and then at the sergeant. "More porn, probably. The amount of dirt getting about is. . . Still, this would be the first porn we've come across on audio tape." He opened the door to his office and, attracting the attention of the officer in charge of porn, beckoned her to join him.

"Yes, Sir?"

"Tapes – audio tapes. We don't know, but probably porn. Can you get a machine in here and we'll give them a listen?"

The tape machines were straightforward, but needed the head cleaned, like most machines for listening to tapes whether in the home or car. After all, who cleans tape machines in their cars? The car, yes – but the machine?

It was switched on, and within the first few feet of the first tape Richards switched the machine off.

"Well, it's not porn, is it? Just leave the player here. I won't need your services, Sergeant."

After she had gone, Richards switched the player on again and listened to them – alone. He found it difficult to believe what he had just heard. Could this be a hoax? It's possible it was a hoax, but if not, the Government would have its hands full. The Official Secrets Act would come down heavily on this one, so before advising the Assistant Chief Constable he would make a few enquiries.

Richards had to know whether anyone else in the Station had heard the tapes, so he made his way to the radio room. Tapes, both audio and video, were copied in a hived-off section of the radio room and filed in the store. It was known which staff were on duty when the tapes arrived. The 'lab' would be different. That was a separate section and was regarded as part of the Civil Service, not Police.

Richards was satisfied that, due to pressure of work, the radio room and the stores people hadn't had time to hear them when the copies were made. That left the forensic laboratories. Nothing like the present, so he phoned them. He knew whom to talk to, as he visited them often when waiting for results and enjoyed watching them work. They were most professional at their task, and their rules didn't let outsiders within a mile of them, but he had contacts.

"The tapes, you say? Tapes, that would be. . . Sean Stone. Can you hold, Superintendent – I'll see if he's available?" He heard the handset hit the desk and a faint 'click' as the HOLD button was depressed.

"Hullo – this is Sean Stone. How can I help?"

"Hullo, Sean – Superintendent Richards here. About the tapes you said were clean – the tapes left in here anonymously – have you anything on them?"

"No, Sir – they were spotless. There was evidence of thorough cleaning, both of the case and the tape housing."

"What of the contents? Any clues on the voices?"

There was silence for a moment. "Sorry, Sir, I didn't check the contents of the actual tape, only the plastic cases. I can arrange to pick them up and do that today if. . ."

"That's all right, Sean. Leave it. I'll get back to you should we need you – bye." Good. Better than good, Richards thought, as it would now be possible for him to sneak off with a copy of the tapes as back up, just in case the Chief Constable closed the lot down and buried them.

The radio room was busy, very busy, as some of the staff were off to lunch, which made it easy for him to make copies.

He would consider passing them on to Chapman. The end of his career would be sudden and certain if he was caught. The RUC could not and must not be seen to be anything other than above board, within the law and clean. That's why the tapes should not be buried by the Chief Constable or any of his assistants. He made copies and left the radio room with them in his pocket without being seen, and returned the originals to the safe, witnessed by the Sergeant.

"Chapman on the phone for you, Sir," the duty sergeant informed Richards. Richards took the call from where he was.

"I've an idea. Can I see you?" asked Chapman.

An appointment was made for Friday morning.

Chapter Fifty-Four

Sutton answered the phone as he was getting into bed. It was Susannah. "Thanks for letting me know, kid. I guess our trip to see Edward is off – right?"

"But I *did* let you know – I wrote and— Don't tell me I forgot to post it. . . Surely not. . . Look, Elmer, I'm so sorry. I meant to phone but there wasn't time – I had to—"

"Tell me about your brother in Dugway, kid – or you can forget about Edward." Sutton could be hard when had to be hard. Right now he believed he had to be. Nobody got away with shooting friends of his and survived. Hunter found that out, so did the guy in Vegas. Sutton was convinced that the girl knew more than she was saying, and he had to find out what she was holding back.

"Dugway? How did you. . . Look, that doesn't matter – how's Edward? Is he all right?"

"Tell me about Dugway – all of it, or I hang up," Sutton responded.

"Don't be nasty, Elmer. I'll tell you, I will, and Edward, but not now. I need—"

"NOW, kid – NOW – Dugway?"

Sutton heard the start of her weeping. He couldn't take it, and held the phone away from his ear for a moment. She was calming down and began to speak. "I can't tell you over the phone. I'll tell you on Tuesday when I get back. That's the best. . ." Sutton hung up.

"You're more trouble than I or Edward can handle right now, kid," he said aloud to the wall and got into bed.

The phone rang again. He ignored it and decided that Mrs Lacy was getting no more from him – or from Edward, if he had anything to do with it.

Susannah didn't wait until Tuesday; she made arrangements to leave Washington on the next flight that her ticket would permit, which was Saturday evening. That would allow her to arrive home at Sunday dinner time. She would go directly to talk matters over with Sutton, after she had destroyed the tapes.

*

Richards liked Chapman's idea of pooling resources, and he offered to provide a safe house where discussions amongst those planning to participate could be held. It would wait until de Courcy was well enough to attend. The arrangement was conditional upon Richards being permitted to sit in on the discussions. Chapman didn't think that condition would be accepted, but he promised to ask the others.

Chapman was right. De Courcy expressed his reluctance to voice his side of the story in the presence of anyone not party to the action, except of course the reporter. What of the agreement where nothing was to be published or acted upon without the agreement of all participants? No policeman could buy into that, de Courcy felt, especially should incidents of criminal activities be made known.

Chapman advised Richards of the failure to procure agreement, and the matter was closed. It was not closed as far as Chapman and de Courcy were concerned. They, with Sutton and the banker, Richmond, could meet in Chapman's house and hold their meetings there. Sutton and Richmond found nothing wrong with that and gave it a go. Out of courtesy to Richards, Chapman advised him that the discussions would take place without him.

"Call sometime before you start your meetings, Willis. I have something that night make a contribution," advised Richards.

*

The days passed, and de Courcy made satisfactory progress. With the swelling gone from his eyes, the black bruises were more noticeable than before. De Courcy managed to walk around the wards more freely, and made frequent visits to Richmond between visiting times.

De Courcy was quietly disappointed to hear of the contents of Sutton's call from Susannah, and was resigning himself to a future without her. The ever-protective Sutton would sort Mrs Lacy out as soon as she returned. He was going to get to the truth of her brother's Dugway connection before making it known how her first husband was killed. That would sort her out, and keep her away from Edward.

The Consul in Belfast had arranged to collect the satellite phone, and Sutton had it ready for him. It was to be collected at midday from the cottage at Brown's Bay. What the Consul didn't expect were the rifles.

"I can't take these. All I will take is the phone."

"You take the lot – the phone and the weapons. I'll retain the handguns and the spare magazines – okay?" as Sutton openly carried them out of the cottage and placed them in the boot of the Consul's Ford Granada. "What you do with them is your business – okay?" Sutton was being intimidating on purpose, and didn't mind being a little rough with the man. "I still remember your underhand methods of the air tickets – so I don't want you to misunderstand this," threatened Sutton by bringing his closed fist up to the Consul's eyes.

"I was only carrying out the instructions of General Laskie, so calm down, Major Sutton." The indifferent Consul ignored the threat and drove off, taking the rifles with him.

Susannah's car arrived as the Consul's left, with Sutton witnessing both. He waited for her to arrive from the car to the cottage gate, before he said anything. She beat him to it.

"I did forget to post the note, Elmer. I found it in my car when I got home." She spoke calmly and had about her the same feeling of mistrust held by the opposing tribes that had infected Northern Ireland for many generations.

Sutton changed his plan. He decided to say nothing – nothing at all.

"Can I come in?" she asked. Sutton extended his right arm towards the door and let her enter. "Thanks," she said as she went in and stood waiting to be invited to sit. "How is Edward? Is he improving?"

Sutton closed the door of the cottage and went to make coffee. He didn't answer her, but set out the two mugs that de Courcy had purchased in Washington, and waited for the water to boil.

"What's wrong, Elmer? Why won't you talk to me?" she asked calmly and sat down in de Courcy's chair.

"You get nothing from me, kid, until the Dugway stuff is cleared up. So, the sooner you start talking, the sooner it gets done – right?"

The tin of chocolate biscuits was nearly empty as Sutton put four on a plate and set the plate on the floor in front of her. He returned to the kettle and poured hot water into the mugs, which already held a spoonful of instant coffee.

"I've got no milk – so it's black – okay?" as he handed her de Courcy's mug.

"This is Edward's mug from the Washington trip, isn't it?" She noticed the similarity to the gift she received from de Courcy. Sutton nodded as he sat in front of her and took a biscuit from the door.

"This is stupid, Elmer – stupid." She put the mug down. "All right, I'll tell you now, Elmer. I can see that you won't be happy until you hear it – ready?"

Elmer had finished the biscuit and he took another from the plate. "Just tell it all, kid – I'm ready."

There was nothing to be gained by hiding anything, so she told it all – from meeting her brother in Green Bay, hearing the tapes, explaining how her brother got the tapes, the contents of the tapes, to destroying the tapes before coming there today.

"Why didn't you tell me on the phone, kid?" asked Sutton without emotion.

"I was in Washington, that's why. There has been such an upheaval with security that I couldn't take the risk. Our conversation could have been monitored." Susannah couldn't make up her mind whether Sutton was being stupid on purpose or not. "What's wrong now, Elmer? Don't you believe me?"

Sutton believed her all right. Nobody could have known the contents of the conversations between MacBride, Hunter, and himself unless they were taped. It was the fact that the meetings were taped that bothered him. If the security of the *Room* was breached, what else had got out? The possibility of secret meetings between heads of governments and their military advisers becoming public knowledge could start wars. That bothered him.

"The information on the tapes stopped the UVF from killing you and Edward, you know. Did you know that?" He didn't know it, but how could he? Now he was starting to let his imagination take over.

"What's that you said? About the UVF? Have they heard the tapes?"

"Yes, Elmer, and by hearing them they knew you were only the messenger. The tapes proved that you were being used."

"You knew about the money too, before we met – no wonder you were not surprised." Sutton stood up and began to pace to and fro in the cottage. She didn't interrupt him and his thoughts. He stopped after about a dozen journeys, turned to face her, and looked her up and down. "You'll do as you are. Come with me, kid," and, leaving her to get out of Edward's chair by herself, held the cottage door open. "Come on, kid – we are going out. Let's visit someone in hospital."

*

Sutton parked the Honda as close to the hospital entrance as was possible for Sunday afternoon visiting, which wasn't close at all, and guided her through the maze of corridors and wards to the waiting area of de Courcy's ward.

"Wait here, kid. Let me tell him first. He doesn't know that your connection with Dugway is clean."

"He knows about my brother in Dugway?"

"Sure does. Wait till I come back for you – okay?" She agreed. She was looking forward to meeting him. What would she say?

"Elmer – is he all right then?" she called out as he entered the ward.

"Wait and see, kid."

De Courcy saw Sutton approach his bed. He wasn't in it but sitting beside it

"You look remarkably well, old boy," commented de Courcy. "Good news?" Sutton sat beside him.

"I'll say. Listen to this," and he told him the outline of Susannah's story. He listened with growing interest, and the weariness left him. And to think I'd written her off, thought de Courcy.

"That is good news, old boy. I can't wait to see her again. Tuesday, you said? She is due to return on Tuesday?"

"Don't go away, Edward – I have to see someone," and Sutton left him sitting there as he went to fetch Susannah. Sutton beckoned to Susannah and told her where she would find him.

"Are you not coming, Elmer?"

"I'll wait here – go ahead, kid," and he gave her a broad smile.

Their reunion was tender, loving, and kind. Susannah was gentle in her caresses and a little shocked at the bruises, while Edward was quiet and emotional.

The pleasant small talk continued until the end of visiting time.

"Time to go, I'm afraid, Susannah dear. Can you call again?"

"Try and stop me," she smiled. "Oh – Edward, will you answer me one question?"

"If I can."

"Where are you going to take me for our honeymoon?"

Chapter Fifty-Five

Patients de Courcy and Richmond were discharged from hospital the following week. Following discussions with Penelope, Richmond decided to accept the offer of early retirement from the bank, which would come into effect at the end of the year. The retirement package was a generous one and too good to refuse.

De Courcy returned to the cottage at Brown's Bay, and was driven daily to the out-patients section of Larne Hospital for his check-up and fresh dressings by Susannah, who was starting to make arrangements for the wedding. The wedding was planned for Monday, 29th August.

Susannah was added to the team, who periodically visited Chapman's house to discuss events. Even she did not expect the surprises. She thought that she knew most of it. De Courcy, unofficial chairman when in attendance, began the proceedings by reminding those present of the promise from Chapman, and he expected the others to reciprocate. Assisted by Sutton, de Courcy gave an account of the events up to the loss of the money. The details of how de Courcy and Sutton acquired the first lot of cash was noted by Richmond, who put to good use the name of the solicitor and bank manager in Carlisle. Travelling by car, Richmond arrived in Carlisle at 2 p.m. and entered the office of Goodrich & Dunn carrying the two containers of money in a holdall. Richmond was able to tell Mr Goodrich how he had acted on behalf of de Courcy and Sutton when the money first surfaced. In order to satisfy the bank in Carlisle that there were no problems of money laundering, Richmond requested that Goodrich accompany him to the bank.

"Do you mean, now, Mr Richmond?" asked Goodrich.

"Yes please, now."

"You have the money with you?"

"That's right. I wish to have it deposited in the bank. It's too dangerous to carry around this amount of cash without proper security protection – a point, I understand, you advised Mr de Courcy on when he was here. Can we go now?" Richmond, holdall in hand, made for the door as Goodrich stood up and just looked at him.

"I should telephone first, to warn them," Goodrich suggested.

"No need. I arranged an appointment some time ago to see Mr Morrell, the manager at 2.15 p.m. We can make it by leaving now." Richmond held the office door open for Goodrich, who grabbed his jacket and put it on as he left.

"I'll be back in a quarter of an hour," Goodrich advised his secretary. Off to see Mr Morrell with this gentleman."

Morrell saw Richmond as arranged.

"I wasn't expecting to see you, Adam," Morrell said to Goodrich and bade them sit. "Well now, Mr Richmond. What can I do for you?" Morrell asked.

Richmond produced one of his business cards and passed it over to Morrell. "Call me Martin. As you see, we're in the same business." Morrell raised his eyebrows, smiled, and set the card in front of him. Richmond told Morrell what he had planned to say, without mentioning anything about making a deposit. Then Richmond, conscious of the strict rules governing money laundering, invited Goodrich to confirm that there were no problems with making such a large cash deposit. Morrell appeared happy with the strangeness of it all. Richmond thanked Goodrich for his services and suggested that he left the two bank managers to talk shop.

"I'll call with you later, Mr Goodrich, and many thanks," said Richmond as he waited until Goodrich had left Morrell's office.

The holdall was opened, the two boxes extracted, opened, and £215,000 in Bank of England notes was placed in front of Morrell. "This is your money returned. They are the same notes. I want to deposit the money, and for you to give me a receipt for my records. Any problem?"

Morrell was pleased to have the opportunity of increasing the Branch's deposit figures, which would put him ahead of his targets. "None. What sort of account had you in mind – Martin?"

The account was opened with an off-shore subsidiary, and a happy Mr Morrell wished Richmond a safe return journey. A relieved Richmond left the bank and entered the solicitor's office to settle the bill. Goodrich charged him £15.

*

The five came and went over the next few days – de Courcy, Sutton, and Susannah holding Chapman and Richmond spellbound with their story. Chapman, with their agreement, made copious notes and nothing was recorded on tape. It all fitted together, with the gaps getting smaller by the day.

When Susannah told of her visit to Green Bay to hear her brother's tapes, Chapman made a note on the large sheet of paper behind him. The paper recorded the story in events, using one or two words for each event.

". . .The tapes are all gone now. The last set I destroyed when I came back from Washington."

Susannah had finished her story. That left two outstanding matters, thought Chapman – the tapes and Richmond.

De Courcy, as chairman, sought help.

"What next, people? Shall we hear you now, Martin?"

Chapman suggested something different, and switched on his hi-fi system, which was set to BBC Radio 4. He changed the selector to TAPE and pushed the PLAY button. The first tape started to roll. The faces of Sutton and Susannah were a picture. Comments from Sutton ranged from, 'I remember that. . . that's Hunter. . . I told you, Willis, I told you. . . Hunter again. . .', while Susannah couldn't move or understand how Chapman had got his hands on them.

"The General must have sent them to you or to the police, who let you have them."

Chapman wasn't saying and used the contents of the tapes with the comments from Sutton to fill in a few more gaps.

The tapes were put away. It was now Richmond's turn.

"I shall limit my input to those areas not already covered. There is no point going over what you already know." He told them about the builder, the frogmen and the torpedo, and how a terrified builder had left his tools behind, and how he had gathered them. And the money. He told them about it and included his recent visit to Carlisle, where he managed to get rid of the cash.

"How, old boy?" asked de Courcy.

"Let's say, it's somewhere in an off-shore account attracting interest until I decide what is to happen to it."

Despite further questions, Richmond refused to disclose anything more about the money. Chapman didn't care for the money. He cared about the story and of getting it published, something they all agreed to, and for his paper, and soon. They left Chapman to work on an article that they could accept and would allow him to publish. It took him two days, but it was worth it. There was no mention by name of those involved in 'Ireland 6' or 'Ireland 7' on this side of the pond. Not so for Washington or Dugway.

The editor was delighted. Spooner tipped off the Fleet Street crowd, ITN and BBC News that his paper, the *Belfast Telegraph*, had something big.

The 'sixth' edition hit the street that Friday afternoon, and the news was picked up by ITN, and the BBC, who used it to open their news broadcasts that night. The American media went mad over it, and the local politicians from Northern Ireland were full of, 'Told you so. . .'

"AMERICAN COVERT ACTION ASSISTS IRA TO KILL 50"

Willis Chapman had made sure that his sources were protected. He also cleared his story with his legal people. Nowhere did he accuse the US Government of anything. Nowhere did he say that the actions came from the US Government. However, he did say:

> '. . .it is difficult to understand how finance can be allocated to covert actions in a friendly country resulting in 50 deaths without the government who supplied that finance knowing anything about it. Perhaps someone in Washington would like to speak to a General Gene Laskie, while others explain to the relatives of the dead. . ."

The paper sold its story around the world, and enhanced its already growing reputation and that of its reporter. Chapman appeared on many current affairs programmes at home and abroad without betraying the agreement made between himself and those who provided him with the story. In addition to this, Chapman committed to paper the background to the scoop, and presented it to those who had provided him with the information. Minor alterations were made before each signed the declaration in presence of each other, and Mr Cole, Solicitor.

After the signing of the declaration, the following came to light. Westminster saw the Commons and the Lords in uproar, with immediate meetings demanded between the US President and the

Prime Minister. Washington was no different, with the European Parliament bringing up a close third.

A joint American-British communiqué announced a total unconditional condemnation of acts of terrorism being carried out on the innocent peoples of Northern Ireland by the IRA and Loyalist groups. Also announced was a meeting between top Government and Civil Service personnel of both countries that would take place within twenty-four hours at the White House. The television networks gave wide coverage of both countries' representatives meeting each other on the front lawn of the White House.

Susannah gasped at the sight of the man beside the Prime Minister. Sutton and de Courcy noticed her wide-eyed open-mouthed speechless stare as she pointed to the television.

"The General," she whispered. "It's the General – the UVF's General. . ."

The Prime Minister introduced the Civil Servant as 'Our expert in Northern Ireland affairs, Mr John Johnston.'

On the American team a certain Major Black Feather smiled contentedly as he fingered his Rolex watch.

Coda

Temple Spooner closed Chapman's manuscript, stood up, switched off the 'Don't disturb' light, and went home taking the manuscript with him. It was getting dark, and for the first time since his appointment as Editor, he forgot to take a paper home with him. Chapman's story had engrossed him. Perhaps there was another scoop, or an opportunity to publish it in serial form in the paper, before Chapman had it released in book form. Spooner phoned Chapman to search out his plans for the manuscript. Chapman didn't have any. There was the idea of a story of foreign funds going to the UVF to help them arm against the IRA. After all, Chapman hadn't covered 'Ireland 7' yet. The story in the paper was 'Ireland 6'.

"What happened since the declaration was signed, Willis? Did they get married?"

"De Courcy and Mrs Lacy? Let me tell you tomorrow. There's another killing that's not in the manuscript. Interested?" asked Chapman.

"Be in my office at 08.30. Of course I'm interested."

"Right. I'll collect my manuscript then – 'night."

*

Chapman continued where the manuscript finished. He started from the Sunday before the wedding, where an invitation was given by the Minister of the Methodist Chapel in Island Magee. During the church service, the minister said, "Any member of the congregation able to attend the short wedding ceremony tomorrow at 11 a.m. and afterwards a beach barbecue organised by Elmer Sutton is welcome to do so. The wedding of Mr de Courcy and Susannah Lacy is a happy occasion. Let us join in their happiness by accepting their kind invitation."

The church was full on that Monday. Susannah was given away by her brother, Owen, and attended by her sister-in-law, Mary Lou.

Sutton had bribed a few local lads to look after the barbecue while he was carrying out the duties of best man by promising them as much steak as they could eat.

The weather was more than kind and for the first time in living memory an open air wedding reception was held at Brown's Bay, where two hundred ate barbecued meats of all types and sizes served by Sutton and Richmond suitably dressed for the occasion. Other volunteers made it a most happy and informal time. That evening Mr and Mrs de Courcy left for unknown destinations, believed to be in Scotland.

Two days later the IRA, using Sinn Fein as a mouthpiece, announced a cease-fire that would be effective at midnight on Wednesday, 31 August 1994. Sutton was watching the TV news programme at 9 p.m. while cleaning the handgun. He was delighted with the news of the cease-fire, which should mean that he could get rid of the weapon, for good. With Hunter gone, there was nobody else after him. He had worn the gun every day since Susannah had warned him of trouble.

He had finished the routine cleaning and assembly of the weapon, so he loaded it and bolstered it.

There was a knock at the door.

Unusual, thought Sutton, and he quickly put on a light jacket to hide the holster and gun. "Be right with you."

He switched off the TV and made to open the door. Too late. It was already open, with a man standing there pointing a Colt .45 at his head.

"General Laskie!" gasped Sutton.

"MISTER Laskie, to you. Sit down," and with the Colt constantly pointing at Sutton's head, Laskie entered the cottage, closing the door behind him. "I hear your Brit sidekick has got himself married."

Sutton was trying to think. His gun was fully loaded but on safety. It would take too long to draw, release the safety, load a round from the magazine, aim and fire. He had no chance against the Colt. Not at that distance. "You hear right."

Laskie, expressionless but alert to Sutton's every move, remained standing. "Where's your gun, Elmer?"

Sutton thought fast. He made what he hoped would be seen as an involuntary glance towards the shower. Laskie saw it.

"Show me. Slow – Mister – real slow," and Laskie stepped back to give Sutton room to move. "Try it anytime, Elmer. Just try it," warned Laskie as the Colt kept its aim and tracked Sutton getting out of the chair. Sutton, slowly as ordered, made his way to the shower.

"It's hidden under the shower tray," Sutton said calmly as he entered the bathroom.

"Stop," shouted Laskie, who took a step towards Sutton. "Like I said, Elmer – real slow."

Sutton didn't move.

"Show me," Laskie said again.

Sutton, moving slowly, knelt down and began to lift the shower tray until it rested fully open against the wall of the shower. De Courcy's gun, holster, and spare magazine could be seen wrapped in a transparent plastic sheet.

"Easy now. . . And slow. . . Lift out the gun," Laskie instructed.

Using his right hand, Sutton reached into the space and caught hold of the plastic. He lifted it out, placed it on the floor beside his right knee, and returned his hand to the shower tray.

"Help me lower this, Laskie. It's heavy," Sutton asked.

"Nice try, Elmer – nice try." Sutton let the tray fall loudly back into place. "Don't get up, Elmer. On your knees," sneered Laskie. "Move back to your chair. NO. Leave the gun."

Sutton hobbled on his knees, feigning pain and discomfort, all the way to his chair. Before Sutton got to the chair, Laskie kicked the plastic package out of the bathroom and into the main room where he could examine it. Sutton began to move back and forward in the chair showing as much discomfort as he could.

"What's the big idea?" Laskie asked, putting a little pressure on the trigger.

"My back, and knees. They give me real pain. . . can't help it. . .," panted Sutton.

"Tough," responded Laskie with his Colt still pointing at the target. "This is how it's going to be, Mister Sutton. Listen if you want to."

Sutton continued with his discomfort act. If I can get one chance, I'll draw on him, Sutton thought. Laskie's eyes never left him. Using his feet, Laskie felt for the package and once he had found it, knelt down, grabbed it with his free hand, and picked it up. All the time he kept his eyes and aim on the target.

"It's like this, Elmer," Laskie stated calmly. "The only person who knows about Dugway and Washington, and who hangs out in Northern Ireland, is you. As far as it goes, in every direction, it's you. That's why I'm going to use your own gun to finish you off. You were behind the papers getting the story, and behind me getting my pension cancelled," shouted Laskie. "Yes – cancelled," he shouted again as Sutton worked hard to keep up his show. "First they close my section down, then retire me. Lastly, they stop the pension."

Laskie had managed to open the plastic sheet from which he withdrew the magazine. He stole a quick glance at it and saw that it was full.

"That will do nicely!" smiled Laskie.

It had to be soon, thought Sutton. He changed his movements slightly and managed to loose one of his shoes, using the other one as a lever. If he had a chance, he would throw it. . . Now. It was now. . . or never. . .

Sutton threw his shoe at Laskie with his left hand, withdrew his gun, removed the safety, got a round loaded and. . . . . .And Laskie fired the Colt. Sutton had moved left and down. Laskie's shot ripped open Sutton's shoulder, throwing him back. Sutton pulled the trigger. The gun was on automatic and let off four rounds in the direction of Laskie. Laskie fired a second shot, and Sutton fell into a lifeless heap, releasing his gun in the process, which immediately stopped firing. Sutton died instantly Laskie's second shot hit him in the neck, snapping the spinal cord. There was blood everywhere, mostly from Sutton's shoulder.

Laskie wasn't much better off. Sutton had found the target twice. First through the aorta, second smashing Laskie's right fibula. Laskie struggled to the door, opened it, then fell dead before reaching the gate.

*

Superintendent Richards was advised of the shootings and made arrangements to meet Mr and Mrs de Courcy on their return from Scotland.

They were badly shaken by the news of Sutton's death, and attended the funeral service in the Methodist Chapel. The church was attended by those who knew him, including the Consul.

Papers in Sutton's belongings included a copy of his will, showing that he had left all he had to de Courcy. Two days after the funeral, Chapman, Richmond, and de Courcy met for the last time in Chapman's house and listened to a proposal from Richmond. It was accepted and came to fruition eight months later.

Six weeks after the IRA/Sinn Fein cease-fire, the Combined Loyalist Military Command announced the end of their operational hostilities as from midnight on Thursday, 13 October 1994. Their statement offered 'abject and true remorse'.

De Courcy, assisted by his wife, put their energy into running a youth club, supported by the leaders of all the churches on the island, that operated from a new hall funded by an anonymous donation of £220,000 and a gift of £50,000 from de Courcy. De Courcy's contribution was half the legacy received from Sutton.

Elmer Hall was officially opened by Mrs de Courcy, and now caters for twenty-five teenagers, who regularly attended twice weekly for various activities.

Susannah and Edward currently live in an extended and modernised cottage overlooking Brown's Bay, and are expecting to add to their family. A new team of three, thought de Courcy. "Let's call him Elmer, if it's a boy, or Lee, if a girl," suggested de Courcy.

Susannah shook her head. "No. Let's not look back. Let's not have any connection with Elmer except the Hall."

Chapman finished his story with that remark.

"Forget your additional material, Willis," Spooner suggested. "Just use what you have in the manuscript, and can you let me have your article on the Pentagon and the UVF in two hours?"